AVENUE OF DREAMS

Chiara dreamed of fulfillment—in the dressmaking business she risked her husband's rage to create . . . and in the arms of the wealthy, worldly man who offered her everything her marriage did not.

AVENUE OF DREAMS

Her husband, Mike, dreamed of climbing to the top in the auto-making jungle of Detroit, where only the strongest survived and the most relentless succeeded.

AVENUE OF DREMAS

Their daughter, Anna, dreamed of love as she fell under the spell of the breathtakingly handsome and charming Italian aristocrat whom her father would do anything to keep her from.

Spanning two continents and three generations, this towering family saga is as heartbreaking and heartlifting as the American experience itself.

AVENUE
of
DREAMS

Lucy Taylor

A SIGNET BOOK

SIGNET
Published by the Penguin Group
Penguin Books USA Inc., 375 Hudson Street,
New York, New York 10014, U.S.A.
Penguin Books Ltd, 27 Wrights Lane,
London W8 5TZ, England
Penguin Books Australia Ltd, Ringwood,
Victoria, Australia
Penguin Books Canada Ltd, 2801 John Street,
Markham, Ontario, Canada L3R 1B4
Penguin Books (N.Z.) Ltd, 182-190 Wairau Road,
Auckland 10, New Zealand

Penguin Books Ltd, Registered Offices:
Harmondsworth, Middlesex, England

First Printing, July, 1990
10 9 8 7 6 5 4 3 2 1

 REGISTERED TRADEMARK—MARCA REGISTRADA

PRINTED IN THE UNITED STATES OF AMERICA

PUBLISHER'S NOTE
This is a work of fiction. Names, characters, places, and incidents
either are the product of the author's imagination or, if real, are used
fictitiously.

BOOKS ARE AVAILABLE AT QUANTITY DISCOUNTS WHEN USED TO PROMOTE
PRODUCTS OR SERVICES. FOR INFORMATION PLEASE WRITE TO PREMIUM
MARKETING DIVISION, PENGUIN BOOKS USA INC., 375 HUDSON STREET,
NEW YORK, NEW YORK 10014.

Dedicated to the memory of my parents, intrepid Italian immigrants Domenico and Antonia Sanitate.

And for their unstinting encouragement and support, to my husband, Bill, and children, Celia, Bill, Christine, Beth, Carol, Mary, Steven, and Suzanne.

Thanks for their help and guidance: Deborah Chrisman, Karen Morrell, Linda Pedder, Kathy Tountas, Joyce Wells.

Special thanks for her memories to Clotilde Del'lera.

— 1 —

Region of Puglia, Italy, 1928

By nightfall I will be engaged to a man I've yet to meet.
With that chilling thought, Chiara Sardanno crept from
the bed she shared with her two younger sisters and
hurried to the tiny balcony. She watched the brilliant sun
floating in a fiery burst over the distant Adriatic as she
murmured a prayer for guidance.

Arranged marriages were the rule in Chiara's Italian
village. But the prospect of marrying a stranger and then
departing for faraway America was terrifying.

Her prayers, she supposed, should be appeals for acceptance. As her mother often reminded Chiara, she
was, at twenty-two, almost past the marriageable age and
fortunate to have a suitor. Judging from the covert, admiring male glances she usually drew, she knew she wasn't
unattractive. Indeed, compared to the olive-skinned village women, her appearance was unusual, with pearly
complexion and sleepy-lidded eyes, blue as the Adriatic,
under ached brows, and thick light brown hair, sun-
touched with traces of reddish-gold. The problem had
been the insufficiency of her dowry. She sighed. Everything seemed to depend on money.

As she ended her prayers, the Italian village slowly
came alive with a baby's lusty wail, the braying of a
donkey, the slamming of a door. She smiled at the wizened goatkeeper who rang his bell and paused under her
balcony to milk his goat with a rhythmic tugging. Women
gathered around him to buy pails of fresh milk and rolls
of creamy cheese.

Chiara beheld the village scene, fixing it in her mind.
The narrow dirt road below, lined with two-story concrete
homes, led to the center piazza. Distant green hills out-

1

lined against a cloudless western sky sprouted clusters of small tile-capped houses, many crumbling with age. To the east, the sun's fiery reflection glittered on the calm aquamarine Adriatic Sea. Tears stung behind Chiara's eyelids but she blinked them away. If her father accepted the proposal, she would leave all this behind her.

She chided herself for the threatened tears. After all, her existence was not so grand. Just the opposite—village life was penurious. But it was an acceptable poverty; familiar, bearable.

Pressing her hands against her plump breasts, Chiara tried to still the pounding of her heart. Her future lay before her like a blank canvas, waiting for the artist to daub on his paints. What sort of scene would Michele Marcassa create on the canvas of her life?

Hearing her mother stirring about, Chiara murmured a final hasty prayer and hurried through the bedroom, where her sisters still slept peacefully, then down narrow steps to the small porch outside the kitchen.

Ripe tomatoes, almost bursting their skins, hung from the porch ceiling to dry, and alongside trailed strings of golden onions, rustling and crackling in the light breeze. Luisa Sardanno sat on the concrete stoop, performing her morning ritual.

Chiara watched from the doorway, taking delight in the familiar hair-combing exercise. Luisa, a round woman with a heart-shaped face, had sad dark-shadowed eyes. A pouch in her black skirt, formed from her spread legs, held a small mirror and three tortoiseshell pins. She hummed a Verdi aria as she drew a gap-toothed comb through waist-length chestnut hair.

Her mother spied Chiara from the corner of her eye. "Ah, *buon giorno, figlia,*"

Chiara took the comb from her mother's hand. "Let me do that. I used to love combing your hair when I was little." She dragged the comb through the coarse, thick tresses, enjoying the tactile connection.

Luisa smiled in relaxed contentment and toyed with the pins in her lap. "You could not sleep thinking of tonight, eh, Chiara? I am not surprised. Marriage is the most important event in a woman's life."

Chiara parted the thick hair into three thick sections.

"Perhaps I won't like Signor Marcassa. Perhaps I'll refuse the offer."

Slowly her mother turned and fixed a piercing gaze on Chiara. "What 'perhaps'? It's almost all settled. You can't back down." Angrily she pulled the dark mass of hair over her shoulder and began braiding, her fingers flying in deft, graceful motions. "It's not up to you to accept, anyway. It's your father's decision. Chiara, we've gone all over this. There's no other way. You must marry this man."

Chiara knotted her hands together. "Mama, I don't want to leave Italy. We hardly know anything about the suitor other than he's twenty-nine years old and works in a factory."

"Figlia, I cried last night, thinking about you going to America. How it saddens me. But you can't refuse this time, like you did the others."

Chiara's mouth curved downward as she remembered the other proposals. "I couldn't marry them. One was a poor widower old enough to be my father, and the other was dim-witted and jobless. Neither had two sticks to rub together."

"What? Will only a prince be good enough for the princess?" Her mother spoke in a shrill singsong voice. "Well, daughter, there is no prince, no castle. There is this!" She pointed dramatically downward. "A floor, a roof, food. You're lucky in life to get your daily bread. *Capisci?"* She wound the thick braid into a coil at the nape of her neck and skewered it with the shell pins.

Chiara dropped the comb in her mother's lap. "Are you so anxious to be rid of me?"

Tears gathered in her mother's eyes and her shoulders hunched, making her look even smaller. *"Figlia,* I don't want to see you end up a spinster, dependent on us for the rest of your days. Come, sit." She made room on the stoop for Chiara. "Life is so difficult." A tear glinted in her eye. Her head wobbled and her mouth formed a tight line. "Ah, Cara, Cara, how mean your mother is, how bitter. It was not so when I was a young girl. Poverty and hard times have made me this way. I was once beautiful, like you, yes, and hopeful. And you see what I have now?" She looked around her. "Madonna! I thought my lot would be better than my mother's, but you see, it is not. It is the same. Maybe even worse. At least she, God rest her soul, had her own teeth." At that Luisa opened her mouth and pointed to the empty spaces.

She laughed, her mood changing abruptly. *"Basta!* Enough! Why do I carry on so?"

"You're used to this life. I have no idea what might be in store for me in America."

"You must trust in God. He will guide you." Her hands came together and she waved them upward in supplication. "Does he not supply us with food for our table, clothing for our backs? That is all one can hope for. One must expect nothing more than to get along and make the best of things."

Yes, that was all one could expect; Chiara had heard it often enough. Trust in God, be thankful for his meager gifts. Observing her mother's lined face and rough brown hands, Chiara marveled at her indomitable spirit and steadfast faith, her lifelong habit of acceptance. Even when Chiara's father had been ill for months, Luisa undertook the backbreaking burden of tending their small plot of land outside the village. The task of caring for their home and the younger children naturally fell to Chiara. The harvest was poor that year and they'd had to rely on her Uncle Nunzio for a loan to buy necessities. Chiara would never forget her father's whipped look. Begging came hard for her parents.

Her mother was chattering on. "They say factory workers make a good living in America."

"Who really knows? Flora says sometimes the workers are laid off, and if they haven't put money by, they're in trouble." Chiara rested her head against her mother's arm. "I'm . . . I'm afraid," she whispered. "This man, Signore Marcassa, is partly American, and Americans are different. Flora said so in her letters. For all we know, he may be mean and ugly. And poor!" She tossed her head and set her mouth. "If I don't find him *simpatico,* I will refuse him. I'll go to the convent."

"Madonna!" Luisa stamped her foot in disgust. "Go, then. Go to the convent. They will throw out such a disagreeable girl. Remember the saying: a child who disobeys her parents *'fa la morte di un cane,'* will die like a dog. You have read too many novels of silly girls who fall madly in love with rich and handsome princes at your

Zio Nunzio's house. Bah! I knew no good would come of allowing you such frivolity."

"Reading isn't frivolous!"

Her mother pulled Chiara to her soft full bosom. *"Figlia mia,* it hurts me to think of you leaving us. Who knows if you will ever return or if I will ever see your children?" Her lips puckered and she made a mewling sound.

Loath to distress her mother further, Chaira said nothing. But her fears of marriage stemmed from her observation of the village women who led lives of drudgery and looked old beyond their years. Too often marriage was the thief of adventure, the murderer of youth.

But what was the alternative? The convent? Though she spoke of joining a nunnery, the thought of imprisonment behind high, dark convent walls, with tart, often bitter old women, made her shudder.

She could remain a spinster, but could she endure the pitying deference paid to unmarried ladies? And could she bear being dependent on her parents for the rest of her days?

She'd had vague notions of eventually taking over the sewing business from her employer, Dona Isabella. Isabella had no daughters, and her sons' wives weren't interested in her little enterprise. But Isabella was not old and would probably continue her work for many years.

It seemed there were no alternatives to marriage.

Her mother stood abruptly. With a typical lightning-quick mood change she said, "No more of this talk. I have work to do, bread and pasta to make."

A bittersweet smile appeared on Chiara's lips. Her mother's habit of acceptance, of forbearance, her avoidance of unpleasant thoughts, was both familiar and distressing. A surge of love welled in Chiara's heart. Life without her mother was unimaginable.

Luisa donned her large black apron, tying it behind her. With the hem she dabbed her eyes. "Come then, and help me. Go to the *fontana* for water before you leave for your work."

Inside the house, curtainless windows, small and deep, shadowed the room in perpetual twilight. Chiara cast a glance about the neat but drab dwelling. A large sooty fireplace dominated one end of the room, and beside it on a shelf stood a collection of blackened pots. Against the wall, a worktable held three earthenware bowls and a jug.

From above came sounds of the four younger children scrambling about, their querulous voices welcoming the new day. How many more days would Chiara hear quarrels and laughter from her sisters, Gabriella and Tonina, and her brothers, Carlo and baby Dino?

Lifting the earthen water jug from the worktable, she started for the stone building that housed the public waterworks. The day was perfect, cloudless and fresh, with only a slight breeze teasing her hair.

"Eh, Chiara," a voice called out. "Wait for me."

Her friend Elena, a jug propped against her hip, came astride, yanking along a recalcitrant child.

"Buon giorno, Elena, Pasquale." Chiara knelt on one knee to greet the beautiful boy. "Hello, Pasquale. What lovely pink cheeks you have."

The youngster grinned and pulled away to pick up stray stones from the road.

Elena flicked back a strand of hair from her forehead. "He's a handful for me. And already I'm expecting another."

Chiara had guessed as much from the slight bulge under Elena's loose dress. "Maybe you'll have a girl this time." Elena had been so pretty in school. Now she looked weary, with downturned mouth and unkempt hair.

"I thought it wouldn't happen because I've been breast-feeding, but . . ." Elena shrugged. "His father is an animal." She tilted her head and laughed, as if it were a great compliment. Leaning forward, she said slyly, "I hear you may be getting married soon."

Chiara reddened. "It isn't settled yet. Signore Marcassa wants to live in America."

Elena gestured with her hands. "Is that so bad? It couldn't be any worse than here." She shifted the jug to her other hip. "Then again, the old proverb says, 'Whoever forsakes the old way for the new knows what he is losing, but not what he will find.' Who knows what to believe?"

"But you're happy, aren't you, Elena?"

Elena's mouth turned down at the corners and she shrugged. "There are good days and bad. Marriage isn't all happiness. And this child . . ." She snatched Pasquale up and inserted her finger into his mouth to retrieve a stone he'd placed there. "Bad!" She shook Pasquale's shoulders and turned to Chiara with an exasperated expression. "You see?"

Chiara clucked in agreement.

"There's no end to the work." Elena looked sullen for a moment, then cheered up. "It really isn't so bad. What can you expect from life?"

Pasquale darted ahead, and his mother scurried after him, calling over her shoulder, "Good luck, Chiara."

As she went on her way, Chiara wondered if she would be like Elena in another year or two. She was well aware of the plight of the village women. Marriage seemed to mean drudgery, bambinos arriving one after another, lack of privacy, lack of money, lack of . . . of hope.

She reached the concrete building where women lined up at the spigots for water. Several shriveled old women in long black dresses and shawl-covered heads gathered to exchange village gossip, their voices shrill and cutting. Chiara accomplished her task quickly to escape their probing eyes.

Back home, she deposited the jug on the table. In her room she reached under the oil lamp for the letter from Flora. Although she knew the contents almost by heart, she read the letter again.

My dear cousin,

Eduardo has found work at a factory; but it is very hard, and he is always so tired. My uncle boarded us until last month. Now we are renting a flat of our own. I am trying to learn the language, which is difficult and harsh on the ears, unlike our speech.

Eduardo says there is opportunity here, but one must be wily and quick. It is a disadvantage to be Italian, for we are often looked down upon and given only the most menial of tasks. But some do well, especially those with a talent or trade.

Chiara dropped the letter to her lap and reflected on her cousin's situation. How bewildering, how lonely it must be to feel unwanted in a strange country.

The letter continued:

The winter here in Detroit is bitter cold. My hands are stiff and chapped. The flat has running water and heat, but the heat is never enough to take the chill from my bones, although it's the end of March. And the sun, when it shines, is too weak to warm anything. Still, the summers are lovely and hot.

Last week Eduardo invited a most charming Italian gentleman, Michele Marcassa, to our home. He was born in Campania, but has lived in America several years. He wants to return to Italy to find a wife and settle down. Please do not be angry, Cara, but I told him about you, and showed him the photograph of both of us at the seaside. Remember the wonderful time we had bathing and laughing and singing? I think of those days often. Anyway, he declared he would write to the matchmaker, Angelina, and ask her to present his case. Both Eduardo and I think Michele would make a fine husband.

I miss my friends, my family, my lovely sunny Italy, and I miss you. Please write to ease my homesickness.

Nothing more. Couldn't Flora have at least described Signor Marcassa? Chiara sighed. It was so like Flora to skip the essential details. Still, Michele Marcassa must be acceptable if Flora and Eduardo found him so.

She pressed her palms to her temples. Her mind buzzed with confusion. She needed to talk to someone wise and understanding. Of course, her Uncle Nunzio.

In the kitchen her mother kneaded dough, her palms pressing the cream-colored mound in a pulsing cadence.

"Mama, let me go to Zio's today. Carlo can drive the cart."

"What about your work? Isn't Dona Isabella expecting you?"

"I'll tell her I'm working only this afternoon. There's not much work anyway."

Her mother gave an exasperated shake of her head. "Go, then; go to your uncle."

Carlo, pleased at an excuse to avoid work, went to the stable attached to the house to harness the mule, Figaro. He shooed noisy, flapping chickens from his path as, tugging and whistling, he urged the recalcitrant gray mule forward. On its way at last, the cart left puffs of dust in the road behind them.

Chiara knew they were close to Zio Nunzio's when the

piscine smell of the sea greeted her senses. Beyond a bend she spied the three-story white stucco villa overlooking the Adriatic Sea. As soon as he deposited Chiara and greeted their uncle, Carlo dashed off toward the beach.

With a warm hug her uncle led her through the cool marble-floored drawing room, where white-painted shutters were drawn against the morning sun. "Come, we'll sit in the garden. It's shady there."

Her uncle was a *professore,* the only one of seven brothers to go to university. Unmarried and childless, he channeled his love of children toward his many nieces and nephews. He was proof that there *was* a better life, gained through education. But he was an exception. A university education was denied to all but a chosen few.

The enclosed garden, ringed with white and pink bougainvillea and pale blue hydrangeas, held a scattering of fig and peach trees. Chiara and her uncle settled on wrought-iron chairs under a small grape arbor where bright leaves provided shade from the punishing sun.

Zio observed his niece through round spectacles that shielded his kind gray eyes. "What is it, Chiara?"

"The matchmaker, Comare Angelina, has arranged for a suitor." She nipped a grape leaf from a curling vine and rolled it around her finger. "Tonight he comes to visit for the first time."

Zio nodded and asked, "Is he a good man?"

She shrugged. "I don't know much about him." Her chin dropped and she covered her face with her hands. "Zio, he wants to take me to America."

Her uncle tipped her chin upward with his thumb, and her hands dropped away. "Is that so terrible? Italy is a poor country. There is surely more work and more opportunity in America."

Chiara's eyes clouded over and she shook her head in a helpless gesture. "I hate the thought of leaving my family and my beautiful Italy for a strange land with strange customs."

"Yes, this is a wonderful country, if you can distance yourself from all the poverty." Zio's white hair trembled in the light breeze.

The housekeeper, a bent old woman with an agony of wrinkles, appeared bearing a lunch of linguine, clams, and fresh fruit, then toddled off, complaining of her aches.

Chiara relaxed back into the iron filigree chair. "I love this place. My happiest hours were spent here with books from your library, reading, reading, as if my thirst for knowledge could never be satisfied."

"You have inherited my love of books," Zio said. "Your parents berate me for encouraging lofty notions through reading. But only good can come of learning. Remember, when you have children, do not disparage school learning, like some *contadini* do. Only through education can you understand your life and better it."

"What good is knowledge when all a woman does is have babies and clean and sew?" Chiara asked. "A woman is dependent on her husband; she is tied to her family."

"That's the old way of thinking, *la via vecchia*. It is not always the better way. Everyone should aspire to better himself, Chiara. You must decide what you want." Her uncle poured wine from a wicker-shrouded bottle.

Chiara pondered. What *did* she want? She tried not to wish for fine things. She had been taught that yearning for the unattainable was folly. One must accept, make do, survive.

She blurted out, "I want a better life! Maybe it's bad luck to wish for that, but I can't help it."

"Chiara, there's marriage or the convent." Zio spread his hands. "Or you could remain a spinster. I think you prefer marriage and children."

"Yes, I want babies—round, dimple-cheeked cherubs like my brother Dino. But marriage to a stranger frightens me." Chiara leaned forward. "I want, most of all, a home of my own, a nice one, like yours, and a plot of earth. I don't want the sort of existence my mother and most of the villagers endure."

"Well, there you are. Home and family are the important things." Her uncle gave an exaggerated shrug. "Someone wants to marry you, yet you hesitate."

"But I want other things too. I want to . . . to accomplish something, to earn money of my own that I can keep. I'll never forget how hard it was when Papa was ill for so long, how destitute we were."

"Well, you have a skill, sewing, to help you along in life."

"I once thought I'd eventually buy Dona Isabella's shop. She's spoken of it. Of course, when I mentioned it to my mother, she said it was idle talk, and there wasn't any money for such a venture. Besides, she said, my job is to get married." The talk of sewing reminded Chiara that she was expected at work that afternoon. "I mustn't stay too long or Dona Isabella will be angry. The sewing work is tiresome. Isabella usually gives me the boring jobs, like basting, hemstitching, and pressing. When I suggest using modern designs like the ones I've seen in your magazines, she disapproves."

"She's getting old. Old people don't like change."

Chiara's smile was sheepish. "Still, whenever I have the chance, I make new designs from the old patterns for the younger girls, and let Isabella rant a bit. If I were running the shop, things would be different." Chiara touched her lips with a linen napkin.

"It's a lovely dream, owning a shop, but not practical right now. A woman needs a man, and this is your opportunity. You haven't much choice."

Chiara sighed. What had she expected?

Her uncle put his arm around her shoulder, hugging her close. "Chiara, meet this man and decide if he is a good man. You can learn to love a good man." They began walking toward the villa. "You know, love is rarely gifted to us as in a magic spell, especially in our culture, where two strangers are usually thrown together. Love is earned and grows."

Their heads turned as Carlo, shouting a greeting, burst into the garden. After he devoured a cold meal, they prepared to depart. Zio settled Chiara into the cart, held her face in his hands, and looked into her eyes. "Don't forget to dream, Cara."

Later, when Chiara returned from an afternoon of tedious stitching, her father called to her from the balcony. Emilio Sardanno, freshly washed and shaved, wore a slightly rumpled suit, his only one, and a shirt with a stiff collar.

Chiara joined her father and kissed his leathery cheek. "Hello, Papa." Taking his hand in hers, she touched the ropelike bluish veins that extended from his knuckles. His huge walrus mustache, once rust-colored, was now shot with gray. Her heart went out to him. The burden of working his small plot of land, eight kilometers away, aged him. His toil produced food for his family's needs and a small amount to sell at market.

"You'd better get yourself ready for our visitor." He observed her with keen eyes, heavy-lidded and deep blue, much like her own. "Soon you will be gone from my home, to begin a new generation, a new cycle of life,"

"I haven't made that decision yet, Papa."

He shook his head sadly. *"Figlia mia,* every woman needs to be married; needs a man to care for her."

He seemed about to say more, but her mother's voice cut through their conversation. "Chiara! Get in here and make yourself ready. It's late."

Chiara hesitated a moment, then hugged her father tightly.

"Go on," he said. "Your mother is upset." His eyes were shining with suppressed tears. As Chiara turned to go, he grabbed her hand. "Chiara?"

"Yes, Father?"

In a gruff-tender voice he said, "This time you can't back out, daughter."

Chiara squeezed his hand, then stepped inside the main room that served as kitchen, dining room, parlor, and even bedroom for Carlo and Dino. The strong, bitter odor of percolating coffee permeated the small house.

"Mama, what time is he coming?" Chiara asked.

"Seven." Luisa, engaged in a flurry of activity, flicked dust from the sideboard. "Can't you see how busy I am? You should be helping me instead of la-la-la-ing with your father."

Chiara ignored her mother's remark, knowing it masked her anxiety. She shook out a crocheted tablecloth and spread it on the table, then took a bottle of anisette and small glasses from a shelf.

"I'll do that," Luisa said impatiently. "Get into your best dress. Go get ready, go!"

Luisa placed a special custard cake on the table. The cake, four rich spongy layers separated with thick almond cream, was usually reserved for important feast days.

Dino and Tonina darted about trying to snitch crumbs from the cake while Luisa, brandishing a wooden spoon, screamed at them, "Get out, you miserable children!"

Chiara glanced about the room, trying to see it through the eyes of a stranger. It was shabby, she thought. The drabness of the walls was relieved by faded holy pictures—the Virgin looking heavenward in anguish, the Christ in pain on his cross, and San Nicola di Bari, the patron, blank-eyed and vaguely pious. But it was neither better nor worse, she supposed, than the surrounding homes.

With a sigh she left the confusion for the comparative solitude of her parents' bedroom. After dressing, she gazed into the flawed mirror that hung atop an ancient dresser. The simple pale blue garment of her own design, stylishly loose except where it belted at the hips, didn't quite hide her tiny waist and ample rounded breasts. She straightened the white pointed collar and studied herself in the mirror. Would Signor Marcassa find her pretty?

She combed her long tawny hair, letting the thick curls swirl to her shoulders, and pinched her cheeks to redden them.

When Chiara returned to the main room, her mother said with a nod of approval, "You look fine."

Luisa seemed finally satisfied that everything was in order. Wearing her best black dress with beading at the neckline, she assumed an air of calm, folded her arms across her expansive chest, and waited.

Chiara returned to the bedroom and boosted herself up on her parents' lumpy bed. Closing her eyes, she crossed herself. Her nervous hands made small pleats in the fabric of her skirt. When the loud knock sounded on the outside door, she started, then clutched her hands together and sat so quietly she could hear the beating of her heart.

Her father's voice boomed in welcome; then her mother chattered nervously. Chiara held her breath until she heard *his* voice. Ah, it was a rich bass, confident and strong; that was a good sign. Her pulse raced as footsteps proceeded toward the table. Chiara peeped through an opening in the curtain, but her father's bulky form obscured her view of Signor Marcassa.

Observing the formal custom, they inquired, each in turn, of the other's family. Chiara knew they would ease into the issue at hand, almost as if it were an afterthought.

"You have a good trade?" asked Emilio after the formalities.

"I've worked in factories. I'm not afraid of hard work or long hours, and I've never been without a job for long. The pay is enough to support a wife and a family."

She heard her mother fluttering around Signor Marcassa, pouring more coffee and urging cake upon him.

For several minutes they talked about his work, about America. Chiara peeped around the curtain again, but could only see Signor Marcassa's back. He was tall, at least, and broad-shouldered. Her thoughts were a jumble of confused questions, of uncertainties. Would he like her? More important, would she like him? Was he kind? Thoughtful? Would he expect total obedience of her, the way so many Italian men did? Would he lift his hand to her in anger? She squeezed her eyes shut, forcing her mind to return to the conversation in the front room.

"I would be most honored if you would deem me an acceptable spouse for your daughter Chiara," Signor Marcassa intoned.

Chiara drew in her breath, her hand flying to her mouth to still the light tremor. When finally her father called her to join them, her heart stopped beating for a moment, then raced wildly. Parting the heavy curtain, she entered the room.

— 2 —

Michele Marcassa stood and moved toward Chiara. His bearing, Chiara noted, was erect, his demeanor proud, almost haughty, and his eyes, dark brown and intense, studied her as she studied him.

Bowing low, he said, "You are indeed more beautiful than I was led to believe."

Chiara's heart quickened as Michele's lips grazed her hand.

week here in the village, if that is Chiara's wish. Then on to Naples to board ship for America. Flora and Eduardo have offered to let us stay with them for a while, until I find a place to rent."

One week! America! The word sent a shiver up Chiara's arms. Across an ocean. So far away. She suddenly felt an overwhelming sense of confusion, of panic.

Emilio slapped his hands lightly on the table. "It's settled, then. My wife will confirm the date with Padre Contrara."

Both men rose and vigorously shook hands. The contract was sealed.

Michele turned to Chiara. "I have your father's consent, *signorina*, but I don't have yours. You have said nothing yet."

His eyes compelled her to speak, to accept him. But her tongue seemed stuck against the roof of her mouth. Though Michele waited with an expression of patience, still Chiara could force no words to her lips.

"Chiara!" her father said sternly.

Chiara remained speechless, her eyes pleading for understanding. The silence stretched and became agonizing, but still she said nothing.

A frown puckered her mother's brow.

Finally Michele said gently, "Perhaps your father would allow us to walk together to the piazza." He turned to Emilio. "*Signore*, do I have your permission to walk with your daughter?"

Emilio looked chagrined. "Yes, go. Carlo can bear the candle."

"Thank you for your respect and trust, *signore*."

Michele extended his hand toward Chiara. "Come, *signorina*."

His voice was soft, cajoling, and despite Chiara's turmoil, she nodded and stepped toward him.

Touching her elbow, Michele led her outside while Luisa shouted for Carlo to act as chaperon. Chiara felt self-conscious walking beside Michele, but even in her flustered state she was aware of his powerful male aura. Her arm brushed his and she felt the warmth of him through the rough cloth. She was careful not to move too close. For them to touch would be unseemly and fuel for the gossips.

Chiara forced herself to nod at the neighbors, who watched, openly curious. A walk was the villagers' entertainment. Some of the women sat outside their stone or concrete houses, facing the doors, with mending or other work occupying ever-busy fingers. Others chatted and fanned themselves with their broad aprons, and a few hung over the bottom halves of their doors, observing the nightly parade and making remarks *sotto voce*.

Close to the piazza Chiara and Michele passed small shops and cafés where men played cards and drank wine or coffee at the outside tables.

At the piazza Chiara focused her attention on the fountain top, where silvery threads of water flowed from the mouths of marble fish. In the center was a voluptuous figure of a woman surrounded by a watery cascade, like a transparent veil, splashing into the waiting pool.

A group of men loitered at the fountain, gesturing wildly as they argued. A couple played *morra*, a hand game that required quick fingers and quicker wits, with onlookers shouting encouragement. A few scattered youths watched the evening panorama with bored faces.

Finally Michele leaned toward Chiara so that his mouth was close to her ear. *"Signorina,* when you walked into the room, I thought: This is the woman I have waited for, the one who will help turn around a life that up to now has been barren. I sensed a goodness in you. You are young and inexperienced. But you mustn't be frightened. I will be good to you."

His sincerity touched her heart, but still she hesitated to speak, to even look at him.

"Look at me, Chiara. You've said nothing. Why are you afraid?"

Chiara lifted her eyes to Michele's. His eyes encouraged her. "I know nothing about you, though you seem sincere," she said quietly. "I don't know what sort of life we would have in America, how and where we would live. I don't know the language. Here, in Italy, at least I know what I have and what to expect; in America . . . I've seen magazines and books at my uncle's house. Everything seems so strange and . . ."

"Signorina, I know the language. I'll teach you. And there are many Italians in Detroit. You would make

friends." His lids lowered and he seemed to weigh his words. "I understand how you feel; leaving family is difficult. But there is little opportunity here. In America there is at least the chance to make a living for someone like me, with little education and few skills. I won't deceive you. I'm not a rich man. But we can have a good life, not riches and a fine villa, perhaps, but enough money to take care of you and the children I hope we have."

At the mention of children Chiara blushed and looked away. A sprinkle from the fountain dampened her cheek. She brushed away the wet drops and turned toward home in the evening dusk.

From the way he looked and talked, Michele seemed to be a cut above the ordinary *contadino*. He had a grace about him, a strength, and appeared to be *un uomo di pazienza,* a man of patience and honor.

Her objection was not so much to Michele himself, as to the move to America. She didn't want to be poor. But if poverty was her destiny, better to endure it in Italy, among family, than in America, among strangers. Yet she could appreciate Michele's viewpoint. His views on "opportunity" echoed her uncle's and Flora's. In Italy there was little chance of bettering one's life; in America at least there was a possibility.

Opportunity. It wasn't a word heard in the village. The familiar platitudes here embraced the notion of "endurance," "forbearance," "patience."

"America frightens me. I've seen pictures of women with painted faces and blood-tipped fingernails, with cigarettes in narrow holders, of fancy cooking machinery, of streets filled with automobiles. Everything is so different. I would be a stranger in a strange land."

"Signorina, there's nothing to be frightened of. You would easily adjust to America."

They had reached her home and Chiara led Michele to the courtyard in the rear. She turned sad eyes to him. "My heart is here."

Michele gestured with lifted hands. "I'm young and strong. These hands have served me well. I'll take care of you."

Chiara stifled an urge to reach out and touch his long-fingered hands. Despite their roughness, they were tapered and graceful, like those of a maestro or a sculptor might be. His sincerity moved her. In spite of all her earlier misgivings, she believed him and wanted to trust him. And truly, she had little choice.

Despite Carlo's nearness, she gave in to her impulse and placed her hands into Michele's. She said softly, "I will marry you, Michele."

Michele's expression softened as a slow smile lightened his features. His voice was tremulous. "I'll see that you want for nothing. I promise, you will never regret your decision. It is too early to speak of love, but in time, love will come."

Looking up into the chasm of his luminous dark eyes, a tremor passed through her. She felt suddenly heartened. Surely she was doing the right thing. Surely this was a good and kind man, a loving man.

During the next week, the young couple, accompanied by either Carlo or Luisa, visited relatives with an invitation to the wedding feast. On several evenings Chiara's father involved Michele in card games with a neighbor or two, while Chiara and her mother sat quietly embroidering. When Michele won a hand, Chiara smiled her approval.

Chiara raised her arms as her mother slipped the wedding dress over her head and tugged it into place. Alternately grousing and crying, Luisa clumsily slid tiny buttons into their slits down the back. Isabella, Chiara's employer, had helped Chiara construct the luxurious silk dress. Chiara knew that Isabella had been saving the material for a special occasion.

"You might as well have it. I have no daughters to pass it on to. And when would a wrinkled old lady like me ever use such fine material?" Isabella had said in her self-deprecating way.

When Chiara thanked her, Isabella sniffed. "I always thought you might own my shop someday, but nothing ever works out, it seems."

Now Gabriella and Tonina tore in and out of the bedroom, flushed with excitement over the celebration.

"Out, out," Luisa shouted to the girls, "and take Dino with you. Can't you see you're making me nervous?"

Three-year-old Dino chewed happily on a *biscotto* and allowed the girls to lead him outdoors. When they left, Luisa pressed the wreath of faux pearls, which she had fashioned from wax, onto Chiara's glowing tresses. Satisfied, Luisa boosted herself onto the edge of the bed. Suddenly tears began falling furiously.

"Figlia mia. My beautiful daughter. There is so much I haven't told you, so many words I have stored up in my heart. But now I can't think of one. I don't even know what's most important to say." She covered her face with her hands, and her shoulders shook with her crying.

Chiara's own tears had been spent. The day after her decision to marry Michele, she had been awake and tearful all night, but after that she resolutely put her tears behind her. Now she assumed the role of mother, placing her arms around Luisa. "It's all right. We need no words between us." She patted her mother's back. "I love you so. I only hope I can be as good a mother to my own children."

"But there are so many things you should know," Luisa said with a hiccup. "So many secret things I feel too embarrassed or too stupid to tell you."

Chiara knew her mother alluded to the mysteries of the marriage bed. They had never spoken openly of the intimate side of marriage, and the thought of what would transpire on her wedding night frightened Chiara. Her knowledge was skimpy at best. If it weren't for her younger brothers and pictures from her uncle's books, she would be ignorant of even the basic male anatomy. She wanted to ask questions, but was always too shy, and now, in the crucial last moments, she perceived her mother's hesitancy.

"It's all right, Mama."

They clung to one another, Luisa sobbing audibly. When they pulled apart, she said, "Remember all the things you have learned at my knee and in the lessons from Padre Contrara. And rememeber *la via vecchia,* the old way, the way of the family. The old lessons are the most valid ones; they have withstood the test of time." She dried her eyes and readjusted the frothy veil on Chiara's softly curling hair. Almost as an afterthought,

Luisa said, "The other . . . I suppose you will learn soon enough."

Chiara composed herself and entered the parlor, the skirt of her gown making a soft swish. At the sound, Michele ceased his nervous pacing and turned. He looked dashing, though a bit nervous, in a closely fitting navy suit and immaculate white shirt. His mouth opened as if to speak, but no words came. In the intensity of his deep, dark eyes, Chiara read a message of promise, of desire, of love.

Chiara's sisters, strewing flower petals from their small baskets, giggled and waved as they led the short procession to the church. The entire village population turned out to witness the happy event. Chiara and Michele walked behind her sisters, and the family and guests followed. Chiara heard her mother directing a fierce whisper at Dino, whose attention was so easily distracted, urging him along.

I must remember this, Chiara thought as they passed through the village—the marketplace that comes alive each morning with its vibrant sounds and smells, the fountain in the piazza, the shoe shop, Isabella's shop, the little ones playing barefoot and sometimes bare-bottomed in the road. *I must remember all of it, for I may never see it again.*

At the church, Padre Contrara, his wrinkled face wreathed in a smile, stood at the altar and beckoned them forward. Chiara glided down the aisle supported by Michele, and felt a moment of panic. What did she know of this man? So few words had passed between them, and now, in a matter of seconds, she would pledge to spend the rest of her life with him. Once they recited the vows, there would be no reprieve and their destinies would be inexorably bound. What was Michele thinking? Was he feeling the same turmoil?

Chiara's anxiety was allayed when Michele took her hand firmly and pressed it into the crook of his arm. As if sensing her fear, he looked down at her and smiled reassuringly.

It took only moments for the old priest—who had baptized and confirmed her, who had heard her confessions —to listen to their vows and raise his gnarled hands to bless them.

It is over so quickly, so quickly, she thought as Michele gently slid the gold band on her finger, then held her hands fast, stilling their tremble. He placed a dry, chaste kiss on her lips.

Outside the church, assorted *comari* and *compari* lined up for a turn to offer heartfelt good wishes and plant loud, wet kisses on the bridal couple, while children flitted among the guests throwing rice and *confetti*, the traditional almond-filled candy. Then the coterie retraced their steps to Chiara's home for the celebration.

Relatives arrived with huge baskets of food atop their heads: roast lamb, steaming linguine, platters of thick sliced prosciutto and mortadella, creamy cakes and crisp cookies.

In the courtyard, Cousin Vittorio took out his accordion and played a few riffs while Emilio poured wine and urged it upon one and all.

Old women with graying hair in tight buns sat and watched, smiles creasing their puckered faces. They fanned themselves with pasteboard fans and waved their dark skirts discreetly against their legs to cool them.

When Vittorio began playing in earnest, Michele extended his hand to Chiara with a courtly bow. She placed her hand in his and he swept her into the first dance. Chiara's limbs moved stiffly at first—she wasn't a skilled dancer—but Michele's muscular arm, warm against her back, guided her firmly. His velvety dark eyes, direct and confident, held her in thrall. The guests clapped encouragement and cheered them, and soon others joined in as the tempo increased. Young people danced with wild abandon, children stepped hesitantly, old people moved gingerly. After the first dance, the young women brazenly vied for a turn with the handsome Michele, and men twirled Chiara, envy of the groom written on their faces. Courteously, Michele danced with Luisa and the assorted *commari*, who twittered and teased the young bridegroom. When she noticed the young girls openly flirting with her new husband, Chiara stifled a flash of annoyance which she realized was jealousy.

After Elena danced with Michele, she patted her damp neck with a handkerchief and said, "Eh, Chiara, I had thought you foolish to refuse the others. Now I see how wise you were. What a fine, courteous gentleman. And those dark, brooding eyes. *Mamma mia!*"

Chiara's low laugh was touched with proprietary pride.

Vittorio's brother, a squat, elfish man, stood and started singing *"Vidi e luna mezzo mare,"* and soon others joined in the song, laughing raucously at its bawdy lyrics. Zio Nunzio stole up beside Chiara and cupped her shoulder in a tight hug. "Ah, Chiara, I'll miss you."

She patted his hand. "I'll miss you too."

"Remember what I've always told you: don't forget to dream, *cara.*"

A young cousin spirited Chiara away to dance the lively tarantella. Her skirts whirled and her limbs pounded in a staccato beat until, at the end of the dance, she collapsed in a paroxysm of giggles. When she found herself partnered again with her husband, she relaxed in the security of his arms, aware of his admiring half-smile.

"Good evening, Signora Marcassa," he whispered.

Signora Marcassa. She was no longer Chiara Sardanno, no longer her parents' charge. Her fate was locked forever, for better or worse, from this day forward, with that of this handsome stranger.

When the last of the guests had finally departed with loud congratulations and louder kisses, Chiara felt suddenly reluctant to see the festivities end. In the house, Luisa, her face flushed with excitement and perspiration, sat with Emilio at the kitchen table, counting gifts of money from *la busta,* the roomy purse. Chiara kissed her parents good night and left with Michele for her widowed aunt's house. Thankfully, her mother had arranged for the newlyweds to spend the week there alone, away from the thin walls and curious children. Her Aunt Lena had discreetly left to stay with other relatives.

Michele took Chiara's hand as they walked the short distance to the house in the still, warm air. He remarked on the brilliance of the full moon that lit their way and cast elongated shadows before them. Only the braying of a donkey and the hooting of an owl disturbed the peace of the village.

"It was a wonderful feast," Michele said.

"Yes." Chiara wanted to make conversation, but her mind was whirling. Her stomach tightened at the thought of what lay ahead. In matters of the bedroom her education had been sparse. She knew so little, only what the girls talked about in whispers and what she heard from the wives in jokes and secrets. It seemed the married women belonged to a secret society and the rites of passage could not be told outright, could only be alluded to. But the message was clear: the coupling was, for women, a duty to be endured, and for men, a right and a pleasure to be claimed at will. Would Michele, like Elena's husband, be "an animal"?

Inside the tiny house, Michele lit the oil lamp. The wick flared, sending eerie shadows dancing around the small main room. Chiara stood motionless inside the door, listening to the creaking wooden shutters, unsure of what to do first.

Michele took his coat off and turned to her, smiling. "Come, Chiara."

She entered the room and lowered herself slowly into a chair. Michele, watching her, still smiling, unbuttoned his shirt, then turned in to the small bedroom. Chiara's mouth suddenly went dry and she wet her lips nervously. She heard water splashing in a basin, the rustling of his clothing. In a few moments he was back in the room, his chest bare. His clothing had concealed a firm, muscular frame and a covering of curly black hair over his chest and sinewy arms. The sight of him quickened Chiara's pulse.

"Chiara, don't be afraid of me." When she didn't move, he said softly, "Put on your nightdress."

In the bedroom, behind the curtain that separated the bed from the toilet area, Chiara poured water into the basin with shaking hands, then slowly removed her clothing, aware that he must be listening to the whisper of each garment as she folded it and laid it across a chair, the swish of the washcloth in water. She washed methodically, delaying as long as possible, until Michele called to her, an edge of impatience in his voice.

No man had ever seen her bare. The nightdress from her trousseau was thin, too transparent, too revealing. She clenched her hands together at the stiff lace edging the neckline as she slowly moved past the curtain.

Michele was in bed, a sheet covering him to the waist.

He raised his hand and beckoned to her, his eyes smiling under lowered lids.

Chiara took a tentative step forward.

"Come, Chiara," he said, seeming to sense her hesitation. "I'll be careful."

She moved haltingly to the bed, and he took her hand, pulling her down next to him. He lifted onto his elbow and with gentle fingers caressed her arms, her face. She shivered involuntarily.

"I won't hurt you," he said, moving his hand to her nightdress. He undid the tie and trailed his fingertips across her breasts. She stiffened slightly as a tremor pulsed through her.

"Don't be afraid of me, Chiara. I want you to enjoy this, to have pleasure from it." His breath tickled her ear.

"This is all so new for me," she said in a hollow whisper.

"I know that. But it will hurt only for a little while, and only the first time." His lips moved from her ear to her cheek to a corner of her mouth, where they lingered.

She let her hand touch his neck, let her fingers flutter through the soft hair lying there. He kissed her fully on the mouth, lightly at first, then more insistently, while his hands wandered over her body.

Chiara hardly breathed as Michele gently lifted the gown and removed it. His gaze roamed over her bare, gently curving form, her full, high breasts, her tawny triangle of curling hair. She flushed under his scrutiny, disconcerted by the obvious pleasure he took in viewing her.

She closed her eyes as his mouth grazed her shoulder and moved downward. The male smell of him—a mixture of wine, tobacco, and perspiration—was heady, and when he lowered his head to nibble her breasts, her pulse quickened and a warmth spread through her. Then his mouth was on her own again, kissing her fiercely, taking her breath away. She found herself caught up in his urgency and wanted the kiss to go on forever, but suddenly he moved on top of her, exhaling in quick, passionate pants. His half-lidded eyes were ardent as he poised above her, whispering her name. His chest hair grazed her tender breasts and she involuntarily whimpered, pushing against him.

"No, sweet Chiara, let me make love to you," he said, his manhood pressing warm and hard against her thigh. "Look at me. I want to see your eyes."

She looked at him and was momentarily startled by the intensity of his gaze and the flush on his cheeks.

Then his knee separated her legs and he pressed against her in a steady pulsing beat. With a driving thrust he entered her, and she felt her muscles tighten under the burning pressure. The gentle yearning his caresses had inspired vanished quickly in the sudden searing pain. His breath against her cheek was rapid, hot. She wanted to cry out, but his mouth closed over hers, his tongue jabbing against hers. She tried to writhe away, but was pinned tight under him. Thankfully, in a few moments the pain dissipated. Before she could adjust to the new sensations flooding her body, her husband gave a low groan, shuddered, and collapsed on top of her.

The small stuffy room was silent except for Michele's long breathy sighs.

It must be over. This was it, then, the act that was both terrifying and compelling. It wasn't unbearable after all. In fact, she liked the feel of him within her.

Michele seemed drowsy, but a smile of contentment played on his lips. "I must be heavy," he said, rolling off with a satisfied groan.

He hadn't seemed heavy. She had begun to enjoy the press of his flesh on her own, the sinewy limbs entwined with hers, and felt disappointed that it was over so quickly.

Michele's perspiration mingled with hers, warm and moist on her flesh. Between her legs she felt sticky and sore. She wanted to rise and wash away the evidence of the consummation of their union, to weep a bit in solitude over the loss of her virginity. But she lay perfectly still, unsure of the convention.

As though sensing her mood, Michele brushed a tendril of hair away from her face, saying, "It will be better for you next time, I promise. I was . . . overanxious."

Chiara lay quietly in his arms and let tears slide down into her hair, hoping he wouldn't see them. The sweet mystery of love had been revealed to her and it wasn't so greatly horrifying. Yet it was an invasion, a trespass.

With that act her childhood had been surely left behind her, and now her lot was cast with Michele Marcassa.

She was embarking on a life's journey to a place strange and distant, with a man she barely knew. Life was fraught with uncertainties. For a long time she lay motionless, listening to the sonorous cadence of Michele's breathing, watching the even rise and fall of his expansive chest. It was almost dawn before she slept.

—— 3 ——

When Chiara awakened, Michele stood over her with a steaming cup of coffee and some sliced peaches and *biscotti*. She felt self-conscious, being served by her husband, but the custom of "bride's week" demanded that the bridegroom coddle his new wife and cater to her needs.

"Come, get dressed," Michele said. "Your father's letting me take the cart. We're going to the seaside, to Sancto Spiritu."

Chiara's uneasiness was quickly forgotten. She was delighted that Michele had made arrangements for their pleasure. It was a portent of things to come. He would take charge; he would be the master.

Before they left, the matchmaker, Angelina, knocked on the door, calling a greeting. "I've come to collect the sheet for your parents' inspection."

Chiara blushed, smarting over the indignity of the age-old tradition, but obediently fetched the bundle. The bloodied sheet attested to Michele's manhood and her virginity. Michele, she noticed, seemed unperturbed by the small drama and unaware of her discomfort. At least her mother wouldn't hang the sheet over the balcony rail for all to see, the way some did.

*   *   *

The week was over quickly, spent in short trips and visits to friends and relatives. It was a rare holiday for Chiara, who had been taught that one must never waste precious moments in idle pleasure.

When at last their possessions were bundled into the worn suitcases and the motorcar had been summoned, Chiara could think of nothing to say to her family. "Good-bye" was such a minimal word, unable to support the weight of her feelings. And yet everything else had already been said. Now there were only tears.

Engulfed in a great sadness, Chiara hugged her sisters and brothers in turn. Her mother's lips trembled with the effort of holding back a wail. She scattered extravagant kisses over Chiara's face, her arms clutching tightly.

"Luisa, they have a train to catch," her father said, forcing his wife and daughter apart. He helped Chiara into the back seat with Michele while unabashed tears slid into his mustache. As the vehicle pulled away, the entire family ran beside it until it picked up speed.

"Good-bye."

"Remember us."

"Write."

"We love you."

Chiara knelt to look out the oval rear window, her hand waving, waving until her family diminished into small specks in the dust.

A few days later Chiara stood on the deck of the steamship *Saturnia* as it rolled steadily out into the endless gray-blue expanse of the Mediterranean. As she watched, the shoreline gradually waned, buildings shrank into miniatures then vanished, Naples retreated, Italy finally disappeared. Gone, gone; her native land had passed into oblivion, taking with it her youthful history, her link to something vital, something elemental. Gone, a part of her heart, along with that boot-shaped lusty land.

Only two weeks ago she was a daughter; now she was a wife.

"You're getting cold," Michele murmured in her ear. "Come to the cabin now."

Chiara turned to look at this man, this stranger to whom she had given over her life. Daily she learned

things about Michele Marcassa. Yet, though she slept
with him, ate with him, talked with him, still there was so
much that seemed a mystery. What sort of past did those
solemn dark eyes hide?

Sometimes, looking sad and distant, he would fall silent in the middle of a conversation. They were polite
and considerate to one another, as strangers are. But
what did she really know of this man?

Now Michele tugged at her hand, pulling her away
from the railing. She turned reluctantly and allowed him
to lead her to their cabin. In bed he was gentle, kind, and
she was submissive, as she should be. In the past two
weeks of their marriage, Michele's lovemaking inspired
unexpected sensations within her, but she was still uneasy
with the urgent feelings that gathered force and momentum, that cried for more. Embarrassment kept her from a
total surrender to this powerful male presence lying next
to her, filling the bed, indeed, filling the small room.

After their lovemaking, Michele propped himself on
his elbow and gazed at her. With an index finger he
traced a line from her temple to her mouth. "I'm a lucky
man," he said with a smile of contentment. "None of
the other women on the ship compare to you."

Chiara's heart fluttered with pleasure. She slipped her
hand into Michele's and he gave it a reassuring squeeze.
Moments later, when he released his grip, Chiara realized he was fast asleep. She lay quietly, listening to his
measured breath, amazed at his sudden and total capitu-
lation to sleep. Gazing at his expression of innocence and
serenity, she was overwhelmed with a feeling of happiness. Impulsively she kissed his cheek, then crept sound-
lessly from bed and pressed her face against the glass of
the round porthole. In the onyx mist that met her eyes,
she visualized her parents and brothers and sisters as they
waved a last brave, tearful good-bye. *Please, God, let me
see them again someday.*

The next day Chiara, wrapped in the soft wool coat
Michele had bought her in Naples, hooked her arm through
her husband's for a stroll on the deck. It was a pearl of a
morning, cold and bright. She noted the unmistakable,
almost smug look of pride he wore when he introduced
her to friends he had recently made. Settling in striped
canvas deck chairs, they watched the roiling waves dash

up toward the ship. Gray smoke twisted from tall funnels and disappeared into the atmosphere.

"Dolce far niente," Michele said, and she agreed. It was sweet indeed, to do nothing.

"Was it like this when you first traveled to America?" she asked.

He threw his head back and laughed. "Ha! Not at all. It was a miracle my family survived. We went steerage for thirty-six dollars each. When we boarded, we were given a tin pan, a cup, spoon, and fork, all wrapped in a blanket. We used the utensils for the whole trip, washing them in a barrel of seawater. They were always greasy. It's a wonder we didn't get food poisoning.

"As it was, I developed a terrible itch on my chest and scratched myself raw. Finally a nurse said it was lice. Lice! My parents were mortified. My poor mother cried." He shook his head sadly, remembering. "The lice must have come from the so-called mattress, which was like a stuffed burlap sack. Who knows how many bodies slept on that mattress before me?"

"Poor Michele. How did you get rid of the lice?"

"I had to throw away my clothes and they gave me another mattress. I can still remember trying to wash in that cold salty water. My lips split from the salt." He looked out, squinting at the horizon, as if searching there for the memories. "The room had, oh, maybe a hundred and fifty people. There was no room for bags, so we had to keep them on our bunks; double bunks they were. It was hard sleeping like that. Cooks would come with big pots of soup or stew and fill our tin pans. We ate sitting on our bunks. People would be seasick, and the stench never left. The smell was so awful from all those bodies, I never felt like eating. We could get only a few minutes of air on deck because it was so crowded."

Chiara gave his hand a sympathetic squeeze. "There are so many things I don't know about you."

"And many things you may never know," Michele answered, jostling her hand up and down in his. Then he laughed, as if his words had been a joke.

A small group of Neapolitan men sauntered by their deck chairs and invited Michele to play *morra*. When it was his turn, Michele and another man each threw fingers out from a curled fist while shouting a number. The man calling the number that matched the total of out-stretched fingers won.

The game was lightning fast and difficult for Chiara to keep up with. A small crowd gathered, encouraging and shouting, and Chiara was pleased to see that Michele was winning. He caught her eye and winked. When the game ended, the men went off to play cards, and Chiara pulled up the collar of her coat for a brisk walk around the lower deck.

The young woman was there again, as she had been each day Chiara walked the deck. She sat alone, wrapped in a shawl, staring straight ahead through large sharp eyes, her black eyebrows a straight row across a face blank and unlined.

On the first day out, Chiara, certain the woman was also Italian, had introduced herself, and they'd exchanged short greetings since then.

Perhaps this morning she would be friendlier. "Good morning, *signora*," Chiara ventured. "It's a bit cool today, isn't it?"

The woman slowly looked up, as if moving her head was painful, but she didn't speak.

Chiara went on, "I hope you are not ill."

"No, no, not ill." The woman nodded, indicating the empty chair next to her.

"You look so lonely sitting here by yourself. Are you traveling alone?"

The woman, Maria Gabriani, stared at the sea and said in a low monotone, "I am going to America to find my husband. We were married two years ago."

"That's good reason to feel pleased, not sad."

"My husband left after a year to find work in New York. I received three letters, then nothing. I have not heard from him since." She sank further into her shawl.

Chiara murmured sympathetically.

"I wrote to an acquaintance in New York, but he tells me my husband left for Chicago. I have no one there to write to, so I am going myself to find him."

There were men, Chiara knew, who went to America and conveniently "forgot" to send for their families. There were others who met with foul play.

"You have my sympathy, *signora*. You are brave to do this. I hope you find your husband."

The woman moved her head, neither a nod nor a shake. "One does what one must do. *Che serà, serà.* One doesn't look for happiness in this life. I have dreams sometimes, visions. I see a meeting in my dreams, not clear, but it is my husband's face. Somehow it is not a happy meeting."

As the daily conversations continued, the woman became friendlier. Chiara learned that Maria's father was a cabinetmaker and had a prosperous shop near Florence. He hadn't liked Maria's husband, had called him an adventurer, a good-for-nothing, but had given him money for the voyage.

"Ah, but he was so handsome, that's all I could see. Love may be blind after all. I still dream of him each night, and long for him."

At dinner one evening, when Chiara related Maria's story to Michele, he was visibly agitated and waved away her words. "I don't want to hear such sad tales."

"But can you believe there are men who would abandon their wives?"

"There are all kinds of people in this world. You think the world is filled with nuns and priests? Perhaps there are circumstances you don't know about."

"But to leave his wife and—"

"I told you to be quiet. I don't like hearing that kind of gossip."

Chiara shrugged, perplexed, but said no more.

After dinner, as they walked back to the cabin, Michele said, "Come now, you must speak the new words you learned today."

Each day since their wedding, Michele had insisted she learn ten new American words. Now he laughed indulgently at her attempts. Miffed by his laughter, she pouted, causing him to laugh even more. She scolded him in a string of Italian.

"Where is the shy, obedient wife I was promised?" he asked in mock anger, leaning against the rail. "Come to think of it, the *ruffiana* said you had a temper."

"What? I have no temper," Chiara insisted, then, realizing the contradiction, laughed along with Michele.

He was patient with her, she realized, and kind. Besides that, he was quite handsome, especially when he

smiled, his white teeth glowing against his dark skin. She
wanted to know so many things about him.

"Why did you wait so long to marry?"

He shifted uncomfortably. "Italian men don't marry
young. You know that. Besides, I was always too busy to
think of women. I worked, ate, slept, that was my life."

Chiara thought that unlikely. She didn't know much
about men, but knew their nature required more than
what Michele had described.

"Tell me about when you were young," she said. "Tell
me about your village."

"It was a simple place, not unlike your own, except
that it clung to a mountainside in Campania. I liked to
look down on the village from a special spot in the
mountains. There was a dry stone wall and large flat
steps leading to the village. I could see the little stone
houses with red tile roofs, the terraced farms and orchards, the springs that sang as they made their uneven
way downhill. It was beautiful."

Chiara edged closer to him. "You went by yourself
into the mountains?"

"No, I would go with Mama to the spring to do the
weekly wash. You would have loved my mother. She was
kind and loving." Michele put his arm around Chiara,
hugging her close. "I remember how she walked, tall and
straight, one hand holding mine, the other supporting the
large woven basket on her head. She'd straddle two flat
stones in her bare feet and whip the sheets up and down
in the rushing water." Michele laughed at the memory.

"I had a friend, Concetta," he continued, "who came
to the spring with her mother. Her skirt would be tied up
around her waist and we'd splash in the lively stream
while our mothers washed and gossiped. Sometimes we
would frighten our parents by playing in the caves. People once lived in those caves." Michele stopped and took
a deep breath. "Concetta cried when I went to America."

A shadow seemed to cross his features while a small
vein pulsed at his temple. He seemed so lost in memory
Chiara hated to intrude.

"What troubles you?" she asked finally.

Startled, Michele turned toward her. He squeezed his
eyes shut, his brow furrowing. "I was remembering . . . remembering. It was so long ago. I was six years old

when we went to America. America. It was a magic word, a place where everything was possible. At the Statue of Liberty my father raised me to his shoulders and said, 'Remember this lady, son.' He said other things I didn't understand, about the value of work, about safety and freedom from want, about never being beholden to anyone. Work and family, he always told me, that's what life's all about. Nothing will come to you without hard work."

This was a new side to Michele, a thoughtful, introspective side. She was fascinated by his story. "Did your father find work?"

"Not at first. Then he got a job in Illinois, on the railroad. When he heard Ford was hiring men at five dollars a day, we went to Detroit. So did thousands of others, from all over the country. There were so many men crowded outside the factory gates, they finally chased them away with fire hoses. They said you had to be a resident of Detroit for at least six months to get a job at Ford."

"Did he get a job?"

Michele turned away from the ship's rail, and taking Chiara's hand, walked toward their cabin. "Finally he was hired at Ford's 'Crystal Palace' in Highland Park. That's near Detroit. His job was to guide the body, the outside of the car, to the chassis, the inside. The body would come down from the second story on top of the chassis, which moved along on the first floor. That's all he did, day in, day out. But he was grateful to be working. 'God bless America,' he'd say after grace each day."

"You admired your father very much, didn't you?"

"Yes, he was a good man. I miss him still." Michele's eyes became hard and steely. "He died after a car body worked loose from its pinnings and fell on his leg, mangling it. There was an infection and . . ." He turned away, swallowing hard. "I was fifteen years old. My mother was beside herself with grief. She scraped together what money she could and we returned to the old country." Michele stuffed his hands into his pockets. The air was turning colder. "I wanted to stay in Detroit, pleaded with my mother. I figured I could get a job and support the two of us. But she wouldn't hear of it."

"It must have been sad for you, leaving your friends behind," Chiara mused. "Then what did you do in Italy?"

"The usual, I worked in the fields. How I hated it. Oh, not the work, actually. It's wonderful to see your efforts come to fruition. No, it was just that I knew there was no future there. I could break my back twelve hours a day and never get ahead." Michele lapsed into silence and Chiara waited patiently to hear more, but he stared vacantly, silently at the endless ocean, lost in his own thoughts. Finally he resumed walking. Chiara kept pace, but he hardly seemed aware she was at his side.

Little by little Chiara stripped the outer shell and glimpsed deeper into the mind of her husband. She was encouraged by what she discovered, but often there seemed to be a secret part of him he wouldn't or couldn't share, and a vulnerable area that required her understanding, her comforting, and even, surprisingly, her protection.

On the day of their arrival, the decks were jammed with passengers, all wanting a glimpse of the Statue of Liberty. Chiara almost hated to see the week-long journey end. Despite some mild seasickness in the mornings, it had been a pleasant passage and the most leisure she had ever experienced.

As they drew near the harbor, the fog rose up in great clouds from the inky water, but soon dissipated in the morning sun. When finally the giant metal woman came into view, Chiara's heart lifted. Golden rays struck the torch and lit the lady's inscrutable face.

In her bearing—the arch of her arm, the lifted breast, the high-held torch—there was hope. What will America hold for the Marcassas? Chiara wondered. Her faith in Michele and in their future had grown steadily firmer; but still when she closed her eyes, she recalled again her mother and father as she had last seen them, and her heart yearned ever homeward.

As the ship drew close to the harbor, her excitement intensified. Ahead, Manhattan Island loomed, with mile after mile of peaks and spires that pierced the clouds.

"Skyscrapers," Michele said.

Chiara thought the island must surely sink with so much steel and concrete weighing upon it. A ferry shuttled them to Ellis Island, where an imposing gray building stood among smaller structures of red brick and white stone.

"It looks like a castle," Chiara said, awed at the sight of the main building that dominated the island.

"Only on the outside," Michele said.

On the island Chiara clung to her husband's arm, fearful of being lost in the sea of humanity. Most of the people were ragtag immigrants from third-class passage, carrying rope-tied bundles and wearing fearful expressions.

In a daze, Chiara was pushed forward among the crowd, into the building. A huge staircase led from the baggage room up to the Great Hall.

"See those men at the top of the steps?" Michele asked. "They're doctors, looking for lameness or shortness of breath. See, they're pulling that poor wretch out of the line. They'll mark his jacket with chalk, L for lameness, H for heart or lung diseases."

"*Madre di Dio,* what stories these steps could tell." Chiara clung to Michele's arm amid the crush of bodies.

The Great Hall, a room roughly one hundred by two hundred feet, had a high vaulted ceiling and steel-mesh cages lining both sides, where, Michele explained, undesirables were detained. Attendants, shouting and shoving, funneled people into the proper areas, and some into detention rooms because of faulty papers or suspected disease.

Michele propelled Chiara through a maze of narrow passages divided by iron fences. At a high desk at the end of each passage sat an inspector, the judge who would with a stroke of the pen decide the fate of those standing humbly before him.

There were thousands of people shuffling through the lines, emitting a babel of strange sounds from many different lands, bewildered, straining to understand. Inoculations were given, papers checked and checked again, questions asked and answered, all the while the cacophony of voices swirled about them, shrieking and yelling, strident voices, insisting, demanding.

"We're almost finished." Michele shifted a suitcase to his other hand. "I'll send a telegram as soon as we get our train tickets, to let Flora and Eduardo know when we'll be arriving."

At last they were directed to the money-exchange area and finally to the railroad room, where they waited for the ferry to the mainland rail lines in New Jersey. From there they would board the train for Detroit.

"How much longer?" Chiara asked, her face haggard with fatigue. They had been on the island for eight hours.

Michele patted her hand. "Soon."

The train to Detroit was grimy and rank with the odor of so many bodies. Chiara started when the shrill whistle blast signaled the train's departure. Slowly gathering steam, the train jerked forward with a low, hollow rumble, then gradually gained momentum, and finally settled into a steady rocking pace. Chiara heaved a sigh and burrowed gratefully into her seat.

The incessant grinding and clacking of the wheels had a hypnotic effect. Through the dirty window she watched the swiftly passing scenery. There were murky rivers pushing against muddy banks, green forests with spiky pine trees etched against the sky, gray shanties and red brick mansions, rusty sumac and Queen Anne's lace, flickering lights on high buildings and low, and vast empty spaces, moving, moving, at a dizzying pace, like life itself. With each turn of the wheels she felt the enormous distance between her and her homeland growing, felt a severing of the chains that bound her. This was another world, a strange world. Touching Michele's arm, her eyes glistening with tears, she asked, "Will we ever go home again?"

He reached across the seat to hold her hand. "Yes, if you want to, but not to stay. America is your home now. You'll see; you'll love America." He settled comfortably in his seat and coaxed her head to his shoulder. "You're overly tired now. Try to sleep."

When they arrived at Michigan Central Station the next evening, Chiara's head pounded from a combination of fatigue and excitement. The noise from trains coming and going rumbled around the cavernous building, intensifying her exhaustion.

"Detroit, Chiara," Michele said, helping her maneuver the narrow iron steps. "Say hello to your new home."

"Look, look, there they are," Chiara yelled, catching sight of Flora and Eduardo Pasini.

The Pasinis strained their necks for a glimpse of their friends, while Chiara waved frantically and called to them. Flora spotted them and ran forward, the feather in her red cloche dancing erratically on her head. Eduardo followed a few steps behind. Chiara squealed out in delight at the sight of her dear cousin, remembering all at once their childhood pranks and jokes, their adolescent exchanges of dreams. The women hugged and kissed noisily, with joyous exclamations, while the men watched indulgently. Then the men clapped each other's shoulders and pressed their cheeks together, first one side, then the other.

Flora, usually the somber one, laughed and chattered, asking questions without waiting for answers, while Eduardo, a thin wiry man with a slightly hooked nose, directed them impatiently toward a cab.

In the cab, to show off her English, Chiara said, "Good morning." When they all laughed, she was bewildered.

"This is night, not morning," Michele explained patiently.

Chiara looked petulant. "And I thought I was so smart."

"Don't worry, I'll help you learn," Flora said. "Though, God knows, I make many mistakes. Still, I try, not like some women, who refuse to even make an attempt." She squeezed Chiara's arm. "I'm so glad you're staying with us."

"You must stay as long as you like," Eduardo insisted. "Flora is lonesome and has talked of nothing else for weeks."

"I haven't made many friends," Flora said. Of the two of them, Chiara was the more gregarious one, Flora the shy one. She had a tendency to look at the mean side of life, Chiara remembered. Sometimes Flora's heavy eyebrows would raise, as if she were looking down upon the world and all the people in it. Her face was round, and the unruly dark ringlets of her bobbed hair were forced into even rows of waves, with a few curls plastered down against her forhead and cheeks. Now she glowed with the happiness of having her cousin with her.

"We will stay only until I'm working again," Michele said.

Chiara craned her neck to look out the window. So many buildings. So many people and cars. Where were they all going? She read the street signs as the cab careened through the bustling, energetic city. The streets bore French names: Lafayette, Dubois, Gratiot, Beaubien, St. Antoine, Cadillac.

"Why are there so many French names?" she wondered aloud.

"Detroit was settled by the French," Michele said. "An Italian, too, named Tonti, but no one ever hears of him."

Flora said, "We'll go shopping together. At Eastern Market you can get fresh vegetables and fruit. And there are many lovely shops for clothing."

"Are there any dressmaker shops?"

"I don't know. Most things are ready-made."

"I thought I could work for a dressmaker, like I did in Italy."

Michele glared at his wife. "My wife won't work! Your job will be to take care of me and our home . . . and our children too, when they come along."

Chiara smarted under his reprimand, but said nothing. She was beginning to realize that she'd have to handle her husband diplomatically in order to get her way.

Flora covered the awkward moment. "We'll take you to the moving-picture show, and to Belle Isle Park."

They moved past Canfield Avenue, and Eduardo said, "Almost there. We rent the upper flat; it's not so bad."

As he helped unload their bags, the cabdriver said, "Eye-talian, eh? I know lots of Eye-talians. Detroit's full of 'em, the east side especially. I *capisce* a little." He flicked the ash from his cigarette. "I love that dago-red stuff."

The men looked at each other and shrugged.

The wooden houses were tall and narrow, and so close one to the other that Chiara was sure they could probably hear a sneeze from the building next door. In front of each house was a tiny patch of sparse grass.

The pungent aroma of *sugo,* heavy with garlic and oregano, greeted them as they stepped inside the flat. A black metal monster with squat legs dominated the dining room.

"It's a stove," Flora explained. "You'll be glad to have it on cold nights." She ushered them through the living room, kitchen, and two bedrooms.

"Sit, sit," Flora commanded when their bags had been unloaded. She slipped on an apron and presided over the supper of veal and pasta.

While they ate, Eduardo talked about the current working conditions. "I hope you get a job quickly. Some of my friends have been laid off." He pushed large platters of food toward Michele. "Some were never called back after the summer changeover."

"It happens with every model change," Michele said.

"As usual, the workers are disgruntled. There are many union agitators. But of course, they're quickly gotten rid of." Eduardo twirled long strings of pasta on his fork. "I hope Briggs takes you back."

"I wish I didn't have to go back to the factory. I always think of my father's accident . . ."

Eduardo shrugged. "What else is open to you, my friend?"

"I suppose you're right. Well, one good thing about America, there's always work."

After they ate, Chiara insisted on helping Flora clean up, while the men went into the front room. Over the rattle of dishes and pots, Chiara heard the men discuss work and mutual friends. During a lull in Flora's nonstop chattering about all the surprises Chiara could look forward to, she heard Eduardo ask *sotto voce,* "Does she know about the *other?*"

She heard Michele's quick reply, "No. And she never will." There was more, spoken in whispered agitation, but the words were lost to her.

Later, overcome with exhaustion, Chiara gave her cousin a grateful hug and said good night. Michele followed her moments later. The wood floor in the neat little bedroom smelled of fresh wax. Next to the bed lay a stiff rag rug, and a crucifix hung over the bed. She unpacked a few essential garments and tucked them into the top drawer of the polished pine chest on which stood a statue of the Virgin.

Chiara slid into the bed murmuring a good night. Lulled by the airy smell of freshly laundered linen and comforted by the softness of the feather pillow agaist her head, she gave herself up to sleep.

Michele's whisper as he slipped into bed jarred her. "Well, Chiara, do you like your new home?"

"It's too early to know and I am too tired to care," she said through a yawn.

"No, you're not too tired yet. There is one more wifely duty to fulfill before you close your eyes," he said, moving against her.

"No, no, they will hear us," Chiara whispered in alarm.

Michele hugged her close. "I don't care. This is a special time—our first night in Detroit."

Chiara sighed and teased, "Don't you ever grow tired of this?"

"Never." Michele's lips moved over her face, kissing first her nose, then her cheek, her lips.

Chiara's hands caressed his back, feeling the tensed muscles. "Michele, what were you and Eduardo talking about?"

His breath was coming faster. "Many things. Work, mostly."

"No, it was something else."

His hand found her breast. "Hush, Chiara."

"Eduardo said something about telling me, Michele. What do you have to tell me?"

In the dark Michele stiffened momentarily.

"What is it?" she prodded.

"I don't remember," he muttered. "Something about his job."

"But you sounded so annoyed."

Michele's hand slid over her belly, to her thighs. "It was nothing. I don't remember." He positioned himself over her, then covered her mouth with his, terminating any further discussion.

Though she was exhausted, Chiara let her husband take his pleasure. It was her duty to yield. Through the first weeks of their marriage she had come to enjoy his frequent and ardent lovemaking, and usually welcomed his advances. But not this night. Tonight she felt strange and displaced. The sights and sounds with which she'd been bombarded throughout the day had left her physically and emotionally spent.

She thought of her tiny bedroom at home and the two young sisters who had shared it and listened raptly as she entertained them with stories while the night noises of nature lulled them. When she shut her eyes, she could almost smell the lemon trees and oleanders, could almost taste the fresh almonds that dropped from overladen branches.

Italy. That's where I belong, she thought, where I want to be.

America will never be home.

4

Flora and Chiara, their heads wrapped in white cotton squares, set flour and eggs out on the oilcloth-covered table. Arms powdered white to the elbow, Flora made a valley in the mound of flour and cracked an egg into it. She added portions of the heaped flour a bit at a time, working it in. Making the sign of the cross, Chiara said, "I pray Michele finds a job. He left early this morning, but Eduardo didn't sound too hopeful about his chances."

"He'll find work. Don't worry," Flora said, scraping dough from her fingers.

The two women gossiped, laughing and giggling like schoolgirls while they rolled out dough for the gnocchi.

"It's not like at home, is it?" Flora said. "Remember how hot it would get, cooking by the fireplace, stirring the big black pot on the tripod? It's easier with the gas stove."

"Yes, everything seems easier here. I'm glad I have you, or what would I do? The way of living is so different. My life changed the moment I stepped onto the boat." Chiara flipped indentations into small balls of dough with her thumb, the way her mother had taught her. "I met a woman on the boat, Maria, who was coming to America by herself, to find her husband. It was very brave of her. I hope she doesn't find a tragedy awaiting, like her husband's death. I gave her this address. Maybe she'll write."

"Probably he has found himself another wife. I've heard of it happening. Men get lonely without family here, and conveniently forget they have wives in the old country."

"Ahh." Chiara nodded with a pained expression. "Look," she said, pointing to the thin stream of water coming from the icebox. "Do you have an animal? A cat or dog, hiding somewhere?"

"No, I just forgot to empty the water from the melting ice," Flora said, wiping her hands on her apron. "It must be done each day."

"So many new things to learn," Chiara said, bewildered.

While Flora emptied the basin, a light knock sounded.

Flora opened the door to a young girl bearing a large cooking pot. Slight as a whisper, but shapely, she had a turned-up nose on her freckled face and an abundance of auburn hair. Her scarlet lips and thin, painted eyebrows gave her the appearance of a cinema star. It wasn't quite "nice" to be painted up like that, Chiara thought.

"Ma says thanks for the spaghetti pot, Flora. She used your recipe. It was swell," the girl said.

"Thank you, Penny." Flora relieved her of her burden. "Come and meet my cousin Chiara, from Italy." Turning, she explained to Chiara, "This is Penny, who lives in the downstairs flat."

"Penny, *sì*, money," Chiara said, rubbing her thumb against the tips of her fingers.

"Yeah, money," Penny said, laughing. "How do you like Detroit, kid?"

Chiara concentrated, then said, "Detroit is nice—a *città*, city."

Penny clapped her hands in delight. "It's so cute, the way you talk. Say, I like your dress."

"*Sì*. You like? I make." Chiara ran a hand from her waist to her thigh.

"No kidding? Gee, you're good." Penny nodded her head in admiration, then opened her mouth wide as an idea struck her. "Say, could you sew me a dress? I need something really swell for tomorrow night. Jimmy's taking me to a speak. I never been there before, but I hear some ritzy folks go. Jimmy's my boyfriend."

Chiara looked quizzically to Flora for her rapid translation, then nodded wildly at Penny.

"*Sì, sì,* I make." It would be good to have something to occupy her time, to keep her mind from dwelling on her homesickness.

"Good, you can use the machine Eduardo bought me," Flora said. "It sits there collecting dust and scowling at me for not using it. I sewed enough in Italy to last me a lifetime. And I hated it, too, not like you. My seams were never straight, my hems always too short or too long."

"Let's go to Hudson's this afternoon for the goods and pattern," Penny said.

"Yes," Flora agreed quickly, "I want to show my cousin downtown."

Later, as the three women exited the streetcar, Flora explained, "Hudson's is the world's tallest department store."

"I've never seen such a grand store, not in Bari, not even in Naples," Chiara exclaimed, lingering before each window display.

Flora pulled her along, saying, "Come, or we'll never get back home before dark."

Fascinated by the diversity of merchandise, Chiara had to be dragged away from counter after counter. She insisted on taking the elevator and stopping at each of the ten floors, where she oohed and aahed in amazement at the wondrous assortments. At the yard-goods department, she fervently wished she could transport Dona Isabella, her old employer, for just one day, to glory in the myriad textures and colors, the silks and moirés, the chintzes and muslins. It was a feast for the senses.

After Penny had made her choices, they returned home and Chiara set to work immediately.

"I'm making a dress for Flora's friend," she explained when Michele returned.

He frowned. "I don't want you working."

"I'm not really *working*. It's just a favor for a friend."

Michele grunted in what Chiara supposed was agreement.

Sewing steadily on Flora's Singer treadle machine, she finished all but the buttonholes and hem by the next afternoon. Penny came by and paced impatiently while Chiara whipped her needle through the cloth.

"Do you have a job?" Chiara asked.

"I worked at the five-and-dime but they laid me off when sales slowed down."

Chiara was confused by the rush of unfamiliar words. Flora entered the kitchen and translated.

"Michele has had no good fortune yet," Chiara said, struggling with the English words, with help from Flora.

"He thought Briggs would take him back, but no." She finished the hem and began working the buttonholes.

"When I got out of high school in June, I thought I'd get a job easy. I wanted an office job, but my typing ain't so good."

"Finite!" Chiara bit the thread and gave a quick shake to the shimmery garment.

Penny wriggled out of her dress, and Chiara thought she looked like a child in her cotton slip, thin-boned and slight.

Penny shimmied into the red satin frock with its deep neckline and dropped waist and did a quick little dance, twirling around until the skirt billowed a bit. Hugging Chiara, she said, "Chiara, you're a champ. Wait'll Jimmy gets a load of this. It'll knock his eyes out."

The next day Penny appeared to report on the party, and Chiara found herself charmed by the girl's expressive pixie face and amusing stories, which, with all the slang, sometimes defied translation. She was Chiara's first introduction to an "American" girl, and though her light-hearted, joking ways were as foreign to Chiara as pasta to peanut butter, she had an undeniable appeal. Chiara's innate suspicion of non-Italians was slowly diminishing.

"They finally let us in, even though we didn't have the right password. And Jimmy was nuts about the dress, and so was my sister, Rosie." Penny paused to light a cigarette.

"Bene," Chiara said, pouring coffee.

"Say, Rosie works for these rich folks, the Austins, and she told me Mrs. Austin is looking for a seamstress. Are you interested?"

"I think, yes," Chiara said with sudden interest, "but I must ask my husband."

"Oh, honey, do you think he'd mind?"

"In Italy, the husband is worker. The woman takes care of the home."

"Well, you'd like the Austins," Penny said. "Mr. Austin, especially. He's real handsome."

Though excited at the prospect of earning money of her own, Chiara realized that Michele might not share her enthusiasm. He hadn't been pleased when she made Penny's dress, had let her know that he didn't approve of women working. Yet he couldn't have a great deal of money left from his savings. Chiara hated the thought of being penniless and dependent on her cousin.

Her husband sometimes puzzled her. Usually kind and understanding, sometimes he became stern or sullen when something she said upset him. She credited his moodiness to his inability to find a job. He'd been so certain he would begin work immediately. He was probably concerned about their finances too.

When Michele returned home that afternoon, he told Chiara and Flora, "I have good news."

"You have a job!" Chiara said hopefully.

"No, not that good." He hung his cap on a hook by the door. "I've rented a flat. We can't impose on our friends any longer."

"Oh, no, Michele, please don't leave us," Flora said, turning from the stove where she stirred a pot of sauce with a wooden spoon. "We've just begun to exchange all the news. It will take another month to finish."

"You two will never finish talking. No, my mind's made up. We're moving in two weeks."

Later, as she prepared for bed, Chiara asked, "Can we afford the rent money? Who knows when you'll have work?"

"I'll have work, don't you worry," Michele said with a flash of temper. "I still have a little money left from my savings."

"I'm not worried," Chiara said quickly. "But wouldn't it be better to stay here awhile, even after you have a job? That way we could save for a house."

"No, I want some privacy."

Chiara was disappointed, but didn't pursue the subject. "Well, I have good news too. Penny told me of a family that needs a seamstress." She rolled down her cotton stockings from thigh to ankle and drew them off her arched feet, then laid the plump tan circles on a chair. "I'm becoming bored with nothing to do. I would so enjoy sewing again."

"If you're bored, you can sew for yourself."

"I don't need more clothes, and it would be a waste of money."

Michele, in his underwear, looked determined. "My wife is not going to work."

Chiara picked up a brush and methodically yanked it

through her hair. Michele was so stubborn. She would have to convince him some way. "What if you don't get work for another month?"

"I'll get work."

"Michele, I would like to do something useful, be of service to people."

Michele laughed. "Only you could view working for others as a pleasure." He hung his pants in the tiny closet, then stretched his long arms to the shelf overhead. "Look, I want to show you something."

"What is it?"

Gingerly he withdrew a guitar and sat on the bed, lovingly stroking the wood.

"What is it?" Chiara asked, sitting on the bed next to him.

"What do you think it is? It's a guitar."

He tipped his ear toward the instrument as he plucked each string, then hummed while he adjusted the keys.

"You never told me you played the guitar." Chiara's voice was accusing.

Michele turned amused eyes to her. "I told you, you don't know everything about me." His fingers teased the strings and he toyed with the keys, tightening and loosening until he was satisfied. As Chiara watched in bemused silence, the frown of concentration eased from Michele's face and he strummed chords until his fingers found an easy familiarity with the instrument.

He began singing *"O Sole Mio"* in a muted baritone, his head cocked, his eyes closed.

When he finished, Chiara placed her hand on his shoulder. "Michele, that's beautiful."

The music had put him in good humor. Now was the time to push her advantage. "You didn't answer me about the sewing job, Michele. Can I do it? This one job, then I'll quit."

He thumbed the D string and sighed.

She ran feathery fingers up his arm. "Please?"

"Well, if you must do it, go ahead." He played a strident chord. "But I don't like it."

Chiara, flanked by Penny and Flora, walked along the winding grass-lined avenue where stately homes of various designs stood on huge green lawns. Some homes had gatehouses; others were obscured by tall trees and shrubs. They were all multistoried, mostly brick, with more windows than Chiara could count. A gardener whistled as he hoed among the shrubs and greenery that hugged a white brick mansion.

Though Chiara was only ten miles from her own home, she could have been on another planet.

"This is Grosse Pointe. You have to have bucks to live here." Penny slid her thumb across her fingers in the "money" symbol.

Chiara, breathing deeply, was struck by the absence of factory fumes. "It looks so different; it even smells different."

"Yes, and it sounds different too. No streetcar noises, no children shouting. It's peaceful here," Flora remarked.

Penny said, "You bet it's different; it's where the rich live. It ain't a city I'll ever live in."

Nor I, thought Chiara. But her uncle's words came to her: "Never forget to dream." Could she dare to dream of having a home like those she passed? Could her dreams ever come true, or were they merely idle and unattainable fantasies? Her dream of buying Isabella's shop had never had the slightest chance of fulfillment.

Several blue spruces towered at the edge of the curved driveway to the Austin home, while maples, Dutch elms, and oaks dotted the spacious lawn. Small clumps of marigolds and a white flower unfamiliar to Chiara edged the shrubbery along the front of the house.

A maid wearing a frilly white cap and white apron over a black dress answered the door and spoke to them in hushed tones, as if they were in a church. The marble-floored foyer smelled of polish and lemons. Several doors circled the vestibule and a wide staircase wound to the second floor. Chiara looked upward at the shimmery crystal teardrops of a huge chandelier. She had never been in such a grand house before.

The women were ushered into a small library lined with bookcases floor to ceiling, with a huge desk polished to a glassy sheen facing them. Even in her uncle's home she'd never seen so many books. In a corner of the room was a grouping of four leather chairs and a round table. The scent of pipe tobacco and leather hovered in the air.

"Jeepers, ain't it grand?" Penny said, her eyes sweeping the room.

"I think I'm in heaven," said Chiara. "All these books. Can one person read them all?"

"Who would want to?" Flora replied.

The woman who entered had neatly marcelled hair and wore a shiny dress that accented her boyish thinness. Chiara's first thought was that it would be easy to fit clothes to such a figure, for there were few curves to sew darts around.

"Mrs. Marcassa?" the woman said, looking from one to the other, and extending her hand.

"*Sì,*" said Chiara, nodding, taking the woman's cool hand.

"I'm Penny Middleton, Mrs. Austin," Penny said, "Rosie's sister. Flora, here, is Chiara's cousin. Chiara doesn't speak English too well, so her cousin will sort of translate."

"I'm pleased to meet you. So good of you to come. Do sit down." Mrs. Austin fluttered a long-fingered hand toward the chairs. "You look too young to be an accomplished seamstress," she continued doubtfully.

Chiara sat on a wine-colored wing chair of soft leather. "I speak not good, but I make nice dress," she said, pointing to her own dress with a small white collar and covered buttons to the waist. "*Bella costuma.*"

"Why, that's lovely," Mrs. Austin said, looking closely at the fine detail of the dress. "I need a gown for a dinner party next week. It's short notice, I know. Can you do it?"

"*Sì,* yes, I do."

At Mrs. Austin's bidding, a maid brought in a package containing a pattern with "Butterick" written across the top, a length of exquisite pale green brocade, and a tapestry-covered sewing basket. Mrs. Austin explained rapidly the changes she wanted while Chiara took notes and measurements.

"You can work here if you like; I have a small sewing room on the third floor," Mrs. Austin said when Chiara had finished.

"No, I will work at home, and return day after tomorrow for a fitting." Chiara preferred to work in privacy, and have the freedom to sing at her work when things went well, or complain out loud when things went wrong.

Later, while they waited for the streetcar and Flora and Penny chattered in English, Chiara's thoughts went back to Mrs. Austin and her elegant home. People really live this way, day in, day out, as if they have no cares, no woes, she thought. They wear silk and fine woolen, they have shiny automobiles and impeccable manners. They have maids who make the meals and clean the floors, gardeners who trim the shrubbery and tend the lawn. What quirk at the hand of fate ordained that some fortunate few should live in splendor and others in poverty? Is there some reason? Do the rich deserve to be rich, and the poor deserve to be poor? Perhaps the rich merely learned to seize opportunity when it presented itself.

She fervently wished there was some way she could direct her path toward a better life. But the habit of *la via vecchia*, of accepting, making do, shackled her.

America was the land of opportunity. God willing, her children would have the opportunities that she and Michele never had.

The sewing room at the Austin home was cozy, with an overstuffed covered-chintz chair in a corner and matching curtains tucked back to let in the sun. Facing the window was the sewing machine, its cast-iron filigree work black as india ink. Well-oiled, it responded readily to Chiara's steady pedaling. She had completed most of the garment at home, and was working now on the finishing touches because Mrs. Austin was in a "dreadful hurry" for the gown.

Chiara frequently halted her work to glance outside. Beyond the window was a large manicured garden where a sea of blue-green grass, each blade perfect, halted at a curved border edged with tiny purple-and-white flowers. There were gleaming white concrete steps leading down to a charming white gazebo containing wrought-iron chairs, a table, and a settee. In the distance, white-capped waves lifted and dropped in the Detroit River. The river fascinated her. She'd seen it up close, gray and angry, but today it was lively and interesting, a vivid blue. Mike— Chiara had adopted her husband's Americanized name— had shown her on a map how the Great Lakes circled the mitten of Michigan. She wanted to see where the river spilled into Lake St. Clair, and then into Lake

Huron, wanted to see the towns on the water's edge.
Someday, Mike promised, when they had a car of their
own, they would drive north as far as Port Huron, where
the lake began. Her gaze went back to the gazebo and
she thought idly how pleasant it would be on warm
summer days to sit there and read or embroider.

Softly Chiara sang to herself as her nimble fingers
guided the cloth through the swiftly tracking needle.

"Hello, what's this?" asked a voice behind her. "Have
we a canary in the house?"

Turning her head, Chiara encountered the soft gray
eyes of a very tall, very thin gentleman. His hands were
at his waist, pushing back the coat of his gray suit. The
watch chain across his vest shone as only gold can.

"Canary?" Chiara asked, puzzled by the new word.

"Ah, you're the new Italian seamstress Audrey told
me about. How do you do? I'm Stewart Austin."

"How do you do?" Chiara repeated, enunciating each
word. She put her hand in his outstretched one. "I am
Chiara Marcassa."

"I used to know Italian. Let's see if I can recall a few
words," he said, staring upward for inspiration. *"Buon
giorno. Comè stai?* How's that?

"Very good," she said, smiling at his effort.

He looked pleased with himself. "Do you do much
sewing work, Mrs. Marcassa?" he asked in halting Italian.

"No, only for Mrs. Austin. I am working until my
husband has a job," she replied, also in Italian.

"Well, perhaps we can steer more sewing your way.
Audrey seems very impressed with you, and she has
many friends she can recommend you to."

Audrey entered the room and slipped her arm through
her husband's. "Darling, I thought I heard you come in.
I see you've met Mrs. Marcassa."

There was something about Mrs. Austin that made
Chiara uneasy, a quality she couldn't quite put her finger
on, perhaps the overly bright smile and the tautness of
her bearing.

"Yes, we've met. A charming young woman."

"Her husband is looking for work, Stew. Do you think
you could help him?"

"Why, yes, I think so. Why don't you tell your husband to come around to the Ford Rouge Plant, and I'll

see what I can do." He fished a card from his pocket and jotted some words on it. "Have him see Harry Bennett, in Personnel. He can show Harry this card."

Chiara took the card. *"Grazie, signore,"* she said, overwhelmed by the unexpected kindness.

"Finding Chiara was a stroke of luck," Audrey said. "It's so tiresome going to New York for shopping."

"A welcome addition, I'm sure."

"Oh, no, darling, she's not staying. She works out of her own home. No, she's just finishing up a gown as a special favor."

Mr. Austin look slightly disappointed. Mrs. Austin steered him out of the room, saying, "Now, we mustn't disturb her, Stew, she has lots of work to do."

"Delightful meeting you, Mrs. Marcassa," he called out as he disappeared around the door.

He reminded her of someone—the wistful smile, the thinness, the bony face—but the memory eluded her. A character in a book, probably.

Finally she finished her work and went in search of the maid to summon Mrs. Austin. Glancing into a bedroom from which emanated shrieks of laughter, she saw Mr. Austin on the floor with a young child. As he advanced on all fours, the child clutched his sides in merriment and threw himself to an opposite corner of the room to evade his "attacker." Chiara smiled at the father-son ritual and imagined Michele indulging in the same sort of game with the child they would have one day. But that was something she didn't foresee for the near future.

"Who did you say this man is?" Michele asked suspiciously.

"I told you; his name is Stewart Austin."

"He's probably nobody. Just wants to act the big shot."

"No, I'm sure he's an important person. I know he's very rich. You should see the fine house they have."

"A fine house doesn't mean anything. We'll see how much influence he has."

Chiara sat on the edge of the tub watching as Michele, in his one-piece yellow-white union suit, performed his morning ritual. He whipped the straight razor up and down the strop hanging behind the door. With a soft white brush he stirred up a lather from the round soap at

the bottom of the cup, then circled the sudsy brush over
his cheeks and jaws and chin. The scritch-scritch of the
razor was oddly comforting as it traveled over his face.

"If I get this job, you can quit sewing. You don't need
to work." Michele's upper lip stretched over his teeth,
accommodating the razor's passage.

"I told you, I enjoy it." Chiara knew her working
offended his masculine sensibilities.

"What are you smiling about?" he asked, toweling
himself dry.

"I love to watch you shave." She kissed his damp
cheek. "You smell so sweet."

"Sweet! Men don't smell sweet!"

"You do."

He laughed and threw the towel at her. His eyes narrowed. "I wish I had more time, I'd teach you a lesson!"

Chiara blushed, aware of the "lesson" he had in mind.

He dressed quickly, tipped his cap at a roguish angle,
and set off for the Rouge plant with a cheerful whistle.
Chiara closed the door behind him and whispered a quick
prayer for his success.

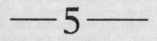

5

"Our luck is changing. We have a new flat and tomorrow
I begin a new job." Michele stood in the center of the
drab cold kitchen, striving for a cheeriness he didn't feel.

Chiara nodded, a forced smile on her lips.

Michele was disheartened by the dismal rental flat on
Chene Street. He wanted desperately to give his new
bride a nice home, a clean, comfortable home, but this
was all he could afford. The paint on the cupboard, once
white, was now a nondescript gray, faded and peeling. He
walked to the sink and noticed the black nicks, like

tiny insects with many legs, that marred the white porcelain. A sagging horsehair sofa and chair stood forlornly in the center of the living room, a remnant from a former tenant.

Out back, a small plot of earth sported a few tufts of grass trying bravely to survive beside a weathered fence. Just beyond, a three-story brick building blocked everything else from view. On one corner of the street stood a barbershop, and on the other a grocery store.

Chiara jumped at the sound of a streetcar rocking along its tracks in front of the house. Michele wondered if his wife would get used to the clacking and grinding noises. By God, he'd make it up to her. Now that he had a job, things would be different.

"It's only temporary," he assured her, touching her shoulder. "As soon as we save for a down payment, I'm going to buy you a house with a big yard."

"I know you will." Chiara stretched both arms around his waist and hugged him close. "Then can we plant tomatoes and onions and parsley? I long for the taste of tomatoes fresh from the vine."

"Of course. There'll be plenty of room for a garden. Maybe we'll plant some grape vines too, and a fig tree."

"A fig tree would never survive this cold climate."

"I know people who have one. In the fall they cover it over with burlap and tarpaulins."

"That would be wonderful, a fig tree."

He saw the lifting of her spirits and made a mental promise: she would have her fig tree one day.

Chiara set about scrubbing immediately, until there was no sign of grease around the stove, and the cracked linoleum floor, black where the pattern had worn away, was as clean as a church altar.

Though the place was drafty and dirty, at least it had cold running water and a proper bathroom with a clawfoot bathtub. Mike smiled at his wife's delight at having a warm bath in the slippery-sided tub, though they had to lug pots of boiling water from the kitchen.

His wife had been bombarded with new challenges, new experiences, but she seemed to be adapting well. Smart; she was smart. Look how quickly she was learning the language. And industrious; always busy cleaning, cooking, sewing.

Sewing. Chiara's accepting that job had nettled him. It should be enough for her to see to his needs. But she seemed so happy with her work, singing, smiling . . . well, it was all right for now. He'd had no idea she was so clever, so talented with her hands. Still, in a few weeks he'd make her quit.

The next day, as his shoes struck the steel steps of the overpass, Michele felt a sense of destiny. The clangor of a thousand feet filled the air. Today he joined the army of laborers in "The Rouge," the vast, bustling complex of Henry Ford that covered eleven thousand acres. It was a city unto itself, a city of smokestacks, steel and brick; of giant pulleys and conveyors; of legions of men carrying black lunch containers; of brains and brawn. Would he take these selfsame steps for the next thirty-some years, punching his card, plodding to his spot, repeating the motions of his job day after day, collecting his paycheck week after week? The thought was at once comforting and strangely alarming.

"This place don't just build automobiles," his foreman said when Michele took his place at the bench. The burly, thick-browed Swede, who had come from the copper mines in the Upper Peninsula, was obviously proud of the factory and of his small place in the order of things. "This here is the world's biggest foundry; we got our own harbor and ninety-two miles of railroad track. Not only that, we got a steel-manufacturing plant and a paper mill too. Buddy, this is some plant!"

"Some plant," Michele agreed as the shrill whistle sounded, summoning thousands of men to action, causing giant machines to whir and grind, propelling the overhead conveyor on its unending journey.

A man called Polack, who chewed continuously on a toothpick, operated a square shear, a voracious guillotine that sliced huge pieces of steel in two with its sharp and shiny blade. Michele's job was to stand behind the shear and pull the steel up snug against a gauge while Polack, on the opposite side, manned the treadle that lowered the blade. A high lift truck hauled away the steel after Michele slid it off the bed and stacked it. His muscles, he realized after a few hours, had gone soft in the time he'd been jobless. No matter, in a week he'd be in shape again. And he wouldn't be a helper for long. He'd move on to a better job.

Every now and then Polack would say, "Move it, dago, we ain't at no Sunday-school picnic."

The men were stripped of personality and reduced to racial and nationality groups: polack, dago, nigger, kraut, mick. Well, so what? It was nothing new. He could endure anything, knowing a paycheck waited for him at the end of the week.

Work. His life was defined in relation to work; that was the Italian way. The twin standards of making your own way and taking care of your own had been ingrained in him from the day he was born. Work was man's destiny; it separated the weak from the strong; it bestowed a sense of self-worth; it empowered one with its monetary reward. Without work, Michele was nothing, and nothing was possible.

When the final whistle blew, he groaned with relief. Outside, the buses were lined up, their doors squeaking as they opened to transport the tired workers back home. Michele was carried forward by the momentum, nudged along onto the crowded bus, where, thankfully, he found a seat. Some sat, reading the paper or a book; others stared into space; some balanced precariously, straddle-legged, hanging on overhead straps. Michele leaned back against the cane seat, and closing his eyes, said a prayer of thanks for his niche in the working world.

He would have to describe his first day to Chiara, he thought wearily, rubbing his hand over his face. He knew she would prod him unmercifully for every small detail.

Chiara. He had to smile, thinking of his lovely wife, the azure eyes, bright and innocent under thick long lashes, the clear pale skin, and light brown hair, the stubborn set of her jaw when she made up her mind. He envisioned the home he would buy, a neat bungalow with his wife inside, presiding over a food-laden table. There would be children, male children, to carry on the family name and the Italian traditions.

A lucky stroke of fate had brought Chiara to him; fate in the form of Flora, with her nagging insistence that he should have a wife. Flora had been ecstatic at the prospect of playing Cupid, and thrilled when the wheels for his betrothal to Chiara had finally been set in motion.

He had never imagined he would fall in love so deeply, so thoroughly, with the lovely Chiara.

Lost in his reveries, Michele started when the conductor called his stop. He jumped eagerly from the top step and almost ran the short block to his house.

Inside his house the smell of olive oil and garlic, nectar of the gods, assaulted him.

"I made risotto," Chiara said when he'd kissed her cheek in greeting.

He warmed his hands over the cookstove with its high curved legs. Inserting a rod into its slot, he lifted the round cover and peered at the darting flames.

"Did you have trouble getting the fire going?"

"Yes, the stove doesn't like me."

Michele laughed. "You'll get used to it."

"I don't think so. It's so capricious; so unlike the stone fireplace in Italy, where we always had a few bones simmering for soup stock, or a pot of beans warming on a tripod."

Chiara ladled out thick, steaming rice onto his plate, then sat across from him, watching him eat, waiting, he knew, for approval. He murmured appreciation, exclaiming over the tastiness of the food. Suppertime was the best time of day. His wife brought a warmth to the kitchen as she ministered to him and urged him to tell about his work.

"There are tiny machines no higher than my head, and giant toggle presses almost touching the ceiling. With one stroke the big presses can form a fender or a quarter-panel."

"Do you use a big machine?"

"No. They didn't believe me when I said I had experience. I'm a helper on a square shear." In between mouthfuls of food, Michele went on to describe his work.

"My poor Michele." Chiara's face puckered in sympathy. "Such hard work."

"It's not as bad as when I was at Briggs," Michele said. "I realize now what a sweat shop Briggs was—not that Ford is so wonderful, but it's an improvement. I got there early this morning and met a guy who used to work at Briggs too. Now he's working tool-and-die at Ford. He's young, but he's tough and smart. Walter Reuther's his name. One of the other guys said to stay away from him; he's a union agitator. But he makes sense to me."

"Michele, I don't like this union business. I heard you and Ed talking the other night. Ed says it's dangerous. He won't have anything to do with unions."

Michele pursed his fingers, rocking them. "You don't have to worry about this. It's man business. You worry about the cooking and cleaning." At her hurt expression his voice softened. "Aren't you eating?"

"I'm not hungry. My stomach's a little upset." She sawed fat slices of bread from a round loaf held firmly under her arm.

Michele took the bread she directed at him from the tip of the knife. "What's wrong? I hope you're not sick."

"I don't know what's wrong. Maybe it's the rain. I haven't seen the sun in a week. That's what I miss most of all, the sun," she said, setting down the knife and bread.

"Tomorrow, I promise the sun will shine, just for you." He knew she was homesick. He reached across the small table and took her chin in his hand. "Come, don't be sad. I thought you would be happy once we had a place of our own."

"I'm trying to be happy."

She reached into the pocket of her apron and produced an envelope addressed in the typical ornate Italian scroll. "I have a letter from Maria Gabriani. In Chicago she found *paisani* from her village and they helped her get work at a restaurant. But no sign of her husband. Now she thinks she has traced him to Detroit, and asks if we can board her for a time so she can continue her search. Sometimes I think it's madness, moving around the country to find this man."

"Where would she stay? We have only our bedroom and your sewing room." He washed down a mouthful of food with a swallow of wine.

"We could put a cot in the sewing room. It would be temporary."

"I don't know, Chiara. It's nice to have some privacy."

"I think we should help her. She's so optimistic about finding Tony."

"Maybe too optimistic. Maybe he doesn't want to be found," Michele said, sopping the last bit of rice from his plate with a chunk of bread. "But I suppose you're right. We should help our countrymen when we can. It will all come back to us. You won't need the room for sewing much longer. You're going to quit working now that I'm earning money."

"I like working."

"Well, you're going to quit anyway. My wife doesn't need to work."

Chiara started to say something, but thought better of it and began to clear away the dishes.

Chiara scrubbed and dried the blue checkered oilcloth and tidied the kitchen, then retired to her workroom. It was Michele's turn to have his friends there for their Saturday ritual card game of *tre sette*.

"You ought to go to bed," Michele said.

"No, I like to listen to the men talk."

Michele seemed nervous. "The men talk rough. Sometimes they end up arguing and almost come to blows."

Chiara laughed. "I'll do some sewing."

She settled under a bare overhead light bulb in her workroom. Needle and thimble in place, she picked up a tiny white satin shirt and worked neat stitches that progressed like a row of ants hastening to their sand hill. "It helps me understand about your work, about factories. Even about men."

When the men took their places around the table, Eduardo said, "You were lucky, Mike, to get a job when you did." He shuffled the cards with quick, slim fingers.

"Lucky, sure," Mike said, squinting in the upward-spiraling stream of smoke from his Lucky Strike, "but when I quit Briggs to go to the old country, I was making more money. Now I'm only making sixty cents an hour. Is that what you call progress?"

"Yeah, but at Briggs you made more because you worked ten, twelve hours a day," Dino said. He was a slight wiry man with a white scar separating his left eyebrow and a great blade of a nose. He made up for his size with a roaring voice.

"I still say you're lucky," Ed persisted, snapping the cards around the table with a flick of his wrist. "Plenty of people are out of work."

Mike shrugged.

Fredo, his large belly pressed against the table, said, "Hell, yes, you're lucky. Look what happened last January. When Ford got ready for full production of the Model A, he advertised for workers and thirty-two thousand men lined up to apply. Only eight thousand were hired. They turned away twenty-four thousand men!" He shook his head. "I wonder what happened to all those other poor suckers, if they ever found work."

Fredo, with his knife-pressed trousers and wavy gray hair in neat rows, was called "the Judge" behind his back, because of his pomposity and his elegant manner of dress.

"Yeah, it was fourteen degrees below zero, too. I know a guy who was there. He got frostbite," Dino said, stubbing out his cigarette.

They finished one set in playful argument, and Mike scooped up the cards for a new deal.

"Factory work's no picnic," Ed said. "It's like being in jail now. We used to have one foreman for thirty workers, now there's one for every fifteen. Still, it's better than the old country, where there's no work at all. I'm not complaining. I make a living; we have food on the table."

Dino popped the meat of a slick *lupino* bean into his mouth and discarded the skin. "Well, I'm complaining. In my section we can't talk, whistle, or even hum, can't even sit down. If we're not working, we have to stand at our benches. One guy just leaned against his machine, and they fired him. Ed's right, it's a jail."

"But wages go up," Eduardo said.

"Bullshit!" Dino banged his fist on the table. "They fire men with five years' seniority, and hire in a green-horn because they can get him for thirty cents less, or even hire back the same man for beginner wages."

The game continued, with cards flying amid shouts of joy or disappointment.

During the next deal, the Judge said, "Our earnings don't buy as much. And where we used to work six days, now we work only five. We go backward instead of forward." He puffed on his cigar. "But I was fortunate; I got into tool-and-die work. That's where the money is."

"Yeah, yeah, we know how rich you are," Dino said, scooping up the cards with a flourish. "We see how nice you dress."

The Judge leaned forward and jabbed his finger toward

Dino to accentuate his words. "Hey, my father put me through Ford Trade School, because he knew the shit you have to take on the line. My father stood with thousands in 1914 when Ford came out with the five-dollar day. There were so many waiting, they put the fire hoses on them, just so the day shift could get through the gates. He finally got hired when they said you had to be a resident of Detroit for six months. Most of those guys came from up north or down south. My father told me, 'You ain't goin' on no line. Tool-and-die, that's the way to go.'"

"Yeah, your father steered you right." Dino fanned his cards, then arranged them in neat order. "But goddammit, you guys think you're the upper crust. Four years ago, when I worked at General Motors, my unit went on strike because they cut our wages, but the tool-and-die men wouldn't support us, and neither would any of the other units. They were all under different unions—body shop, metal finishers, painters, all different. So they fired us. That never woulda happened if we'd all stuck together. Lucky for me I got a job at Chrysler."

"That's the problem; we're all divided," Mike said, snapping a card from his hand to the table. "We have to organize into one big union. There's a guy in our plant, Reuther's his name, a socialist, that's what he keeps saying. He's a tool-and-die man too; a smart fellow. We need to form one union, he says; everybody together."

"You'll never get all the different sections to agree." The Judge squinted past the smoke curling from the cigarette that dangled in the corner of his mouth. "If you talk to the other tool-and-die men, you'd see. They think they're special. Same thing with the painters and grinders—they want their own group."

Dino said, "Face it, there will never be a union at Ford. Not with Henry Ford and Harry Bennett running things. I joined a union one time, the Auto Workers Union, but they got nowhere. They couldn't get enough members."

"The unions have no power. All they can do is pass out leaflets, and then they get hounded." Mike toggled the cork on a jug of dark red wine, filled his glass, and passed the jug along. "If one of Harry Bennett's 'spotters' thinks you're a union 'troublemaker,' you get pushed around and maybe even fired. The whole plant is filled with thugs and ex-convicts that Bennett hired for his Service Department. Bennett's the one hired me. I thought he was okay, but now I know different. I still think one of these days things are going to change. One of these days Detroit will be known as a union town."

"We'll probably never see it," Eduardo said.

Mike snapped back, "No, not if everyone runs scared."

"I ain't scared, just cautious." Eduardo sounded offended. "Listen to me, Mike, don't get mixed up in no union. It means trouble, big trouble."

Before Mike could retort, the Judge said, leaning forward confidentially, "Well, none of us will get rich working in a factory. You wanna get rich, do like I did. Get into the stock market."

"Yeah, sure. You think we've all got money, like you," Dino said sarcastically.

The Judge smiled and nodded as if he had a secret. "You don't need much money. Buy on margin. That's what I did. I bought RCA and it went from eighty-five to four-twenty. I'm cleaning up."

Eduardo was obviously impressed. "What're you doing with all that dough?"

"I don't have it yet. I get it when I sell. But the beauty part is that it's like a loan. You make installment payments."

Eduardo said, "I don't trust that kind of thing. It's not the Italian way, to borrow money. It doesn't even sound legal. If I get a few bucks ahead, I put it into postal certificates."

The Judge reared back, his paunch bouncing, and said with a smirk, "That's why you bums'll never have any money."

Dino jumped to his feet, "Bums, eh?" he yelled.

"Yeah, bums!" The Judge labored to his feet and stood glaring, nose to nose with Dino across the table. Their evening, as always, degenerated into a shouting match, all of them yelling, none listening. And, as always, it ended in good-natured back-slapping and raucous laughter as they left.

Chiara, unable to sleep, had tried to read the Detroit *Times*, but the effort of translating was too great. She picked up *La Voce del Popolo*, the Detroit Italian-language chronicle, in an attempt to block out the men's lively conversation. Soon their shouting distracted her completely and she gave up trying to read. The men sounded disgruntled, but resigned. All but Michele. He sounded . . . What? Determined? His conviction about a union frightened her, though she hardly understood about unions and their purpose. It was clear the bosses didn't want unions. It was also clear that those in favor of unions put their jobs in jeopardy. What was Michele thinking of? Why would he risk his job for an ideal which would probably never work? The bosses always had power and control. Why couldn't Michele just be satisfied to have steady work? She would try to persuade him to give up this union talk. As Eduardo had said, it could only lead to trouble.

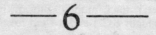

—— 6 ——

"The hem's almost finished." Chiara whipped her needle in and out of the flowered curtain panel.

Flora squinted as she directed thread through the needle's narrow eye. "These hands were not made for sewing."

"What do you like to do, then, if not sewing?"

"I like to cook and play with babies. I'm not like you, needing to be busy all the time. See these hips?" she said, patting the ample sides that seemed to billow below her tiny waist. "They're designed for having babies. But God hasn't seen fit to answer my prayers."

It was a familiar lament. "You have time yet; lucky you married young." Chiara bit the thread and gave the cloth a quick shake. "Everything happens for the best."

Flora scoffed. "So they say, but I haven't found it always to be true." She helped her cousin thread a rod through the new curtains.

Chiara positioned a chair beneath the window and snapped the curtain rod into place. "I appreciate the loan of your machine. As soon as I've saved some money, I'll buy my own and return yours. Michele's savings have gone to buy the kitchen table and chairs and the bed. He says we will buy our own home soon. It won't take long to save three or four hundred dollars for a down payment, especially with my sewing work."

"Do the Austins give you much work?"

"Not only them. They've sent me to others, who are pleased and recommend me to still others. I have plenty of work to keep me busy. And the women let me make changes in the patterns. I look at magazines for new styles, then draw a picture of my designs. My patrons are delighted. It's not like when I worked for Dona Isabella and did the boring jobs."

Chiara loved entering her clients' homes; enjoyed the feeling of opulence and serenity in the high gloss of the dark wood, in the plush pile of the carpets, in the muted brilliance of the Oriental rugs. She would catch herself fantasizing that she was the mistress of those homes.

"I thought Michele wanted you to quit."

Chiara shrugged. "I try not to work when he's home. He doesn't realize how much work I'm really doing. What does it hurt?" She poured coffee into plain white cups, her hand shaking slightly.

"What's wrong?" her friend asked. "Are you upset about something?"

Chiara's eyes misted. "I don't know what's wrong with me. I suppose I'm homesick, Flora. I miss the sunshine and the flowers and the blue, blue sky. I miss my family, especially little Dino. I long to hug him and smother him with kisses."

Flora nodded with a resigned shrug. "I know. I was the same. You'll get over that."

"Nothing sits right with me; even the coffee doesn't taste good." She pushed her cup away, making a face. "My stomach is upset. It feels like the seasickness I had a few days on the ship."

Flora shook her head. "It certainly can't be seasickness. Have you had the bleeding this month?"

"My times have never been dependable. Sometimes I'm early, sometimes two or three weeks late."

Flora threw her hands into the air. "Chiara, you are probably pregnant, you silly thing. My sister couldn't drink coffee when she was pregnant. It made her sick."

Pregnant. Of course, the thought had entered her mind, but for some reason she had pushed it aside. She hadn't wanted it to happen so soon, before she'd even had a chance to adjust to all the changes in her life. And in a vague way, she felt reluctant to share the little time she and Michele had, just as they were beginning to really know each other. Pregnancy restricted one so. In Italy, women were closeted inside their homes for the last few months, as if hiding a shameful condition. She dropped her head into her hands and let out a small sob.

Flora looked bewildered as she rushed to her friend's side. "Aren't you happy?"

"Yes, of course I'm happy." Chiara's words were muffled into her hands. She lifted her face. "But I'm frightened too."

"There's nothing to be frightened of. I envy you," Flora said with a trace of bitterness. "I wanted to be first."

Wiping her eyes on the handkerchief Flora had fished from her sleeve, Chiara said, "I don't know what's wrong with me. I just don't feel ready."

"Of course you're ready. This is what marriage is all about. I only wish it were me."

"I *have* been acting foolishly lately. One minute I laugh, the next minute I cry." Chiara blew her nose noisily. "I suppose I didn't expect it to happen so soon. Sometimes I feel like such a child myself. I wish I could share this with my mother. Aren't you ever homesick, Flora?"

"Oh, yes, I was at first. But that goes away. You adjust. You take what life hands you and make the best of it."

"I don't know if I'll ever truly adjust, if I can feel that this wretched place is home. Sometimes I feel so alone. Oh, I know, I have Michele and you, but . . ." She wiped away a tear. "I wonder what Michele will say."

"He'll be pleased. I know Michele."

Yes, he probably will be pleased. It was understood that they would have children; that's what happened to married people, and he often mentioned the son they would have, a male to carry on the family name. But they had never *really* discussed it, though she had wanted to. Michele was often guarded about his own childhood and family life.

She would tell him when he came home tonight, after supper. He was always relaxed and happy after supper.

After Flora left, Chiara planned what to say, but Michele returned home tired and out-of-sorts, and the evening passed without her mentioning it.

In bed, she snuggled next to him. "Michele?"

"Yes?" He brushed a long strand of hair from her cheek. "Yes, what is it?"

For some reason, she couldn't quite say it. After all, she wasn't absolutely sure she was pregnant, and wouldn't be until the midwife visited. Somehow, she wanted to keep the feeling of "specialness," this warm, cozy secret that seemed to throb under her breastbone. A baby, she thought, hugging her arms around her middle protectively. She imagined a tiny downy-headed infant cradled against her chest.

"It's nothing. Just good night."

For the next several days she kept her secret. Tonight, she thought, tucking a maroon velvet suit for the Austin child into her shopping bag, tonight she would tell him.

It was Saturday, high noon. The light dusting of snow on the ground, the first she'd ever seen, delighted Chiara. She had tugged the new brown rubber galoshes on over her shoes, glad that Michele had bought them over her objections.

"They're ugly," she'd said.

"Never mind, you'll be glad to have them when it's freezing and there's snow on the ground."

Chiara hadn't eaten much breakfast, just a bit of toast and milk, but she felt well when she left the house for the Austin residence. Mrs. Austin had specifically requested the outfit be completed for an activity tomorrow.

As she walked to the streetcar the next day, Chiara spoke to the infant she imagined taking form inside her, expanding her waistline, disrupting her calm. *Darling child, why did I cry when I found out about you? I suppose I was excited and frightened at the same time. I'm pleased as can be now, and can't wait for you to begin punching inside me, which won't be for a while yet. Next*

*week I see the midwife. Already I'm sewing little dresses
and knitting little boots for you. You will be so well-loved.
Even your Comare Flora is crocheting a sweater. Tonight
I will tell your father. I wonder what he'll say. I suppose
he'll want a boy, but for me it doesn't matter. Just be well.*

The cold air felt refreshing at first, but soon she became
nauseated from the fumes from the vehicles crowding the
streets. On the streetcar the seats were all taken. She
held on to a strap, swaying unsteadily, until a fat man
with a leather shopping bag exited.

She gazed out the window. There were so many buildings of wood and brick, so many concrete roads. Where
were the vast farmlands, the fruitful orchards, the open
meadows that Michele assured her dotted the state? Someday, he promised her, he would take her north to see
them. She longed to feast her eyes on green fields and
verdant trees like those she used to see when riding in
the cart alongside her father on their way to his fields.
She would hold on to his arm, the sack of bread, cheese,
tiny sweet green olives, and tomatoes in her lap, while
her father sang to her in his gravelly voice, urging her to
join in. She longed to kiss his leathery cheek, to see his
reaction at the news of his first grandchild. He would
probably cry.

Finally, the ride over, she plodded along on the tree-
lined, winding road where the Austins lived. Her usually
bright eyes, barely visible under the gray cloche hat,
looked faded under the bleak, leaden sky. Her quickened
breath hung in white clouds. Hunching her shoulders, she
was grateful for the thick hair that bunched around her
neck, helping to keep her warm. Usually she enjoyed the
long, energizing walk after the wearisome trolley ride,
but today she felt exhausted. Inhaling gulps of fresh air,
she tried to dispel the slight queasiness that danced around
the pit of her stomach. Skirting small patches of ice that
glinted like scallop-edged mirrors, she trudged up the
long, curved walk to the front door.

Mr. Austin answered the door, his year-old son on his
shoulders. He was dressed in casual weekend attire, a
thick maroon sweater and sharply pressed gray trousers.

"Mrs. Marcassa, our Italian songstress. Do come in,"
he said, sliding the squealing child from his shoulders into
his arms. "Say hello, Sonny," he said to the boy, who

responded with gurgles and smiles. He called down the hall, "Molly, please come and take the little fellow. It must be time for his nap."

Chiara took a deep breath, which seemed to quell the nausea.

Mr. Austin balanced the child on his hip. "Sorry to tell you after you've come all this way, but Audrey isn't home at the moment. She's at some luncheon, a charity function, I think." When Chiara didn't answer immediately, he said, "Oh, I am sorry, *scusa*, you don't understand everything, do you? *Non capisci, eh?*"

"I understand very much. My husband speaks only English to me and makes me answer in English also." She tried to ignore the rumbles that pulsed again in her stomach.

A tiny woman with a chirpy Irish voice came and took Sonny into her arms and up the wide, circular stairs while he wailed and stiffened at being rudely separated from his father.

Chiara was feeling weaker by the moment. Her breath came in short pants, and beads of perspiration dotted her forehead. She wanted nothing more than to sink to the floor and rest awhile.

Mr. Austin turned to her, saying, "Audrey should be back before long. Do you want to just leave the package or do you need to talk to her?"

Chiara pressed the parcel into his hands. "I'll go now," she said, her voice sounding faraway.

"I say, you look awfully pale. Are you all right?"

"Yes." She leaned against the door frame. "No. I . . . I'm only tired."

"You're not well," Stewart Austin said, dismayed. "Come along and sit down for a moment."

He led her willingly into the library and sat her on the closest chair, where she leaned her head back and closed her eyes. When he began unbuttoning her coat, her eyes flew open, and she put her hand out, stopping him.

"Look, you mustn't be frightened of me. I'm harmless. I just want to help you get your coat loose." He unfastened the last button and pulled the coat back from her shoulders. His hand grazed hers. "Why, you're cold as ice. You need a little something to warm you up."

At a sideboard he poured liquid into a small stemmed

glass. "Here, this should do it. Drink up," he said, handing her the glass.

Her hand trembled as she took the goblet. The drink was dark, like wine, but sweeter and thicker.

"It's sherry," Mr. Austin said.

Going down, it felt warm, but it met her stomach with a sickening thud. Perspiration dampened her neck and underarms. Her head felt fuzzy. *Oh, dear God, I think I'm going to be sick. Please don't let me throw up all over this beautiful carpet. I would die of shame.*

Wondering if she could navigate toward the door, she made a supreme effort to rise. "I think I'll go," she said in a small, constrained voice.

"You're not going anywhere. Why, you look positively green. Are you going to be ill?" Without waiting for an answer, he took her arm and hustled her down a dark hall to a small bathroom.

She motioned him out and knelt on the white-and-black tile floor just in time. The sherry flew out in a vile stream, and she remained on her knees for a few moments longer, trying to gather her strength.

"Mrs. Marcassa, are you all right?" Mr. Austin asked, knocking lightly on the door.

"Yes," she mumbled. She stood unsteadily and opened the door.

He moved past her and filled a glass with water. "Here," he said, handing it to her, "take this and just swish it around and spit it out."

When she did as she was told, he said, "Atta girl," and yanked a towel from the bar. He dampened it and pressed it against her cheeks and forehead.

Chiara loosened the top buttons of her dress. Taking the towel, she pressed it against her throat. Gradually she felt revived.

"I'm so sorry, Mrs. Marcassa," he said, leading her back to the library. "It was my fault for giving you that sherry. I'd no idea it would make you sick. There's an influenza going around, you know. I hope it's not that."

She sat in the chair she'd recently vacated. "No, I'm not really ill." She looked downward. "I'm with child."

"Oh, now I really am sorry." He ran his fingers through his hair, looking stricken. "I mean, not that you're pregnant; that's splendid. I'm just sorry about the sherry. That was a sorry mistake. Are you a bit better now?"

"Yes," she said, anxious to leave the scene of her humiliation and hurry to the comfort of her own home.

"Just stay put a moment. I'll help you with your coat and take you home."

"No, no, I take the streetcar." She began pushing herself up.

He stayed her gently, his hand on her shoulder. "Nonsense. I won't hear of it."

Going to a boxy cabinet by the door, he turned some knobs. "You just relax and listen to the Victrola while I tell Molly I'm leaving. I have some Caruso records here somewhere." He ran his hand over the stack of records, pulling out several. Finding the one he wanted, he set it on the turntable and positioned the needle on its edge, filling the room instantly with the sound of Caruso's rich tenor voice.

Resting her head against the chair back, Chiara closed her eyes, marveling at the remarkable music box. How fortunate he was to own so many marvelous things. "*Ridi, Pagliacci,*" Caruso sang with his tragic laugh. But at the moment, the laughter seemed out of place. She felt deeply fatigued and mortified at her accident.

Mr. Austin held Chiara's coat and led her to the door. She heard a voice from upstairs, Mrs. Austin's voice, she thought. But she must be mistaken. It was probably the maid.

The garage housed two sleek, shiny automobiles such as she'd seen only in pictures. The car Mr. Austin handed her into was maroon, polished to a sheen, with a white wheel tucked against the fender.

"It's a Lincoln Sport Phaeton," he said.

The leathery smell in the roomy, comfortable car had a calming effect. But Chiara was still somewhat uneasy: fearful of throwing up again and embarrassed to be sitting in close quarters with a man who was not her husband.

As the car glided down Jefferson Avenue, he asked, "Are you quite all right now?"

"Yes, I'm fine, thank you." Her shallow voice belied the words.

Mr. Austin shifted his eyes toward her in an apprehensive glance.

To put his fears to rest, she said, "My stomach is settled now."

After a few moments of silence Mr. Austin asked, "Where did you live in Italy, Mrs. Marcassa?"

She knew he was trying to put her at ease. "A small village in Puglia. There are mostly *contadini*, farmers, in my village. Do you know Puglia?"

"On the Adriatic side, isn't it? I've been to southern Italy, but not that far east. Actually, I stayed in Milan a couple of summers when I was a teenager, with an aunt and uncle. I fell in love with all things Italian, including a lovely young girl, and learned to speak quite well. Of course, now I'd have a hard time coming up with the proper words. But I would love to brush up a bit. You must speak to me in Italian, so I can relearn. Will you do that?"

"*Sì.*" Chiara closed her eyes, realizing she was very sleepy. Her bones seemed to melt into the cushiony leather, and a sense of peace engulfed her. She had to force her eyes open, had to concentrate on making conversation, to keep from falling asleep. "Does your aunt still live in Milan?"

"No, she passed away. I remember her fondly. Those two summers were the best of my life, happy and carefree. Up to that time I was so terribly restricted. I'm afraid I was a real bore; did nothing but study. I thought I had landed in paradise with Aunt Marietta. My cousin Gilbert and I palled about with the gardener's son and got a few lessons in real life." He smiled a secret faraway smile, obviously transported to a time made more precious as it was reclaimed from his memory's store. Chiara could see the tight lines on his brow disappear as he spoke. For some reason her heart went out to him. A tension seemed to ease from him, a burden lightened, as he talked of a long-ago time that obviously meant a great deal to him. He seemed to forget she was sitting there. Then, suddenly aware, he glanced at her and gave a self-conscious laugh.

"And the girl?" Chiara asked.

"The girl? Oh, I don't know. Got married, I suppose, to one of the youths of her own class."

Yes, she thought, that was one of the rules. We all marry our own. He, too, married one of his own class, not some peasant girl from a town outside Milan. Audrey was the sort of woman he *would* be attracted to—sophisticated, polished, accomplished. Still, for all his wife's qualities, Mr. Austin seemed lonely, somehow.

Directing him to her street, Chiara was keenly conscious of its air of poverty, the streetcar tracks, the shabby buildings, the beer gardens. He must be thinking that this was a humble neighborhood indeed, a far cry from his own prosperous, well-tended community.

"Well, your color's back, Mrs. Marcassa," he said as he helped her from the car. "Do take care of yourself— and the little cargo too. And you really should call before you come next time. Audrey is . . . well, she's very busy with her charities, and benefits, and such."

Too busy to care for her husband and son, Chiara thought, feeling suddenly sorry for him. "We have no telephone," she said.

"Oh, yes, of course. Well, I can always stop by to drop off or pick up items. It's not far out of my way." He slid back into the car, tipping his hat, a plushly expensive gray fedora. "Good day, Mrs. Marcassa."

"Good day, Mr. Austin. And thank you for your kindness."

"Indeed, it was my pleasure."

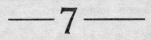

—— 7 ——

Michele was at the stove stirring *sugo*. "I've started cooking," he said with a pleased expression.

Chiara was grateful that he hadn't seen her alight from Mr. Austin's automobile. She didn't want to explain about being ill; but she would have to tell him now about the baby, especially since Mr. Austin, who was practically a stranger, knew her secret.

After supper, she cleared the table and poured hot water from the kettle into the basin. Shaking soap flakes into the water, she said, "I think I know why I've been feeling ill, Michele."

At the stove he jiggled and rattled a bar, shaking down the ashes, then stuffed wood into the gaping hole. "Why?"

Very quietly Chiara said, "I think I'm going to have a baby."

She waited for a reaction, but there was utter silence for several moments. Finally Michele approached and gently turned Chiara to face him. "Chiara, a baby?" He moved her an arm's length away and searched her body, as if looking for proof.

She held her dripping hands aloft. "There's nothing showing yet."

"A baby! That's wonderful!"

She laughed, wiping her wet hands on her apron. "I wasn't sure how you would feel."

"Why? What could be better? A son. We'll have a son, to carry on the family name." Michele pulled her to him in a bear hug. "He won't be a simple laborer, either. No, he'll be a mayor, or maybe a governor or a senator."

"You're a dreamer. I'll just be happy if he's healthy and smart and can work for a living, make his way, like his father." Chiara spoke softly against her husband's shoulder.

The next day, when Michele returned from work, he threw open the door and shouted, "Close your eyes. I have a present."

Chiara covered her head with her apron, and as soon as she heard a squeaking noise, pulled it down. Michele dragged in a large white wicker baby buggy, bouncing on its springs, shiny in its newness.

"Look at this," he said, folding the hood back on silver hinges.

Proudly he wheeled it to a corner of the kitchen, while Chiara squealed in delight. She ran her hand over its smooth side and put the satin-covered pillow next to her cheek.

"It's beautiful, Michele, beautiful. But it's too early. They used to say in the old country that it's bad luck to buy something so soon."

"Bah." He hugged her. "Every Sunday we'll take him for a walk."

She gave the buggy a little push. It must have been very expensive. Had Michele taken money out of their meager savings? "It's so fine. What did it cost?"

"What does it matter? You always worry too much about the money."

"One of us has to worry."

"Nothing's too expensive for our son. He'll have the best."

Chiara made a mental note to skimp a bit on the groceries. She was determined to save for a house, and it was obvious Michele wasn't very good at saving. It was a miracle he'd accumulated the money for his trip home and the honeymoon. He'd lived cheaply, he'd explained, in a boardinghouse, but he made it clear he was through scrimping like that.

Chiara's pregnancy proceeded without event, through the long and lonesome winter months, until the last frigid vestiges of winter disappeared and March bequeathed an unseasonably balmy day.

With a hint of spring in the air, Chiara opened the kitchen window. Leaning on the sill, the dry, whispery wind blowing against her face, she noticed a promising touch of greenery on the winter-drab earth. Most likely weeds, she thought, but green nonetheless.

Across the alley Laurelia hung sheets on the line, taking the clothespins from her mouth and snapping them in place. Chiara called out a greeting to the tall walnut-skinned woman who, soon after the Marcassas moved in, had knocked shyly on the back door. Because she'd never had experience with colored people, Chiara had been suspicious of the dark-skinned stranger, but as they talked, she realized they had a common bond: they were strangers to Detroit. Laurelia had come from a place called Mississippi. The two women remained friends, but Chiara was aware that other white neighbors had little or nothing to do with colored people.

Now Laurelia returned the greeting, hoisted a heaping laundry-filled bushel basket to her hip, and went indoors.

Back at the sewing machine, Chiara guided a luxurious emerald silk fabric into the ever-pulsing needle, wondering to what sort of fancy party Mrs. Austin would choose to wear the dress. She'd seen scenes at the cinema, or moving pictures, as Michele called them. There were men in tuxedos, smoking cigars, drinking cocktails, and slender women with marcelled hair and painted nails punctuating their words with cigarettes in long holders, laughing shrilly at the conversation.

Arching her back to ease the strain, Chiara pushed herself up laboriously from her chair. Carefully she placed the finished dress on a hanger. Stroking the smooth fabric, she wondered if she would ever have such a fine gown, imagining herself dancing, smiling, even flirting. Then she chided herself for that foolish thought. When would she ever have occasion for such a garment? "Perhaps at your wedding," she said aloud, to the child churning in her womb.

Resting her hands on the shelf of her belly, Chiara talked to the child inside. "Go ahead, move about if you like. It makes me happy to know you're so lively. Two months more, that's all. Coma' Lucia tells me all is well and I should have no problems. Good hips, she says. No problems. But I remember my aunt's childbirth; there were problems at the end. A breach birth. I remember her screams. Still, I mustn't worry. Her child grew fat and healthy."

In the kitchen she drained the cod that was soaking in a pan of water, and sliced an onion thinly.

Stewart Austin's Lincoln rolled out of the Rouge onto Michigan Avenue. He had left the office early. Though he knew Mike Marcassa wouldn't be home before six, he didn't want to take any chances. Chagrined at his own actions, he seemed incapable of using common sense. Like a lovestruck schoolboy, he invented reasons to drop by Chiara's house. Before he left for work this morning, even as he'd reproached himself, he'd intentionally ripped the hem from a pair of trousers.

Chiara. She had captured his interest from the first moment he'd heard her charming mangling of the English language. There was no mistaking the melodic accent. Or for that matter the looks, though she hadn't the typical olive-toned, dark-eyed look one associated with Italians. But the facial contour, the shape of the eyes, the expressive hand movements, and, once she had gotten over the shyness, the frank direct eye contact—they were characteristically Italian. Her earthy essence brought a sudden whispered recall of his enchanted stay in Italy, the way a scent can recall something distant and pleasurable, though ephemeral. Somehow Chiara embodied the spirit of those wonderful halcyon days.

He couldn't help himself; he was enamored of all things Italian. The love affair had begun when he was sent off to visit with his Great-Uncle Regis, who had gone to Italy on business and never returned. The relatives (his parents included) would laugh when recounting the tale of Regis, declaring he had been struck by lightning or touched with a magic wand, which, indeed, to hear Regis tell of it, was exactly what had happened. He fell in love with Marietta, who called herself "La Contessa" (whether the title was authentic, they never discovered), and was so smitten he married her within two months of their meeting.

Uncle Regis had undergone a transformation, as who would not, with a constantly warming sun, heady luxuriant flora, sustaining diet, and mellowing wine. He had four sons, the eldest of whom was just one year older than Stewart. It was decided, when Stewart was sixteen years old, that the boys should spend some time together, thereby each learning the other's language.

Stewart's "learning" encompassed more than the language; it took in life itself, with an abandon only a repressed boy can feel.

The boys were given free rein, a license he had never known before.

Languid summer evenings were spent at supper, which stretched from eight o'clock to midnight and included discussions of all manner of lofty subjects, which began in politeness, escalated to shouting, and lapsed into friendly back-slapping, no doubt aided by the effects of the fruity wine and the tropical breezes.

There was a girl . . . What was her name? Renata? Yes, Renata, an overripe, round-eyed, red-cheeked servant girl, who probably thought to winnow her way out of a life of servitude with a rich American. It was a short but sweet alliance that ended in her flood of tears when he went back to the States. The once-staid Uncle Regis chose to ignore the antics of his eldest son and grandnephew. That sort of uninhibited behavior was, after all, expected of healthy Italian boys.

Stewart was taken by this gregarious family, their ebullience, their enjoyment of good food, their encompassing love of children—their own, and any others who happened through their lives.

Perhaps his memory had repainted the scenes with the golden brush of reminiscence that made the happy events happier and the unpleasant ones fade away. Ah, but still, those happy days . . .

He had envied Gilbert, who was swathed in an enveloping adoration from his mother, and in turn exhibited an almost reverent love for her. A far cry from Stewart's own bridge-playing, luncheon-going mother, who gave him a perfunctory bedtime kiss. *No more hugs now, you'll muss Mummy's hair.*

Gilbert, in turn, spent a summer with Stewart, but the summerhouse on Mackinac Island, though beautiful and tranquil on a bluff facing magestic Lake Michigan, was no match for Gilbert's villa and the surrounding lush valleys, the Milan Opera House, the cathedral with its countless ornate spires kissed with gold, the sense of history. And, most of all, their boyish adventures.

Later he was drawn to Audrey with her patrician bearing, her clever wit. They were perfect together; or so said the others in their clique. Her cool beauty and sophistication had enticed him. Of course, the match was sanctioned by both sets of parents. And yet she was so unlike the picture of womanhood his mind had drawn from the lovely, intense "Contessa" and the joyous Renata.

When had he and Audrey become blasé? When had the union become jaded? Or was it jaded only for him? Audrey still found it "terribly exciting, darling," to discover the "in" places where teacups held bathtub gin and the jazz was hot and spicy.

He'd been back to Italy several times, one time being his honeymoon, but never again could he capture the essence of joy that marked that first excursion. And how could he? It was a time of awakening for him, of burgeoning sensuality, a kindling of the senses and the intellect, an awareness of his masculine power. It was a time and place his memory captured as if in fantasy, a place resplendent with richness and charm. He smiled to himself as he recalled the carefree days.

Chiara . . . she was different. She had a sensual beauty, a Madonna's smile, a peasant's rigid code of social behavior, a keen, pragmatic intelligence. Occasionally her mouth would take on a small pout when unable to formulate the proper English word, and she'd lapse into Italian. At those times he longed to kiss the pout away.

Her face betrayed nothing but friendship, while his own body cried out almost painful messages of need, lustful need.

Now here he was on her doorstep, like a smitten schoolboy, seeking only a smile from his secret *inamorata*, knowing she would be both disconcerted and pleased to see him, would flutter a bit.

When the doorbell rang, Chiara knew it would be Mr. Austin. After her mishap at his home, he had taken to stopping by every few weeks or so to pick up any finished work she had for his wife. Even when she told him there would be nothing for a while, he would come, usually at the same time, with trouser seams to be repaired or hems to be lifted or lowered.

She always flushed with embarrassment in his presence, keenly feeling the disparity between her living conditions and his; contrasting his obviously expensive suit with Michele's work clothes. He drove a sleek Lincoln; Michele took the streetcar. He wore a fine fedora, creased just so; Michele wore a cap.

She removed her apron before answering the door.

He tipped his hat. "Good afternoon, Chiara."

Chiara flushed and nervously tucked a tendril of hair behind her ear. "Come in, Mr. Austin. Do you have work for me?"

"Just something small." He handed her the parcel and glanced at her waist. "Are you feeling well?"

"Yes," she said, putting her hand protectively on her abdomen. "No more sickness."

"Good. You'll enjoy a baby. I love children. I'd like to have another, but Audrey, well . . ." He trailed off, unwilling to finish the thought.

Little by little during his visits he divulged small details of his life, a life vastly different from her own. An only child, raised in affluence, he'd had everything he could wish for, everything except the attention of his mother and father. Nurses, servants, boarding-school staff—they were his family for the most part. He spoke fondly of holidays in Italy. For all his poise, his impeccable manners, his wealth, there was something sad about Stewart. That was why Chiara welcomed him into her kitchen, where he loved to taste and to make comments and suggestions. He was, he told her, a gourmet cook and often at his home he would take charge on the cook's day off, sitting his small son on a high stool with wooden spoons and a bowl to play with.

"It smells delicious, Mrs. Marcassa. What is it today?"

"I'm having fish. You smell the onions. No matter what I fix, if I put in onions and parsley, it smells good."

"What sort of fish is it?" he asked, following her into the kitchen.

"It's *baccalà*, dried cod. I fix it with tomatoes and onions. There's a song that talks about it; '*pesce fritto e baccalà*.' "

She sang a few lines of the ribald song, with a slight blush of embarrassment, and Stewart threw back his head and laughed.

"This is a new side of you, I must say." He smiled with obvious delight.

She went to the workroom and brought out the newly finished silk gown, holding it up against her for his inspection.

"You like?"

"It would be beautiful on you," he said. "That color makes your eyes sparkle. You should have a gown like that."

"I hope your wife will like it."

"You look like a painting, a Raphael Madonna," he said in frank admiration.

Aware of the color rushing across her cheeks, she wrapped the dress in tissue paper, then placed it into a box. Quickly she thrust the package into his hands and said, "Thank you for picking up the dress."

He took her hand, and in a courtly gesture put it to his lips, kissing it. "Thank *you*. Not only for the sewing but also for . . . well, for letting me visit, and for making me laugh with your little song."

She pulled her hand away and put it to her throat,

feeling the warmth, the rushing pulse. "Good-bye," she said, ushering him to the door.

She closed the door swiftly, aware of the quickening of her heart. She put a cold cloth to her face to diminish the heat. Why did he upset her equilibrium so? And why did she feel that she heard words he wasn't saying, words locked in his heart? So often she felt like patting his head, like mothering him. He seemed, somehow, so needy.

She busied herself with setting the table. Michele would be home soon, and she was sure he wouldn't approve of Stewart Austin's visits.

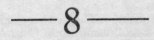

"Breathe!" The midwife, Comare Sophia, commanded.

Chiara complied, clinging fiercely to Sophia's hand as the pain absorbed her. The contractions were getting stronger. At first they ebbed and flowed like the tide, a gentle knotting and hardening. Now the wave of pain gathered force and pushed to a climactic peak, then receded.

"Don't hold your breath," Sophia instructed, more gently this time. "Breathe in and out, slowly."

Sophia's quiet air of authority, her obvious knowledge of her profession, inspired confidence. Her full cheeks and plump arms lent a soft look which belied her competency. Her eyebrows were permanently raised, giving a questioning look to her intelligent dark eyes.

When the throbbing receded, the midwife bent and put her ear to Chiara's abdomen. "A nice strong heartbeat."

Chiara eased her hands to the small of her back and massaged the ache.

"Your back hurts?" Sophia asked, inching cool hands under the arch of Chiara's spine.

"Yes, that's the worst of it, my back." Chiara's voice was strained.

Sophia massaged the area at the tip of her patient's spine. "There?"

"Yes, there. It feels better when you rub it."

"Hm," Sophia said, her lips pursed. She pressed firm, knowing hands on Chiara's abdomen, palpating lightly, a frown of concentration creasing her brow. Her hands moved slowly along the sides of the mound, from top to bottom, side to side. "Hm," she said again.

Chiara noticed the subtle change in Sophia's expression. "What's wrong?" she asked, propping herself up on her elbows.

"Nothing. Lie back and rest. You need all your strength."

Flora entered quietly and hugged her cousin, then wiped her brow with a cool, damp cloth. Chiara's eyes filmed over in teary gratitude.

With her back toward Chiara, Sophia whispered something in Flora's ear. Flora's eyebrows lifted and drew together.

Chiara eased herself partially upright. "Something's wrong, isn't it? Tell me."

Sophia stroked her chin thoughtfully, then plumped the pillow behind Chiara's head. As she eased Chiara's head down to the pillow she said calmly, "The baby's head isn't in position. It's lying this way, across, instead of this way, up and down." She positioned her hands on Chiara's abdomen to illutrate.

Chiara's eyes widened with fear. "What will happen?"

"Often the baby turns. I've seen them turn even in the last hour."

"What if it doesn't turn?"

"It will turn. It will turn." Sophia nodded.

But her tone didn't sound convincing to Chiara. "If it doesn't?" she repeated.

"Then we'll have to get the doctor."

Flora grabbed Chiara's hand and squeezed it. She released it, saying, "I'm going to make some coffee."

Another contraction began around the periphery of the taut mound. At first teasingly light, soon it clutched Chiara in a fierce spasm. Tears formed in her eyes as the pain reached a crescendo, then dipped.

"Now take a deep breath," Sophia said when the contraction ended.

Chiara drew in a gulp of air and blew it out slowly through trembling dry lips. The window was open, but the air that stirred the lower half of the lace curtain was warm and offered little comfort. "It's so hot, and it hurts so."

"Of course it hurts. Your muscles are stretching, opening up." With her broad, powerful hands, one on each side of Chiara's abdomen, Sophia began manipulating, one hand easing downward, one pushing upward. "I'm trying to move the baby, but it's stubborn."

After several minutes of concentrated effort, she shook her head in a gesture of defeat. "No change," she said.

Chiara's limbs tightened as Sophia parted her knees and examined her. "It's almost time. Do you feel like you want to push?"

"No. Where's Michele?" Chiara asked. "He should be home from work by now."

Seconds later the back door slammed and Michele's voice called out, "Chiara!"

"She's in the bedroom, Michele." Flora's voice was excited. "She's in labor. It began six hours ago."

Michele flew into the room and was at Chiara's bedside in two long strides. He knelt beside her.

"Are you all right?" The anxiety in his voice was shaded with excitement.

"I'm so afraid. The baby isn't in position." As the pain began again, she clutched the sheet with a wail. "Aaah."

Sophia handed her a small white towel with a knot at the end. "Here," she said in her soft, soothing voice, "bite on this. It won't be long now."

When the contraction subsided, Chiara sobbed quietly and threw her arms around Michele's neck, clinging fiercely to him.

"It's all right, Chiara, I'm here. You'll be all right," Michele said, smoothing her damp hair back from her face.

He turned to Sophia. "What is this about the baby's position?"

"Come into the kitchen. Flora's made fresh coffee."

Chiara's arms were clasped, tightly as a vise, around his neck.

"Cara, I'll be right outside," he said, firmly unlocking her arms."

Chiara finally released him.

"Will she be all right?" Michele turned pleading eyes to Sophia.

She nudged him toward the door and followed him out, while Flora straightened the tangled sheet from around Chiara's legs.

Sophia returned a few minutes later, her arms loaded down with fresh linen and two enamel basins.

"The pain is beginning again." As another contraction racked her body, Chiara bit the knotted towel to keep from screaming.

Sophia placed her hand on Chiara's abdomen, gauging the strength of the spasm.

Now the pain began in earnest. No one had told her it would hurt so. Was there a conspiracy among women to keep this terror a secret? She wished her mother were here to give her comfort and encouragement. It seemed like days had passed since the first niggling spasms. The pain was peaking now. From her constricted throat came a guttural sound, an unfamiliar groan. Dear God, why doesn't this child come? Why does it resist leaving its warm haven for entry into the unknown?

But why not? If it's a girl, she will repeat this same cursed life cycle. The light seemed to brighten and dim and brighten again. Had she fainted? Mother of God, let it end; let me out of my misery. I know I will die from this pain. Let Michele in to kiss me good-bye.

Sophia intruded into Chiara's absorption when she examined her again. "Very soon you will want to push."

Moments later a compelling urge engulfed her, like a giant hand manipulating her insides downward. She drew up onto her elbows while hoarse animal sounds rose from deep in her throat. "I have to push now," she said, panting.

"Go ahead, push, child, bear down," Sophia urged.

"I can't bear seeing you suffer." Flora's face floated above her.

"Why doesn't it end?" Chiara moaned in anguish. "Dear God, release me from this pain."

Sophia raised the sheet from Chiara's legs and examined her again. Chiara watched her anxiously, but the midwife's face betrayed nothing.

"It's not going well, is it?" Chiara asked.

Sophia frowned and mumbled, "This baby is stubborn. It doesn't want to right itself."

"The pain is beginning again." Chiara whimpered as another contraction racked her body. She reached behind her and clung to the cold metal of the bed frame. Squeezing her eyes shut, she bit her lip.

"I'm going to try to turn this stubborn little creature," Sophia said.

Chiara felt Sophia's fingers lubricating the area. With an agonizing pressure and tugging, her hands stretched into Chiara's vagina. Chiara suppressed the wail pressing the muscles of her throat. *Please let it be over soon.*

"I feel something, a little hand," Sophia muttered. "That's not what I want, I want to nudge the little bottom upward . . . ahh, yes . . . I think so . . . yes . . ."

Chiara drew in her breath sharply as suddenly there was a churning and tumbling, and then a subtle alteration of pressure. The tension against her spine lessened somewhat.

"What's happening?" she cried out in a frightened voice.

Sophia's head emerged and she shouted, "Thank God! The baby just fell into place. All it needed was a little coaxing." She clapped her hands together and raised them upward. "Thank God."

Licking her parched lips, Chiara breathed, "Thanks to God and thanks to you, Sophia."

"Come on, push, once more," Sophia coaxed.

Chiara lifted onto her elbows and with a supreme effort bore down. Again and again she pushed, while the room seemed to swim around her. Her mouth felt full of dry cotton. The strain taxed every muscle in her body.

Sophia murmured encouragement. "Ah, that's fine, Chiara, not much longer; very soon now; I see a dark head, lots of hair," she gurgled with delight. "You'll have a beautiful child, you're doing fine, just fine."

Just when Chiara was sure there wasn't an ounce of strength left in her, she felt the baby's head pushing through, sensed Sophia's guiding hands, and heard her muttering to the emerging child, "Come along now, you're almost home."

She heard a faint mewling, then a single wail. Flora laughed and cried at once, and Sophia shouted, "You have a son."

A fine film of perspiration covered Chiara. Her entire body smarted. She collapsed onto the pillow and pleaded, "Let me have him, please, let me have my baby." Her hands trembled as she reached out for the child.

"Wait, be patient, he's not ready yet." Sophia lifted the crying bundle upward, the pulsating umbilical cord still attached. "I must cut the cord and take care of the afterbirth."

"His cry is strong. Is he all right?" Chiara asked.

"He's perfect," Sophia said. *"Un bambino bello, Chiara.* You did well. Look how strong. Look how beautiful."

Sophia cleaned her hands on the wet linen towel Flora handed her, then reached into the tiny mouth, removing mucus. The child's miniature penis emitted a small stream of urine.

"Already he wants to show us that everything's in working order," Sophia said, laughing. "The males often do that."

With dispatch she clipped the umbilical cord and in a moment the slick little body lay quietly curious on Chiara's chest. She inspected him, uncurling the delicate fingers, touching the screwed-up red face, smoothing the inch-long damp, dark hair.

Flora dabbed at the perspiration on her cousin's forehead and hugged her through her tears.

"He is beautiful, isn't he?" Chiara asked in a breathless voice, raising her head to kiss the downy cheek. "He looks like Michele."

"Yes, and like you too," Flora said.

"Here, give me that child," Flora said, gently lifting the baby from Chiara's chest. "Let me get him all dressed up for his father." She cooed to the infant as she slipped his tiny limbs into a cotton wrapper.

Chiara felt the afterbirth sloughing away and realized how exhausted she was.

"Get Michele, quick," she said, dropping her head weakly to the pillow.

Sophia dipped a cloth into a basin of warm water and wrung it out. "Wait, wait, I'm almost finished cleaning you," she said. "Just lie still and rest now."

Flora swaddled a blanket around the baby, crooning, while Sophia bathed Chiara, murmuring kind words. "You're fine now, you did so well, and the child is healthy. What more could you ask? A lucky little one he is, with two such loving parents. Yes, yes, he will be quick and bright, mark my words. I have seen so many, thousands. I can tell."

With efficient, economical movements, she disposed of the soiled sheets and rubber mat and placed fresh sheets on the bed, then discarded her blood-splattered white coat.

Flora, one arm curled about the baby, opened the door and beckoned to Michele. He hurried in, his eyes looking stricken, his hair awry.

"Your son," Flora said, moving the blanket from the infant's face.

Michele gazed at the baby in astonishment. His mouth opened and closed, but no words came.

Chiara held her hand out to him. He grasped her hand and kissed the palm and Chiara saw the wet brightness in his eyes.

"Michele, I've never seen you cry before."

He folded her hand into both of his and pressed it to his cheek. "I'm not crying," he said gruffly, kneeling by her side. "I was so worried about you."

"The men, they always act like they are the ones who go through such pain," Flora said with mock sarcasm. "Here, brave one, take your new son."

When the sleeping infant was placed in Michele's stiff arms, he shook his head in wonderment. "He has your mouth and chin, Chiara. He's so small." He examined the child, peeking into his diaper as if to assure himself that all the proper parts were in place. "Take him, Flora, I may break him."

"Give him to me," Chiara said sleepily, turning on her side and cradling her arm for the child.

Michele gingerly placed the baby at Chiara's side, and kneeling, circled his muscled arm around them both. "June first, a day to remember," he said. "Roberto. We'll name him Roberto, after my father, according to the custom. He'll want for nothing. I'll take good care of you both." His voice was rough with emotion.

Chiara rubbed her cheek against Michele's. "I miss my

mother. If only my family could see him. Do you think they ever will?"

Michele patted her head. "Of course."

Chiara cooed to Roberto in her special mother voice while she dressed and wrapped him in the blanket Flora had crocheted.

"Aren't you ready yet?" Michele asked, ever impatient.

"No, I had to prepare the food and bathe Roberto, and—"

"Here, give me my son," Michele said, tucking the blanket around him and lifting him high into the air.

"You're frightening him." Chiara thought Mike was a bit too rough for the child.

"No, look, he's laughing," Michele said, smiling at the chortling child. "We have to toughen this boy up. You get ready. Ed and Flora will be here any minute."

Chiara had to smile at her two males. The baby's birth seemed to have transformed Michele, infused him with new energy. Though he still returned from work exhausted each day, after dinner he seemed to revive, and spent an hour or two with Roberto, singing Italian verses, playing pony boy. The baby always responded with gurgles and smiles. "See?" Michele would say. "He knows me. He loves me."

Chiara marveled at how swiftly her loneliness had diminished since Roberto made his appearance. Her days had beauty, order, and purpose to them now. The pleasant warm weather helped too. Winter had left her pale and depressed, always longing for the sun, which sometimes didn't appear for days at a stretch. Now there were Sunday walks with Michele pushing the baby carriage proudly, showing Roberto off to all interested passersby, while smoking his Sunday cigar, and visits with *paisani* on the east side.

Chiara dressed quickly in a navy dress with a low waistline and white sailor collar. She wished fleetingly that women could wear trousers for picnics. It would be so much more comfortable than the dresses and skirts that required constant tucking around and under for modesty's sake. She laughed to herself at the incongruous idea of women in trousers, though she had occasionally seen pictures of fashionable women in pants or knickers.

"Maria is coming too," Chiara told Michele while she gathered up sweaters and put them in a sack. After coming from Chicago, Maria had stayed a short time with Chiara and Michele, then rented the upstairs flat when the tenants moved out. Ever resourceful, she had found a job as cook and housekeeper with a wealthy Italian banking family, and had a boarder for her spare bedroom.

Ed and Flora pulled up in the old Dodge and the women got in the back seat with Robbie while Mike gave the crank a few turns until the engine sputtered to life, then hopped in.

"Penny and Jimmy are coming to the island later, so I told them to look for us." Flora held her arms out for the baby. "You know Penny—she loves babies. I wish those two would get married. It's not good to have a long engagement."

Ed called over his shoulder, "Eh, it's none of your business about their engagement."

Flora waved a dismissing hand at the back of Ed's head and whispered to Chiara, "They're so much in love. It's dangerous." She nodded her head signifiantly.

The car chugged onto the wide bridge from East Grand Boulevard and across the blue expanse of the Detroit River to Belle Isle. Chiara loved the lush island. It was a peaceful respite from the noisy city. On prior trips she had delighted in the aquarium, with its fascinating array of wide-eyed and colorful aquatic creatures. She'd never seen such sights before. But her favorite place was the "glass house" filled with exotic plants and bright-hued flowers.

They settled on a picnic spot near the bank of the Grand Canal, on whose shores towered huge weeping willows that tossed their branches like so many silky green ribbons. While the men scouted for a good level spot for the *boccie* game, the women attended to lunch. On a cloth-covered picnic table they laid out hard-crusted Italian bread, sharp, tingling gorgonzola and provolone, mortadella and prosciutto still in their brown store wrappings, dry red wine, hard, shiny *biscotti*, and from the package that Chiara's family had sent, almonds and dried figs. The main course, *mostaccioli* drenched in meat sauce, was still warm in its cloth-wrapped pot.

Roberto lay on a blanket, amused by the antics of two

gray squirrels chasing one another in a zigzag pattern up a Dutch elm tree.

"Hello," a chirpy voice called out. Chiara turned to see Penny, her sun-bright auburn hair shiny as a copper coin, strolling toward them hand in hand with a tall, broad-chested man.

"Oh, I'm so glad you have the baby here," Penny said, kneeling by the blanket. "I been telling Jimmy how cute he is." She chucked Roberto under the chin. "This here's Jimmy. Jimmy, this is Chiara and Maria. You know Flora."

They nodded or called out a hello.

Penny's crimson Cupid's-bow lips were small and pouty, her eyebrows thin half-circles. Though Chiara disapproved of Penny's painted face and cigarette smoking, she loved having her around, enjoyed her constant laughter, her love of life.

When the men rejoined them, Penny introduced Jimmy, saying, "We have something to celebrate. Jimmy just got a job."

Ed clapped him on the shoulder while Michele extended his hand, saying, "Good for you. Where's the job?"

Jimmy pumped Mike's hand with his beefy one. His nose, humped at the bridge, was slightly off-center. His eyes, a deep blue, were wary, softening, Chiara noticed, only when he gazed at Penny.

"I work at Ford."

"Ford, eh? What plant?"

"Rouge."

Penny piped up, "Ain't that where you work, Mike?"

"Yeah, I'm at the Rouge."

"Jimmy was lucky. Mr. Bennett put him on right away. He got laid off from Briggs."

"I was at the Waterloo plant, 'The Slaughterhouse.' " Jimmy put his hands in his pockets. "When they laid me off, I wanted to celebrate; that's how bad it was."

Mike asked, "What building you in? What job?"

Jimmy seemed to hesitate slightly. "Building four. I'm a . . . a sweeper."

Mike looked closely at Jimmy but didn't speak.

"Come on, the food's getting cold," Flora scolded.

They scrambled to the table, the men exclaiming over the abundance and excellence of the food.

"God bless America," Eduardo shouted when they'd blessed the meal.

After they ate, the men, satiated, went off to play *boccie* while the women cleared away the debris.

"Tell us what you see, Maria," urged Flora, stirring a spoonful of sugar into her coffee. "What's in the future? Do you see a baby for me soon?"

Maria shook her head in irritation. "Flora, I keep telling you, I don't see everything."

"Bah, you see plenty; you just don't like to tell it all. Maria has dreams and visions," Flora explained to Penny.

"What about me?" Penny hopped out of the seat she had taken in the low, spreading branches of a giant willow tree. "Will me and Jimmy ever get married?"

Maria looked out over the water, her eyes taking on a glazed stare. Finally she said, "You and Jimmy will marry, but not for a while."

Penny's skirt whipped about her legs in the breeze. Quietly she said, "Oh, we ain't hardly talked about it yet."

"Yes." Maria nodded her head. "A little trouble, first. But you'll marry." Abruptly she turned away and stared at the water. "They said in my village that I had the evil eye. Such a superstition. It's because my eyebrows meet across. I do have dreams that far too often come true."

"You could pluck your eyebrows," Penny said. "But then maybe the gift would leave you."

They all laughed.

"What else do you see in my life?" Penny asked, intrigued.

"Nothing more than marriage for you, Penny. But Flora . . ." She narrowed her eyes and stared intensely at Flora. "I see sadness in your life. Eduardo . . ."

"What?" Flora's eyes darted to her anxiously.

Maria's heavy lids dropped and she turned her head away, shaking it. "Nothing."

"Yes, you see something. What is it?"

"Just an . . . an illness. Nothing more." But her face had turned a pasty white.

Flora said with an imploring voice, "But, Maria . . ."

"No, nothing more," Maria said, getting swiftly to her feet and walking away.

Flora twitched her shoulders and flipped her fingers under her chin, a gesture meaning "So what?" They all remained silent for a few minutes.

Chiara rarely asked Maria questions. If there were happy events in her future, she wanted to be pleasantly surprised. If there was bad fortune . . . well, better she didn't know about it.

When Roberto began squealing, Penny and Flora argued over who should hold him first. Penny won. She cooed to him, nose to nose, and patted the little dark head. She toyed with the locks spiking down his forehead and neck. The deep blue of his eyes had begun shading to a smoky gray. When she played "This little piggy . . ." he looked merely bewildered. She tried "pony boy" and he kicked vigorously against her stomach.

"Look at my godson kick," Flora said. "He's very strong."

"The doctor told me to put a binder around his middle, but I didn't do it for long," Chiara said. "He could hardly move about and turn. It wasn't natural."

"The doctors know what they're doing, Chiara," Penny said. "Look at him smile. I adore babies."

"The doctors don't know everything. He said babies should be fed every four hours, but Roberto cries sometimes in three or even two hours. I feed him when he's hungry. 'Are you a mother?' I asked this learned man. 'Did you give birth? No. Then about my child, I know more than you.' He threw up his hands and told me to do as I wish."

Flora laughed. "Good for you."

When Roberto cried out, his little fists punching the air in agitation, Chiara took him.

She leaned back against a tree, arranging her dress over her cotton-stockinged legs. With a towel over her shoulder to conceal her breast, she unbottoned the top of her dress and began nursing.

"I got a letter from my mother; from Carlo, really, because she can't write," she said. "But the words were hers and they made me cry. She wants to see Roberto so badly. 'I shed tears of joy and sadness,' she says, 'joy that all is well, sadness at not being able to see and hold my first grandchild.' "

"Have you heard from Mike's family?" Penny asked.

"He has no family. We never hear from anyone in Michele's village. He was an only child and has few relatives. He says there is no one he cares to write to. When I tell him it's strange, he says I should be quiet, and he doesn't want to talk about it."

Maria had rejoined them and looked surprised. "You're sure there's no one?"

"Yes, why?"

Maria was pensive. "No reason."

Chiara patted the contented infant's back, then handed him to Flora and went off to watch the men play *boccie*. She nodded encouragement when Michele looked to her for approval. He was good at sports, agile and strong. After the game, he insisted on taking Chiara for a canoe ride.

"Let the others watch Roberto," he said when she demurred because of the baby. "You'll enjoy a ride."

"I'll watch the baby," Flora said. "You go; go and have a good time."

When Michele rented the canoe and pushed away from the shore, Chiara sighed with contentment. She loved to watch Michele's muscles ripple as he dipped and pulled the paddle through the water. His face was relaxed and smiling. The heavy look he always wore when he returned from work, the furrow in his forehead, were gone.

Dangling her hand over the side, Chiara relaxed, basking in the feeling of peace that engulfed her. Weeping-willow branches dipped gracefully at the water's edge. The only sounds came from the birds as they flitted among the leaves, and the soft plop of the paddle as it sliced through the water.

"It's so lovely here. I'm happy when the sun is shining, sad when it's so gray and gloomy. I hate the thought that winter's coming."

"Don't think about it, then."

"Michele, you don't like Jimmy, do you?"

"I like him okay." Mike's eyes narrowed. "But he said he's a sweeper. Only coloreds are sweepers. I got an idea he's working in Bennett's service department."

"Is that bad?"

"Most of those guys are pugs, ex-convicts. Their job is to spy on everyone, keep the rank and file in line."

"Well, you don't have anything to worry about, do you?"

Mike snorted. "I could get fired for being Italian, for parting my hair wrong. I could get fired for just mentioning unions."

Chiara's high spirits were suddenly deflated. Nothing was safe, nothing sure; everything seemed so tentative. She had never had this feeling in Italy, this feeling of impermanence. "I don't want you talking about unions at work, Mike. You be careful."

"Don't worry. Nothing's going to happen to my job; I'm safe as can be." Mike dipped his hand in the canal and playfully sprinkled water on Chiara's face. "Come on, smile, Chiara. Life is good. We're two lucky people."

He dragged the paddle alongside the canoe and sang snatches of "Return to Sorrento." "Like in Venice, eh? This is our gondola."

"Michele, you've never been in Venice."

"No, but one day I'll take you there, I swear it."

"When did you become such a millionaire?"

"I may not be a millionaire, but who knows? This is the land of opportunity. In America everything is possible." He squinted into the sun and hummed a few more bars. "My first concern is a home of our own, in another year or two. Then some good furniture, and then a new car—a Ford, of course.

"Oh, Michele, do you think we can have all that in another two years?"

"Of course. Things are looking up for us. When things go well for the Ford Motor Company, they go well for us. Sales of the Model A are booming. Why, Ford may outsell General Motors! I may not end up a millionaire, but don't you worry, I'm going to see to it that you have a good life."

Chiara's face softened. "I know you will." She trailed her hand in the water. "You're such a dreamer."

"Yes, I *am* a dreamer. I dream of a good future for our son. What's wrong with that?"

"Nothing. I'm a dreamer too. Do you think we'll ever have a house in Grosse Pointe?"

Mike laughed. "Grosse Pointe! You *are* a dreamer."

"We have to save our money."

"I'll take a few dollars from each pay and put it in the

bank. You'll be surprised at how fast it'll grow. Life is good, Chiara."

She lifted her face to the sun. Yes, life was good, and yet . . . An involuntary shiver coursed through her. Superstitiously, she was almost frightened by her feeling of well-being, by Mike's hopefulness. Life was going too well. She was distrustful of too much happiness.

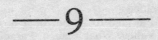

The streetcar mesmerized Mike with its swaying and rolling, clacking and roaring. It had its own peculiar odor: fumes and perspiration and stale tobacco that lingered on the passengers' wool coats. Unable to concentrate on reading in the dim overhead light, Mike folded up his newspaper and gazed out the grimy window into the silvery haze of dawn. He tuned in to snatches of conversation amid the coughing and occasional snoring.

Next to him a colored man sat slumped, dozing. Mike recognized him as a neighbor, Mortimer, and fellow worker at the Rouge. Mortimer's wife, Laurelia, had brought them a sweet-potato pie after they had moved in. Mike remembered Chiara's appreciation of the southern delicacy.

When the trolley stopped suddenly, the man, jolted awake, rubbed his eyes.

"You work at the foundry?" Mike asked.

"Yeah, that's the only place hires niggers." Mortimer looked down at his hands, large and brown as newborn puppies. "You always readin' the paper on the bus, ain't you, Marcassa?"

"Yeah, I got into the habit of reading the paper when I was a kid," Mike said. "My father made me read to him every night, because he couldn't read. He bought an old secondhand dictionary for me, and made me look up words I couldn't understand."

Mike remembered laboring over the newspaper, remembered his father's insistence that he use the dictionary. "Ahh," his father said. "You see, Michele, if you read, you learn. But remember to use this." He jabbed a finger to his head. "Not everything you read is the truth. You have to think for yourself."

Mortimer, next to him, yawned and said, "I don't read much. I only went to fifth grade in Mississippi. And there wasn't much readin' goin' on on Hastings Street."

"You lived on Hastings?" It was the black ghetto, the area whites avoided.

"Yeah, but I'm glad to be out of it now. Black Bottom; Paradise Valley. What a laugh, Paradise." He cackled, with his head tilted upward, his teeth gleaming in his dark face, then fell silent.

Mike turned his attention again to the scene darting by outside his window. The city was just awakening; lights were flashing on in the row of squat buildings, in a barbershop with its spiraling red-and-white pole, in a grocery store with its pyramid of oranges in the front window. Still asleep were the beer gardens, a pool hall. Mike smiled to himself at the comforting sight. The city was almost an entity to him; an adolescent sustaining growth pains, stretching its joints, reaching, fumbling, striving toward maturity; capable of greatness; powerful yet flawed.

"Paradise Valley," Mortimer repeated almost to himself.

"It's not such a bad city," Mike said. "You're working, aren't you?"

"Yeah, I'm working. It ain't so bad; better than where I come from, where you could get lynched just for not movin' off the sidewalk for whites." He nodded his head. "It ain't a bad city. You know, I seen the General Motors Building go up in 1919. The biggest office building in the world."

Mike remembered his awe at the buildings that had sprouted like dandelions in the twenties: the forty-six-story Penobscot Building, the Fischer Building, the Cadillac Tower, the Bell Telephone Building—all magnificent structures lording over Detroit's downtown.

It was natural that he'd be overwhelmed. He'd been a child from a primitive village in Italy when he first came to Detroit. He had studied in the city's schools, played in its streets, worked in its factories. As the auto industry thrived, so did Detroit. It was a workingman's town, growing, expanding. Here a common laborer had a chance for a decent life, could buy a home of his own, and a car as well. Everything was possible in Detroit. There were dreams to be dreamed, and now, as never before, they were attainable dreams, thanks to industry, thanks to the installment plan.

Even before the likes of Henry Ford and General Motors' William Durant, Detroit was a major production center, particularly in manufacturing wheels, axles, frames, and bodies for railroad cars, and before that, with the state's vast lumber resources, in producing carriage bodies. From those beginnings Detroit became a manufacturing colossus. The city held an endless fascination with its hidden resources, like the vast salt mines tunneled below the city.

Mike felt a special kinship to the city. It was strong, vital, growing, advancing. Oh, there were imperfections in the labor structure; the sweat shops still prevailed. But the movement toward unionization would surely gain momentum. Eventually the wrongs would be righted; management would be forced to offer better wages and working conditions, more benefits and equality. Right now his earnings bought fewer goods today than they had in 1926. Mike was sorely tempted to take an active part in the formation of a union, but he couldn't risk losing his job. He had a family to support—that was his prime responsibility. He couldn't jeopardize his job. Still, a union would come to pass. It would just take unity and cooperation.

Mike roused himself from his reveries and transferred from the trolley to a bus loaded with workers all heading for the Rouge. He hung on to an overhead strap as the bus lurched down Miller Road, past the Michigan Central railroad tracks.

When finally the bus screeched to a stop, the men rushed out the door and up steel steps polished smooth by a million feet. Mike jostled against the men from the night shift stampeding from the opposite direction, anxious to get home. Hurrying through the double doors to his section, he punched the time clock and finally arrived at his bench with two minutes to spare. With its piercing wail, the starting bell shrilled through the plant and another workday began.

The familiar symphony of the factory began—the roaring cacophony of discordant sounds; a din that reverberated through the plant and had gradually seeped into his very bones. The racket became so routine it was all but ignored; it was a backdrop for Mike's thoughts as he repeated the motions of the job, minute after minute, hour after hour.

The job was infinitely monotonous, as well as dangerous. The risk of accident, due to fatigue and inattention, was ever-present. So far, Mike had avoided that problem. More insidious was the other peril—spotters and goons who watched, especially for union agitators. He had seen a man in his section fired simply because he praised John L. Lewis, president of the mine workers' union. No explanation was given for the firing, but they all knew.

But there were worse jobs. At least the area was clean, the floors well-scrubbed, the walls freshly painted. Henry Ford prided himself on the cleanliness of his plants.

It was almost quitting time. Mike could tell by the dull ache in his arms and legs. If he could only take a moment to stretch, to lean against his machine for a few seconds, but he couldn't risk even that. His stomach pained him too; it was "Forditis," a stress-induced ulcer, the bane of the workers.

No one could move before the bell rang. Just last week a worker bought coffee from the lunch wagon a few minutes before the signal. His job was driving cars off the assembly line to inspection and he hadn't enough time for another delivery before lunch. When he went to punch his card, he couldn't find it. He had been fired because of those few "stolen" seconds.

At last the bell sounded and Mike was finished for the day. Without conscious effort, like a robot, he followed the long line of weary men, punched his time card, and retraced his morning steps to the bus. He dozed, exhausted from the work, the sameness, the long hours.

At last the steetcar stopped at Chene Street. Another day had ended.

Mike was almost past the shoe-repair shop when he remembered to pick up the shoes he was having half-soled.

The proprietor took his stub and turned to the shelves behind him for the package with the matching number.

"Ah, here it is. Marcassa." He slapped the package on the counter and peered into Mike's face. "Marcassa. I thought you looked familiar." His hand, blackened in the creases, shot out and gripped Mike's. "Verdano, Joe Verdano, from Ramolita. Don't you remember me?"

Mike sifted through old memories to place the broad, open face and familiar name. Yes, yes, he remembered. Joe's father had had a small shoe shop in his village.

A smile spread over Mike's face as he pumped Joe's hand vigorously. "Joe. Sure, I remember."

"I though I knew all the *paisani* in Detroit. I guess I was wrong. You live around here?"

"Yeah, on Chene." Mike's head tipped in the direction of his home.

"How long have you been in Detroit?"

"I lived here when I was a boy, then went back to Italy with my mother after my father died in 1915. I came back in 1921."

Joe narrowed his eyes at Mike, then pointed a finger. "Hey, I remember now. You married Concetta and then there were problems. Yeah, my buddy told me about it. He was related in some way, a distant cousin or something."

Mike closed his eyes painfully. His neck grew warm.

"It was unfortunate, very unfortunate, my friend." Joe's voice softened. "And she was never found, eh? Simply disappeared. Strange. And a terrible thing for you."

Mike fished into his pocket for change, then flipped the correct silver on the counter. "My wife's got dinner waiting," he mumbled.

Joe reached across and placed a hand on Mike's shoulder. "Ah, I shouldn't have said anything. I see the memories are not happy ones. It was stupid of me."

"Nah, it's okay. It's just that I remarried and . . . well, my wife knows nothing, and, well . . ."

"Eh, I understand, pal."

"Look, Joe, it's been good seeing you, but I gotta get going. I'm sure I'll see you again." He picked up the package and left.

"Yeah, yeah. *Arrivederci—*" Joe called after him.

Yanking his cap down over his eyes, Mike hurried

away. Strange how you could never quite put your past behind you, how it reared up unexpectedly when you were sure you'd excised it from your life.

His earliest memories of life before he came to America were happy ones. His village clung to the mountainside in Campania, where a dry stone wall and large steps led to terraced farms and orchards surrounding clusters of stone houses with flat rust-colored tile roofs. He remembered the olive trees. When the olives were ripe, all able-bodied people—men, women, and children—worked from morning to dusk to pick the valuable crop. Michele and the other children would pick olives from the ground.

Lively mountain springs gurgled and chortled as they made their uneven way downhill. He would go to the springs with Mama to do the weekly wash. He imagined his mother, walking tall and straight, a large woven basket balanced on her head with one hand. He skipped along beside her, singing, chattering, whistling. If there were others washing at the spring, Mama would hurry above them, so that the dirty suds from their clothing wouldn't wash down on hers. His mother straddled two flat stones on her bare feet and whipped the unwieldy sheets up and down in the rushing water. It was there that Michele usually saw Concetta. He'd call to her and they'd splash in the lively waters while the women washed and gossiped. Concetta's long skirt was tied up around her waist as they played barefoot in the shallows. She clung to his hand and looked at him adoringly. Her hair when newly washed made a dark, cloudy halo around her tiny face. He remembered that she cried when he left for America. They were just babies and it was so long ago; but he remembered.

America. There were work and opportunity and money in America. A magical place. Everything was possible in America.

Then, when they arrived in Chicago, the only work available was on the railroad, laying ties and driving spikes.

Michele remembered waiting impatiently for his father's homecoming after twelve hours of steady labor. Although bone-weary, his father accepted his fate, grateful to have work, no matter how hard. He was sure their lot would improve. "Work," he would tell his small son.

"Work and family. Those are the important things. That is what we were put on this earth for. Nothing will come to you without hard work. Never forget that."

His mother, Anna, would massage his father's back, clucking sympathetically and murmuring soothing words. He took his young family to Detroit when he heard there were plenty of jobs in the auto factories. But it was over a month before he found employment at Detroit's first automobile factory, Ransom Olds, on East Jefferson Avenue, next to the Belle Isle Bridge. Later he graduated to the assembly line of the Ford Motor Car Company, the "Crystal Palace" of Highland Park, where his wage was twenty-six cents an hour. "God bless America," he would say at least once a day, ever grateful for the ability to earn his way, to be self-sufficient.

"They treat us like animals on the assembly line," he told his son, "but I shut my mouth and do my job, even when they call me 'dago,' or 'wop.' That's the only way to survive."

His father was proud of him—he was quick and bright, not only at book learning, but at the alley sports and playground games, baseball and "red rover" and "crack the whip."

Michele was fifteen years old when his father died from a work accident. His mother, beside herself with grief, and still a foreigner in this strange land, scraped together whatever money she could and returned with her son to the old country. They stayed with a cousin and Michele worked in the fields.

By then Concetta had grown into a woman; fragile, lovely, shy. He remembered her enticing glances when they chanced to meet at church or in the piazza.

He would casually stroll by her house, hoping to glimpse her on the balcony. She would dazzle him with her smile but they could never converse, for there was always someone around. He was feverishly infatuated. He had to have Concetta for his wife. In due time a marriage was arranged, though his mother was against it.

"You know nothing of this girl," she admonished him. "No one does. They keep her hidden away, as if she were a rare flower."

"You've been listening to the village gossips, old woman," Michele admonished his mother. He was blinded by love, caught up hoplessly in his carnal urges, like a fly in a spider's web. Until the engagement they hardly spoke, and were never alone, even for a moment. But the mere sight of Concetta caused ripples of desire in him and a fierce craving to touch her, protect her, make love to her.

They were both nineteen when they married, and gradually he discovered that his mother had been right. Concetta hid away inside herself, in a secret world of her own. Childlike and insecure, she hardly spoke, and performed only the simplest household tasks. Being young and inexperienced himself, he was often impatient, and unable to understand her ways. Though he was enamored of her, he was perplexed by her. The marriage was not even consummated until several days after the wedding, because of her unreasonable fear. He could still recall how she huddled on the edge of the bed, her eyes shut tight in terror. His words did nothing to allay her dread. When she finally allowed him to make love to her, he felt ridden with guilt.

He envisioned her now, the frightened doe eyes in a porcelain face, the delicate features, the hair hanging in ringlets. At first her innocence was endearing, her dependency flattering, but soon he felt strangled by her inability to make the smallest decisions, and by her weakness, both physical and emotional.

They lived with his mother in her tiny one-room house. His mother vacillated between impatience with Concetta's dreamy ways and pity for her.

"I fear for you if she should have a child. How will she care for it? She is such a child herself. Somehow, the wisdom and maturity of womanhood have not visited this unfortunate creature."

Michele worked with Concetta's father, Mario, in the small fields hacked out of the mountain. It was discouraging to chop away at the unrelenting earth that, despite backbreaking toil, yielded little. The olive trees, however, produced well, and there was usually a small profit to be made on the oil. But Michele wasn't happy, knowing it would be years before he could afford a house and some land of his own. He dreamed of returning to America.

After a few months he confided to Mario that he could

no longer accept his charity and planned to return to America. Mario agreed; after all, he wanted a better life for his daughter. He'd heard the tales of riches in America, where there were jobs for everyone. Michele, with his mother's and Mario's blessings, scraped together money and, with a loan from Mario, booked passage for America.

When Michele told Concetta about their trip, she merely smiled her sweet smile; but as the time to leave drew closer, she whimpered and pouted and refused to consider leaving. When the day arrived, she screamed invectives at him and adamantly refused to leave her bed. In the end he went alone, but with her promise that when he found work he could send for her and she would join him.

Back in Detroit, Michele found work immediately and lived frugally in a boardinghouse in order to send money home and save a little.

Although he wrote faithfully, Concetta's letters to him were few and far between, and finally stopped altogether. After months with no word, he received a long, painful letter from his father-in-law. It told of a series of deplorable occurrences. Several months ago Concetta had been raped by an official in the village. The official, whose name was Bendari, had claimed that it was Concetta who had come to him and seduced him. No one was willing to confront this vile man; and truth to tell, there was nothing one could do, for he was powerful, and people professed to believe him rather than to invite his ire. Distraught and confused, Concetta succumbed to a deep depression. The villagers, in their backward and insensitive fashion, ostracized her, claiming she had the "evil eye." In her confused state of mind, she left to live in a cave at the outskirts of the village. No amount of persuasion could convince her to return home. Her father beseeched Michele to return and use his influence to help Concetta, before she became so entrenched in her dementia she would be unable to return to a normal life.

Michele booked passage immediately. Back in Italy, he was saddened to see Mario's face had grown old and lined in the intervening months. The two men hurried toward a dusty path that wound to a cavernous area beyond the village. Unmoved by the brilliant beauty of the day or by the comforting sound of cedars gently swishing in the breeze, they trudged on. Mario paused, puffing, and fanned himself with his straw hat. He took a huge blue handkerchief from his pocket and wiped his sweaty brow.

"You won't know her, my little sparrow, she's so thin, so sad . . ." Mario's voice faded away in a guttural sob. "The priest tried to talk to her, as well as the doctor, and of course all her *comari*. Her mother took to her bed and has been unwell since this happened. I've gone to her and begged, screamed, cajoled, all for nothing. She is not herself; no, she's someone I don't even know." He seemed lost in thought for a few moments, then continued. "She was never a strong child, not like the rest of our children. In school, well, it was difficult for her." As they approached the stark rocky hills, he slowed his steps and said in a quiet voice, "There it is, see? That's where she chooses to live." He pointed ahead and motioned Michele to stop.

Michele's gaze followed a short weedy path to an opening in the craggy gray wall. Sparse vegetation dotted the mound.

A crow, sitting on a promontory above the cave, flapped its wings and cawed eerily. Its flight created dark darting shadows on the ground. An omen, thought Michele as he slowly approached the uninviting black yawn of the cave entrance.

"Concetta," her father called out. "It's your father."

His voice echoed through the valley. They stood as still as the rocks around them. There was a movement, a stirring, then a singing sound, but with strange, unintelligible words. They waited. Mario put his finger to his lips, signaling Michele to be still.

Finally a figure appeared at the opening of the cave, but the wild-eyed, disheveled creature who stared without recognition was a stranger to Michele.

"Concetta," her father said in a pleading voice, "Michele's here, come to take you home."

Her eyes widened in fear, and she began backing away. Michele sprang forward and grabbed her by the wrist. She tried to pull free, scratching and hissing like an animal.

"It's me, Michele. I'm your husband. Don't you know me?" he pleaded.

She spat at him and writhed about, trying to break his grip.

He clasped her from behind, pinning her arms, and spoke quietly, intensely, into her ear.

"I'm taking you home, Concetta. You're my wife and you belong with me. I'll take care of you. No one will hurt you again." He kept up a patter of soothing words until she stopped struggling. Finally she collapsed in tears and he and Mario supported her on the long walk home.

Back at his mother's home, Michele began the tedious battle to bring Concetta back to health. With his mother's help he forced her to eat properly, bathe, and care for herself. Little by little she began functioning in a semblance of normality, and although still shunned by the superstitious villagers, she was at least able to communicate with her husband. In three months she had regained her health, and if she wasn't happy, at least she had lost the fearful, vapid look she'd had when Michele found her.

But she was not the same girl his youthful fantasies had invented and embellished.

Concetta lay next to him, her long hair tickling his shoulders. She was so frail. He could easily reach his thumb and index finger around her birdlike wrist.

"You won't leave me again, will you, Michele?"

"No, I won't leave you. When I go, you're coming with me."

"You shouldn't have left me before."

"I had to go. You know I couldn't stay here. I should have forced you to come with me."

She whimpered a little, but said nothing more.

He kept pushing away the thought that wound its way insistently to the front of his brain: would he ever have a normal life? Would she ever be able to cope in a new country, perhaps with a child?

He hugged her a little closer. "We're going back to America. I had a good job there; I had friends. Even your father thinks it would be better for both of us."

She shivered and shook her head. "I'm afraid."

She was such a child; with a child's mentality in a woman's body. Were his expectations too high?

"I can't stay here. There's no way to make any money. I get more depressed by the day, living this way. This time you're coming with me. No arguments. Do you understand me?"

She was quiet for a moment, and Michele nudged her. "Do you understand me?" he repeated.

"Yes," she murmured, but her look was dark and brooding.

He booked their passage once again for America. But when it was time to leave, she was nowhere to be found.

Michele, along with her family, searched the village, the caves, and the byways, to no avail. Impossible as it seemed, she had disappeared.

"It's no use. I've no idea where she could have gone," her father said breathlessly after returning from a frantic search. "Certainly she's nowhere in the village, nor in any of the caves I know of."

"It's time to leave," his mother said. "You can't wait any longer." The automobile was waiting in the piazza to take him to the train station.

"I can't leave without her," Michele said.

"Go with God's blessing, my son," his mother said between her tears. "You are better off without her; God forgive me for saying it."

"She is my daughter, and I love her. But your mother is right. You must leave without her. We'll find her somehow, then see that she comes to America."

Though her parents never gave up hope of finding Concetta, she never returned to the village and was never heard from again. Michele should never have left her. Who knew what misfortune might have befallen her? He should have continued to look for her; she was a child, an innocent.

Her father wrote to him:

I have searched, and others have helped, but all in vain. There is nothing to be gained in your returning, for we have done all that can be done. I fear she has met with disaster. Her mother is heartbroken, and I continue to bear up, but with a heavy heart. Don't grieve and don't be remorseful, for there is nothing you can do. Go on with your life.

10

"Did they deliver the radio?" Michele asked as he burst in the door.

"Yes, it came." Chiara couldn't hide her disapproval. She had been waiting for Michele, to hear an explanation of this extravagance. He had just begun to make a little headway with his savings, and now he'd bought a radio. "Why didn't you at least discuss it with me?"

"I wanted it to be a surprise." A pleased grin erased the tired lines from Mike's face as he hurried to the front room, where the large oak box with squat carved legs sat like a scowling child. Kneeling, he ran his hand over the cloth-covered speaker and began twisting dials.

There was a static screech, and finally, voices. "There. Listen, it's *Amos n' Andy.*"

Chiara gestured in exasperation. "I can't understand that dialect. It's another language, not English. I don't know why you bought this, Michele. We don't have enough money for playthings."

Michele looked annoyed. "Don't you worry about the money. It's on the installment plan."

"Installment plan? You mean you pay a little each month?"

He stood, beaming at the radio as if it were speaking directly to him. "Yes. It's not much money."

"Now we're debtors! You've really become an American, haven't you?" she said with disgust. "I don't like it. If we can't afford it, we shouldn't buy it."

"We can afford it. It'll just take us a little longer to pay for it. Why should we wait for the things we want? We'll have pleasure from it while we're paying, and beyond."

"It sounds wonderful when you say it, but it's not right.

It goes against the grain, contrary to everything we've been taught. We'll never save the down payment for a house."

Michele waved his hand to still her objections. "Quiet! It's done, and I don't want to hear any more about it."

Chiara tried to swallow her displeasure as she went back to the kitchen. Setting a steaming bowl of pasta on the table, she called to him, "Come and eat, then, while it's hot." When Mike took his place she said, "I just don't think it's wise to be in debt to anyone."

His dark eyes flashed as he said sternly, "I said, that's enough."

"All right. But I think you should at least talk to me before you go ahead and do something like this." At his angry look, she said quietly, "All right, I'm finished." She knew better than to pursue it any longer. He was usually slow to anger, but now she could see he was at the limit of his patience. And what was done, was done.

It was obvious that Michele wasn't disciplined enough to save. This purchase shored her determination to add to the savings she'd begun with her very first job. The money grew slowly but steadily, and the knowledge of its existence was a source of comfort to her. The deception caused an occasional pang of guilt. She quelled it by imagining Michele's pleasure when she presented him with the money.

Still, in the following weeks Chiara had to admit to a fascination with the radio. Like all of America, she and Michele gathered around the set each evening and tuned in to Bing Crosby, Paul Whiteman, Ed Wynn, Rudy Vallee. So much of the patter was lost on Chiara because of the language barrier, but she kept the set on for "company" during the day. As time went on, the radio more than anything else contributed toward the improvement of her English and her understanding of American mores.

On a Sunday evening Chiara joined Michele in listening to Father Coughlin, pastor of the Shrine of the Little Flower in Royal Oak. With his inspiring and hypnotic voice, the priest denounced Wall Street and the international bankers, sure they were pushing the country toward disaster. She wondered if he was speaking the truth.

"Don't believe all you hear and read," Michele told her.

A few days later, Michele twisted the dial past intermittent static until he found what he wanted.

"Come here, Chiara. This is a historic day, Monday, October 21, 1929. It's the celebration of the fiftieth anniversary of the light bulb. Shh, listen."

Henry Ford hosted the festivities, attended by the President and Mrs. Hoover, J. P. Morgan, Albert Einstein, Madame Curie, Orville Wright, Will Rogers, and the man of honor, Thomas Edison.

"It's at Greenfield Village, the museum Henry Ford built. We'll go there one of these days," Michele said. "It's a remarkable event with all these great men gathered together. Listen, Chiara." He sat forward, hands on his knees, intent on the speeches. "What a great land this is, full of great people. And it's still a new country. Who knows what wonderful things are in store for us?"

Chiara, properly awed, agreed. "Yes, it *is* a wonderful country." She laid Robbie on the floor atop a blanket with a stuffed animal to amuse him, and cooed, "What wonders are in store for you, Berto? Ten years from now, twenty, thirty?"

"Soon we'll buy an electric refrigerator and a telephone. I'm working steady; we'll have the money," Mike said expansively.

"One thing at a time, Mike."

"And Edison said, 'Let there be light!' " the announcer intoned.

Just a few days later, on Thursday, October 24, Michele flipped the radio dial to hear newscaster H. V. Kaltenborn report, in shocked tones, the stunning news of a three-billion-dollar loss on the stock market.

Michele listened intently through the broadcast, then clicked off the radio and shook his head. "From greatness to disaster. I don't know what's happening to this country." He whipped the Detroit *Times* open to the business section. Since September he had followed the spastic fluctuations in the market with some slight concern.

Chiara put Robbie to her breast and murmured to him as he nursed. "What is all this talk of the stock market?" she asked. "Why are people frightened?"

"When people buy stock, they're investing their money in big companies. When the prices go down, they lose money; when they go up, they make money. If the prices fall too fast and far, it means trouble. That's what's happening now."

"Is it like a regular market?"

He smiled. "Not exactly."

"People should take their money back when it goes up," she said with sudden enlightenment.

Michele laughed. "Now you got the idea. People always hope it will go higher. No one knew it would drop so suddenly, not even very smart and very rich people."

Chiara made a face. "It's like gambling. I don't believe in gambling." With her little finger she released Roberto's mouth from her breast. Hoisting him to her shoulder, she rubbed his back in circular motions. Suddenly worried, she asked, "Surely you don't have any money in that market?"

"No, of course not, but I know people who do; factory workers, cabdrivers, even Fredo. Some people buy on margin. They owe money for the stock." He stood and paced restlessly. "When the stock market drops, it affects the economy of the whole country."

It sounded serious. "It's so complicated. But as long as you're working, that's all that matters."

Michele opened his mouth to say something, but thought better of it. Why bother her with his concerns? They were probably unfounded anyway. In a day or two the market would be up again. Still, he couldn't help feeling a little nervous. Cars were the leading product bought on credit. Sales of automobiles were the weather vane of the American economy. What would this do to car sales, to the Ford Motor Company, and ultimately to him?

By the next Tuesday, at the end of the day stocks were valued fourteen billion dollars less than at the beginning of the day. Now they were calling it a "crash."

During the following weeks, there was talk of nothing else. The city seemed suspended in a cloud of apprehension.

But in November, Michele told his wife, "I think things are looking up; Henry Ford is reducing the price of the Model A. Maybe things aren't as bad as we think."

"He's a wise man, Henry Ford."

"Sure, it's a smart move. He'll sell more cars with a lower price."

Shortly after that, Michele reported, "Old Henry's done it again. He increased the minimum wage to seven dollars a day. By God, Henry Ford has faith in the country. And I got faith in Henry Ford. Look what he says in the Dearborn *Independent:* 'The storm of the depression is but a passing wind which will soon blow over.' "

With blind optimism, Michele, along with the rest of the workers, believed Henry Ford, and indeed, the stock market rallied briefly. When days later it dropped again, so did the hopes of the city.

Michele's fears seemed submerged for a while in the excitement of the wine-making. Chiara watched from the front door as Michele and Ed hoisted boxes of precious cargo from the curb to their shoulders. Lush clusters of purple grapes, blushed with a dewy white film, spilled over the top and through the slats of the plywood crates. The men laughed and whistled as they moved the boxes to the back door and down the basement stairs.

Michele took a break and stopped in the kitchen for a glass of water.

"I don't like this," Chiara said.

Michele and Ed had bought a wine press a month ago, before the crash, before the future looked so uncertain.

Michele wiped his brow. "There's nothing wrong with making our own wine."

It seemed strange to Chiara that in all other matters Michele was scrupulously honest, but in this, he was willing to overlook the rules. It frightened her. "But it's against the law."

"Bah! A man should be allowed to drink what he wants in his own house. Gasoline if he wants it!" Michele gulped the water down and wiped his mouth with his sleeve. "We need our wine. Wine is the staff of life, more so than bread. In Italy babies drink wine at their mothers' knees; that's what puts iron in their blood." He patted Chiara's behind. "It's not like Italians are drunkards. When do you ever see an Italian falling down from drink? Rarely."

Chiara nodded her agreement.

He grinned. "Wine mellows a man; drowns his woes for a short time. God sanctions wine. Remember the Bible story of the wedding feast? When they ran out of wine, Christ performed a miracle and increased the wine so the festivities could continue. If wine is good enough for Jesus Christ, it's good enough for me."

Michele's justification did nothing to dispel Chiara's anxiety. "What if the police see this?" she asked. "What if you get caught?"

"They won't catch us. It's not like we're going to sell it. It's just for our own tables, and some for our friends. You worry too much."

"Someone in this family has to worry." She didn't complain of the money it cost, though that rankled too.

He shook his finger under her nose. "When it's time to worry, I'll worry." He hurried past Chiara and outside for another load.

"*Presto*. Make it fast," Michele urged Ed, who preceded him down the steps with his own load. "I don't want these boxes out in plain sight for too long."

Michele plucked a bunch of grapes and offered them to Chiara. He popped a plump grape into his mouth. "Mmm, they're delicious, bittersweet, zinfandel, the best California grapes, almost as good as in Italy. Almost, not quite."

Chiara tasted the fruit and agreed that it was excellent, then went to Roberto, who had begun stirring in his crib. Holding him close, she rocked as she watched out the window. Michele went to the barrel standing in the yard and pulled the cork, sending the water arcing out in a curved, steady spray. The oak barrel, ringed with dark metal bands, had been filled with water to swell and seal it. When the barrel was empty, Michele and Ed rolled it down the cellar steps.

For the next several nights the men took turns rotating the handle that pressed the juice from the grapes. The deep purple liquid oozed from the slats of the press and trickled into the waiting wooden bucket. When the bucket was full, it was emptied into the barrel. Soon the entire house reeked with the heady smell of fermenting grapes.

"Don't let any women into the basement if they're menstruating," Michele warned. "It'll ruin the wine and turn it into vinegar."

Chiara scoffed at the ancient superstition, but was unwilling to put it to the test.

"It's going to be good wine, I can tell," Michele said, rubbing his hands together.

*　　*　　*

The doorbell rang several days later while Ed and Flora were visiting. Chiara opened the door and saw two strange men in dark suits and brimmed hats.

"Excuse me, ma'am," said the one nearer the door, tipping his hat. He was a tall, gaunt man with sparse hair slicked straight back from a middle part. "Your name Marcassa?"

"Yes." Chiara stepped back in alarm. There was something ominous about the men. "What is it?"

"Me and my partner, Larsen, hear you got wine here," the second, shorter man said, with lips that were twisted in a permanent sneer.

"Michele!" Chiara called out.

"What's going on?" Michele came from the kitchen, with Ed and Flora at his heels.

"You Marcassa?"

"Yes. What's it to you?"

"Who're you?" the man called Larsen asked, glaring at Ed.

Eduardo hesitated a moment, then said, "Ed Pasini."

While the short one jotted Ed's name in a notebook, Larsen reached into his pocket and withdrew a leather folder. "Federal agents," he said, flipping open the folder to reveal a badge. "We want to see your wine barrels."

They pushed past the group and marched into the kitchen.

"Wine barrels?"

"Yeah, in the cellar."

They reached the cellar steps and their footsteps clattered as they hurried down the dark, narrow stairway.

Michele scurried after them, shouting, "Wait, you can't do this."

"What are they going to do?" Chiara asked, twisting the edge of her apron as she followed Michele.

"Haven't you heard of Prohibition?" Larsen asked, sarcasm dripping from his words.

"Prohibition?" Michele said. "I don't know about that. I'm from Italy. I only make wine for myself and my friends."

"Sure, play stupid," said the shorter man.

The agents stood in the dank cellar, before the barrel, hands on their hips. "What's this, sody pop?" asked Larsen as he turned the spigot, releasing a stream of sparkling purple juice. He stuck his index finger in the spray and licked it. "Not bad," he said. "A shame it's all going to waste."

"It's not even ready yet." Michele winced as he watched his precious wine hit the crumbling concrete floor. "It needs to age. In a month come back and I'll give you some wine, the best you ever tasted."

"Are you trying to bribe me?"

"What bribe? I'm just offering you some good wine."

"Come on, Al, we don't have time to watch it disappear. Throw something in it."

"Yeah," Al said, looking around him. "What's this?" he asked, his eyes fastening on a gallon can sitting on a shelf behind them.

"Kerosene," Larsen answered. "Just the thing."

The men turned the barrel on its side and quickly removed the plug. Al lifted the kerosene can to the opening and emptied the contents into the wine barrel while Michele winced and groaned as though he'd been hit in the gut.

"My God, it's all ruined," Ed said.

Chiara turned and ran, wailing, up the steps. What would happen now? Would Michele go to jail? All this work and money wasted. Nothing ever seemed to go right.

A week later, Michele returned home from his court appearance and told Chiara the bad news. The judge had fined him fifty dollars, but would take payments of ten dollars a week.

Chiara moaned. They took one step ahead and two steps back. It seemed they would never get ahead.

Michele's confidence in the economy flagged as the year crept to an end, and the beginning of the new year brought no relief. He read the papers voraciously, looking in vain for signs of an upturn. Forecasts were bright. The Department of Labor predicted that 1930 would be a "splendid employment year." In March, President Hoover predicted their problems would be over in sixty days. But each month saw an increase in the list of automobile manufacturers that were falling by the wayside like rotten apples from a tree. In a solemn voice Michele read aloud the names of the auto companies that had folded. The litany included Stearns, Moon, Gardner, Locomobile, Jordan. The good news was that with so many companies gone, Ford had a greater share of the market, and even outsold General Motors.

"Isn't that good?" Chiara asked.

"Yes, it's good for Ford, but what about all those others out of work? People who aren't working aren't going to buy cars."

Though the city was in the grip of fear, still they all clung to slim threads of hope, wanting to believe President Hoover's declaration on May 1 that "we have now passed the worst and . . . shall rapidly recover."

By mid-year the depression was worldwide. Hoover carefully avoided the use of words like "panic" or "crisis." It was, he said, a "depression," which had the connotation of a dip rather than a drastic crash. "Buy" was one solution. "Buy something for somebody: we all prosper together," a utility association advertised. "Go to the movies—that's one way to spend," an ad said. Prohibition should end, some papers insisted. Legalizing beer alone would employ more than a million people.

Nightly Michele searched in vain for evidence of an upturn; news of bankruptcies peppered the papers.

"This is madness," he told his wife. "And Henry Ford keeps expanding. He's building plants across the country and adding to the Rouge powerhouse. What is he thinking of?"

By mid-year the news was even more discouraging. Henry Ford's show of confidence notwithstanding, Mike knew car sales were down drastically. More and more businesses folded and the welfare lists swelled.

Michele turned constantly to the radio, hoping for an optimistic report, but the creature dispensed only discouragement and stood as an angry reminder that it wasn't totally his. It grinned its knobby grin in a cloth face that mocked him: *Pay up, pay up.*

With each passing day, Michele's anxiety increased. The other big plants were laying off workers; Ford would almost certainly do likewise. Michele's fear gradually shadowed his every action.

He performed his job robotlike, spoke to Chiara hardly at all.

She chided him. "You never talk to me anymore. What's wrong?"

"Nothing. I only want peace and quiet when I come home!"

He didn't like what was happening to him, but couldn't seem to help himself. The thought of losing his job was forever on his mind, fogging his brain, numbing his emotions. How long until he was fired? It was only a matter of time.

—— **11** ——

Chiara wasn't fond of doing laundry, though hanging it outside on warm days was a rather agreeable chore. She rubbed Fels Naphtha soap on the clothing and scrubbed energetically against the washboard, her reddened knuckles scraping painfully. She washed in one large galvanized tub and rinsed in another. After wringing unwieldy sheets a section at a time, she loaded them into baskets.

When Roberto whined his displeasure at being left to his own devices in his high chair, Chiara fetched and dressed him, then set him outdoors at a blanket-covered spot where a few sparse tufts of grass grew. He amused himself by filling a battered tin cup with sooty earth.

The March wind stung Chiara's cheeks and whipped her skirt against her legs as she ran a damp cloth along the line. Removing the wooden clothespins from her mouth, she snapped them into place on the wet laundry, then blew on her fingers to warm them.

It was the first time this spring she had attempted to dry her laundry outside. She turned her face toward the weak, cloud-filtered sun, welcoming its warming rays. Thank God for the sun. All winter she'd had to drape damp sheets and diapers across ropes strung around the kitchen.

"Hello, Laurelia," she called out to the tall woman who was performing the same chore across the alley.

The brown-skinned woman with chestnut eyes made her way toward Chiara, saying, "Ain't seen you all winter, Chiara, how you been?"

"I've been well, and you?"

"As good as I can be, considerin'. I ain't seen your baby in quite a spell. What a darlin' chile," she said, chucking Robbie under the chin. "I guess we be goin' soon, 'cause Mortimer loss his job. They put a white man in his job. The niggers is the first to go."

Chiara clucked her disapproval. "Where are you going?"

"Down home, to Mississippi. Mortimer's pa has a farm, so's at least we can work the land some. There sure ain't no jobs here. Your husband still workin'?"

"Yes." Chiara shook out a workshirt and hung it on the line. She was almost embarrassed to admit Mike was one of the fortunate ones.

"He shore lucky."

"Yes, he is."

"Well, maybe we see you if things gits better and we come back."

"I hope so."

As Laurelia turned to go, Chiara touched her arm and said, "I wish you good fortune."

After the last towel was hung she led Robbie inside, fed him, and settled him down for a nap.

At the sound of the doorbell, she peeped through the lace curtains and was surprised to see Stewart's car at the curb. His visits always made her a little fluttery. After a quick glance in the mirror and a pinch of her cheeks to redden them, Chiara whipped off her apron and went to the door. She hadn't seen Stewart since before Robbie was born, though she'd been to the Austin home for work several times. Mrs. Austin would greet her in a slightly haughty, brittle way, with the separation between employer and employee clearly implied in her manner.

Stewart's smile lit his angular face. "Hello, Chiara, I hope you're keeping well." He gave an almost courtly bow.

"Yes, I'm well. And you? You're thin." His skin looked sallow and tight across the cheekbones.

"Thin? Yes, well, I suppose I've lost a bit of weight.

There have been a few problems." He shifted a large package from one hand to the other.

She opened the door wider. "Come in, come in. Problems. Everyone around us has them." Nervously she tucked a strand of hair behind her ear. "The man in the flat above is unemployed. He looks for work every day, and returns looking beaten. The people across the way are going home to Mississippi because the husband lost his job." She continued while Stewart followed her into the kitchen, "At least you don't have to worry about that. Mike worries all the time. He's still working, but it probably won't be for long."

"Don't worry about your husband's job. I'll see to it that he stays on."

She was touched that Stewart had spared her the embarrassment of asking that favor.

He frowned and hesitated before going on, "But things are very uncertain at the plant . . . there is some agitation for a union; and of course, Henry Ford is adamantly against it. And rightly so. After all, he has always looked after his men, has been a champion of the laborers. He still considers himself one of the working class."

Chiara looked incredulous. The great, wealthy Henry Ford a workingman? She had seen pictures of his huge estate, Fairlane, and read of his family in the society pages of the paper.

"If he is for the workingman, why are the wages cut? And the days? Michele is working only three days a week now."

"Some things can't be helped. The economy . . . I'm sure there'll be an upturn. Meanwhile, it would be better for your husband if he stayed clear of the elements who are making waves, the communists and socialists like Walter Reuther."

Chiara frowned.

"I don't want to upset you, but . . . well, so many are losing their jobs, and he shouldn't give Bennett any more reason to put him on the list."

Chiara nodded slowly, her face crestfallen.

"I'll do what I can, Chiara." Stewart reached out and touched her shoulder, his eyes softening. "Don't worry."

His touch stirred her, causing a small heat rush over her neck and face. Softly, she said, "We are grateful to you."

When his hand dropped, she said, "Won't you sit a moment and have some coffee?"

"No, thank you. I don't have much time." His eyes darted about nervously, until they lit again on her. "Your hair. It's different."

"Yes." She touched her locks, which fell from a side part in unruly waves just below her ears. Michele hadn't seemed to notice the new style.

"It's very becoming."

Chiara flushed at his frank admiration, but said nothing. An undefinable undercurrent filled the air, a vague tension. Did he feel it too?

"Did you bring work for me?" she asked finally, pointing to the package.

"Oh, yes . . . yes, I have something." It was as if he had forgotten for a moment where he was. "Audrey wants some skirts taken in. They're pinned. She seems to be losing weight. She hasn't been very well." He handed Chiara the parcel. "There's also something for the baby. How is the baby? I'd love to see him."

"He's asleep." Chiara unwrapped the package and drew out a stuffed blue bunny. She ran her hand over the soft plush ears. *"Che bello.* He'll like this. But you already sent a blanket. I thank you for that also."

"The blanket was from Audrey. This is from me. I chose it myself." He smiled with satisfaction.

Chiara was touched. "Come, you can see him if you like. He sleeps soundly."

They tiptoed into the room and gazed at the slumbering child. His thumb was tucked firmly in his mouth, his pink, damp cheek pressed into the pillow.

Stewart's face softened. "He's beautiful. He looks like you," he whispered.

Chiara's eyes were adoring. "He has Michele's mouth and chin."

Roberto opened his eyes and smiled dreamily at his admirers, then was instantly asleep again.

"He has your eyes; lovely eyes." He leaned close and looked into her eyes, then rested his hand lightly on hers.

Chiara was warmed yet disturbed by his touch, his look. She moved her hand to tuck the blanket close around Roberto's shoulders.

She turned away and he followed. "Would . . . would you like some coffee or tea?" she offered again, flustered.

"No, thank you. I haven't much time. I just wanted to see you . . . see how you were faring since they've cut hours back at the plant."

"We're managing. Like everyone else, we only buy what's necessary." She thought of the radio and silently reproached Mike for the purchase. The payments were ever harder to make.

Stewart sighed. "I'm afraid things will get worse before they get better."

At the door he took her hand in his and held it gently for a moment. "Good-bye, Chiara," he said, then turned swiftly and left.

She watched him through the thin curtains, wondering why he looked so troubled, so uncertain. Was his job also in jeopardy? Again she felt a tug at her heart. She sensed his vulnerability and suppressed the urge to stroke his cheek, to offer him solace. His kindness and concern for her family touched her. Despite the disparity in their backgrounds, he had offered her an openhearted friendship. But now there was something more in those searching gray eyes than merely friendship; something that disquieted her and made her blush. When their glances had met in Roberto's bedroom, she'd read disturbing messages. Were they messages from his heart?

"Look at the little animal Mr. Austin brought," Chiara said, holding the soft plush bunny up for Michele's inspection.

He looked up from the paper and squashed his cigarette out in the ashtray. "I don't want you taking gifts from those capitalists."

Her eyes widened in surprise. "They've always been kind to us."

"I want nothing to do with those people."

Chiara held her tongue. In his present mood she didn't want to remind him that he owed his job to Stewart Austin.

He snapped his head toward her. "Are you still sewing for them?"

She hoped he wouldn't notice her guilty flush. He had no idea how much work she was actually doing. "Yes. I have time now that Roberto takes two long naps. And we can use the money."

"I don't want you working. I can support my family."

"You know I hate being idle. I do it just to keep busy. Besides, now that you're working only three days a week—"

"We're managing!" He crushed the paper and threw it on the floor, then ripped the cellophane from a fresh pack of Lucky Strikes. "We're eating every day, aren't we?"

"Yes, yes, we're eating." Chiara didn't want to set him off again. He was understandably worried over his job. To distract him she said, "Play with the baby while I make a *frittata* for your lunch tomorrow. You can smoke later. I don't think it's good to have smoke around the baby."

Reluctantly he put the cigarette out and lifted Robbie onto his lap. But instead of playing with him and talking to him as he used to, he merely jostled him about with little interest until the child slipped impatiently off his lap.

Chiara hesitated mentioning Stewart's warning, because lately Mike's temper flared for little reason. Finally she said, "Mike, Mr. Austin told me that they fire people for talking about the union."

"I know that. You think I'm stupid?"

"Of course you're not stupid. I just hope you're being careful."

"I'm careful." Mike paced the floor, then turned the radio on, switching the dial from station to station. Restlessly he turned the radio off again.

"What's wrong, Michele?" Chiara asked.

"Nothing, dammit. Why do you nag all the time?"

Robbie, playing under the table with a wooden spoon and tin bowl, began to cry. Mike picked him up and jiggled him absently on his knee.

Tears of anger and frustration sprang to Chiara's eyes as she cracked eggs into a bowl and whipped them with a fork. The change in Mike had been subtle and gradual. Now his churlishness was the rule. Whenever she urged him to speak of his concerns, he became angry and then withdrawn. She was aware that he was worried about money and about his job, but why did he vent his anger on her?

Only by listening when the men played cards and talked did she surmise the extent of his distress. Indeed, all the men seemed to hang on the edge of despair. Supposedly asleep, she'd heard Fredo, the Judge, confess he was deep in debt because of buying stocks on margin. Michele had lent him money, much to Chiara's chagrin. She and Michele had argued fiercely about the loan. The Judge had made his bed, let him lie in it, fool that he was.

She finished her kitchen work and prepared Robbie for bed. When she'd tucked him into his crib, she folded back the spread and plumped up the pillows on her bed.

Returning to the kitchen, she heard Mike shout as he waved the newspaper in the air, "Look at this. There's no justice. Kroger warehousemen are making only thirty-two cents an hour, and that's just for the actual hours worked. They hang around all day and wait for work and maybe get four or five hours in."

Chiara bit her tongue, wishing he would stop reading the newspapers. They held nothing but bad news.

"One kid with guts refused to go on working until they hired back two men they'd laid off for no reason. He got the others to stick with him, and management finally gave in. Now they're negotiating. The kid's name is Hoffa. Jimmy Hoffa."

"Don't get all upset about these things."

"Union. That's what we need. A union. But there's not a damn thing we can do. Even if we all got together and struck, they'd get scabs in."

Union. It was his recurring chant, a remedy for the ills of the country, a symbol of justice, a force that would right all wrongs.

"Forget all that now. It's dangerous talk," she said in a hushed voice, as if the walls were spying. "Come to bed, Michele. You're tired. You need your rest."

"Why do you do that? Tell me when I'm tired; when to go to bed. I know when I'm tired."

"So don't go to bed, then." She threw her hands into the air.

After undressing and washing, she donned a thin cotton nightgown and slipped into bed. But she was lonely.

Mike rarely touched her anymore, and when she snuggled up to him, he was unmoved and seemed to resist her. "I have things on my mind," he would say, excusing his lack of interest. The all-too-familiar worm of anxiety wriggled in her stomach. Her husband had changed. When she was fortunate enough to get his attention, he shouted at her for no reason, but more often he sat morosely staring, unaware of her presence. He was animated only when he ticked off the wrongs being perpetrated by the company bosses.

She wanted her old Michele back—the laughing, confident man she had married. She wanted his body touching hers, his mouth kissing hers. She wanted him to make love to her again—healing, satisfying love.

She slipped out of bed and went to the kitchen, where Mike sat drinking wine and reading.

Touching his shoulder, she said in soft Italian, "Michele, it's cold and lonely without you."

He looked up at her, then turned back and drained his wineglass. His lids dropped slowly, like blinds being drawn.

"Come to bed," she said, her voice an enticing murmur next to his ear.

His eyes still closed, he said, "Later, Chiara. Later." With deliberate movements he picked up the jug and poured more wine.

She placed her hands on his shoulders and massaged, her thumbs kneading the tension from his knotted muscles.

"Ah, that feels good," he said. "Don't stop."

Silently she worked her hands over his sinewy shoulders and back. If only she could ease his mind as well.

Mike placed his hands on top of hers when she stopped. "I'm . . . I'm afraid, Chiara. A man in my section was fired today for wearing a union button."

She knelt in front of him and saw tears forming in his eyes. The only other time she'd seen him cry was when Roberto was born.

"Every day I think it will be my last day of work," he said. "They're firing men all around me."

"You must have faith. God won't let us starve."

"God? Where is he now? He's not helping those miserable people in the soup lines."

"Things will get better. I heard President Hoover say so on the radio."

Mike rolled his eyes and shook his head. "I wish I had your faith. Go to bed, Chiara. I'll be there in a little while."

Back in bed, Chiara waited, forcing her eyes to stay open, but when she looked at the clock it read midnight. Finally she fell into a fitful sleep.

The next morning, as she handed Mike his lunch box, she said, "I need a little money for soup bones and bread."

"Again? Didn't I just leave you money the other day?"

"Yes, but it's gone. We eat every day, you know."

"Can't you try to cut back a bit? I'd like to save a little in case . . ."

"I have cut back. The meatballs are mostly bread now, and the bread is stale. Haven't you noticed you get *pasta e fagioli* twice a week?"

She had a bit of money put by from her sewing, but she could hardly utilize that. It would mean admitting that she flouted Mike's orders not to work. Besides, it was her little emergency fund. Mike hadn't been disciplined enough to save. She often wondered how he had accumulated the cash for his trip to Italy.

He threw a dollar on the table and left, slamming the door. There was a slump to his shoulders she hadn't noticed before.

— 12 —

Grudgingly, the months sloughed away, 1931 giving way to 1932. Always there was "evidence" of an upturn, of prosperity just around the corner. Optimism was the narcotic that dulled the painful wound of economic disaster.

President Hoover declared, "We have now passed the worst and . . . shall rapidly recover." One of his cures was enacting a tax cut that simply put more money into the pockets of the upper-income groups. Despite the encouraging words, the unemployment lines grew longer each day.

Mike's stomach ached from what he was sure was an ulcer—"Forditis," the bane of the workers. The days dragged on with a mind-dulling sameness; up at dawn, the long trip to the Rouge, the monotonous work, a quick lunch of the sandwiches and hot coffee that Chiara prepared, back to his machine, then home to begin the same routine the next day.

Mike noticed Chiara's dried, chapped hands as she poured his coffee. His eyes traveled upward to her red-rimmed, heavy-lidded eyes.

"You were up late last night. I heard you," he accused. "You were sewing."

Chiara turned away. "I wanted to finish some rompers for Roberto."

"Rompers aren't made of satin. You're working for others, aren't you?"

"I'm not doing much. Just a little alteration."

"How many times do I have to tell you to quit?"

Chiara was silent as she placed thick slices of toast before him.

"Do you hear me, woman? I want you to quit."

"We need the money, Mike."

He slammed his cup on the table, sloshing coffee over the rim. "I've told you before, I can take care of my family!"

"You should be glad I'm helping out, instead of—"

Mike threw his toast against the wall and it dropped in a scattering of crumbs. Jumping up, he raised his hand and struck Chiara, catching her across the ear.

Her face went white, her eyes widening in shock.

He snatched his hand away, as if he'd touched a hot stove, and stared at it, horrified. Oh, God, he'd never done that before, never hit his wife. If only he could take it back. But why did she provoke him? Couldn't she understand that her working made him feel less a man? He grabbed his coat and lunch and rushed out the door into a blast of frigid air.

He pressed a hand against his stomach, where fiery arrows of pain stabbed—the ulcer reacting to his argument with Chiara. It was no more than he deserved for his beastly behavior. He had no call to target all his frustrations on his wife.

This wasn't the first time he and Chiara had argued. Mike was aware of the many hours she worked, though to escape his ire, she tried to hide it. She was often up before him in the morning, sewing. What kind of man was he if he could barely support his family? It was useless to explain to Chiara how he felt; it would be admitting failure. Caught up in the frustration of his helplessness, he often lashed out, then regretted it. Chiara's mournful eyes would tear up, but she usually remained silent.

She would probably disobey him and continue working. Her defiance angered him, yet perversely he was grateful for it. They *did* need the money. His pay for three days' work each week barely covered the rent and utilities.

Mike turned up his collar as he swung off the trolley and trudged across the snow-packed pavement of the factory grounds. Head down against the cold January wind, he joined the swarm of men almost locked into step, lunch boxes clutched in their gloved hands. He thought of them as an army of ants, moving instinctively to their hill, doing their job, whatever it might be, with mindless dedication. But the army had thinned, and those remaining were shabby and fearful. And for good reason: their wages were cut to four dollars a day, and their days to three a week. But as Chiara kept reminding Mike, he should be grateful to be working at all. But for how much longer? he wondered. *My turn next, my turn next*, the small voice kept saying. *I can't be lucky forever.*

Where were all the politicians now? Why wasn't anyone doing anything about the joblessness. Flowery words were spoken: "Prosperity is just around the corner," "a car in every garage, a chicken in every pot." The songs were falsely optimistic: "Keep Your Sunny Side Up" and "The Sunny Side of the Street." On the silver screen the Marx Brothers and Laurel and Hardy clowned and cavorted in an attempt to divert the common folk from their wretchedness.

But the misery was evident. "Hoovervilles"—communities of flimsy, tacked-together structures made of scrap—

abounded at the city dump. "Hoover flags," empty pockets turned inside out, flapped in the breeze for all to see, and hungry people ate horsemeat "Hooverburgers."

Mike was more fortunate than many of his friends. Dino had been out of work for several months and moved in with relatives. Ed, too, was laid off. He had a hard time selling the Dodge. Who had money to buy? Finally he let it go for fifty dollars. The last time the men had played cards, Mike learned that the Judge lost money in the stock market. But as usual, he'd landed on his feet. In order to pay up what he owed from margin loans, he had taken a job rum-running from across the river in Windsor, Canada.

"I'll see if I can get you in on it, Mike," the Judge had said. "There's big money in rum-running."

"No, thanks. It's bad business," Mike said, shaking his head. "Aren't you afraid of getting caught?"

"Nah, the police look the other way. They like their booze as much as the next guy."

Mike preferred to close his eyes to such goings-on. The less he knew, the better.

At the sound of the lunch bell he sat beside O'Malley, a squat Irishman whose once laughing eyes were now darting and anxious. He had worked beside Mike for the past year and had always been good for a joke or two during their hurried fifteen-minute lunch.

"Every day I look for the pink slip," O'Malley said, tearing through the wax paper encasing his sandwich. "Why don't President Hoover do something for the workingman?"

"He's gutless; won't even look at a public-works program. He's all for the 'rugged individualist.' What a laugh, as if an ordinary workingman could establish a business when big businesses all around us are failing."

"Ya know, it makes you think of going commie or socialist."

Mike's eyes darted around suspiciously. "Keep it down, O'Malley. You never know who's listening." Others were saying the same thing. Walter Reuther had advsed Mike to vote for the Socialist candidate, Norman Thomas. Reuther was taking a chance just mentioning Thomas' name. "Henry Ford says, 'A vote for Hoover is a vote for Ford.' Don't you see the signs tacked all over the plant?"

"Ha," O'Malley snorted. "Anyone's better than Hoover. With any luck, Roosevelt will win." He wiped his mouth on his sleeve. "At least Mayor Murphy's trying to help. He opened up some empty factories for people with no place to go."

"Yeah, he has feeding stations too." Mike had seen the throngs of destitute men lined up at the Capuchin monastary on Mount Elliott, grateful for the meager meals distributed. He'd also seen hungry people gather behind the Book Cadillac Hotel, and watched them scramble for discarded scraps of food. He saw their wretched faces projecting hopelessness. He'd seen it all and had become increasingly frightened. Where would it all end?

Lunch over, they went back to their jobs. When the shrill whistle signaled the day's end, Mike walked out behind O'Malley. The Irishman reached for his time card and came away with a pink paper.

"Jesus Christ," he muttered. "Laid off!"

Mike watched O'Malley turn away, shoulders drooping, head bowed. His lunch box seemed to weigh him down. There were six children to feed in the O'Malley home, besides his wife and mother. How would he manage?

As they walked out together, Mike put his hand on O'Malley's shoulder and said, "Look, as long as I'm working, if you need a few bucks . . ."

O'Malley shrugged Mike's hand off and shot him a baleful look. "I don't need nothing from you. Why are you still here, Marcassa? I got more seniority than you. Why ain't you been laid off?"

"I don't know," Mike said, shrugging his shoulders. "You know seniority don't mean shit."

"Some wop higher up must like you," O'Malley said, spitting on the ground.

Mike flipped his fingers under his chin in the Italian gesture of disdain, but O'Malley had turned away and headed in the direction of Corey's Bar.

Each week that went by without the fearful layoff notice was a reprieve. But the phantom hung over Mike, causing a knot in his stomach, a throb in his head. It wasn't a question of *if;* it was a question of *when*. Last Friday, six more of his mates had been dismissed. He had held his breath, waiting for the ax to fall, but miraculously, he'd been spared. Why, he couldn't say. He was one of the least senior employees, but there was no such thing as seniority anyway. Men went or stayed at the whim of Harry Bennett, who had a reduction quota to fill and did it with no equivocation and no qualms.

The days peeled away, and Mike worked and worried. Toward the end of January, on a frigid, snowy day, he trudged to the time clock to punch out and found it—the dreaded pink slip; a ticket to despair.

He walked out into the biting crystal air clutching the slip. He had anticipated the fearful lay off for so long that now, in its reality, it was almost anticlimactic.

Chiara hummed as she set soup bowls on the table.

When Mike entered he tossed his lunch box on the splintery wooden drainboard.

"You won't have to bother fixing me lunch anymore. I'm laid off."

Chiara's heart plummeted. "Madonna! What are we going to do?" She gripped her hands together. She had been sure they would be spared. Stewart had promised her!

Robbie clung to Mike's pant leg, begging attention. "Papa, Papa."

Mike swung his son up in the air and hugged him tightly, burrowing his face in the child's shoulder.

Putting on her most determined face, Chiara said, "Well, we'll just make the best of it. You can look for another job." Her voice sounded tentative.

Mike gave her a sarcastic glance as he set Robbie on the floor. "Chiara, don't you know what the hell's going on? There are no jobs. This state is filled with men looking for jobs. Farmers come to the city; city men go to the farms, each looking for greener pastures. They're all disappointed."

She'd heard all that, but they must remain hopeful. She put her hand on his shoulder. "Don't worry. We'll manage."

Mike snorted and shook his head with pity at her optimism.

Chiara grasped the soup-pot handle with the edge of her apron. She ladled chicken soup with pastina into their bowls and sprinkled on a heavy coating of freshly grated Romano cheese. "I know, I know—it's bad. Penny's father hasn't worked in six months. Each day he stands for hours in a bread line."

Mike waved his fist at her. "You think I would stand in a bread line?" His eyes were wide, glinting with anger as he pounded the table and sent the sugar bowl dancing. "Don't ever mention bread line in this house. Never, never will this family be degraded in that way. I can take care of my family without charity. I have my pride."

Pride. He had too much of that. "You don't have to scream at me. I didn't mean you should join a bread line. I'm making a few dollars, Michele. We'll manage." She spoke softly. It wouldn't do to anger him.

He winced when she mentioned her earnings. Then the hard line of his jaw softened and he sighed. "Yes, we'll manage." He shook his finger at her. "But, goddammit, I'll never accept charity, do you understand?"

"Yes, yes, I understand. Just eat now. You'll feel better when you eat."

Chiara chewed her food slowly, tasting nothing. She knew her husband, understood his ways. Just the expectation of being jobless had kept him skittering on the edge of fear. That fear was the reason he had struck her that awful morning. She dreaded the future, having him idling at home, facing the day-to-day reality of his joblessness.

Chiara's worst fear was coming to pass, the fear that they would be left destitute. The memory of that hapless year of her childhood when her father's broken leg rendered him helpless intruded into her thoughts. Her mother had been forced to work the land while Chiara, eleven years old, took over her mother's chores and cared for the family. She had vowed she would never be in that predicament. Now it seemed history was repeating itself. Except that Chiara's work wasn't in the fields. All she had was her sewing, which didn't bring in much money and probably wouldn't last.

But sewing wasn't the immediate problem. Mike's misery was what concerned her now. And she could alleviate some of that misery. Always conscious of Mike's disapproval of her work, she had acknowledged only a small part of her earnings. The rest she tucked away into a

DiNobili cigar box and hid at the bottom of her sewing drawer under a pile of cloth remnants. She'd had vague hopes that the hard-won gains might be a down payment on a home of their own, or perhaps rental on a small dress shop, or even the fare back to Italy someday. Every few weeks she would count her little hoard and smile, despite the twinge of guilt at her deception. She enjoyed the heady feeling of having cash as a buffer against the hostile fates that could turn against one, as they were doing now.

It was time for a confession.

"Michele, stop worrying," she said, finishing the last of her soup. "I have something. Wait."

She hurried into the sewing room, then reappeared with the cigar box and placed it in front of her husband.

He stared at her with a quizzical expression. "What? You bought cigars, when we have . . ." His thumb flipped the cover and his mouth opened in surprise. He lifted the sheaf of bills neatly bound with a thin scrap of satin, and sifted the coins through his fingers: dimes, nickels, quarters, half-dollars.

Chiara stood beside him, beaming, hands on her hips. "Well? What do you think?"

"Where did you get this?"

"From my sewing."

"There must be over two hundred dollars here," he said, running his thumb down the edge of the stack. He looked at her suspiciously. "How did you manage it?"

She shrugged. "I saved it a little at a time, from the sewing."

He looked from the money to Chiara and back to the money, a narrow thread of a frown creasing his brow.

"Well, aren't you glad?" she asked, the smile fading on her lips.

He stared at the box and nodded soberly. "Yes, of course. Yes, I'm glad."

With elaborate care he stacked the cash back into the cigar box and arranged the coins in order. "Two hundred thirteen dollars and forty-five cents."

He closed the lid. "Put it away for now. Soon enough we will run out of my money; then we'll use yours."

"It's all 'ours,' Michele," Chiara said softly, "not mine and yours."

She bent down and kissed his unyielding lips.

Mike turned his collar up against the bone-numbing cold. It was a long walk downtown, but what did it matter? He had nothing better to do. He stepped briskly, in newly resoled shoes, over the hard-packed, soot-darkened snow, with no real destination in mind. He knew his quest for work was hopeless. Most of the small factories and stores were boarded up, but now and then he would find a place with signs of life. He turned into a small tool shop and spoke to the owner, a fat man with a large mustache.

The man laughed derisively. "Work, you say? Hell, I'm laying off two more men at the end of the week." He turned away. "Sorry, pal."

After the fourth turndown, Mike decided it was ludicrous to continue courting rejection. There were no jobs in this city; nor in any city.

He had joined the army of jobless, the newly impoverished, the helpless, hopeless people. He was luckier than most. Many of Chiara's sewing clients hadn't felt the tightening vise of unemployment, so there was money coming in from that source. Bile rose in his throat when he thought of it: Mike Marcassa's wife had to support them. If it wasn't for Chiara, they'd be destitute. He shook his head to escape the upsetting thought.

When Chiara had presented him with her nest egg, he felt both grateful and resentful. Why had she kept the money a secret? That had hurt him the most. She said she'd saved it for a house. That dream would never see reality, not as long as this blasted depression continued. Damm it! It was *his* job to provide for his family. He had let them down.

He released his breath in a long steamy puff and turned into a cafe with "Bar-B-Q Ribs" spelled in red neon on its grimy window. The radio played the happy tune "Keep Your Sunny Side Up." The cheerful words only served to plunge Mike further into depression.

After he ordered coffee at the linoleum-covered counter, he felt a hand on his shoulder. He turned to see a familiar face.

"O'Malley! How you been?"

The older man looked shrunken, grayer since leaving the Rouge with his pink layoff slip clutched in his hand.

"I'm okay. You finally got yours too, eh?"

"Yeah, a couple weeks ago. I'm looking for work."

"Ha, that's a laugh."

Mike detected the sour odor of liquor on O'Malley's breath. That's what it comes to, he thought—obliterating your troubles with a bottle. It was O'Malley's way of coping. Some of the jobless resorted to stealing; still others turned to crooked activities like rum-running or numbers; most went on relief. The specter of hunger arose with them in the morning and went to bed with them at night. Survival—that was what it amounted to. Anything was preferable to starvation.

O'Malley said to the waiter, "Coffee, black and strong." When the coffee came, he lifted the thick white mug with shaking fingers, sloshing the dark liquid over the sides.

"How're you managing?" Mike asked.

"Welfare, what else? The wife sews buttons on cards, one of the kids sells papers. And me, I drink." He looked for a moment as if he would cry.

Mike patted his shoulder.

"Last month I packed us all up and went north to Alma, where my sister has a farm. Big old house with lots of room. We found the family living in the barn because the house was repossessed. They wasn't even certain how long they'd be allowed to use the barn." He shook his shaggy head back and forth, back and forth, then brightened. "Let's finish up and go to Grand Circus Park. Some guy is talking there. They say he's damn smart. Name's Foster. I wanna hear what he's got to say."

"Why not." Mike drained the cup and set it down with a bang. "It'll help kill the day."

Foster's talk stirred Mike, revived his basic beliefs in society's responsibility to its poor. Mike convinced Eduardo to join him a few nights later to hear Foster speak again.

They pushed their way through the double doors to Danceland on West Grand Boulevard. Tonight the usual frivolity was missing from the huge hall. There were no swinging strains of sweet jazz, no couples whirling and bouncing on the waxy dance floor, no gaiety in the air with men ogling and women flirting. Now the hall was filled with scores of grim-faced people, desperation written on their faces.

"Christ, there must be over six thousand people here," Ed said with a whistle. "I don't even know why we came."

Mike unwound the woolen scarf from his neck. "I'm telling you, Ed, I saw this guy at a rally at Grand Circus Park, and he knows what he's talking about."

"Yeah, William Z. Foster. I read about him." Ed took his jacket off and held it in the crook of one arm. "He's a communist."

"I know that. I don't give a damn about his politics. He's from the Unemployment Council, the group I joined. They're interested in getting food and jobs. Isn't that what we all want?"

"Hell, yes, I want a job. You know what I get on the dole? Thirty cents a day. You think we can live on that?"

"I told you, Ed, you can come and stay with us. We have room. And I still have a little money left. . ."

Ed looked away. "No. No handouts."

"This isn't charity," Mike said. "We stayed with you when we came from the old country. I owe you. We help each other."

Ed jerked his chin forward. "Look, he's coming on stage."

Foster strode to center stage to the accompaniment of cheers and wild applause.

With arms held outward, as if he were parting the Red Sea, Foster waited until the audience calmed. Then in a resonant voice he exhorted them to join together in a united front.

"The people of Detroit are living in hard times, under deplorable conditions of need and hunger," he cried out. "It's time we made ourselves heard! Time we did something to alleviate the poverty and unemployment in the city!"

Again and again the audience yelled and cheered at Foster's words.

"Tommorow the Unemployment Council and the Auto Workers' Union will march together," he shouted. "The people of Detroit refuse to take this lying down. We're marching to the mighty Rouge in Dearborn!"

The audience cheered in agreement, stomping their feet and clapping their hands.

Foster continued, "When we get to the gate, a small committee will present the set of demands to Henry Ford. He'll have to listen."

Among the demands were jobs for laid-off Ford workers, a seven-hour day without reduction in pay, the slowing-down of the deadly speed-up, the abolition of factory spies, and the right to organize.

Again the crowd thundered their approval. They seemed transformed, energized by the prospect of action. Anything was better than waiting futilely for an upturn in the economy. Glancing around, Mike noticed that the spectators were losing their glazed, downtrodden look for one of animation and hope. Someone wanted to help! Someone had a plan! Mike, too, was caught up in the excitement, regenerated by the contagious spirit of enthusiasm around him.

When the speech ended, Mike and Ed jostled their way out into the bitter March wind to the streetcar stop. The talk around them was optimistic.

"Hell, yes, I'm going; why not?"

"Count me in."

"I wouldn't miss it."

White puffs of steam accompanied the heartfelt words and Mike punched Ed's arm. "Let's do it, Ed. Let's join the hunger march. Whatta ya say?"

"I don't know. . . ."

"You don't know what? We got nothing to lose. It beats sitting home all day." Mike pulled his frayed overcoat collar up against his ears. "Ed, Foster said all the things I believe in. And there's power in numbers. We can make a difference."

Ed stuffed his hands into his pockets and lowered his head against the wind. "Look, Ford ain't going to listen. What does he care about us? He sits there in Fairlane with all his servants and money . . . he don't give a shit about us."

The streetcar ground to a halt and they surged forward, cocooned in the crowd. The doors slid closed behind Mike and Ed. They were propped up by the press of bodies around them.

"You saw what happened to the Hunger March on Washington, didn't you?" Ed snorted. "That was peaceful too. Machine guns is what they got."

"This is different. You heard Foster. They're getting a permit."

Ed looked reflective. "Do you really think it's safe?"

"Why not? We'll just be a crowd of citizens, without weapons, trying to make ourselves heard. Like I said, we've got nothing to lose."

"I don't know, Mike." Ed still looked doubtful. "What if they have police there?"

"So what? It's a peaceful, legal demonstration. I'm going. Are you with me?"

Ed shrugged. "What the hell. Like you say, we got nothing better to do."

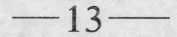

13

The next morning, when Chiara refilled Mike's coffee cup he noticed her appealing morning-mussed hair and musky smell and wished he had more time. His urges weren't urgent any longer, and he rarely felt moved to make love to his wife.

The chenille of her housecoat was worn away at the elbows. If he had a little money he'd buy her a new one. Money. It was always on his mind.

He downed his hot coffee and bundled up against the near-zero weather.

"I don't like this, Mike," Chiara said, handing him his cap. "I think you'll only make Mr. Henry Ford mad."

He sighed. It was a continuation of her complaint of the night before. They'd argued a long time. As usual, she was against anything that seemed to oppose authority.

"I told you, nothing's going to happen." He took the cap and donned it at a jaunty angle. "It's just a friendly march. No one's carrying weapons."

Her mouth was grim. "Whenever there's a gang of

people together, there's trouble. Why do you have to be in the middle of it?"

"Can't you understand? This is something I believe in. There won't be trouble."

Chiara gave him a reproachful look, then took his face in her two hands and kissed him on the lips. "You be careful, Mike."

"I'll be careful. You worry too much." He opened the door.

"I know, I know, I worry. It's because I love you."

He turned back and touched her cheek. "I love you too." Then he hurried out, his head high, his shoulders back, a man with a mission.

When Mike hopped on the streetcar he was surprised at the jam of noisy, good-natured people, all heading for the meeting place at Fort Street and Oakwood. Despite their ragged appearance and their sorry plight, they laughed and joked. When they reached their destination, some of the men refused to pay their fare, shouting, "Charge it to Ford!"

The conductor tried unsuccessfully to keep them from alighting. Policemen, stationed outside, tried to intervene as the men rushed out through the doors, but the waiting marchers sprang forward, protecting their comrades. Mike suspected many of the lawmen were sympathetic to their cause, but were duty-bound to carry out their orders.

At the Fort Street meeting place people were converging from every direction. Mike knew there were workers from the nearby "Ford towns"—Dearborn, Lincoln Park, Melvindale, Ecorse. He nodded to a band of serious, fresh-faced young men.

"We're from Detroit City College," one red-cheeked boy said. "My dad is sick, so I came."

The icy air blowing in from the river seemed warmed by the marchers' high spirits. Most of them, Mike noted, were men, some in overalls and caps, some in suits and felt hats. However, a few women, bundled up against the cold, mixed into the crowd. The wind caught and snapped a variety of banners that declared "Give Us Work," "We Want Bread, Not Crumbs," "Tax the Rich and Feed the Poor."

Scanning the mob, Mike spotted Ed and shouted his name. He elbowed and sidestepped in Ed's direction, exchanging back-slapping greetings with acquaintances along the way, O'Malley among them. It was as if they all belonged to a fraternity, the brotherhood of the unemployed, inexorably linked in their misery.

Al Goetz, one of the leaders, ordered quiet and read the list of their demands.

"Are you with us?" Goetz shouted.

"Yes, yes," the people shouted back.

"Then let's go! But I'm warning you, the Dearborn police might try to stop us. Remember," he cautioned, "no rough stuff. We don't want any trouble."

A tremendous cheer went up and, eight abreast, the marchers proceeded toward the Dearborn city limits.

As Mayor Murphy had promised, Detroit police were on hand to escort the marchers to the Dearborn city line, and they did so with friendly good spirits, kibitzing with some of the men. The crowd moved forward under a dark sky and bitter wind, with banners waving, as if they were going to a picnic. Snatches of song and laughter arose here and there among the group. Someone began singing the "Soup Song," to the tune of "My Bonnie Lies Over the Ocean." Mike joined his baritone with the rest.

I'm spending my nights at the flophouse
I'm spending my days on the street
I'm looking for work and I find none
I wish I had something to eat.
Sooo-oup, sooo-oup, they give me a bowl of sooo-oup
Sooo-oup, sooo-oup, they give me a bowl of soup.
I spent twenty years in the factory
I did everything I was told
They said I was loyal and faithful
Now, even before I get old.
Sooo-oup, sooo-oup, they give me a bowl of sooo-oup
Sooo-oup, sooo-oup, they give me a bowl of soup.
I saved fifteen bucks with my banker
To buy me a car and a yacht
I went down to draw out my fortune
and this is the answer I got.
Sooo-oup, sooo-oup, they give me a bowl of sooo-oup
Sooo-oup, sooo-oup, they give me a bowl of soup.

The song went on for interminable verses; then they

swung into "Solidarity Forever," and Mike felt a rising sense of purpose, of pride. In the distance he saw the giant silver smokestacks of the Rouge plant rising up into the cloudy, granite sky. Henry Ford would *have* to respond to a crowd of this size.

As they crossed out of Detroit to the Dearborn boundary, a contingent of stony-faced Dearborn and Ford Company police met them. Weapons were raised, at the ready across their chests. They looked grim, like they meant business, Mike thought, a prickle of fear rising up the back of his neck.

"Turn back," the leader shouted.

"Christ, they've got guns," Ed said. "I don't like this, Mike. There's going to be trouble."

"I don't like it either, but hell, what are they going to do, shoot us? We're unarmed."

"You know this won't do no good anyway," Ed said with a nervous laugh. "It'll just make old Henry mad."

"That's what Chiara said." Mike wondered if he shouldn't have given Chiara's warning more consideration. "But we've come this far; we have to keep on. If nothing else, it'll get some attention."

The men plodded resolutely onward toward the police barrier. "You're not stopping us," they shouted. "We're moving on. Get out of our way!"

"Who are your leaders?" an officer yelled.

"We're all leaders," the marchers shouted back.

Without warning, the police fired off tear-gas canisters. The sudden sting brought tears to Mike's eyes. Some of the men in the front lines fell back, choking and blinded by the gas. Others grabbed whatever they could get their hands on, frozen mud or sticks, and hurled them toward the police. Many tried to escape by running up a railroad trestle on the side of the road. Luckily, the wind dissipated the gas before it did much damage. The police advanced, their nightsticks drawn, but the marchers, with even greater resolve, pressed on.

Ed sputtered angrily, "Jesus Christ. This is supposed to be a peaceful march. What in hell are they doing?"

There were shouts of "Get 'em" and "The sons of bitches'll never stop us now." They scattered into small groups, all running in different directions toward Dix Road and Gate Three, with the police in hot pursuit.

Mike darted into a vacant field with Ed close behind, and others followed. Ed halted his run long enough to pick up a rock.

"Here, Mike, take this," Ed said, reaching down again and grabbing a rotting fencepost. His eyes glinted with anger.

The men ran forward, fired with bitterness and resentment. At the overpass, within sight of the plant, they were stopped by two fire engines. Ed urged the pack on, yelling, "Come on, don't let 'em scare us."

Mike had never seen Ed like this before—rock-jawed, with fire in his eyes. He looked impassioned, bent on vendetta. Mike's own blood was racing; from exertion, from excitement, from fear.

All at once the fire hoses let go with a frigid spray. Those caught in the surprise shower yelled and gasped. Fortunately, most of it skirted the pack, landing below the overpass, but the side of Mike's face was frosted. He brushed away the water and pushed forward, enraged now, a fury of epithets streaming from his lips. He was separated from Ed and spotted him up ahead next to Joe York, one of the leaders. With a burst of speed, York finally made it to the plant entrance, where Harry Bennett was just emerging from a car.

Planting his feet firmly, hands on his hips, Bennett began arguing with York. Suddenly a piece of slag hit the side of Bennett's head. Blood spurted from the wound. Bennett threw a punch and York scuffled with him. Moments later shots rent the air. Joe York fell to the ground, instantly still. Mike stood frozen, watching in horror as the dramatic scene unfolded. Gunshots thundered in his ears. Men, writhing in pain, dropped to the cold wet pavement. Others, gasping in disbelief and terror, turned and bolted in the opposite direction while bullets continued exploding behind them. In the confusion, Mike lost sight of Ed. He'd been in the forefront, close behind York. Where was he now? Mike pressed forward frantically, fighting against the retreating pack, in search of his friend.

Mike forced his way through the mob. "Let me through," he yelled. Around him people were falling to the ground. Through an opening in the crowd he saw Ed, running toward him.

"Thank God," he groaned with relief. A barrage of shots cracked and Ed's mouth and eyes opened wide with a look of shock. The look changed to terror as he pitched forward and lay still.

"Ed!" Mike screamed. "Ed!"

With shots blasting all around him, Mike raced to Ed's side. He dropped to his knees and saw, with growing horror, a scarlet stain spread rapidly through the back of Ed's jacket, making a brilliant circle around a blackened hole. Ed moaned in agony. Mike whipped off his scarf and stuffed it underneath Ed's jacket, covering the wound. He pressed down to stanch the flow of blood and looked around wildly for help.

The shots, mercifully, were abating. Policemen dashed about, handcuffing whomever they could grab. Mike turned Ed over on his back and, hands hooked under his arms, began dragging him out of the way.

O'Malley appeared suddenly at his side, saying, "Jesus Christ, he's hurt bad." He took Ed's ankles and together they hauled him to a side street. O'Malley dropped Ed's feet and waved frantically to a slow-moving car. It halted and the driver jumped out, while the passenger called after him, "What the hell are you doing, Austin?"

"This man is hurt," the driver shouted over his shoulder.

"You okay, buddy?" Mike asked, chafing Ed's hand.

Ed groaned pitifully, his eyes rolling back in his head, his face a gray shroud.

The driver leaned down quickly and placed his fingers at the side of Ed's throat. "There's a pulse. Is he conscious?"

"Just barely," Mike said. "He's lost a lot of blood. The bastards shot him."

"Come on, let's get him to the hospital." The well-dressed stranger motioned them toward the car.

Mike and O'Malley pulled and tugged Ed into the back of the Lincoln while the driver jumped into his seat and revved the motor.

The passenger hissed, "Are you crazy, Austin? Whose side are you on, anyway?"

"Shut up or get out of the car. I'm not leaving a man to die like a dog on the street." He jolted the car to action and sped around a corner on two wheels.

"Okay, okay, take it easy," the passenger said.

As the Lincoln whirled in and out of traffic at high speed, the sound of ambulance and police sirens mingled in an eerie shriek through the chill air.

"What's your name, friend?" the driver called behind him.

"Marcassa," Mike said, then jerked his thumb toward his friend. "He's O'Malley."

Engrossed in trying to revive Ed, Mike didn't see the driver's eyes dart to the mirror.

"This is my pal Ed. The bastards shot him." Mike groaned as if in pain. "I don't know if he's going to make it."

"My God, who's responsible for this carnage?" Stewart Austin muttered half to himself as he manuevered through the busy streets and finally skidded to a stop at Receiving Hospital on St. Antoine and Macomb streets. O'Malley dashed inside and returned with two white-coated men and a stretcher. Ed was placed on the stretcher and quickly transported inside.

The hospital was alive with images in white: white-garbed nurses streaking along the halls, white-smocked doctors darting in and out of emergency rooms, stark white lights assaulting Mike's eyes.

"Flora. His wife," Mike said. "Someone should tell her, but I don't want to leave, in case . . . in case . . ."

"I'll go get her," O'Malley said. "You stay here."

"Can you stop at my house and tell my wife? She'll be crazy with worry."

O'Malley gripped and released Mike's shoulder. "Yeah, pal."

After O'Malley left, with no place to sit in the gloomy, packed waiting room, Mike paced the floor. The antiseptic smell bit into his consciousness as he smoked one cigarette after another. On the wall the round clock ticked loudly, but the hands moved hardly at all.

It seemed like hours later when Flora burst into the room, her face stricken and tear stained.

"Mike! Where is he? How is he?"

Holding her, Mike tried to reassure her. "The doctor just came through and talked to me. They had to operate and they think he'll pull through. Stop crying now." Roughly he patted her shoulder.

"I want to see him."

On the third floor Mike talked to a nurse with gray wisps of hair escaping her wide-winged cap.

"His condition is serious. He hasn't quite come out of the ether," she said softly, ushering them down a hall.

At the door to his room she admonished them, "You can stay only a moment."

Tears streamed from Flora's eyes at the sight of her husband. She held her fisted hand to her mouth to stifle any sound. Ed's face was ashen and still, his upper body sheathed in snowy bandages. When Flora leaned down to hug him, his eyes fluttered open and he smiled weakly. Though his mouth moved, no sound came. Flora murmured tearful words of love and encouragement, but there was no other response.

"He'll be all right," the nurse said, gently pulling Flora to her feet. "He needs to sleep."

The nurse led them out into the hall, where Mike noticed a policeman leaning against the wall, speaking in low tones to a weary-eyed doctor. The policeman, wearing his hat pushed back on his shiny, hairless head, punctuated his words with a thumb pointed toward Ed's room while the doctor stared at the floor and nodded.

When Michele finally reached the sanctuary of his home, Chiara's shadowy form was outlined against the half-drawn shade in the front window. The door opened and he almost collapsed against her, suddenly weak-kneed and drained of energy. Chiara stroked and patted his back, and murmured comforting phrases in Italian. In bed, the entire story rushed from his lips in a torrent of misery and anger. When he finished, Chiara drew him against her breast and he cried silent, anguished tears, until finally, like an infant in the comfort of his mother's arms, he slept.

The next day, a starched nurse firmly escorted Mike out of Ed's room. "He's still critical. He may be like this for several more days."

It was his fault that Ed was here; he had persuaded him to go on the march. *Goddammit, Ed, you've got to get well, you've got to!* Mike hadn't been the sort to pray. But now he murmured desperate pleas to the God of his childhood.

During the next two days Ed fluttered in and out of

consciousness. Mike haunted the hospital corridors, slipping into Ed's room whenever he could manage it.

When Mike and Flora returned on the morning of the third day, Ed was stirring about under the covers. He smiled at Flora and held out his hand. Flora rushed to his side and showered him with grateful teary kisses. With sudden weariness Mike heaved a great sigh. Ed had survived. He would make it.

That evening when they pushed into the room, Flora drew in her breath with horror. Ed's eyes were sunken and glazed. One of his hands was shackled to the bed.

"*Madre di Dio!* What have they done to you?" Flora burst out.

"What the hell's going on here?" Mike said.

Ed focused slowly on Mike, then waved his free hand upward and managed a weak smile. "They think I'm one of the communist organizers."

Flora's hands flew to her heart. "*Dio mio.* What's going to happen?" She bent to clutch at Ed's hands.

"Jesus Christ. I can't believe this," Mike said. "When did this happen?"

"This morning." Ed eased his head up to explain. "This cop comes in and asks me all kinds of questions . . ." Out of breath, he dropped his head back to the pillow, then rasped, "Mike, I'm scared. I got a record on account of the wine, remember?"

"You don't have a record. *I* got the fine."

"They took my name."

Mike clenched his fist and pounded the wall. "They're not getting away with this."

"But, Mike, what can we do?" Flora implored.

"Don't worry, Flora, I'll take care of things." Mike turned on his heel and headed for the door.

Flora grabbed his arm. "Where are you going?"

"Never mind where I'm going. I'll handle this."

He stomped out to the reception area and made a hurried phone call.

After Mike saw Flora safely on a streetcar, he went back and waited in front of the hospital. He leaned against the brick building, pulling his cap low on his head, huddling into his coat. Restless, he paced, puffing on a cigarette, while he scanned the visitors who came and went. Where the hell was Fredo? He'd said he'd be right here. Mike had lent Fredo some money when he was down and out; now Fredo owed him, and it was time to call in the debt. Because Fredo supplied police officials with bootlegged whiskey from Windsor, he had some influence.

Finally a familiar bulky figure strode up to Mike, and the two men embraced. In silence they went up the steps and to the third floor.

"The copper is meeting us here," Fredo said.

In a few minutes a burly policeman in dark blue uniform and dark beaked hat lumbered up to them and shook Fredo's hand.

"Hello, Hagarty," Fredo said.

Hagarty pushed his hat back on his head. "Where's he at?" he asked from the side of his mouth.

"Room 309," Mike said.

Hagarty glared at Mike. "Who's this guy?"

"A friend," Fredo snapped. "It's okay. Come on, let's get going."

Hagarty strode to the desk and talked to the nurse in charge. She shrugged and pointed to Ed's room.

As the men entered the room, Ed's eyes widened with fear. A weak moan gurgled from his mouth.

"It's okay, Ed, take it easy," Mike said. "We're getting you out of these cuffs."

Fredo went to the bed and greeted his friend with sympathetic words, then motioned for Hagarty to come forward. Hagarty removed a key from his pocket and fitted it into the slot of the handcuffs.

When the bands slid away, Ed rubbed his reddened wrist and his eyes darted from Mike to Fredo to Hagarty.

Mike patted his shoulder. "You're going to be fine, Ed, just fine," he said. But the wild spark of fear didn't leave Ed's eyes.

—— 14 ——

A dull drizzle fell, but Mike hardly noticed it. At Ferry Street he joined the funeral procession for the four men killed in the march. The crowd moved slowly, solemnly, a sea of red berets and banners bobbing to a muffled drumbeat. Fifteen thousand strong, they trooped down the rain-slicked streets, following the red-draped caskets headed for Grand Circus Park. Stifled sobs could be heard, and, occasionally, piercing through the air, a woman's wailing. Someone started singing. Soon the strains of the *"Internationale"* reverberated through the city. Strong men wept unashamedly. It was a day of ignominy for the city of Detroit.

At Woodmere Cemetery the band played the funeral march of the 1905 Russian revolutionaries. The dead were laid to rest in graves just inside the border of Woodmere, within sight of the looming bulk of the Rouge. Mike doffed his cap and watched the dark clouds rolling from the Rouge smokestacks. They drifted over the graves of those four who rested, before their time, in martyrdom. Mike had known one of the men—a countryman, Joe DeBlasio, dead because he believed in righting wrongs. This was where his fierce passion had landed him—in an unmarked grave. March 12, 1932. Mike would not soon forget this day.

A few days later, when Mike pushed into the hospital room, Ed started, his eyes wide with alarm. Though he seemed to be gaining strength, he was jumpy, nervous.

"Relax, Ed, it's just me. How are you doing?"

Ed slumped back on the pillow. "I guess I'm healing okay." He beckoned Mike closer and said in a whisper, "The nurses are spying on me."

Mike pressed Ed's shoulder. "Take it easy, buddy, nobody's spying."

Ed raised himself on one elbow. "You don't know what's going on. They think I'm a communist."

"You're safe, Ed. Don't worry."

Ed grabbed Mike's lapels, his eyes flitting to the door. "Mike, you gotta get me outta here. They're going to arrest me again."

Mike loosened Ed's hands and gently pushed him back on the bed, a knot of concern tightening in his gut. Ed wasn't himself. "No one's going to arrest you. Fredo fixed that."

"I'm scared, Mike." Ed looked as if he might cry.

"Look, Ed, we'll get you out just as soon as the doctor says it's all right. Meanwhile, you're safe."

Ed lay back, breathing heavily, his eyes closed.

Mike went to the window. "Look, it's a great day. No clouds, the sun is out, the trees are greening up."

Without warning, Ed sprang out of bed and staggered to the small closet near the door. "If you're not going to help me, I'll get out by myself," he said, wild-eyed. Panting, he slumped against the closet door.

Mike rushed to his friend. "Ed, for God's sake, get back to bed. You're in no condition to go anywhere." With his arm around Ed's waist, Mike led him back to bed. Ed's skin through the cotton gown felt damp, and perspiration beaded on his forehead.

"Mike, get me outta here," Ed pleaded. "I'm leaving with or without you. This place ain't safe. There're spies everywhere. I'm getting dressed and walking out."

Mike was frightened by his friend's irrational panic. "You don't have any clothes here, Ed. They were all bloody, remember? Anyway, you're too sick to leave."

"I don't care what you say," Ed said doggedly. "I'm going home. Tell Flora to bring my clothes. I'll go in this damn thing if I have to. When you come tomorrow, I'll be gone. Tell Flora I'm coming home."

In his hysterical state, Ed was likely to do just that. Mike ran his fingers through his hair. "Okay, pal, I'll talk to the nurse. If she says it's okay, I'll get you home tomorrow."

Mike left and found the sympathetic gray-haired nurse with whom he'd spoken several times.

"When can we take Ed home?"

"Your friend's been delirious and seems agitated. The fever does that sometimes. But I'm afraid it will be at least another week before the doctor will release him."

"Don't you think he'd be better at home, with his wife to nurse him?"

"No, he still needs special care and medication."

"I'm worried about him. He's acting strange because he's afraid the police will come in and arrest him."

The nurse's mouth quirked. "Who knows? Anything's likely."

When Mike returned to Ed's room, Flora was there. She took Mike aside and said, "He's acting crazy, Mike. Every day he tells me he wants to go home. You know how stubborn he is."

Mike hugged Flora's shoulder. "I know, Flora. Do you think you could care for him at home?"

"I . . . I don't know. What if he gets worse?"

"I'm afraid he's going to leave whether we like it or not."

Flora looked perplexed, then nodded with determination. "We'll bring him home. Tomorrow."

The next day, over the doctor's objections, Ed signed himself out and Fredo once again came to the rescue with his car.

Back in his own home and bed, Ed looked paler than ever. When Mike left, Flora was fluttering about Ed, plumping pillows, heating soup, and chattering about inconsequential matters.

Chiara wrapped a loaf of freshly baked bread in a Silvercup wrapper and jabbed a hatpin through her brimmed felt hat. She was anxious to get to Flora's.

"Christ, why did I have to talk him into that damned march?"

Mike was more concerned than he admitted, Chiara thought, noticing his nervous, distracted movements.

She squeezed his arm. "You didn't know how it would end."

Flora greeted them with red-rimmed eyes. "Thank God you've come."

"What's wrong?" Chiara asked.

Flora put her hands to her head and rocked it. "He's

worse. I think he's lost his mind completely." She beckoned them inside with the edge of her apron. "Come in."

Chiara tiptoed into the bedroom with Mike following
behind, and touched her hand to Ed's forehead. Even in
sleep he tossed restlessly, wearing an uneasy, worried
frown. "He's very hot, Mike. I don't like the way he
looks."

In the kitchen, Flora poured coffee and set a sugar
bowl on the table. "I left him for a little while to go to
the store. He was sleeping soundly, so I thought he
would be all right. I wanted to get a little fresh air, and
really, to get away from him. He calls me all the time; I
don't have time to breathe." She emphasized her frustration by waving her extended hands. "When I got back,
the door was open and his bed was empty. I was so
scared. I ran out looking for him, up and down the
streets. Finally I saw him on Gratiot, walking slow and
talking, talking as if he had a friend with him."

She stopped and blew on her coffee, then took a sip.
"I went to him and tried to get him to turn around and
come home, but he wouldn't listen, just kept on talking
foolishness. I had to almost drag him back. He was
delirious, talking crazy, his eyes like a madmans'."

Ed's scream rang through the flat, bringing the three of
them to their feet.

"I'm here, Eduardo, I'm coming," Flora called, running into the bedroom.

Ed sat bolt upright, staring at the crucifix on the opposite wall, mumbling unintelligible words, his arms raised
to the ceiling.

"Hey, pal, it's okay." Mike settled Ed down, covering
him with a sheet. Checking his forehead with the back of
her hand, Chiara shook her head.

"He's burning up with fever, Flora. You must get the
doctor."

Flora wrung her hands. "I don't have money."

"I'll take care of the money," Mike said grimly. "I'm
going to the corner to call Dr. Catrone."

Chiara brought an enamel basin of cool water from the
kitchen and sent Flora for a washcloth. When Chiara
drew near, Ed shrank back fearfully. Though the women
tried to calm him, Ed continued to mumble incoherently.

Finally he let Flora sponge him down and soon fell into an uneasy sleep.

It was almost ten o'clock when the doctor arrived. He apologized for the lateness of the hour and listened to Flora's short explanation, nodding his white head and stroking his chin. He looked weary and a bit rumpled, unlike his usual fastidious self. His clothing looked loose on his bulky body and there was a pink sheen to his skin, as though he had just scrubbed. A vague medicine smell enveloped him.

"There was an emergency at the hospital," he explained as he quickly strode into the bedroom. He examined Ed, probing with sensitive fingers, while Flora wrung her hands at the foot of the bed. Chiara and Mike left the room and waited nervously in the kitchen.

Afterward the doctor stood by the kitchen table, sipping the requisite cup of coffee.

His heavy-lidded eyes were keen and sympathetic at the same time. "Your husband must go to the hospital. His wound isn't healing properly, and with the fever . . ." He shrugged to indicate his helplessness. "Besides, I can see how agitated and upset he is. He needs constant watching."

"He'll never go back to the hospital. He's afraid he'll be arrested," Flora said woodenly, dropping her head into her hands.

"He isn't safe here, my dear. There is no choice."

Flora's voice was constrained. "I don't know what to do."

Mike said, "Flora, his life is in danger. We must get help. I'll come in the morning with Fredo's car, and we'll get him to the hospital."

The next morning, when Mike approached Flora's door, he heard her voice rising and falling in an eerie keening. It was a sound he'd heard before, a sound that seared itself into his brain. He forced himself to open the door and step inside. Flora sat next to the bed in a chair, huddled into herself. At the sound of Mike's footsteps she became silent. She didn't rise, or greet him, but tipped her head toward the still white figure on the bed. Mike caught his breath and proceeded slowly toward his friend. He touched Ed's hand and drew away quickly. The flesh was cold.

* * *

At the front door of Flora's flat a bouquet of lilies tied with a black ribbon proclaimed the message of death. The casket, half-filling the small front room, was banked with flowers and held the waxen figure of the man who had been Eduardo. A mordant odor, only partially masked by the scent of fresh flowers, pervaded the flat.

With each new arrival Flora retold the story of Eduardo's demise, punctuating her tale with sobs and moans.

"He was a good man," she lamented, "a saint." And the sympathetic mourners joined her cry. When one tearful mourner ended her woeful wail, another one began. The unceasing dirge ebbed and flowed through the night.

Women in black hung over the casket, fingering their beads, mumbling their Aves in a muffled buzz, sorrowing bees in a joyless bower.

"*Povera Flora,* poor Flora, what will she do now, with neither children nor parents to comfort her?" a woman asked Chiara as she walked into the room.

Chiara patted her hand. "She needs her friends now. There's coffee and cake in the kitchen."

She stood beside Mike. He had been greeting visitors, commiserating with friends and relatives, telling the how and why of the tragedy, cursing the police, Henry Ford, Harry Bennett, and the all-powerful fates that converged in one time and place to bring about the deplorable disaster.

Men with black silk bands on their arms gathered outside, drinking wine, smoking cigarettes as they recalled stories of a happier time, some remembering boyhood pranks with Eduardo.

Mike looked tired, Chiara thought. He had made the funeral arrangements, had talked to the priest, had consoled Flora. He was a rock, strong and supportive.

The next day, after the interminable and solemn Requiem Mass, they proceeded to Mount Olivet Cemetery. When the priest finished the blessing, Flora threw herself across the coffin with a shrill cry that echoed through the graveyard. Mike dragged her from the coffin, restraining her, while Chiara held her arm tightly and tried to console her.

When it was over, Mike and Chiara propped Flora

between them as she stumbled in her teary blindness
back to the car.

Chiara wet her finger on her tongue and tested the
iron. The hiss told her it was hot enough. There was
comfort in the steady swish-swish of the iron, in the
warm damp smell that rose in puffs of steam. The May
freshness crept into the open kitchen windows, suffusing
the room with light and energy.

When Flora came in, the two women hugged, and
Flora moaned, as she always did, about her wretchedness.

Chiara brewed fresh coffee and comforted her friend.
"Time heals, Flora. And you must pray. *He* never gives
us more trouble than we can bear."

"So they say." Flora sniffed. "I think about my Eduardo
all the time. How changed he was at the end. I try to
remember him in happier times."

"You need something to do, some work."

"I spend my days in weeping and cursing the fates. I
cook and bake, wash and iron, just as though I had my
man."

Repetition of the mundane tasks defined Flora's existence, Chiara thought. But there was no one to appreciate her efforts. "You could help me with some sewing."
Chiara unrolled a damp pillowcase and pressed the iron
over its surface with an accompanying hiss. "I have a big
job to do, a wedding."

"I just can't think about doing any sewing now." Flora
slumped back into the chair. "I could never have managed without your husband, Chiara. Mike's been my
crutch. He's a good man, a wonderful man."

"Yes, I know that. But, Flora, Mike's changed. He
seemed to gather enough strength to see you through
this, but the very next day after the funeral, he changed.
Some days he just follows me around the house like a
puppy. I have to push him out of bed in the morning. I
tell him to get dressed, to eat, to go outside. He says
nothing. I used to hate it when he would get mad listening to Father Coughlin on the radio, and argue and holler
back at him. Now I would give my heart to hear him yell,
to show some life."

The heat from the iron caused a damp strand of golden-
brown hair to drop down her forehead, and she paused

to push it back and anchor it behind a bobby pin. Lifting the heavy iron with an effort, she went on, "He goes from the bedroom to the kitchen to the radio. He listens to the radio for a while, then goes back to the bedroom. I don't know how to help him, what to do. He blames himself for what happened to Ed."

Flora took two ends of a freshly ironed muslin sheet and helped Chiara fold it with a smart snap to align it properly. "It wasn't Mike's fault. Ed wasn't one to be led so easily. He did what he wanted to do."

"I wish I could convince Mike of that. If only he could find some work, something to take his mind off this."

"Yes, work is the answer. Can't your friend Mr. Austin help him get back to work?"

"I suggested going to him, but Mike won't hear of it. He says Mr. Austin is the enemy, one of 'them.' "

"Foolish pride. Go anyway. Mike doesn't have to know."

Chiara folded a freshly ironed cotton petticoat and set the iron on the stove. "He stays awake late into the night, drinking wine, more than is good for him. When he finally comes to bed, he doesn't even touch me." She raised her eyebrows and gave a resigned shrug, to punctuate her meaning.

"Maybe he should see Dr. Catrone."

"I suggested that. He only gets angry. I don't know the answer, Flora." She sat heavily onto a chair and dropped her head in her hands.

Flora hugged her friend, and they both cried softly in their misery.

"We all have our crosses to bear. At least you have your man," Flora said.

Strengthened by her friend's support, Chiara squared her shoulders. "I'll be all right, Flora. You're the one with problems. Come, let me heat up your coffee."

She knew what she had to do.

─── 15 ───

The dank outside air filtered into Dr. Catrone's office through a half-open window, accentuating the heaviness Chiara felt. The tiny, stuffy office was a study in gray— dull gray file cabinets, gray oversize chair on a gray rug, faded prints on the wall next to the diplomas—all gray, like the weather, like Chiara's own heart.

The doctor finally shuffled into the room looking harried, his stethoscope dangling from his pocket. He sat heavily in the swivel chair behind his massive cluttered oak desk, took off his glasses, and rubbed his eyes.

"And what's the problem, *signora?*" He cleaned his glasses on the edge of his white coat.

Chiara twisted a handerchief between her fingers and turned wide pleading eyes to him.

"You're not pregnant again, are you, Chiara?" This time his voice was gentle.

"No, no." She shook her head. "It's not for myself that I come to see you. It's . . . it's my husband, Michele."

"Is he here?"

"No, and if he knew I was here he would be very angry. He's not sick, not in his body. It's . . ." She shrugged her shoulders and pointed to her head. "It's up here. I pleaded with him to come to see you, but he won't, and he's upset with me for even talking about it. *There's nothing wrong with me,* he says." She took a deep breath and went on. "He is miserable all the time. Sometimes he won't talk at all, other times he shouts at me. Lately he just follows me around the house with a terrible scared look on his face . . . he hardly eats. I . . . I just don't know what to do."

"He's out of work, isn't he?"

"Yes, since January, four months now."

Dr. Catrone passed his hand over the mesh of fine lines etched on his face and shook his head. "Your husband has a sickness, but it isn't something I can treat. It is a sickness of the spirit. I see men with this malady all around me, every day. It's born of joblessness and poverty, and hopelessness. It's more paralyzing than a disease and harder to cure." Wheezing, he pushed himself from the chair and patted her arm. "There is no medication for this ailment. I wish I could help you, but there is very little I can do."

He went to a small closet and rummaged in a box containing small packets of pills. Taking Chiara's hand, he placed a packet into it. "If you can, convince him to take these. But I doubt they will do any good." He took her arm and led her to the door. "And you, Chiara, you look tired. Take care of yourself too. Get enough rest."

"Yes, I am tired. I don't sleep well."

Dr. Catrone shook his head and said with a sigh, "I know; I know how it is. You women are the ones who bear your crosses in silence. So much rests on your shoulders. Italian men are more fragile than they would have you think. The burdens of a new land, of being responsible for their families . . . when they can't work, it destroys them." Opening the door, he ushered her out. "You must remain strong. He needs you. God bless you, child."

"*Grazie, dottore,*" Chiara said.

She made her way through the waiting room, crowded with blank-faced people and whining children. Why did she thank him? she wondered. The pills were probably useless; he had said so himself. And even if they were effective, she doubted Michele would take them. She supposed the thanks were for a sympathetic ear, for a kind word. His sympathy had brought a catch to her throat. It was scant sustenance for her spirit.

He needs you, the doctor had said. But she needed someone too. She and Robbie both needed Michele. Some days she wanted to scream out and beat the walls with her fists in frustration. But of course she did neither. She coped; she managed. Would their lives have taken a different course had they remained in Italy? Somehow, poverty was manageable with family to support one.

She knew what medication Michele needed. It came neither in pills nor in bottles. Work. That was the antidote for his ailment. Work would cure his lethargy. But there was no work to be found in this pathetic city.

If Dr. Catrone couldn't help them, she would find someone who could.

Stewart Austin's face flashed across her mind. Stewart had told her not to worry, that Michele's job was safe. She had believed him, trusted him. Had he forgotten? Michele was proud; he wouldn't like her going to Stewart. But she couldn't afford to bow to that stern master, pride. She would go to Stewart Austin now, while she felt needy and courageous.

The clouds had disappeared and left a humid, unrelenting heat. As Chiara plodded up the walk of the Austin home, she was struck by its unkempt look. Against the surrounding neatly groomed areas, this one looked neglected, the grass longer, weedier, the shrubbery uneven. Spikes of green grass pushed up between the flagstones. It was a far cry from the well-tended yard she'd seen when she first came to the Austin home.

Along the side of the house, the fragrance from huge banks of white and purple lilacs wafted through the air. Tulips were shedding their vivid red and yellow petals while peonies bravely spiked up through the debris. Dead leaves, limp and colorless from the battering of winter, still clogged the earth at the roots of trees and shrubs, though it was May.

As Chiara approached the wide double doors of the house, she noticed that the draperies were drawn. The house looked forlorn and empty, and she worried that Stewart might not be home, though it was Saturday. In the tinted glass of the door, her reflection revealed the tension she felt. She riffled a hand through her wavy hair and moistened her dry lips. She looked attractive, she knew, in her rayon print dress with its flared sleeves and the plate-shaped hat tilted off her face. Taking a deep breath, she forced her lips into a smile.

When she pressed the doorbell she heard, faintly, responding chimes. If Stewart wasn't home, she could leave a note, she supposed. But writing in English was a chore, and she couldn't express herself well. Perhaps she should have telephoned.

If Mrs. Austin answered, she wouldn't know what to say, though she had a gift for her, a sort of premature gratuity, for Stewart's help. Mrs. Austin was never unkind, but her arch manner made Chiara uncomfortable. A gift for Stewart would have been better, but that wouldn't have been proper.

Michele would be angry if he knew she was here. For whatever obscure reasons, though he had never met them, Michele disliked the Austins; perhaps because he hated "owing" anyone, or because Chiara worked for them in a subservient position. She dabbed a handkerchief at her forehead and neck. Michele's fate, their future, was hanging in the balance, and that overcame her hesitancy.

When Stewart himself answered the door, Chiara smiled with relief.

"Chiara! This is a surprise." He ran restless fingers through his rumpled hair. "I wasn't expecting you."

He usually looked dapper, but now his tieless shirt was rumpled and his cheeks sported a shadowy stubble.

He opened the door wide. "Do come in."

Stepping inside, Chiara was struck by the unusual quiet. The ticking of the great gilt-faced grandfather clock that stood guard over the foyer sounded like noisy, intrusive heartbeats. Something was not right.

"I don't like to bother you, but . . . well, I've come to bring a gift for Mrs. Austin and to, well . . ." She hesitated and swallowed, finding the words difficult to utter.

He rescued her from an uneasy moment. "Come, let's talk in the library. Seeing you is no bother at all. In fact, it's refreshing." He took her arm and led her into the book-lined room she'd found so fascinating on her first visit.

"You're just what I needed, like a spot of sunshine on a dreary day." He whisked newspapers from a chair and swept up a cushion that had fallen to the floor.

"The place is a bit of a mess, I'm afraid. Rosie comes in only once a week now, and of course she can't get around to everything. We had to discharge Molly, but . . . well, I'm not completely helpless. I can manage to make us some coffee."

Why had they discharged their servants? Chiara wondered. Surely Stewart hadn't lost his job too. He had an important position at Ford. Chiara noticed the tightness around his mouth, the small lines around his eyes, the furrows across his forehead. Had all those telltale lines been there before? She thought not.

"No, don't bother with coffee just for me," she said.

"Nonsense, I know how you love your coffee. I've found I'm quite capable of handling household jobs. Come along into the kitchen." He gestured for her to follow.

The spacious kitchen enthralled Chiara. An array of cooking equipment hung in plain view: strainers and dippers and spatulas in many sizes. Copper-bottomed pots, dangling from the ceiling, cheered the room with their russet glow. The black-and-silver range had six burners and two large ovens.

"I could prepare a feast for a king in a kitchen like this," Chiara said with a sweeping gaze around the well-equipped room.

"Plenty of feasts have been prepared in this kitchen, perhaps not for kings, but for some of Detroit's royalty. Actually, I did meet royalty once: the Prince of Wales, when he stayed at the Detroit Athletic Club. The joke went around that he had asked for a sprinkle in his room. It finally became clear that he meant a shower." His accompanying laugh held a touch of irony. "Oh, well, best not to dwell in the glorious past."

He filled a coffeepot with water and searched the cupboard. "Ah, success," he said, a can of coffee in his hand. He carefully measured out grounds into the metal basket.

"Mrs. Austin isn't home?" Chiara asked, though she felt sure the house was empty.

"Ah . . . no, not now."

Chiara set a package on the countertop. "I have a small gift for her."

"Well, that's very nice," Stewart said, turning the gas jet under the pot. "Shall I open it?" he asked.

"Yes, if you like."

The tissue inside the box crinkled as he moved it aside and drew out the evening bag, an elegant envelope of white velvet with a silver fringe.

"Why, this is beautiful," Stewart said, holding the bag aloft. "You're so clever. You should be a designer.

Audrey'll love this. She happens to be at a . . ." He paused and dropped the bag onto the box. Stuffing his hands into his pockets, he said, "Why do I lie about it? She's gone. Took Sonny and left. We had a terrible fight over her taking him, but I would've had to hire someone to watch him while I'm working, and well, with everything else that's happening . . . I suppose he's better off with his mother in the long run. Or so I tell myself."

He slumped into a chair and sighed.

"You mean your wife has left you, left this house?" Chiara asked incredulously. How could she leave a man like Stewart? He was a kind and thoughtful man, a gentle man, a man of intelligence and stature. And this beautiful house! How could she leave this house?

"Yes, I'm afraid so." Stewart stared at the floor so long she thought he'd forgotten she was there. Then he said very quietly, "Audrey drinks. She's an alcoholic. Oh, Sonny's all right, because she had the good sense to go back home to *Mummy and Daddy*." His mouth twisted into a sarcastic grimace when he said *Mummy and Daddy*.

He jumped up and turned the flame low under the wildly percolating pot. "Of course, they've been part of the problem all along. *Mummy* has always closed her eyes to Audrey's drinking, as if in denying it, it would disappear. And *Daddy* always made things right for his little girl."

Stewart fell silent and Chiara was uneasy about intruding. What could she say to this surprising revelation of family secrets? The musical bubbling of the coffeepot invaded the quiet.

Almost as though he were talking to himself, Stewart continued, "Daddy got her out of jams and gave her money, and never let her stand on her own two feet. Yes, it's always been dear Daddy to the rescue. Actually, her mother's all right. A bit of a drudge, but at least she's sober, and her heart's in the right place. She couldn't help spoiling Audrey rotten, I suppose, because she lost a child in childbirth, and another one at an early age. Anyway, she'll see Sonny's well taken care of."

Chiara felt bewildered by the words that tumbled from Stewart, but the disclosures explained her uneasiness around Audrey, the nebulous feeling of something askew. Now that Chiara understood, she felt contradictory emotions of contempt and sympathy for Audrey, who seemed to be a victim of her parents' misguided love. For Stewart, who was so obviously distressed, though he tried to hide it with his glib, sarcastic tongue, she felt only empathy. Poor Stewart, his wife's departure was probably bearable under the circumstances, but his son—he was so attached to the boy.

Chiara touched Stewart's arm. "I'm so sorry about all of this. Perhaps she can't help herself."

"Oh, don't be sorry. You're right, she can't help herself. But she won't even admit there's a problem. I honestly tried to help her. But lately I've reacted with anger or sarcasm, which does no good at all. And I realize I helped perpetuate the thing by hiding it from everyone. We were co-conspirators, involved in this intricate game: 'Audrey likes to have a good time, ha, ha,' 'She's in her cups,' 'She tipples,' 'She's under the weather,' as if it were a cute trick . . . never exploring the underlying causes, acting as if it wasn't something very important, and one day we'd wake up and she'd be fine."

"So you made her leave?"

"Oh, no, I was prepared to continue the game. She's the one who decided to leave. When the crash came . . . well, you see, that was the other thing." Stewart yanked a kitchen chair forward and straddled it. "I lost everything. Took her father's advice and gambled heavily in the stock market. On margin, of course, like all the other fools. But that old bastard must have had inside information, or he got lucky, because he pulled out before it was too late. But not old Stewart." He shook his head deprecatingly. "To give the devil his due, he did suggest I pull out, but by that time the market was already sinking, and I made the bad decision to stay with it. Not that I was alone. I certainly had company." He gave a short laugh, but the downward curve of his mouth gave lie to the sound.

"Poor Stewart," Chiara said, her eyes shiny with a hint of tears. No one could have guessed that beneath the smooth veneer of sophistication and lightheartedness the Austin family had been laboring under a cloud of unhappiness, now compounded by money problems.

The pot gurgled a cadence as Stewart burrowed in a cupboard. The two thin china cups tinkled as he placed them on matching saucers. He half-filled one cup with whiskey, saying, "Care to join me?"

Chiara made a negative gesture with her hands. "No, thank you."

"Well, I don't usually imbibe in the middle of the day, but for some reason, circumstances seem to call for it today. I suppose you're thinking, 'Aha. He's no better than his wife.' "

Chiara shook her head gently in denial.

"I'm not really a drinker, don't even like the stuff." He looked into the cup, as if seeking agreement.

He looked so forlorn, she wished she could console him in some way. "I'm very sorry, Stewart."

"No need to be sorry. One copes."

"Yes, we all have to make the best of things." She folded her hands tightly in her lap, remembering her mission.

Stewart looked up, a startled expression on his face. "I'm so thoughtless, rambling on about my troubles. And I know you have troubles of your own. How are you managing?"

"Michele is laid off, you know. My sewing brings in some money, but it's not much. That's why I came, to talk to you about Michele's job. You've helped us out before, and I thought . . ."

Stewart's brow furrowed. "I didn't realize about your husband's job; I've been so absorbed with my own problems."

He turned off the heat under the coffeepot and it abruptly ceased its clamor. "I know Mike. I was the one who drove him with his friend to the hospital the day of the hunger march. He's a brave man, your husband."

Chiara looked startled.

"Oh, he didn't know who I was. At least I don't think he did."

So it was Stewart who had rescued Ed. "Mike told me how someone risked trouble by helping him. You're brave, also, to go against Henry Ford and help those who protested his policies."

"I don't always agree with Henry. But there's nothing I can do. The Ford organization is too big, too powerful, and I'm just a small cog in the wheel."

"My husband . . . he needs to work."

Stewart brushed restless fingers through his hair. "I don't know if I can do anything. I have little influence." He poured hot, dark brew into the cups and pushed a sugar bowl toward Chiara.

"I'm afraid there's not much by way of refreshments in the house." He took a bottle of milk from the Frigidaire and poured the thick top cream into a silver creamer. "I'll see what I can do for your husband, Chiara."

"Please, please try. I would be so grateful."

"Things are bad at the plant," Stewart said. "No one has any influence with Henry except Harry Bennett. I can't stand the man. His methods are appalling. Just talking to him infuriates me. But Henry relies on him completely." He leaned against the table and stuffed his hands in his pockets. "We're all afraid of Bennett, even Edsel. Edsel hates his father, you know. I don't blame him. With all that money, Henry wouldn't let Edsel go to college. He'll never be forgiven that."

"But couldn't he have gone anyway?"

"Go against Henry Ford?" He looked incredulous. "Edsel was just a kid then, eighteen years old. He did what his parents told him."

"What about his mother?"

"Clara? She just does what Henry says, I suppose." Stewart stood abruptly. "Come, let's go into the parlor; it's more comfortable there."

Chiara had never been in the parlor before, and was shocked by its stark look. The wood floor was bare, with a subtle but revealing change in color bordering the room, indicating the recent removal of a carpet. The walls were bare as well, with the same telltale color contrast, where pictures had previously hung. Two matching lilac velvet wing chairs flanked the fireplace and a long damask-covered sofa faced it. A few tables were scattered around, almost haphazardly.

Stewart indicated the sofa and she sat at one end, while he went to the Victrola and selected a record from the storage shelf underneath, then carefully placed it on the turntable.

A pleasing baritone sang "Sweet and Lovely," and Chiara pressed herself into the sofa, but was unable to relax. Though nearly empty, the room intensified her uneasiness—the rich damask draperies, the smell of good wood furniture and furniture polish, the Boston fern with bright green fronds reaching the floor; all reflected an aura of breeding, of manners, of gracious living.

Stewart sat across from her with his hands clenched between his knees. "I'd sell the house, but who can buy these days? I'd have to take a loss. No, I'm going to hang on as long as I can." His voice dropped to almost a whisper. "The Aubusson carpet is gone. The paintings too."

Poor Stewart. His problems appeared as overwhelming as her own. Gone was the assured carriage, the sprightly walk. Even his hair, she noticed, showed streaks of gray she hadn't seen before.

The tinny sounds from the Victrola, happy, carefree words about love, echoed around the room. How false the words sounded in the light of Stewart's and her own unhappiness.

Chiara forced herself to return to the subject of Mike's job. She needed Stewart's help. He was her only hope. In his present distracted state, he might forget all about her request by tomorrow. She took a deep breath and began, "About my husband's job . . ." Her voice seemed overloud as it competed with the sounds from the Victrola. She cleared her throat. "I'm hopeful that you can help us again. Now that he's laid off, he has become very . . . How can I say it?" Her eyes darted around the room, searching for the correct word. "Melancholy." It was difficult to speak of Mike's state of mind, as though it were a terrible disease, like leprosy. "I fear if he doesn't find work soon, he may . . ." She swallowed hard. "He may lose his mind."

There. The words she had thought but dared not say were finally out. They seemed to remain in the room and bounce about off the bare walls and floor: *lose his mind, lose his mind.* The specter of Eduardo seemed to haunt her.

Suddenly it seemed more than she could bear. She burst into tears, covering her face with her hands.

Stewart sprang to her side. "There, there, you mustn't cry. Please, please don't do that." Distraught, he pulled a handkerchief from his pocket and patted her cheeks.

She took the handkerchief and put it to her mouth, but her sobs continued despite her attempts to muffle them.

Stewart dropped to one knee and pulled her close. He patted her back as if she were a child. "Go ahead and cry, then. I suppose you need a good cry. They say it's good for you." Gently he moved a stray strand of silky hair from her forehead. "We're a sorry lot today, you and I."

Chiara clung to him desperately. He was a raft in her sea of misery.

"Now, come on, dry the tears, I may not be able to help myself, but I can certainly try to help you. There may be a few strings I can pull for your husband."

Her tears finally subsiding, Chiara slowly raised her face, hardly able to look at Stewart. The crying had left her weak and embarrassed.

"I'm so ashamed," she whispered.

"Don't be. Tears are an honest reaction to your woes. I wish I could cry like that. It might do me good."

She tried to pull back, but Stewart's hands held her elbows taut. Softly she said, "Strange that I came to tell you of my husband's distress and find you distressed as well. Perhaps it's even worse for you, with no one to comfort you."

Overcome with compassion for him, for both of them, she raised her hand to touch his shoulder. Before it reached its destination, Stewart intercepted it and placed the palm to his lips, kissing it hungrily, his eyes squeezed shut. He kissed each finger with infinite tenderness, then folded her hand in his.

"Look at me, Chiara."

Her eyes met his and she was drawn against her will into the depths of his shiny gray orbs edged in darker smoke. She glimpsed beyond the dark centers, into his very soul, fathoming his sorrows and fears, his hopes and dreams, sensing his need for sympathy and . . . and, yes, his love.

For a long moment she remained under the spell of his hypnotic eyes, eyes that stirred, deep within her, an urgent passion. Her lids lowered, but the spell remained. She wanted to pull away, but couldn't. Gently she ran her free hand over his cheek, tracing the jaw with her fingers.

"I need you," he said, his voice a caressing hum against her cheek.

A warmth suffused her body. Afraid of her wayward emotions, she dredged up a grain of control and pushed away. "No, no."

His soft lips gently touched her forehead, her eyes. "Yes. I loved you from the first time I saw you."

He loved her. He wanted her. Just as she wanted him, though she'd denied her disturbing yearnings, her sinful fantasies. She turned her head away. "No."

He held her face in both his hands, forcing her to look at him, searching her eyes. "Yes. Surely you knew that?"

Of course she knew. A special bond had grown between them, unbidden, hardly nurtured—a love she had not even dared to think of. "You mustn't say things like that." Again she tried to draw away, but he held her firmly.

"Yes, since that day I heard you singing in the sewing room." He kissed the corner of her mouth. "My little Italian songbird. Remember that day?"

Of course she remembered it, remembered the smile on that handsome, aristocratic face, remembered the small ripple of her heartbeat. "No, please don't." Her hands on his chest, she resisted his pull.

"Hush."

He stroked her arm upward to her shoulder, her neck, brushing away the wispy hair that rested at her ear. Her skin tingled at his touch. She closed her eyes, afraid to look at him, lest it break the spell.

He kissed the hollow at her neck, then nibbled at her earlobe. She knew she should move, run away, she knew she was in danger. But she wanted him, needed him. Every nerve in her body yearned for him.

Helplessly, expectantly, she waited for his mouth to reach her own, an agony of desire churning inside her. Pressing close, she circled her arms around his shoulders, her spread fingers feeling the tensed muscles in his back. She moved her fingers upward through his hair, urging him closer.

His mouth wandered to her eyelids, down her nose, her cheek, her chin. Finally his mouth found hers. With an urgent pulsing his tongue parted her lips and moved sensuously inside while her body quivered with passion. His lips moved against hers rhythmically for an eternity; then he eased her gently down to the sofa.

"Chiara. Chiara." His voice was like a breeze riffling through her hair. "I love to say your name."

Her hands moved now of their own volition, touching his face, his neck, urging his lips to close on hers again. His mouth was soft, tender, as it rested again on her eager lips. The kiss inflamed her, filling her with liquid fire. Fiercely she clung to him, as if she would drown if she let him go. She returned his kisses with an ardor she had never felt before. She had no will, no conscience, she only wanted him inside her, filling her center, quieting her compelling need.

Stewart groped at the small buttons down the front of her dress, impatiently undoing them. She was suddenly aware of her plain cotton underwear—did his wife wear silk lingerie, edged in lace?

The dress fell away and he moved the straps of her underclothing from her shoulders, exposing her generous breasts. With a sharp intake of breath, his hands roved over the rounded, milky mounds, arousing the dark nipples. She felt a rare ecstasy, a euphoria, as she threw her head back and guided his mouth back to her own.

Swiftly he undid his trousers and sloughed them off. She felt his hands move under her cotton slip, exploring her bare skin, felt his hardness against her hip. He lifted the slip over her head, slowly, slowly, then pressed her legs apart. Nothing could stop the swell of passion that had risen like a tidal wave within her. She wanted him, needed him desperately. She loved this man, had known it from the beginning. Her body arched upward toward him, inviting him. He entered her cautiously, arousing a hunger that was exquisitely, almost painfully, intense. Their bodies moved together in a harmony that knew no time or space; they were at one with the tides and the seasons and the universe. Low, earthy moans sounded and Chiara realized they came from her. A series of spasms shuddered through her. Intertwined, they rocked until the ebb and flow subsided. He murmured sweet love sounds into her hair. They remained clasped together, damp and spent, while the Victrola needle scratched away on the record long after the melody had ended.

As if in slow motion, he eased himself away, brushing his hand over her cheek, kissing the valley between her breasts. "Chiara . . . I'm sorry, I shouldn't have . . ."

"Oh, Stewart." Chiara's voice was ragged as she sat up, breathing in the mingled earthy fragrance of their spent passion.

He pulled her close and touched the moist valley between her breasts. With nervous fingers she adjusted her underclothing, aware of Stewart's loving gaze. She turned away, forcing her chaotic thoughts to focus on the reality of the situation. Almost to herself she said, "This is madness."

Stewart took her hand, kissing each finger. "Chiara, it isn't madness. Was it so awful for you?"

Her eyes softened. "No, it was wonderful. But we're married people. It was wrong."

"We could hardly have stopped ourselves. It was me. I forced you. You didn't want to, but I made you . . ."

She pulled her hand away. "No, it wasn't only your doing. I lost all control." With shaking fingers she drew her dress on and fumbled with the buttons. "I can't forgive myself for this . . ."

"Don't do this to yourself. You and I . . . we were meant to be together. It wasn't such a terrible thing . . ."

"It *was* terrible, a sin. I should have stopped you, stopped myself." With shaking fingers she tried to smooth the tangle of her unruly hair. She searched about the room, looking for her purse. She snatched it from a nearby table and started for the door.

Stewart hurried after her. "Wait, I'll get the car."

Chiara turned pleading eyes to him. "No, you mustn't. You can't let Michele see you."

"Please let me. Part of the way, then." He took her arm.

She wrested away and ran for the door. "No, I must never see you again. Let me alone, let me go."

Stewart, sounding stricken, said, "Please, Chiara, don't leave like this . . ."

She didn't wait to hear the rest of his words, but ran out the door.

—16—

On the streetcar Chiara sat stiffly, staring ahead, her hands in her lap. Her mouth was parched, so dry she could barely summon saliva. What had she done? Wantonly, knowingly, she had given in to her urgent lust, thinking only of the moment, forgetting the husband who awaited her. She loved her husband. He was her man, for better or worse. And he loved her too, though there had been little evidence of it for a long, long time.

She mentally relived the events that had led to her disgrace, dissecting each moment, each touch, each word, thinking: God forgive me, I didn't mean to do it, I couldn't help myself. Then another thought intruded accusingly: I could have left at any moment. He didn't force me, I let it happen. Though she had tried to deny it, she had wanted him long before it happened, even before the trouble with Mike. She had wanted his flesh against hers, his lips exploring, his hands caressing. And when he touched her, her passion was a whirlwind, impossible to stop. Even now, remembering, she grew warm with desire.

Stewart had become a romantic fantasy, an ideal—successful, capable, sophisticated. Even when his powerlessness, his fallibility were exposed, she was unable to resist his spell.

He said he loved her; she believed he meant it. And what about her? Did she love him too? Impatiently she shook the thought away. She couldn't examine her feelings too closely. Love was an emotion she was unable to deal with right now.

What must Stewart think? That she was no better than a whore? Did he imagine she was making a trade with him? Her body for Mike's job? No, surely not, surely his emotion was genuine, his love real.

The streetcar was too warm, the stench of people crowded together making her nauseous. The strangers seemed to look at her, then turn away, as if they knew or guessed at her shame. It must be written on her face, a mark on her forehead, like that of Cain. Smoothing back her hair with nervous fingers, she tried to shut out the sea of faces around her. She closed her aching eyes, forcing the thoughts away. The interminable ride finally ended and she proceeded toward home with heavy foot-steps, reluctant to face her husband.

"You were gone so long," Mike grumbled. "Robbie was crabby and cried for you."

She glanced at him, then looked away, unable to meet his eyes. Unshaven, his hair awry, Mike was not the same proud man she had married. It struck her that the wounded look in his eyes was similar to that in Stewart's. Were they all paralyzed with the bitter venom of anger against a system not of their making?

Mike was sinking steadily into a sea of hopelessness, and instead of throwing him a lifeline, she had betrayed him. *Mea culpa, mea culpa. May God forgive me, for I will never forgive myself.*

Robbie reached chubby arms to her, calling out glee-fully, "Mama, Mama."

She scooped him up and buried her face in his neck, willing the quiver that pulsed through her body to stop.

"What's wrong?" Mike asked, as if alerted to a subtle difference in his wife.

"Nothing. I'm tired, that's all." Her voice was strained from the dull ache in her throat. Could Mike guess at her sin by the look of her? She put Robbie down and hung her coat on the hook behind the door.

"Did they pay you?"

"No. I left the work with the maid," she lied glibly. "They'll pay me next time."

"That's fine," he said with a sarcastic grunt. "That's the way the rich do it. Pay next time. But there's no next time at the grocer's. First we pay, then we eat." He paced around the room. "Get the box," he said.

She slipped her apron over her head and tied it behind her. She knew what box he meant. The cigar box; their little hoard, which had been dwindling steadily, despite her late nights at the sewing machine, her careful stretching of their simple foods.

"Later," she said, lifting the latch on the icebox door. "Let me get our supper first." She wanted to postpone the tortured look he would display when he saw how little money was left.

"Now."

She shot him a measured look.

His eyes regarded her with steadfast intensity. "I said now."

Taking the box from its niche in the bottom drawer, she squeezed her eyes shut and wished for a miracle, like the ones told about the patron saint of their province, Saint Nicholas, and the bounty he gifted to the poor and needy. Such a wild fantasy it seemed now, though as a child she had believed every word.

Mike passed his hand over the box. The once-bright colors on the cover seemed faded now. With deliberate slowness he lifted the worn lid and sorted through the bills. He snorted at its paltry contents.

Chiara reached down and picked up the money. She counted purposefully to make the total appear greater, then spread the bills on the table.

"Six dollars and sixty cents," Mike said mournfully, scooping up the money and placing it back in the box.

"I'll get more," she said quietly, looking at the floor. "I have a coat almost finished for Mrs. Morrison. It should bring in five dollars. And she wants two summer dresses."

He picked up the box and threw it against the wall. The bills fluttered down in slow motion and the coins jangled to the floor. Robbie began shrieking at the commotion and Chiara hurried to pick him up and comfort him.

"Shut up, dammit, shut up," Mike yelled at the frightened child.

When Robbie screamed even louder, Mike pushed the chair back, toppling it, and stomped out of the house, the door slamming behind him.

Chiara rocked Robbie from side to side, patting his back. I deserve Mike's wrath, she thought; I understand his misery. If he struck me, I would accept it. I almost wish he would strike me.

"Oh, why did we ever leave Italy?" she asked Robbie. "At least there we could always feed ourselves from the bounty of the earth, and I could find comfort in my family." A small sob escaped her lips. "My marriage is a loveless shambles. My husband is ill. All my dreams are gone; the plans for a little dress shop, a home of our own, a visit back to Italy—all gone."

The child searched Chiara's face, then clung to her tightly.

In the following days Chiara tried to lose herself in her sewing and in the delightful antics of Robbie. His baby talk was a charming mixture of Italian and American. Mike was adamant about using correct American grammar, and Chiara was equally adamant about speaking Italian, so that Robbie would be conversant when they returned to Italy. She banished images of *that* Saturday, and hummed as she pedaled furiously, anxious to finish the Communion dress for Rosa's daughter. Robbie mimicked her, and she had to stop to laugh at the sturdy little boy. Absorbed as she was in her son and her work, thoughts of Stewart had, thankfully, little chance to intrude.

Mike left the house at noon. He was in no hurry to reach his destination. This trip was one he had been dreading for weeks.

The drab, crowded welfare office, once a grocery store, now housed cubicles where overworked clerks asked their endless questions.

There were three people standing for every one seated, and despondency hung over them like a heavy fog, displayed in the droop of their shoulders, the empty stares in their lowered eyes. They looked down or straight ahead, as if fearful of making eye contact. There was a similarity in their faces, a look of despair.

Mike loosened his collar against the oppressive heat. He thought he recognized a tall, lean man in a threadbare coat as one of his department co-workers, but he kept his eyes steadfastly averted. He wanted neither to see nor to be seen in this place.

What am I doing here? How did I reach this sorry state of affairs, he wondered. I have always managed somehow to find work, as my father did before me. This is the ultimate humiliation.

A tiny woman with faded red hair broke into uncontrollable sobs. No one looked at her. It was as if she didn't exist. Another woman dabbed at her eyes with a crumpled handkerchief and sniffled. The men looked uncomfortable at the displays of emotion.

The line never dwindled, for as some moved up, others attached themselves at the end. It was like a living thing, a centipede weaving a path to an uncertain destination.

Finally it was Mike's turn. The woman at the window chewed gum and pushed a straggly strand of hair back from her face. She asked questions in a bored singsong voice. Mike stared in fascination at the dark red line of lipstick outlining her lips—the rest was chewed away. She had to repeat the questions, for suddenly his mind had gone blank. He blinked and forced himself to concentrate, then mumbled barely coherent answers to her questions. *Yes, a wife, Chiara. One son, Roberto. Ford Motor Company.*

She scribbled on a printed form, then said something he didn't understand, something about papers. *What? Papers? I forgot to bring papers?*

"I'm sorry, you'll have to come back tomorrow. I need verification of your layoff date," she said finally with a weary sigh. Half the people in line heard the same evasion, or a variation of it. The city was out of money, he knew, and this was a delaying tactic. He was neither angry nor upset, merely resigned to his fate, the fate he shared with all the shabby, gray people around him, all players in this tragedy of a social order. They were a new society, superfluous people, the helpless indigents; willing to accept any work, no matter how menial, and lacking that, any dole the city would mete out.

Mike moved slowly from the counter, unsure of what to do.

"It's closing time, you'll all have to come back tomorrow," a burly guard shouted, trying to herd the people outside.

"No, no," one woman shouted, "my children are hungry." Others joined in, shouting, "We're not leaving."

Several men blocked the door, refusing to leave, until

finally the interviewers agreed to see emergency cases only. Mike was one of the few who shuffled out.

Back on the street, suddenly sickened, he leaned against the rough bricks of the building, breathing deeply. Nothing had come easily to Mike; he'd worked hard for what little he had. But he'd always been sustained by faith and hope. Now, after today's ignominious experience and with the phantom of Ed hanging over him, it was almost more than he could bear.

The next day he left for the welfare office at dawn and repeated the experience of the day before. Dark had descended by the time he shuffled back into the house.

"Sit. I'll warm your dinner," Chiara said.

He tossed papers on the table. "These are the papers that attest to our poverty, the papers that'll keep food on our table and clothing on our backs." He fell into a chair, put his head in his arms, and wept.

Seeing him this way—this too-proud man, once so strong, so intense, now weakened, diminished, cowed, his will broken—it tormented Chiara's very soul. And this was the man she had betrayed, wantonly, lustily. Pangs of guilt and sorrow descended upon her like a storm, the thunder of it filling her head. A silent scream rose in her throat. Suddenly it was more than she could bear, and she burst into a gale of tears that racked her body. She ran into the bedroom and threw herself on the bed. Never before had she released her own anguish in such a way. Always, she had been the buffer for his distress, allaying his fears, offering him hope. It hadn't been difficult for her to comfort him in these months of misery, for poverty was something she could deal with; it was manageable. Her natural optimism had made her confident that their condition was only temporary, that things would improve.

What she couldn't face now was the dual torture of seeing Mike's spirit being splintered away daily and the breakdown of her own moral code. Her faithlessness, she was sure, would torture her the rest of her life.

Mike raised his head, astonished, while her sobs rent the air. Finally he went and sat on the bed beside her, touching her shoulder.

"Chiara, please. I'm so sorry, my dearest. Don't do this. We'll manage, I promise you. Please don't cry."

She tried to choke down her sobs, causing a violent hiccuping.

He picked her up and cradled her in his arms, patting her head. "I'll get a job, by God, I'll take care of you."

He rocked her and with his large handkerchief dried her cheeks, while she whimpered and sobbed. Kissing her face with small pecks, he tried to comfort her. "It's all right, please don't cry."

He laid her on the bed and removed the clothing from her unresisting body, her cries continuing at regular intervals, heaving her chest, trembling her chin, chattering her teeth. In bed he held her close, murmuring words of love, until finally the tears ceased.

With his arms tight around her, his sympathy and love surrounding her, Chiara felt desire stirring her blood. She needed his love. But when she nestled closer against him, he stiffened.

"You don't love me," she said in a constrained whisper.

"Don't say such a thing. Of course I love you."

"Then why don't we make love?"

Mike released his hold on her and sat up, pushing the pillow upright against his back, a woebegone expression diluting the strength of his features.

Chiara sat up and pressed against him. "Why?" she persisted.

Abruptly Mike rose and fumbled in his pocket for his cigarettes. He sat on the edge of the bed, inhaling deeply. Chiara slid over to him and ran her hand up and down his back, feeling the tension ease away as he slumped forward, his breathing deep and audible.

Finally he shook her hand away and rose. "I don't know why," he said. "I just don't know."

In the days following, Chiara thought often of Stewart. The memory of that day invaded her mind unbidden, and she would shut her eyes, willing the memory to leave. But the visions would cling to the edges of her awareness, flustering her. "Jesus, Mary, and Joseph," she prayed, "don't let me think of him." She wanted to see him again, to feel his touch, his hand on her skin, but vowed she wouldn't. She had her life, her place, and he had his. They existed on different planes of reality. Never could their lives really intermingle.

The first morning she arose feeling ill, she tried to deny it, to explain it away as influenza or spoiled food. By the third morning, when the smell of coffee and cigarettes upset her, she could no longer hide from the truth. She was pregnant with Stewart Austin's child.

Mike didn't seem to notice her fatigue or her paleness. His concern for Chiara's welfare after her uncharacteristic outburst a few weeks ago was short-lived. A few days after that he resumed his pattern of helplessness. Several times Chiara had attempted to talk to him, to convince him there was hope, but finally she gave up trying.

She wept silent tears for the child within her, the love child. To what would she bring it forth? To a world of proverty and strife? And how would she explain it to Mike? Even in his present benumbed state, he would surely realize that he was not the father.

Chiara dried her hands on her apron when she heard the knock. She was surprised to see Stewart standing at the screen door looking apologetic.

"May I come in?" he asked politely.

She had been determined never to go to his home again, and to turn him away if he came to hers. But now, seeing his dear face, realizing that she cared for this man, that now there was an inexorable bond between them, though she wouldn't tell him so, Chiara couldn't turn him away. He looked assured, his gray eyes penetrating, assessing. She stood aside and let the screen door clatter shut behind him. They gazed at one another uneasily.

"I hope you've forgiven me," he said finally.

Chiara put her finger to her lips and pointed toward the bedroom, where Mike was sleeping. "My husband," she whispered.

"Yes, well . . . I've come with some skirts to lengthen. I guess the new fashion is longer." He held out a package. "Audrey's back. Nothing's changed, of course, but she decided to give me another chance." He gave an uneasy laugh.

Chiara took the parcel and set it on a chair. "It's better for the boy."

"About your husband's job. I've talked to someone. That's all I can do. We'll see what happens."

"That would be wonderful." Chiara locked her fingers together in a gesture of hope.

"No promises. It's a very touchy situation."

"Whatever you can do."

They both fell silent for a moment; then Stewart grabbed for her hand. "Are you all right, Chiara? You look so pale. Please don't be angry with me."

Chiara snatched her hand away and led him through the house and onto the back porch, out of earshot. A backless chair stood on the uneven paint-flecked boards, tomato plants stretched their leaves optimistically toward the sun from their home in a rusted galvanized tub.

"I'm not angry with you. It's just that . . ." She caught her bottom lip between her teeth and shook her head.

"What? You haven't told your husband, have you?"

"No! I would never do that." She wrung her hands and blurted, "I'm with child!"

Oh, God. The shameful secret she'd carried for several weeks had burst from her unintentionally. "I didn't mean to tell you."

Stewart caught his breath. "You mean that one time—"

"Yes." Chiara lifted her hand wearily to shade her eyes from the late-afternoon sun. "That one time."

"Good Lord." Stewart stared at her for a moment, then looked away. "Your husband, does he know you're pregnant?"

"No," she said fiercely. "I can't tell him. We haven't . . . been together for a long time. He would know . . ."

Stewart turned and paced the small porch, then halted in front of Chiara with a resolute thrust of his jaw.

"Chiara, I love you. There's nothing between Audrey and me anymore. What little love we started with is long gone. I'll get a divorce—I've been thinking of doing it anyway. You can get one too, then we'll get married."

Chiara recoiled in horror, stumbling against the chair. "No! I can't do that!"

"Yes, you can. I want our child." He reached for her hand, but she pulled away.

"No, it's unthinkable." The shameful word "divorce" was never uttered in an Italian household. People married for better or worse. "Mike . . . I couldn't leave him. He's my husband. He needs me."

Stewart turned his hands outward in a helpless gesture. "*I* need you."

Chiara hung her head, shaking it slowly.

After a moment's silence Stewart asked, "Then what will you do?"

She sat heavily on the chair. "I don't know."

He reached again for her hand, and this time she let it lie limply in his. "I'll give you money. I'll pay for the child, pay for the birth, for clothes, for an education."

Chiara shook her head. In a dull, hopeless voice she said, "You can't do that. How would it be explained?"

"Chiara," Mike called tentatively from inside the house.

Jumping from the chair, Chiara said, "You must go. You mustn't see me again. Don't come here anymore."

"Chiara!" Mike's voice sounded closer. "Is someone here?"

"No, it was just Laurelia from across the way," she answered, wondering when and how she had learned to lie so convincingly.

She pushed Stewart toward the steps. Just as he slipped around the side of the house, Mike came out on the porch and sat heavily on the chair.

"Where's Laurelia?" he asked.

"She left."

"I thought she went down south."

"They came back. At least here they get welfare."

He nodded. After a moment he said, "Did I hear a car?"

"I didn't hear anything," she answered.

She knew what she must do. She must convince Mike to make love to her, then somehow carry out the deceit that the child was his.

"Come, help me with dinner," she said, extending her hand to Mike. When he took it, she pulled upward, and he followed her obediently into the house.

The veal cutlet she had managed to buy for their dinner was cooked to perfection, golden brown, delicately seasoned with herbs and bread crumbs. After dinner she poured him another glass of wine and had one herself. When Robbie was safely tucked in bed, she bathed and put on a fresh, transparent nightgown, one from her trousseau, that clung to her breasts, now swollen in preparation for a new child.

When she urged Mike to come to bed, he followed her docilely. She leaned over him and let her fragrant hair, now grown to her shoulders, fall over his face. He blew it away and smiled at her. She pressed against him, sliding her foot along the length of his lean, muscular leg. Frowning, Mike turned his face away, but Chiara was persistent, kissing his neck, reaching down and caressing his taut belly, his thighs. Before she could reach further, he turned and sat up suddenly.

"Stop," he said. "It's no use."

Chiara knelt behind him, circling her arms around his shoulders, pressing closer to him. "I love you, Michele," she whispered, holding back the tears kindled by his rejection.

He shook her away, and stood, his hands balled into fists, his head lowered. "I . . . can't. I just can't." He grabbed his clothes and hurried out of the room. A few minutes later she heard the front door slam.

When Maria came to visit the next week, Chiara broke down and said, "Maria, I don't know what to do. I'm with child again."

"I thought so." Maria nodded knowingly. "You don't want this child, do you?"

Chiara shook her head. "I feel sick all the time, not only morning. It's worse than the last time."

"That will pass."

Will it? she wondered. But the mental agony, the knowledge that this child would be a daily reminder of Stewart Austin, would that pass?

"I can accept it, but what of Mike? We can hardly feed ourselves, much less another child."

"What does he say?"

"I can't bear to tell him. You see how he is. He hardly wants to get up from bed in the morning, and when he does, he follows me around the house like a puppet. I have to tell him to wash, to eat; he's like a child." She grabbed Maria's arm. "What's going to happen to us? Dear God, help me." She dropped her face into her hands and sobbed.

Maria tried to console her friend. "Shh, it's all right. Look at your Robbie, what a beautiful child. Things will be better soon."

How could Chiara confess to her friend that this was not Mike's child? She lifted her head, her wide eyes spilling over with fresh tears. "What if things don't get better? What if Mike doesn't ever get well?"

Maria shook her head sadly. "One prays. One hopes."

Chiara clutched Maria's hands. "Tell me, Maria, what do you see for me? What's in my future?"

Maria closed her eyes, and when she opened them they held a look of ineffable sadness. "I see children, but not this child. Not this one."

Chiara gulped and whispered hoarsely, "I've heard there's something you can take, a purgative, but I don't know what it's called or where to get it."

Maria stiffened. "That's a dangerous thing to do."

Chiara wiped her eyes and stood. "I've made up my mind. Will you help me?"

A few days later, Maria came with a bottle. "I got it from a friend of Comare Rosa's. She asked no questions. What do they care? It's none of their concern—it's a business. They sell, we buy; what we do with it is none of their concern."

"Stop, stop." Chiara put her palms to her ears. "Please, Maria, just go now."

"Let me stay with you."

"No, I want to be alone."

"If you need me . . ."

"I'll be all right."

"God help you, my dear."

"God has deserted me."

When Maria left, Chiara turned the bottle slowly in her hands. The label read "French Lunar Solution."

She called to Mike, who sat on the front step, watching with unseeing eyes as the traffic rolled by.

Chiara put a dollar bill into his pocket. "Go to the fish store on Gratiot and get some fish. Make sure it's fresh. Take Robbie with you."

Putting Robbie's hand into Mike's, she pushed them out the door.

She closed her eyes and uncapped the bottle.

Her mother's face swam before her, an incoherent vision, the eyes moist and sorrowful, pleading.

I want to go home, back to Italy. I want my mother,

the grassy hills and waxy-leafed trees, the song of the birds and the brilliant blue of the Adriatic. I want to be a little girl again, with no anxieties and no frustrations; with no bodies clinging to me for salvation, for existence . . . .

Quickly, she tipped the bottle to her mouth and drank the vile dark liquid.

When the pain came searing through her belly, she welcomed it; gladly she suffered the cramps that clutched her insides. She wanted to suffer. The suffering was obligatory, a required catharsis that would purge the sinful act from her mind as well as her body.

Silent screams tore at her throat, but there was no weeping; there had been too many tears shed already, too many sorrows. Mother of God, was there no end to the depths of her degradation, her wretchedness?

—— 17 ——

A breeze trembled the lace curtains and stirred the warm summer air that washed into the bedroom. Chiara wanted to get up, to go the the window and soak up the sun that filtered in. The sun would heal her. But she was too weak; too weary. There was something she should think about, but she couldn't remember what it was. Michele's face floated in, his palm touched her forehead, his lips grazed her cheek, but when she mustered the strength to lift her hand to him, he was gone.

A hand supported her head and forced a bitter pink liquid past her lips and down her throat. A whispery voice, Flora's voice, wafted in and out along with smells, tea, chicken soup, oranges. Roberto's clatter startled her, causing her eyes to fly open, but he was sternly hushed, and her eyes, so heavy with sleep, closed against her will.

Dreams flitted in and out of her consciousness, dreams of the vibrant blue water and white sand on the Adriatic shore. She saw herself splashing about, and suddenly dark clouds moved in and the waves were higher than her head and she couldn't find the beach. A gray figure swam toward her, a man, and then another man struck out from another direction, but the current drew her farther and farther out. Just as she took her last gasp of air and the sea prepared to claim her, she awakened.

Soon sleep engulfed her again, and the dreams took over. This time she was in pursuit, running, faster and faster, trying to catch something or someone, while the eerie cries of a hundred newborn infants rang in her head, louder and louder, until she had to cover her ears. Her own weak scream awakened her and a cool wet cloth dampened her forehead and a voice, Michele's voice, whispered comforting words in a troubled rasp.

It was dusk now. Had she been in bed all day? She rubbed her forehead and ran her hand to her chest. A light perspiration filmed the flesh between her breasts. Why was she sleeping so long? What day was it? Oh, yes, now she remembered. She had taken the potion and had bled so long, so profusely, that Michele, distraught, called Dr. Catrone.

Ether. The remnants of the sickly-sweet odor remained in the room and she remembered the doctor's voice drifting away, telling her she would be fine, then fading into nothingness.

Now she heard, faintly, the doorbell ringing and Dr. Catrone's voice. A moment later he entered the room with Michele.

"Ah, you're awake," the doctor said, seeing her fluttering eyelids. "Are you better today, *signora?*"

"I'm fine," Chiara said, though her head was heavy and her stomach upset.

The doctor helped her to a sitting position and motioned Michele out.

Chiara said nothing as she watched him draw the stethoscope from his bag. The metal felt cold against her flesh. After his examination, the doctor studied Chiara with keen eyes. His expression betrayed nothing. But he knew, he knew. "You had a scraping," he said.

She had averted her face, unwilling to meet his eyes.

"Does your husband know about this?"

She shook her head.

He sighed, his thick white eyebrows lifting slightly. "These are hard times. One must survive the best he can." Catching sight of her stricken face, he continued, his voice low and sympathetic. "I am not God; I am only a doctor. God sees and forgives."

He patted her cheek. "I'll leave some medication with Michele. I'll come to see you in a day or two." He snapped the heavy black bag closed and waved as he left the room.

Had it been only yesterday, only one day?

Michele stole softly into the room and touched her cheek with a troubled look. "Are you better?"

She mustered a weak smile and nodded. He had something in his hand, an envelope.

"What's that?" Chiara asked.

"A letter. From the Ford Motor Company."

A spark of hope flickered in her heart. "Do you think they're calling you back to work?"

"I don't know." Mike's voice was quiet. For several moments he stared at the envelope as if it were alive, then tore the end off and drew the stiff sheet of paper from it. His eyes raced across the typewritten lines. Wordlessly he handed the letter to Chiara. She managed to make out enough of the words to understand. Report to work Monday morning.

At first he flushed; then his jaw tightened and almost imperceptibly his chin rose. The very air about him seemed to lighten. With this stark typewriten page his life was reclaimed, his future assured, at least for a while. Their siege of discontent was over. He would once again take his rightful place as the head of the household, the patriarch, the wage earner.

Chiara held out her hand and he bent to her and lay in the warm, comforting circle of her arms. They remained that way for several moments, gaining strength from each other. It's one day too late, she thought, tears rolling silently down her cheeks.

One day.

Had she waited one day, yesterday might not have happened. With the knowledge that Mike would be working again, she might not have felt pushed to perform the wretched deed. Now she would have to live with this monstrous sin, this loss of faith, for the rest of her days.

She had already seen the lifting of Mike's spirit, the lessening of the frown that had imprinted permanent ridges in his brow. Work and all it represented—wages, self-respect, independence—would hasten his recovery.

But how had she allowed herself to lose faith, to abandon the moral fortitude of her forebears? She had forgotten the lessons learned as a child from Padre Contrara, and from her parents; the lesson that one must accept the vicissitudes of fate, must believe in the goodness of God. When had she forgotten God's admonition to be like the lilies of the field, his assurance that he would take care of them? *Dio vedi e provedi,* it was said; God sees and provides.

Yet how could one maintain faith when all around there were hungry people with vacant eyes, dirty children wearing ragged clothing, living in hovels that passed for homes? How could one believe that an all-caring Father watched over them with vigilance and sympathy, when so many were starving and homeless?

A tumbling of light footsteps sounded in the room; then Flora's voice whispered, "Come, little one, your mother is resting."

Chiara opened her eyes slowly, wearily, for they were as heavy as if they bore weights. She pushed a loose strand of pale hair from her moist forehead. "No, let him in, Flora."

Robbie leaned as far as he could reach onto the bed and grabbed her hand. "Are you sick, Mama?"

She pulled his hand to her mouth, kissing it, and, grabbing his little rump, boosted him up onto the bed. He nestled against her with a pleased smile, patting her face.

Robbie needed her. Michele needed her. She was their rock, their strength. "No, I'm not sick, Robbie. Not anymore."

She must put this deed behind her, along with the ignominy of her lustful act; submerge it into the deepest part of her memory, into a niche reserved for unspeakable deeds. She must attend to her family, for that was her duty and her destiny. Let the monster of remorse pay solitary visits at night, when sleep would elude her and when her dreams, as they had last night, would reveal shadowy, wraithful infants calling out to her in a sorrowful chorus.

Pushing herself up onto her elbows, she sighed wearily, then hugged Robbie and called out to Flora, "Bring me a cup of coffee, please, Flora."

"Bene, bene," Flora said. "Life goes on, my dear, your family needs you. Italian women are nothing if not resilient."

Chiara let the strong coffee seep into her bones and blood, reviving her. Gingerly she slid from her bed and forced her shoulders back. One day. She'd had one day to mourn this child whose father had no idea of its demise.

Life is a struggle that is endured but never won.

She had one chore she must attend to. The following Saturday she went to St. Elizabeth's Church, a few blocks away. Usually a sense of peace engulfed her when she entered the red-brick, twin-spired building, but not this time. This time her footsteps, echoing through the dim, high-ceilinged structure, seemed to say, "Sinner, sinner."

A suffused, hazy glow entered the church through stained-glass windows. The fact that the pastor, Father Palumbo, a grave, pale second-generation Italian, did not know her, afforded her a shield of anonymity. She thought of Padre Contrara, back in her village, and imagined confessing to him. No, she wouldn't have been able to tell him of her shame. He would die of shock at the depths of degradation into which his pure, sweet child had fallen.

She waited toward the back of the church until the last penitent went into the cubicle. Then she took a deep breath and entered the opposite side. As soon as the little door slid open, she began.

In a low whisper she spilled her sins, the words tumbling out one upon the other, with small gasps of breath in between, so low that he had to say, "What?" and, "Excuse me?" several times, but she talked steadily, right through his interruptions, until she was finished. Then she bowed her head and waited; waited for the wrath of God, justly deserved, to rain down upon her. For long moments his breathing was all that could be heard through the thick cloth in the dark cell.

He cleared his throat. "My child, the worst sin is loss of faith. You must believe that God is everywhere, that he is by your side, that he will forgive you, that he will help you."

Chiara wanted to believe, but if God was everywhere,

how could he allow the poverty and suffering, and how could his children sustain their faith?

"I know by your anguish that you are repentant. God forgives his sinners. You must forgive yourself also." He mumbled the Latin absolution in a singsong voice, then said, "Go and sin no more."

On her way out Chiara genuflected, dipped her fingertips in the basin of warm holy water, and crossed herself. God's forgiveness would be easy to accept. Her own would be harder.

The Fox Theater was crowded with people, all there to see a darling curly-headed moppet, Shirley Temple, in her first movie, *Red-haired Alibi*. Mike had been working for several weeks and insisted they celebrate with a trip to the opulent cinema. He glanced at his wife in the darkened theater. Her beauty warmed his heart. She wore the new red dress with square shoulders that he'd bought her. The dress brought out golden highlights in her hair. He loved touching her thick silky hair, watching her luminous blue eyes light up with laughter. But there hadn't been much laughter lately. He had been concerned about Chiara and perplexed by her moodiness. His return to work hadn't seemed to elevate her spirits the way it had his own. His heart quivered at the thought of the past months. Only in retrospect did he realize the pit in which he had allowed himself to wallow. That would never happen again, he vowed, no matter what path his life might take.

Glancing at his wife more closely, he saw that her eyes were closed. What price had she paid? he wondered. Most probably, he would never really know. She had responded to his misery with strength and love. Only once had she broken down and wept in front of him. Now, taking her hand, he folded it under his arm and held it tightly, caressing it.

She squeezed his hand and whispered, "I don't feel well, Mike. I'm going to the rest room."

He looked alarmed. "Shall I come with you?"

"No, I'll be fine. Just a little headache. Enjoy the picture."

Chiara hadn't felt well since *that* day. She tried to hide her unhappiness from Mike, but she was sure he sensed that something was wrong. Sinking down on a plush seat in the lobby, she took a handkerchief from her purse and dabbed at her brow. She studied the lions guarding the staircase, Italianate in their beauty, and the massive ornate columns gilded with intricate Balinese dancers. Feeling the pressure of a hand on her shoulder, she jumped. She turned to see Stewart's face above her own, observing her with arched brows, unspoken questions in his eyes.

Chiara's heart lurched in her chest. For a moment she couldn't speak. She had expected to see him again, and, yes, had yearned to see him, but at the same time dreaded a confrontation. What would she say to him? *I have destroyed my . . . our child. I'm sorry, but I had no choice?*

"I saw you walking up the aisle and followed you," Stewart said, seating himself next to her. "I've been thinking of you constantly." He glanced significantly at her waist. "Are you all right?"

Chiara swallowed hard and nodded.

His eyebrows arched into a question, but she couldn't bring herself to explain. She had to turn from his eyes, those clear gray eyes that could so easily undo her. Finally she said, "I'm fine. Mike's back to work again, thanks to you. I . . . we appreciate your help."

"It took a bit of doing, but I was glad I could lend a hand."

"You've been very kind." She had to keep talking, so she chattered about inconsequential things, anything to keep from talking about herself. "I saw your picture in the paper—with your wife." The picture, in the society section, was of the Austins and the Edsel Fords. They wore tasteful evening clothes, the men looking dapper, the women stylish; and all sported bright, not-a-care-in-the-world smiles.

A shadow passed over Stewart's face. "Yes . . . we're still together, though nothing's changed." He hesitated, then added, "Her father's helping me through this money crisis."

Money. The world revolved around money. Everyone depended upon it, craved it.

Stewart took her hand and whispered fiercely, "Chiara, what about the baby? What are you going to do about the baby?"

She looked around uneasily, yanking her hand out of his. "I must get back. Mike will be worried."

"The baby, Chiara," he persisted, this time more urgently.

Her eyes shimmered as they filmed over with tears that threatened to spill. *Oh, please, God, don't let me cry. If I start, I'll never stop.* Summoning up a fragment of control, she said with a slight quiver, "There is no baby."

For a moment he looked perplexed. Then he said, "You lost it?"

She looked down, fastening her gaze on the watch fob draped across his vest, and nodded slowly.

Stewart's probing stare held questions Chiara was unwilling to answer. The silence between them lengthened uncomfortably, until finally she turned frank, sober eyes to his, daring him to say something to shame her.

Finally he said very quietly, "I see."

What could he see? He was a man. He had never felt the joy of a fluttering life in his belly, the burden of a new responsibility crowding his brain. She wished wholeheartedly that she could hate Stewart, purge her heart of any desire for him. But it was impossible to do so. Because of that one impetuous act, their lives were inexorably linked.

"I must go now. Mike will be worried." Her voice was clear and low.

"Chiara." A muscle jumped in his temple; his jaw was set. "I didn't want this to happen. I wish things could be different for you . . . for us."

She reached up and touched his cheek. A welling-up of bitterness and tenderness joined in her heart. "We are what we are, two different people living in two different worlds. It was a strange accident that brought us together. What happened, happened, but that will never be again."

Quickly she rose and walked away, her head erect, her shoulders straight, her heels sinking in the deep pile of the dark red carpet. She was thankful that he couldn't see the tears, held in check so long, finally spill over and roll down her cheeks.

A few months later, Chiara lifted the cigar-box lid and slipped in five dollars. Since Mike had returned to work, she had resumed accumulating her little stockpile of dollars. She closed the lid, patted the box as if it were a child doing a good deed, and placed it back in its hiding place beneath a length of bleached muslin. Perhaps they could plan again to buy a house.

As she prepared supper, she hummed a Verdi aria, a secret smile playing on her lips. She thought of the house they would buy. She envisioned a peaceful neighborhood, with spirited children at play, with women taking a breath of air on their front porches, with men striding home spent and weary, but smiling with the knowledge that peace, comfort, and hot meals awaited them.

While the sauce simmered, she went to the mailbox, and was distressed to see a black-bordered letter from home. Ripping it open, she scanned its contents, then sat down to read it thoroughly. When she finished reading, she dropped the thin paper with the flowery scrawl onto her lap and cried silently. Her beloved Zio Nunzio had passed away peacefully, as he had lived, in his sleep. She remembered the excitement of choosing a book from among the dozens lining his library wall, looking at pictures in "forbidden" American magazines. She remembered the long hours passed reading in the grape arbor of his garden, the sun filtering through the thick foliage, making lacy designs on the pages. She remembered his cheery, newsy letters filled with words of hope and encouragement. For all the spiritual nourishment he had given her, his memory would always be alive.

"Mama?" Robbie tugged at her skirt.

Chiara spread a dried chunk of bread with *sugo* and handed it to her son. "He would have loved you," she said, pressing Robbie close to her bosom.

Though it wasn't strictly required, out of respect, Chiara wore black for a month.

Not long after, on a bright October day in 1932, Mike joined an excited throng on Woodward Avenue. He shouldered his way to the edge of the street in order to get a good look at the *Great Man*. Digging his hands into his pockets, he waited until the caravan glided into view. The crowd yelled and cheered when finally the open touring car passed at a measured roll. Franklin Delano Roosevelt sat waving at the crowd, acknowledging the accolades, his head tilted at a rakish angle, a cigarette in a tortoiseshell holder clenched in his prominent white teeth. He was the savior, the messiah.

A stranger nudged Mike. "Think he'll follow through on his promises?"

"At least Roosevelt's offering us a New Deal," Mike said. "Hoover thinks we're all 'rugged individualists' who can be successful with no help from the government."

"He don't know nothing. He ain't seen the unemployment lines and the Hoovervilles." The stranger pushed his hat to the back of his head. " 'Course, he did cut taxes."

"Sure he did—for the wealthy."

The stranger agreed. "That's right. But I don't pay taxes. The tax on nothing is nothing." He laughed at his joke.

"Roosevelt's talking about a jobs program that'll put people to work. He says it's time the government stopped worrying so much about the welfare of business and started thinking about the welfare of the little man, the *forgotten American*."

"If he does what he says, well then, maybe there's hope. I sure would like to be working again." The stranger moved away whistling "Happy Days Are Here Again."

When the last car disappeared, Mike remained rooted to the spot letting the crowd jostle past him, reluctant to move on. Finally, when the crowd had dispersed, he roused himself and went doggedly on his way.

On November 5, when Mike read in the morning *Free Press* that Roosevelt had won the election, he let out a roar that woke the baby and sent Chiara flying from her bed.

"We won," he yelled, claiming it as a personal victory. "We won!"

That evening, as she served Mike and Robbie great bowls of steaming soup, thick with fat vegetables, Chiara said, "Maybe things will get better now." She fussed over her family, making sure there was enough bread sliced, pouring the wine, and finally, assured that all was well, sitting down to her own meal.

"Roosevelt has his work cut out. Last week they cut wages ten cents an hour," Mike said. "But we should see some changes." He shook his finger at his son, saying sternly, "Don't play with the bread; eat it. In Italy only children of kings eat as well as we do." He turned back to Chiara, "Would you believe it, today they fired Walter Reuther."

"Who is this man Reuther you talk so much about?"

"I told you. He's a socialist, a tool-and-die man, but he's not like the others, who want the craft unions kept separate from the rank and file. He's always talking union. He claims until we have a union that takes in the entire plant, we'll be forced to accept only what the bosses want to give."

"Did he do something to get fired?"

"You don't have to do anything to get fired. Maybe they don't like the color of your eyes! Harry Bennett probably fired him because a spy heard him talking about unions. Or maybe because he campaigned for Norman Thomas, the socialist." Mike speared a slice of bread and buttered it thickly. "There were posters all over the plant saying 'Vote for Hoover. A vote for Hoover is a vote for Ford.'

"I thought this was a free country. Nobody can tell you how to vote."

"Henry Ford tries. You'd be surprised how many people think he's a brilliant man."

"You used to think that, not so long ago."

"Well, I know better now. At least he can't follow us into the voting booth to see how we vote. Thank God Roosevelt won." He took the napkin from his knee and wiped his mouth, then cleaned off Robbie's food-smeared hands. "Chiara, I want you to go downtown to the Federal Building and apply for citizenship."

Chiara rolled her eyes. It was a long-standing bone of contention between them. "I will. One of these days."

"You keep saying that, but you don't do it."

In a tentative voice she said, "Maybe we'll go back home, to the old country. What if you lose your job again?"

"You think there's no depression there? All over Europe there's a depression."

"Poor Mr. Reuther," Chiara said, changing the subject. "We know what it is to be out of work. I suppose he's angry."

"Not at all. He says it's a perfect time to see Europe and Russia. He's wanted to work in the Russian factories, to see what they're like." Mike pushed his chair back and stretched. "The Russians need skilled workers since Ford sold the Gorki Auto Works all his old equipment for making the Model A. We're through with it anyway. Lots of Ford technicians are there in Russia now. Ford lent them to Russia to teach them how it's done."

"Stop talking and sit down," Chiara said, pouring thick dark coffee into his mug. "I got a letter from home today and didn't even have a chance to read it yet." It had become her habit to read mail from home at suppertime.

Now she reached into her apron pocket, drew out the letter from her father, and began reading. After inquiring solicitously into their health and expressing his longing to see them, he continued: " 'I don't like writing bad news, but your mother has been feeling poorly, though she wouldn't let me mention it in letters before this. You remember old Dr. Ariella, who was old when I was a child and not always very alert even then. He said I should take your mother to a doctor in Bari, which is what I did, last week. The doctor in Bari said she has a tumor in the womb and it must be removed.' " Chiara fumbled in her sleeve for her handkerchief, and wiped her eyes. The thought of her always robust mother—laughing, yelling, taking charge—now lying in bed, ill, distressed her. For a few moments she couldn't go on.

Mike joined his sympathy with hers, shaking his head sadly and saying, "Poor Luisa. A good woman."

"Don't cry, Mama," Robbie said, his own eyes sad.

"Ah, I can't help it. My dear mother." She reached over and patted Robbie's cheek. "She loves you dearly, Robbie, even though she's never seen you." She gulped and read on. " 'This doctor, who appears very learned, says he does not foresee any difficulties, and has scheduled the operation for February, but of course your mother is very upset, and cries for you. She refuses to have the operation until she sees you and her grandson. "I don't want to die without seeing my firstborn again," she says. She is so fearful she won't survive.' "

Again Chiara snuffled into the handkerchief, then read on. " ' "Tell her," Luisa says, "that I will die happy if I can see my little grandson." We would like to see you all again, but understand that Mike cannot leave his job, especially since he was out of work for so many months. We would be so grateful if God would allow us this wish, to see you and little Berto, for who knows what the future holds. There's a little money from your uncle's inheritance that we could lend you for the fare. Please consider it. With many kisses for you and also Mike and Roberto, Affectionately, Your father.' "

She dropped the letter in her lap and sniffed again, wiping her damp eyes, then heaved a great sigh.

Mike sipped his coffee slowly and thoughtfully.

"Well," she asked, "what do you think?"

"What do *you* think?" he countered. "Do you want to go?"

She pursed her lips. "I want to see my mother. What if . . . what if she should die?" She shook her head in an effort to dispel the ugly thought. "We have a little money saved." It was the house money, dollars that had grown from her stringent saving; by reusing basting thread, by baking bread, by turning worn collars, darning and redarning stockings. It would take many months to replace the savings.

"I don't want to take money from them," Mike said. "Your mother must feel despairing, for Emilio to write like that, to offer a loan."

"You know how my mother is, so dramatic. Maybe it's not so bad." Chiara rose and began clearing the table. "My sewing business is picking up a little. I have two wedding gowns to sew right now. That would help with the expense of a trip." Using her own earnings would lessen her guilt at taking Mike's savings from the bank.

Mike looked pensive. "If your father wants you to, I suppose you should go; he's the patriarch and should be obeyed. *La via vecchia.*" He tapped his spoon against the mug and said thoughtfully, "You've never been truly happy here. Maybe it will do you good to go back home, see things with a fresh eye."

Chiara was taken by surprise. She had tried to make the best of things, had tried to curtail her complaints. Mike was more aware of her feelings than she had supposed.

"If I go, I'd want you with me. Who would take care of you?"

Mike pushed his chair back and stood, smiling. "I can take care of myself. I didn't always have you, remember? I couldn't leave my job; it isn't so secure as it is."

"I can't imagine you cooking and cleaning for yourself. You're so helpless," she chided, patting his cheek.

Mike rolled his eyes, in exasperation. "It's settled, then. By February there should be enough money in the bank. It won't be long before it builds up again." Since he'd returned to work, Mike had saved frantically along with Chiara, putting every spare dollar into savings, determined that Chiara would have a home of her own, away from this rough-and-tumble neighborhood with its noisy trolleys and shouting children.

Chiara put her arms around him. "Thank you, Michele. You're good to me." The thought of going home, of seeing her family and her beloved Italy again, filled her with joy, overriding her worry over her mother and her reluctance to leave Mike.

At the train station, Flora and Maria fussed over Robbie and gave Chiara last-minute instructions while Mike stood in line for tickets.

"Don't forget to bring back dried figs and almonds," Flora said.

Maria joined in. "And some of the good olive oil, first pressing."

"I'll need a special room just for all the goods I'm bringing home," Chiara said in mock annoyance.

Maria touched Chiara's arm. "You must go?"

Chiara looked startled. "The train is waiting! Of course I must go. My mother needs me, and . . . I long to see them all again, Carlo, little Dino, the girls, my father."

"Of course she's going," Flora said. "What do you think we're doing here at the station?"

Maria narrowed her eyes and pouched her lips. Slowly she moved her head from side to side, then picked Robbie up and hugged him fiercely, with a mewling cry. "Goodbye, little one." When he wiggled impatiently, she set him down.

Chiara stiffened. "What is it, Maria?"

"Don't go. Or if you must go, leave the little one here with me, or with Flora."

"I would never leave my son. Are you crazy?"

Flora piped in, a hint of alarm in her voice, "You see something, eh? A dream? What do you see?"

Maria screwed her eyes shut and said nothing.

"What is it, Maria?" Chiara shook her arm.

"Nothing; an illness. Sometimes I'm wrong. Why can't you leave him here?"

"I can't go home to my family without Robbie." Sometimes Maria went too far with her wild imaginings.

Mike strode up to them, waving the tickets. "Come on, they're loading up. Better get on before I change my mind." He swung Robbie up on his shoulder and hoisted a large suitcase with his free hand.

Chiara preceded him up the narrow train steps and turned to wave a last good-bye to her friends.

Flora waved madly, saying, "Good-bye, good-bye. Be a good boy, Robbie, and don't forget your Aunt Flora."

Mike enveloped his wife and child in one last bear hug and smothered them with noisy kisses.

Maria stood quietly, watching them go, her face expressionless.

—— 18 ——

The first glimpse of her father brought tears to Chiara's eyes. He stood at the station, scanning the train windows as they rolled by, his straw hat in his hand, his dear face a little more sun-beaten, his hair a bit grayer. Before Chiara and Robbie were off the last step, her father swooped them up in a tight embrace.

"Ah, what a fine little man," her father said, plastering kisses all over Robbie's face.

"It's good to be home again," Chiara said when he released them.

Her father hugged Robbie to him again, but the child hung back, frightened by the strange man with the large mustache.

"He'll be used to me in no time," Emilio said, chucking the child under the chin.

When he'd settled them and their luggage into the cart,

Emilio snapped the whip, and the mule, Figaro, trotted away from the train station.

Chiara drank in the sweet fresh air of her homeland and squinted toward the sun. "There's no doubt—in Italy, even in February the sun is brighter, the sky clearer, the water bluer than any place else in the world."

Robbie mimicked his mother, sighing and lifting his face toward the sun. Emilio, delighted with the child, amused him by singing a song.

"Have they narrowed the roads?" Chiara asked when the cart finally turned down the familiar stone-paved corso toward the piazza. Everything seemed strangely small as if in the intervening four years a shrinking process had settled upon the town.

"Nothing changes here," her father answered as they pulled up to her old home.

Luisa, waiting at the door, wept profusely at the sight of her daughter and clung to her, saying over and over, *"Figlia mia, bella figlia."* She released Chiara and smothered Roberto with wet, noisy kisses.

Chiara's brothers and sisters clustered around, all speaking at once. The shrinking hadn't extended to them. They had shot up so that she hardly recognized them. Chiara basked in the warmth of their welcoming love, which included the bewildered Roberto.

In no time, Dino, a chubby toddler when Chiara had left, and now a thin, energetic seven-year old, had coaxed Roberto from behind Chiara's skirt.

"Gabriella, you're so pretty," Chiara said, holding her at arm's length. Her sister was a rounded, peach-skinned thirteen, a little shy, not quite comfortable in her newly burgeoning flesh. "And you, Tonina, so sweet, so tall." An elongated replica of her mother, Tonina chattered and giggled and tried her best to lure Berto away from Dino.

Missing was her brother Carlo, who was fulfilling his military duty. Chiara missed his presence keenly.

"I despair of his ever coming home again," Luisa said with a little sneer. "He is spellbound by the fancy big city."

When supper was over and a quiet had settled over the village, Chiara threw a shawl over her shoulders and sat on the balcony with her mother.

"I've been so worried, Mama," Chiara said, reaching over to hug her mother. "How are you feeling? You look so well."

"I've suffered, daughter." Luisa's eyebrows arched and her head tilted in a resigned nod. "There has been too much bleeding, woman troubles—from a tumor the doctor says. But just seeing you has made me forget my ailments." She brightened immediately. "And you? Michele treats you well?"

"Yes, he is a good husband."

"It seems so. Such a lovely dress," Luisa exclaimed, rubbing the material between her thumb and index finger.

Chiara lifted the skirt toward her mother. "It's rayon, and the skirt is cut on the bias."

"Is everything so fancy in America? *Viva l'America.*" she dropped the skirt. "Have you forgotten *la via vecchia?*"

Chiara laughed, "No, of course not. But sometimes we have to mix the old with the new."

A few days later, Luisa prepared to leave with Emilio for the hospital in Bari. "You will be mother to the little ones while I'm gone," she admonished Chiara, amid her sniffling and prayerful lamentations. "I may never return."

"Dio mio," said Emilio, raising his eyes upward with a pained expression, "the doctor said you will be fine, that it is not a serious operation."

In her most dramatic voice Luisa said, "No one knows what's in store. I've heard so many tales of doctors who take out the wrong organs. May the merciful Lord spare me." She made a sign of the cross.

Emilio shook his head in exasperation and hurried her out the door. "Don't worry about her," he said to Chiara as he hoisted the battered cardboard suitcase. "As soon as I have news I will place a telephone call to my friend Giuseppe at the village hall, and he will get the message to you."

Late the following day a distinguished gray-haired gentleman came to the house with a message from her father. The operation, he told them, had gone well. A small tumor had been removed and Luisa was resting comfortably. The doctor had assured Emilio that there would be a speedy recovery and no more problems.

The rooster's trumpeting at dawn had frightened Roberto the first few days, but to Chiara it was as welcome as an old friend. In no time the domestic routines once again became habit: the making of bread, the hauling of water from the fountain, cooking at the fireplace, the distasteful job of carting the urns of excrement out to the road for the twice-a-day collection.

In a week Roberto was speaking words in Italian; in two weeks he spoke complete sentences in the dialect that Chiara had taken great pains to drop.

One day she and Roberto rode the cart with her father, out to the fields, to see the additional five hectares of land he had purchased with his portion of Nunzio's estate. The fertile land yielded good crops and he had to employ a laborer to help him work it. Chiara was gratified to see that life was somewhat less burdensome for her father.

In ten days her mother was brought home in a hired car. "You see, it takes being ill to live like the rich," she exclaimed as Emilio helped her into the house.

Luisa's recuperation period was a time of peace and happiness for the two women. While Luisa was waited on by her daughter, she entertained Roberto with old children's tales. Changing her voice for the various characters, Luisa recited Chiara's favorite story of an ant who lived in a church and met a tragic fate when he fell into a pot of soup.

Chiara, washing dishes, smiled at the sound of the familiar tale. "You tell it exactly like you did when I was that age." She went to the door and tossed the dishwater out onto the street. After storing the supper dishes on an open shelf, Chiara sat next to her mother. "It's so good to be home. If only Michele were here, it would be perfect."

"Chiara, much as I want you to stay, you must think of leaving in a week or two," Luisa said, nodding in a sage and knowing manner. "Your husband is a young man with a young man's needs, and his wife should be nearby. Your place is with him."

Chiara colored, knowing the "needs" to which her mother referred. "Yes, you're right, of course. I miss Michele." She thought of him every day, wondered if he missed her and what he was doing. "I'll have Father book passage for me. I'll leave in three weeks."

"Tell me again how it is in America. Is there food for everyone?"

"It's like everyplace else. When there's work, there's money, and everything is fine. When Michele wasn't working, it was terrible." She wouldn't burden her mother with tales of their past woes. It was better to put the bad times behind her. She touched her mother's arm. "But now we're happy."

Luisa snorted. "Happy. What's that? You try to survive, that's all. You thank God you're alive."

"That's the old way of thinking, *la via vecchia*. There should be more to life than just surviving."

Luisa shook her head. "You're young. What do you know of suffering?"

Chiara didn't answer. How could she tell her mother of their misfortunes, of Michele's sickness of the mind, of her own shameless acts? No, it would break Luisa's heart to know these things.

Luisa went on, "I should never have let you spend so much time reading books when you were young. It put strange ideas in your head."

"This way of life is the only way you know," Chiara said quietly. "There are others who live differently, who don't work so hard and long. Life should contain a little joy too."

Luisa shook her head with an expression that clearly implied her daughter was not too bright. "I try to find a little joy in my children, and so should you. You need more *bambini* in your life."

"Oh, yes, we want more children. Mike wants daughters now that he has a son."

Luisa sighed. "Children are a joy, but they bring pain too. Like when you left home." She picked up a pillowcase that she had made for Gabriella's dowry, and commenced embroidering on its border. "You'll learn. Life is a battle," she said.

The next morning Luisa greeted her sleepy-eyed grandchild as he stumbled to the table. *"Buona mattina,* sleepyhead." She pulled him to her lap. "What a beautiful boy. He looks so healthy. Look at those roses in his cheeks."

Chiara left the fireplace, where she stirred a pot of *polenta*, and went to Robbie. His eyes were bright above ruddy cheeks, but he seemed lethargic, and that morning he'd slept later than usual, long after the rooster's crow.

"His cheeks are too red. He must be sick," Chiara said, feeling his forehead. "He's a little warm."

With a large wooden spoon she scooped *polenta* into a bowl and laced it with milk, but Robbie sat in a slump, a small pout on his lips. "I don't want it," he said.

"What? It isn't like you, your belly's always gurgling and asking for more food," Chiara teased, poking a finger into his stomach.

Luisa lifted Robbie to her lap and said in a plaintive voice, "What is it, little one? Are you sick?"

"No, I'm just sleepy," Robbie answered, snuggling against his grandmother's bosom. "And my head hurts," he added, yawning.

"What's wrong, Berto?" Dino said, stooping to Robbie's level, with his hands on his knees. "Don't you want to go out and play?"

"All right," Robbie said, brightening somewhat. He slipped from the chair and allowed himself to be led outdoors.

"He's not himself," Chiara said. "He doesn't seem to have any pep."

"He'll feel better in the fresh air." Luisa waved away Chiara's worry.

He did seem improved the next day, though not as rambunctious as usual. But the following day he awakened with a temperature which increased gradually until evening. When he fell asleep hours before his usual bedtime, Chiara became alarmed.

"Maybe we should get Dr. Ariella," Chiara said, pressing her palm against his forehead. "He feels very warm."

"If he's not better in the morning, we'll get the doctor," Luisa said.

When Chiara put her cheek against Robbie's the next morning, it felt cooler than it had the previous night, and he appeared a bit livelier. Luisa drew the thermometer, a precious possession, out of its case, shook it down with four quick snaps of her wrist, and handed it to Chiara. Gently Chiara placed the thermometer under Robbie's arm.

In a few minutes she withdrew it, rolling it around to catch sight of the silver thread. "One hundred. Not too bad. How do you feel, Robbie?"

"I feel fine." But his eyes were listless, his skin dry.

During the next night, Robbie's crying woke his mother.

When she lit the oil lamp, she saw a red trickle from his nose, and bright red spots staining his white nightshirt. After Chiara washed and changed him, she stroked his warm head until he fell asleep, resolving to get the doctor the next morning.

Early the next day, while Luisa hovered over them, Chiara again took Robbie's temperature. She held and rocked him, singing a little song that usually made him laugh. But now he lay inert in her arms, forcing a small smile to his dry, peeling lips.

Luisa took the thermometer and squinted as she held it to the light, rotating it. Finally she proclaimed, "It's one hundred and two. That does it. Tonina," she shouted, "go tell the doctor we need him. Little Berto is sick. And don't play around in the street, or you'll get this." She waved her fist in the air.

Tonina returned with the message that the doctor would come that afternoon.

Robbie ate little during the day. When Chiara bathed him, she was alarmed to see small rosy spots on his abdomen.

The sun was setting when Doctor Ariella arrived, shuffling in with stooped shoulders. His cheekbones, prominent in a sallow face, shone white. How old he is, Chiara thought. Does he still have all his faculties? Will he be able to treat Robbie?

Though lean and gaunt, the doctor still looked distinguished in his neat black suit and spotless white shirt. He bowed to the women, saying, *"Buon giorno, signore,"* then kissed Chiara's cheek. "I remember you as a child, Chiara. You have grown into a beautiful woman." Then he answered her unspoken question. "I am old, but I have seen many things in my lifetime, almost every illness known to man." He placed his black bag on the table. "So now you are an American. And do you like America?"

Chiara endured the small talk, hiding her impatience. "I like it well enough, but I am still an Italian."

"Brava," he said, nodding, a pleased smile on his pale lips. "I always wanted to go to America," he declared, "but it's too late for me now. Death is snapping at my heels, an old man like me."

The coffee gurgled at the fireplace, and Luisa set cups out on the table.

"The coffee later," he said to Luisa. "Let me see the young gentleman first."

When the doctor entered the bedroom, Robbie stirred, and his frightened eyes darted to his mother.

Chiara took his hand and patted it. "It's all right, this is our good friend the doctor. He is going to make you well."

"*Sì, sì,* I will make you well, little one," the doctor said, placing a thermometer under Robbie's arm.

"Hm," he said a few minutes later as he read the slender glass rod with old, watery eyes. He flashed a light back into Roberto's throat. "Let me see your tongue."

As he peered into Robbie's throat, he said quietly, "His throat looks all right, but regard the tongue, Chiara. See how brown it is?"

His tongue looked coated in chocolate, with reddened edges. "Yes, but what does it mean?" Chiara asked in a tight voice.

Dr. Ariella turned back the bedcovering and lifted Robbie's nightshirt, exposing the pale, flaccid body. The child stiffened as the doctor's gnarled hands touched the rash on his trunk and probed his abdomen with sure, knowing fingers. Robbie coughed, his eyes beseeching his mother.

"It's all right, Robbie," she said with a forced smile, pressing his hand.

"You see, the abdomen is distended. Has he been coughing?" the doctor asked.

"Just a little."

"Some nosebleeding?"

"Yes, last night."

He shook his head almost imperceptibly as he recovered Robbie. Shuffling into the kitchen, the doctor ran his hand over his jaws and chin.

Chiara followed at his heels. *"Che cosa?"* She twisted her hands anxiously while the doctor lowered himself wearily into a chair. He poured milk and two teaspoons of sugar into the coffee Luisa had poured, then stirred it deliberately, as if it took all of his concentration. He cleared his throat and spoke very quietly.

"In America, with your good sanitation system, children are not exposed to certain germs and therefore do not build up immunities."

The women hung on his every word.

"Now Roberto has come into contact with these germs and his body cannot resist, and so he has contracted a disease."

Chiara stiffened. "What kind of disease?"

Dr. Ariella coughed, covering his mouth. "Typhoid fever."

Chiara's hands flew to her mouth, stifling her shriek. Luisa cried out, *"Madonna!"*

The old man pushed himself up from his chair. "I can give you some medication, but . . ."

"Will he get well?" Chiara asked, her eyes pleading.

"We hope and we pray. That's all one can do." He handed her a bottle of amber liquid and snapped his bag closed. At the door he hesitated. "I'll be back tomorrow."

The next day Robbie developed diarrhea, and his fever rose to one hundred and three. Chiara sponged him down, singing a song to mask her worry, then sat and rocked him while Luisa fingered her rosary beads and mumbled Ave Marias. That night Chiara wrote a long tearstained letter to Michele, telling him of the illness and of her fears. "If only you were here, I could bear it. I'm so afraid. I cry myself to sleep each night."

The next day and the next, Robbie's temperature climbed. Dr. Ariella made daily visits, but shook his head sadly and offered them scant words of hope. "Sometimes they rally," he said. "Keep sponging him down. Give him the medication and aspirin. I'll come tomorrow."

Luisa sat in her chair next to the window murmuring repetitious prayers in a mournful whisper.

The diarrhea continued and Robbie's temperature climbed steadily the next day and the next until it reached one hundred and five. Frantic, Chiara sponged him with a cool linen towel, which quickly absorbed his body heat. In and out of delirium, Robbie called for his father and muttered unintelligible words. Flailing, he cried out in terror at some frightening dream. He remained in that condition for several days; then suddenly his temperature dropped.

Relieved, half-dead with fatigue and worry, Chiara fell to her knees and whispered a prayer of thanks.

Finally, that night she allowed herself a peaceful sleep on the narrow cot next to Robbie's. Just before dawn, hearing him moan, she shot out of bed. "Mama's here, what is it, Robbie?"

As she lifted him onto her lap, his frail arms reached around her neck. She rocked him and dozed for a moment, then slowly realized his body had grown limp and heavy.

She put her cheek to his mouth, anticipating the warm breeze of his breath. She felt nothing. "Robbie! Wake up!" she commanded. She shook him and screamed, "Robbie!"

The small white form shook like a rag doll, but there was no response. Frantically she called his name again and again, then screamed for her mother. "Mama, Mama, my baby!"

Luisa ran into the room, her long hair, unwound, trailing behind her. She snatched the child from his mother and with eyes wide in disbelief stared at the inert form that hung lifelessly in her arms.

The sun beat down relentlessly, though the air was cool. Six men carried the casket on their shoulders from the church to the cypress-edged cemetery where the grave had been dug. Townspeople gathered around the casket. Two youngsters sat on the stone fence surrounding the graveyard. Chiara lifted her heavy head and looked around her. So many people. Who were all these people? Many she recognized, but others were strangers. They had come yesterday to the house to kiss the child lying white and still on the bed, and to weep and curse the fates as they listened to the oft-repeated litany of the events that took his life.

Michele should be here. She needed his strong arms around her, needed to share her tears and grief. How would he manage his own grief without the finality of saying good-bye to his beloved son? Alone, Michele's all alone, reading and rereading the insufferable wire, probably tearless and angry in his solitary mourning. No, Flora would be there, making him eat, giving him coffee; and Dino and Fredo, in their awkward way, saying sorrowful words, Italian words, soft words that flow and ebb with sadness, that lilt with sympathy.

Words. She had heard so many words, so many wailing women, mourners in black dresses, with black shawls that half-covered their anguished faces. Mourners summoning up their own sad memories in order to do justice to their maudlin duty.

Emilio was beside himself. All his own children were healthy, strapping youngsters, but his grandchild . . . gone to an early, undeserved grave. He was to blame, he said, he had insisted that Chiara come home. She never should have left in the first place; then this misery would have been averted. *Miseria, miseria.*

Luisa had taken immediately to her bed, and spent half a day in weeping, then arose, gathered her strength around her like a large cloak, and comforted her firstborn. Chiara's brother and sisters were uncharacteristically quiet, unable to voice their anguish.

Now Father Contrara sprinkled holy water over the small casket while his solemn voice chanted the Latin words that would guard this innocent soul on its journey.

Slowly, slowly, the casket was lowered into the ground, while the mourners wailed and cried.

Chiara fell to her knees and buried her face in her hands. Her sobs shook her thin body. *Blood of my blood, heart of my heart. My firstborn son. Gone. Disappearing into the earth.* Two men took up shovels and in alternating rhythm tossed dirt on top of the casket, while the ululations continued. Soon the mourners turned and made their way slowly back to town.

The black soil covers his wooden home, his eternal dwelling place. My heart is buried here in the Italian soil, with my child. Good-bye, my heart. Chiara's mother and father gently pulled her upright and supported her as they made their plodding way down the hill, three huddled figures in black.

Packing for the return trip seemed a monumental chore. Chiara's fingers closed over the blue rompers she had sewn for Roberto. Burying her face in the cloth, she stifled a sob and crumpled into a chair.

Her mother gently took the clothing from Chiara and set it aside. "I wish you would stay longer, daughter. You need your family to comfort you. It's been just one day . . ."

"No, I must go. I'm Michele's family." Chiara stood and straightened her shoulders. "He needs me."

When the packing was finished, Chiara and her mother stood locked in an embrace for several minutes, both crying silent tears, comforting each other with pats and caresses. Finally her father pried them apart. "It's time to go. Come, the train won't wait."

At the station Emilio twisted his hat in his hands. The train whistle announced its arrival in a shrill burst.

"I should never have insisted you come home," he said miserably.

"How could you know, Papa? It wasn't your fault."

He seemed relieved to have her forgiveness. Bending, he kissed her cheek. "Now you must be strong for Michele."

Chiara said nothing. What good, after all, were words? She had heard so many words; words that were meant to comfort: "He is with God" . . . "He is in a better place" . . . "He is an angel now." The words meant nothing.

The porthole was a large eye peering at her in its brilliant whiteness. Her head ached from the light. What day was it? Had she lain in bed the entire trip? No, she remembered being led to the deck and bundled gently into a deck chair. Someone had tucked a blanket around her and put a book into her hand. Who was that coming in and out? Someone in white; a nurse, pushing food between her lips, broth and tea. *You must eat*, she'd said. *You must live. You are a young women and will have other children.* But other children would not be Roberto. What potion was given her that made her head fuzzy, her eyelids dry and heavy?

Did it matter if she lived or died? Her heart was dead already, the rest could die too. Had it been eleven days ago that she stood at the graveside, keening in her grief? It seemed only moments ago. How was Michele? How had he reacted when the cable arrived? She visualized him opening the front door, puzzled at the uniformed messenger. Then alarmed, knowing a costly message such as this would be sent only in an emergency. She imagined him ripping open the message of death. Did he pound on the walls? Did he curse? Did he cry out for his son, for his wife?

He needed her. She must be strong for him. And she needed him too, dear God, how she needed him.

*　　*　　*

"We are docking soon, Mrs. Marcassa. You must get dressed." The voice was a soft one in a soft face, wearing a soft dress. Calm, assured. A nurse.

"Here, my dear. It's coffee. Come, I'll help you sit up." Her face was small and pointed, her eyes pale and kind.

Chiara's arms were leaden. Lifting them took all her strength. The nurse propped pillows behind her head and put the cup to her mouth.

"You have to pull yourself together now, Mrs. Marcassa."

"My baby's dead." Chiara's voice was toneless.

The nurse turned her head away for a moment and shook her head. "Yes. Your baby's dead, my dear," she said softly.

She rustled some clothing out of the tiny closet and laid it on the bed. "As soon as you finish the coffee, get dressed. I don't know why the doctor insisted on giving you that medication for so long. It dulls your reality. You're healthy and strong; now you must face the rest of your life."

The nurse went to the door and stood for a moment, then went back to the bed and hugged Chiara. In Chiara's trembling hands the coffee cup rattled against the saucer, chink, chink.

Why had misfortune stalked her, dogged her steps. Was she so deserving of this, the worst of punishments?

Slowly she donned the clothes the nurse had laid out for her, the woolen suit of periwinkle blue that Mike had picked out for the trip. He loved her in blue. "They'll think you're a rich American," he'd said when she had balked at the price tag. Now she buttoned the skirt and it drooped to her hips. Her hipbone felt sharp through the cloth.

She stood unsteadily and placed her feet into shoes that felt too roomy. Exhausted from the effort it took to dress herself, she dropped heavily to the bed.

Michele sprinted to the cabin, a huge bouquet of fresh flowers in his arms, anxious, unsure in what state he would find his wife. He rattled the doorknob, then opened the door and burst inside. He stood there for a moment staring at his beloved wife. Her face was pearly, her lips white; her eyes, so large in her thin face, were ringed with dark circles. Taking one giant step, he threw the flowers on the bed and then they were in each other's arms. She collapsed against him and he could hear, from deep in her throat, a wailing that gathered force and erupted in an unearthly keening.

Shivers ran down his spine at the sound. He picked up her wraithlike body easily in his strong arms. She was so slight, so fragile; he was afraid her bones would crack at the slightest pressure. Sitting on the bed, he gathered her close, rocking her back and forth, back and forth, listening to the convulsive, heartrending sobs bursting from her. He had been so afraid she would be mad with grief that his own misery was submerged. But now his own sobs joined with hers and the pent-up tears tumbled freely down his cheeks, until finally the crying subsided and they were both spent.

"Our son, our baby." Chiara turned wet, stricken eyes to Mike. He kissed her full on the lips, tasting the salt, drinking in strength from her love.

"You're going to be all right, eh?" he said. "You're strong. Italian women are strong."

"I'll be all right," she said, for the first time believing it. "But you, Michele, how are you? I've thought only of myself, of my loss. At least I had my family around me. You had no one." She patted his cheek. "My poor Michele."

"Now that you're back home, I'll be fine."

"Why did I take our son and leave you? It was folly. My place was with you. I knew it; but selfishly, I went home. The fates are against us."

"No, don't blame yourself, or the fates. You went for a good reason, and I allowed it. Never, never blame yourself, or your life will be a hell."

"But that horrible disease would never have happened here. Why has God deserted us?"

"Stop this," Michele said, putting his hand over her mouth. "We'll have another child. We'll have many children."

"But not Robbie. Robbie's gone. He's gone."

— 15 —

The high-pitched whir of the sewing machine was somehow comforting. Chiara's feet pedaled rhythmically, ceaselessly, her head dipping forward as, mesmerized, she watched the needle darting through the cloth in a blur of movement. Her fingers deftly fed the yards of frothy white tulle that billowed around the machine into the hungry needle. The wedding dress was for Fredo's eldest daughter, Marcella. The job had been thrust on her soon after she returned from Italy, and she hadn't wanted to take it on, a big job like that. But Mike, for once, urged her to do it.

He was right. If felt good to be busy; busy mind, busy feet, busy fingers, too busy to dwell on . . . But there! She was doing it again, thinking of Roberto. Fishing into her sleeve, she withdrew a handkerchief and wiped away an errant tear. Flora and Maria had been staunchly supportive through the agonizing past three months; had said, in an effort to comfort her, "You'll have another child." It was scant comfort.

Still, she realized she did want another baby, and so did Mike, but their frequent and tender lovemaking hadn't produced any results. What if it didn't happen? More tears gathered in the corners of her eyes. She could have had another, Stewart's child, but . . . Was God punishing her? Had her deed destroyed something vital inside her? Was she destined to remain childless? She shook her head, banishing the disturbing thoughts, and rocked her feet on the grilled pedal as if the devil himself were after her. She mustn't think, she mustn't think . . . .

She was startled by Mike's strong arms folding around her chest, cupping her breasts. Her movements came to an abrupt halt.

208

"Come to bed, Chiara," he said gently. "You can't keep driving yourself like this."

"I promised Marcella I'd have this ready by tomorrow."

He wore a concerned frown. "I thought Flora and Maria were going to help you."

"They're helping me with the seven bridesmaids' dresses. But I'm the only one who can do justice to the wedding gown." She gave the wheel a turn and pumped the pedal. "I'm almost finished."

"You'll exhaust yourself." Mike had been solicitous since her return, and hovered over her, despite his own heartbreak.

"That's what I want to do, exhaust myself. I want to fall asleep as soon as I touch the pillow. That way I won't think about . . . things."

Mike tipped her chair on its back legs and turned it, then gathered Chiara up into his arms. "I'll give you other things to think about," he said gruffly.

Chiara nestled her head against Mike's neck and forced herself to relax against his powerful chest.

"You must stop this grieving, Chiara, and the over-working. Look how thin you've become." He kissed the collarbone protruding at her neck's edge.

"I know. I'm trying. I'm much better, don't you think? I don't cry all day anymore."

Mike placed her on the bed and lay beside her. She touched his cheek. "You too, Mike. You work too hard." There were new furrows across his brow, and flecks of gray in his hair. Though his body was hard and powerful, she wondered how much abuse it could take, with the long hours of constant toil. His strong, handsome features softened at her concern, and he stroked her arms, then undressed her slowly, admiring her soft flesh. When he kissed her, her fatigue seemed to dissipate, and she yearned her body toward him, eager for his love. His gentle caresses stoked her desire until, at last, he entered her welcoming body. Perhaps this time, she thought, it will be a baby. Please, God.

Afterward, content and exhausted, she fell asleep in his arms.

A few weeks later Chiara listened to Penny's chatter as they waited for the elevator in Hudson's department store. Chiara loved shopping at Hudson's. Sometimes she would take the elevator and stop at every floor, from the first to the tenth, just to look at the wonderful assortment of goods available to those who had the means to buy. Curved glasses with long stems, dishes painted with feathery flowers, furniture fit for kings, shimmery gowns of every hue. She promised herself that someday she would serve Mike wine from a delicate and elegant stemmed glass. Someday she would buy all new furniture to befit the grand house for which they were saving diligently. But today there wouldn't be much time for browsing.

In the bridal department Penny scrutinized each gown. "This one," she said finally, with a pleased smile.

Chiara examined the dress closely, trying to memorize the details. "Remember these tucks, and how the collar stands up in the back," she whispered to Penny.

In the yard goods department Penny prattled as they meandered among the various bolts of material. "I know it ain't a good time to get married, but we've waited so long, and it seems like there's never going to be a good time for it, so we're just going to do it."

"Dio vedi e provedi," Chiara said. "It means God sees and provides." Even as she said it, she wondered at its verity. How many times had she been in need? God had provided, eventually, but at what cost? Had he been testing their faith during those trying times? It wasn't good to question too closely.

Leafing through a pattern book, they found the one that most resembled the finished gown Penny had admired.

"Do you think we're doin' the right thing, getting married?" Penny asked, her usually lively green eyes turning serious.

"If you love him, then you should get married." Chiara thought of her own arranged marriage; love hadn't been a requirement. Still, a love had grown between them, surely and steadily, despite their trials. "Jimmy has a steady job, doesn't he?"

"Yeah, and he's got some money saved, but I worry about his job, you know? Sometimes I think it's dangerous. He don't tell me what he does. He hates to talk about his work, but I know a lot of people don't like him."

The salesclerk, a neat lady in a dark dress collared and

cuffed in white, lugged to the counter the bolt of creamy white satin Penny had picked. She flopped it over and over on the counter with a soft thud and measured the cloth against a yardstick. "It sure is pretty, honey," the clerk said with an admiring glance. "Gee, you'll make a swell bride."

Back in her kitchen, Chiara took a pad and pencil and made a sketch of the dress she and Penny had seen at Hudson's. Painstakingly she added and deleted details according to Penny's instructions.

"Perfect," Penny squealed when at last the sketch matched her vision. "Do you think you can make the veil too? I want little flowers and pearls around the top, and a train."

"Yes, I have just the veil in mind." Chiara narrowed her eyes, imagining the finished product. "It will have lace along the edge to match the lace inset at the bodice."

"You're so clever, you ought to have a shop of your own." Penny leaned across the table, her thin legs twisting together like a vine. "Someplace where you could put a couple of your dresses in the window, so people would see the nice things you can do. A place near Grosse Pointe, where the money is."

"How I would love that." Even Stewart had once suggested she open a shop, but she had all but scrapped that fantasy. "I used to dream about it."

"I suppose it would take a lot of money."

"I guess it would. But I'm not thinking about that right now. I have other things on my mind." Chiara smiled a sweet secret smile and hugged her waist protectively.

"Chiara! Are you pregnant?"

Chiara's eyes sparkled with happiness. "Yes, I think so."

Penny hugged her friend. "Oh, honey, that's swell. What does the Sheik think?"

Chiara laughed at the playful name Penny had given Mike. "I haven't said anything yet. I want to be very sure." She didn't want to risk raising Mike's hopes, only to have them dashed. Her eyes clouded over. "He wants a son so badly."

Chiara unfolded and smoothed out the crinkly pattern on the kitchen table. When she'd made the adjustments according to her sketch, she spread the material and pinned the altered pattern to it. The scissors cut cleanly through the tissue and the satin material with a swish-swish.

"Are you still working at Kroger's?" Chiara asked.

"Nah, I got canned. I'm at Motor Products Company. They finally hired me after I went there every day and waited around the gates with a hundred others. A foreman would come out and say, 'I need you, you, and you, and the rest of you go on home.'' I figured one of these days it'd be my turn. I kept a smile pasted on my face, as if I thought the foreman was cute. Sure enough, after a week, I got a job. I feel sorry for anyone over forty—they get passed over every time."

"It's not fair, is it?" Chiara gently folded the cut-out sleeve section and set it aside. "Do you like the new job?"

"It's boring. I screw in screws. All day long, I screw in screws. And that ain't the worst of it. In order to keep my job, I gotta put up with the foreman's damn pawing. I do a fast dance to keep out of his way."

Chiara threw her hands in the air, an indignant expression clouding her face. "That's terrible. I don't like it, a young girl like you having to go through that embarrassment just to make a living. I wish you could find a better job."

"I just told you. There ain't no jobs." Penny removed pins from the piece Chiara had cut out and punched them into a pincushion. "It was okay for the first couple of days; then he starts making remarks."

"What kind of remarks?"

"Oh, you know, 'When we gonna get together, babe?' and he moves his slitty eyes up and down my body. It makes me shiver. What a person has to go through just to work!"

"Can't you tell the big boss?"

"Ha! He don't care. He probably does the same thing."

Chiara clucked her disapproval. *"Que animale!* It's degrading."

"Yeah, well, I gotta work," Penny said defensively.

Chiara patted her arm. "I know. I understand how it is. But it's so unfair."

When the cutting was finished, Chiara folded the sections and put them in her sewing room. "I'll start first thing in the morning. Come next week. I'll have it all basted, and we'll see how it fits."

She would make this gown special for Penny, with elegant touches: seed pearls at the neckline, the best lace at the wrists. Mr. Nussbaum, who owned the five-and-dime on Mack, had told her how to get lace and material from a manufacturer for a lot less money. If her business continued to expand as it had been, she could save money by purchasing several bolts at a time.

As she closed the door behind Penny, Chiara felt a sudden wave of nausea. This was the sign she had been waiting for. Please, God, let it be a baby, she prayed.

The work on Penny's dress had gone well, though Penny had come for the first fitting three weeks late. She hadn't come back at all for the final one, and with the wedding just two weeks away, Chiara was a bit worried. She decided to go to Penny's house as soon as she finished the mother-of-the-bride dress she was currently working on. Her mouth full of pins, she hemmed up the bias-cut dusty-rose skirt that fell to the floor in soft swirls. From the same material she cleverly fashioned a flower to place at the shoulder. It seemed that suddenly Chiara's services were in great demand. That so many families were willing to spend large amounts of cash on wedding celebrations amazed Chiara. It was a sign that the depression was not quite as devastating as it had been. Of course, those who worked steadily simply hadn't felt the effects of the depression. "Them that has, gits," Laurelia had said, and it seemed to be true.

Chiara put on her hat, skewering it in place with a long hatpin, and proceeded to Penny's house.

Penny's mother, a slender woman with faint freckles across her nose, answered the door with a soft drawl. "Why, do come in, Chiara. Penny's feeling poorly lately. She's down on her back."

Penny's mother was unsmiling, with thinning faded red hair bobby-pinned off her face, but Chiara could see the echoes of a former beauty. Penny's father had brought his family to Detroit from Kentucky fifteen years ago in search of a "lucrative" factory job. He had just recently returned to work after a two-year layoff.

"I thought I heard your voice, Chiara," Penny said, greeting her with a wan smile.

"Penny, I was worried about you. I expected you weeks ago."

"Y'all go on in the front room and I'll bring some tea." Penny's mother turned on the flame under a kettle.

"Wait until you see the dress, Penny. It's just beautiful. Flora embroidered flowers at the neckline and I sewed in the pearls." Chiara opened the box and drew out the gown, waiting expectantly for Penny's gush of excitement.

But Penny sat perfectly still, a small frown creasing her freckle-dotted brow. Noting her pallor, Chiara asked, "Have you been sick?"

Penny shook her head. "Nah, I'm okay."

"Come on, then, let's try it on."

Penny stood quietly as Chiara slipped the dress over her head and fastened the row of small buttons down the back. "You'll be a beautiful bride, with that hair, like an Italian sunset, so red." She tugged and coaxed the buttons toward their loops. "My, I'll have to move the buttons, Penny. Either I measured wrong or you're getting fatter."

When Penny's mother entered, she set the tray down and put her hands to her cheeks, shaking her head with pleasure. "Lord a mercy, if that ain't the purtiest dress I ever did see!"

While her mother poured tea, Penny forced a smile. As soon as she left, Penny slumped to the sofa and burst into tears, hiding her face in her hands.

Chiara stared at her friend. "What's wrong?"

"Nothing," Penny burbled behind her hands.

Chiara put her arm around her friend's shoulder. "Something must be wrong with you. Tell me." It could just be pre-wedding nerves, but it wasn't like Penny to cry like this. She was strong, tough. Chiara handed her the tea. "Here, drink this; you'll feel better."

"Ugh, I don't want it. It makes me sick."

Chiara's eyes opened wider. So that was the problem. She should have guessed. A year ago she would have been shocked; now it didn't seem the worst of sins.

As though to confirm Chiara's suspicion, Penny said quietly, "I'm . . . I'm pregnant."

"Is that it? Well, it's not the first time a woman's been pregnant before the wedding. I'll let out the side seams. No one needs to know."

"You don't understand. It's not Jimmy. It's Bull, the foreman. I don't dare tell Jimmy. He'd kill him."

"Dio mio, that beast," Chiara said. "He should be killed!" She gathered her friend in her arms. "Poor Penny. You'll be married next week. Your baby will be born a little early. It happens all the time. Jimmy doesn't need to know."

Chiara stood to ease the pressure on her back, then took up her sewing and sat on the easy chair by the window. Mike had moved the chair from the living room so she would have a comfortable spot to do her handwork, but it was wedged next to the ironing board and a worktable. Resting her arms on the shelf of her belly, she reflected that this pregnancy was more uncomfortable than the last, and there were three more weeks to go.

Without actively seeking it, Chiara had had a surprising increase in her business. Word of her skill spread through the Italian community, and those who could afford a traditional wedding celebration sought her services. It amazed her that families with modest means chose to spend their small savings on wedding paraphernalia. But they excused their extravagance by saying their children needed a good start, a fine wedding to look back on when times were bad.

Times *had* been bad for quite a while. Could they get worse?

She had to finish this job quickly, before the baby came. This was the first of four powder-blue rayon bridesmaids' dresses she was completing for the March wedding of a wealthy Italian banker's daughter. Her needle flew through the cloth, the silver thimble glinting in its forward thrust. She sighed and looked around her.

The accoutrements of her business were overrunning the small bedroom workshop. Crowding the room were bolts of material stacked precariously on a small table against the wall; two "forms" that didn't seem to replicate any actual person's shape; an ironing board; and a second used machine for Flora, whom she had pressed into more or less regular service. Even Maria and Rosa, Dino's wife, helped out in a crisis.

"You ought to have a bigger room," Mike observed, walking in. "When we have a home of our own, you'll have a big sewing room, I promise."

A home of their own. It had become a catchphrase. She wondered if it would ever come to pass. So often their plans were dashed. Though she was saving steadily, she felt that Mike's hold on a job was precarious. She'd heard many tales of unjustified firings.

"People say I should have a shop, that I should design clothing."

"What foolishness! Soon enough you'll have your hands full with the baby." Mike patted Chiara's belly affectionately. "Then you'll probably give up sewing altogether."

"No, Mike. I *love* my work." Sewing gave her a sense of pride, of accomplishment, but Mike couldn't understand that. And the money. She received a great deal of satisfaction from seeing the dollars pile up in the cigar box. Mike had urged her to put her savings in postal certificates, but she was as distrustful of government agencies as she was of banks. She shuddered, remembering that they'd just missed losing their savings when Mike withdrew the money for her trip a year ago, in February 1933. A few weeks later the banks had all folded like a deck of playing cards standing on end. The closings had precipitated a food panic and skyrocketing prices. It had all happened while she was gone.

"A shop would be nice, Mike." Chiara shifted her weight and the homemade wraparound dress fell open, revealing her still-slender thigh. She extended her hand to Mike and he helped her up. "I'm sure I could make a lot of money with a shop."

"Are you crazy?" Mike pursed his fingers and rocked them. "Where will you get the dough? Shops cost money."

"Maybe we could borrow."

He laughed. "What a babe in the woods you are. You need collateral to borrow."

Chiara's lips tightened and her eyelids lowered.

Mike said, "You have no head for business anyway. As it is, you don't charge enough money. You do it for charity! What you got from Penny hardly covered the price of the cloth."

"She's my friend."

"Friend! That's no way to run a business."

Mike was right, though she wouldn't admit it to him. Because most of her clients were in modest circumstances, she was reluctant to charge them much.

But when money seemed to be no object, as with the Morrisons, she charged high. And at that they obviously thought they had gotten a bargain.

"All right, Mike. You have a business head. You do the business. You could bargain over rental prices, figure out what the wages should be for help. And you could build shelves and partitions and fitting rooms . . ."

"I give up! Did you forget you're having a baby?"

"I don't mean right away. Maybe next year."

"I'm not arguing with you anymre." Mike turned and stomped from the room. *"There will be no shop!"*

Chiara waddled after him. "There will be no shop," she mimicked, lowering her voice. "This isn't Italy, Mike, it's America. Women can say what they think here. It's a free country."

Mike turned suddenly and laughed at her. "Where do you hear such talk? The radio? I'll have to lock it up in a closet. Now, get my dinner."

"But—"

"Basta!"

Chiara knew Mike was at the end of his patience. For all his modern ideas, and despite the fact that he had been educated in America, Mike still clung to the notion of *la via vecchia*. A woman must stay home and take care of her husband and children. As long as Mike thought of her sewing as something to idle away the time, he could accept it. He was a strange mixture of the old and the new.

Chiara surprised herself when she argued instead of just accepting his decision. His point about her lack of business sense was well-taken. But she could learn. And maybe Maria would help her. Maria had told her that in Italy she had tended to the business end of her father's small furniture store.

When the labor started, Mike sent for Comare Sophia, the midwife. There was none of the panic Chiara had felt the first time. Now she knew what to expect, knew that though it seemed endless, the pain was actually brief and quickly forgotten.

Sophia entered briskly and removed the instruments from her black bag, layng them on the clean towel-covered dresser top. She set about her tasks in a confi-dent, matter-of-fact manner.

"You, Mike, don't stand around looking sick, go get me more towels. Then make coffee." She closed the door after him, whispering to Chiara, "It's best to keep them busy. They can be such a problem." Her examination produced a pleased grin in her round pink face. "Not long, Chiara, a few hours and it will all be over. Everything looks fine." She handed her patient a knotted cloth. "Here, bite on this when the pain is too bad."

Chiara thought of her first child and felt a tear form and drop down her perspiring face. Another tear dropped with the remembrance of the one who had never had the chance at life. With trembling lips she murmured prayers of contrition and ended with, *Please, God, let this one be healthy. I've suffered enough.*

"My, my," Sophia was saying as she examined Chiara again, "this one's in a hurry, Chiara, it won't be long now."

In a scant half-hour her daughter, a black-haired, dark-eyed replica of Mike, was born.

The baby cried out her objection to air, light, and cold before Sophia even had a chance to coax a response with a smack.

"Ah, she's not going to let anyone tell her what to do," Sophia said. Chiara smiled happily as she reached for the slippery infant, and wondered if Sophia's words were prophetic.

She looked the infant over carefully, uncurling little fingers, counting little toes, then kissed the dark, downy head. *Thank you, God, for forgiving my sins and blessing me with this beautiful child.*

Mike hurried in and lifted the babe from Chiara's arms, gazing with total amazement at the tiny features. "I'd forgotten how small babies are. She's beautiful, Chiara. We'll follow the custom and call her Anna after my mother."

Chiara raised her hand to Mike. "Are you disappointed it's not a boy?"

Mike took her hand and pressed it to his cheek. He hesitated just a moment before he said, "Of course not. We'll have a boy next time."

When Chiara finished nursing Anna, she removed the newspaper from Mike's hands and laid the baby in his lap. She had cooked linguine with clam sauce and earlier had baked a round loaf of bread. Afterward she'd poured him more wine, hoping to mellow him even further.

Turning down the volume of the radio news, she said, "Mike, I looked at some shops on Gratiot today."

"Look, she smiles when I tickle her chin." Mike's sturdy bronze finger fluttered under Anna's soft flesh, causing a chortle. "What a beauty, eh? Isn't it early for her to laugh like that?"

"Yes, a bit." Chiara pulled a chair closer to Mike's and touched his shoulder. "There's one shop that looks pretty nice. It's a good size, and wouldn't take too much . . ."

Mike swiveled his head toward her. "What are you talking about? Are you still thinking about a sewing store?"

"No, it would be a bridal shop. I would specialize—"

"Chiara, are you crazy? You don't have enough to do with the baby and the house, cooking and washing and ironing?"

She stood and paced behind his chair. "I'll get someone to help with all that. A young girl, maybe Rosa's daughter."

"What would you use for money? Look, if you have time on your hands and you want to sew, then sew at home. I don't want to hear any more about a shop." Then, as if to himself, Mike muttered, "Madonna, where does she get these ideas? People are out of work, on welfare . . ."

"Mike, they still want wedding gowns. I could have so much business . . ."

He stood and angrily handed Chiara the baby. "I said no, and I don't want to hear any more about it. Understand?"

One look at his set jaw, his glaring eyes, told Chiara she had better not pursue the subject. But she smiled to herself. She would bide her time.

Managing the baby wouldn't be difficult. She would put a crib in the shop. A contented, smiling baby, all Anna did was sleep and nurse, and when she was older . . . well, Chiara would face that when the time came.

Chiara had worked furiously on the gowns for the Morrison wedding party and was surprised and delighted when she received an invitation to the wedding. Mrs. Morrison said Chiara should be able to watch her handiwork go down the aisle, especially after acceding to the bride's last-minute request to fashion a gown for her grandmother. She was a crotchety old woman, hard to fit and harder to accommodate. It had required working late into the night to finish on time.

Getting Mike to the wedding had been a problem. She'd had to use all her feminine wiles and the argument that this might be the only society wedding she'd ever have a chance to attend. He had balked at "hobnobbing with those pompous bluebloods." In the end he gave in, as she had known he would.

On entering the ballroom, Chiara caught her breath. Crystal chandeliers hung like tiers of elongated diamonds and huge round linen-covered tables were awash with fine china, delicate stemmed goblets, and silver in various shapes and sizes. Leafy palms trembled in giant pots as members of the orchestra, dressed in sleek black tuxedos, set up shiny brass instruments, and women floated in wearing furs, on the arms of men in double-breasted suits.

Self-consciously, Chiara's hand flew to her throat, then to her hair, light brown hair which had grown long and hung in natural, shimmery waves with ends curling under. Was it out of fashion? She glanced at the other women, comparing. Was her dress too bright? She fumbled at the folds of the skirt, licking her lips, covered with creamy new Tangee lipstick.

As if reading her gesture, Mike bent to her and said, "You're the prettiest woman in the room."

She smiled her thanks up at him. He'd disapproved of the lipstick at first, but accepted it now. The dress, at least, was of the newest style, aquamarine, with an oval neckline and a fitted top that accented her full breasts and tiny waist. The skirt moved gracefully as she walked. The sapphire earrings her Uncle Nunzio had given her as a wedding present dangled enticingly when she moved her head. Seeking support, she took Mike's arm and they proceeded to the reception line. Glancing at her husband, she thought how handsome he looked in his new navy-blue suit and red-flecked bow tie. At thirty-five, he seemed at his prime. His newly shaved cheeks were devoid of the blue-black hue that shadowed his jaws on his return from work each day, and his teeth shone white and even in an easy, self-confident smile. He could be a banker or a doctor, just like the other guests, who, she was sure, must be professional people.

They reached the wedding party and accepted the warm handshakes of the newlyweds and the whispered thanks of Mrs. Morrison. "Everything is perfect, my dear."

Even old Mrs. Morrison, wizened and beady-eyed, tried to be gracious as she rasped, "You managed to make me pretty, Chiara."

Finding their name cards, they sat at the empty table. In a few moments a tall black man joined them, a beautiful beige-skinned woman at his side. Chiara recognized the man as Thomson, the Morrisons' butler. After introductions were made, they were joined by two other couples who, Chiara soon realized, were all workers on the Morrison estate. There was a clear separation between the haves and have-nots; how could she have thought otherwise? No matter how they looked, they were categorized, marked as the laboring class.

After the tables were cleared from dinner, the band began to play. Mike nudged Chiara's elbow and tipped his head toward the dance floor. As he guided her onto the slick waxed surface, he said *sotto voce*, "You notice we're sitting with the lower class, the servants."

Chiara's pointed chin edged upward. "But that *is* what we are, after all."

"You know how I feel about the monied class, Chiara. I didn't want to come, for just this reason."

"The Morrisons are not bad people just because they

have money. Probably they thought we might be uncomfortable with some of the others. They've been very kind, and very fair to me. They even paid me more than I asked."

"That's because you never ask enough."

Mike, a smooth dancer, guided Chiara in a fox-trot. Chiara was less accomplished, having had little practice. The next number, the big apple, had the dancers scuttling over the floor with toes, then heels together and index fingers circling in the air. After a few minutes, Chiara, flushed and breathless, begged off and they returned to their seats. The others at the table congratulated them on their performance, and they were all soon conversing easily. The woman, a maid for the Morrisons, spoke with a Scottish brogue that clashed with Chiara's Italian accent, causing good-humored teasing.

Laughing at the butler's mimic of her dialect, Chiara was startled by a tap on her shoulder. She turned and found herself looking into the lively gray eyes of Stewart Austin.

"Good evening, Mrs. Marcassa. It's nice to see you again." He looked poised, a half-smile on his lips.

Chiara was momentarily flustered, then regained her composure. "Good evening, Mr. Austin. This is my husband, Mike."

Mike stood, hand extended, a questioning arch to his eyebrows.

"Mike, you remember Mr. Austin. His wife was my first customer."

Mike nodded as he and Stewart shook hands.

"Would you mind if I borrowed your wife for a dance?" Stewart asked.

Though Chiara detected a slight scowl on Mike's face, he said, "Not at all."

"I'm not a very good dancer," she demurred.

"Nonsense. They're playing some great songs." Stewart took her elbow and urged her upward.

On the dance floor he turned her gracefully into his arms while the orchestra played "Smoke Gets in Your Eyes."

"You look stunning, Chiara. That color suits you," he murmured close to her ear.

"Thank you." She arched away slightly, trying to ignore the way her heart quickened at the sound of his voice.

"How have you been? Are you happy? You look happy." His hand on her back was warm and pulsed gently, guiding her forward and back with practiced ease.

"I'm fine. I'm very busy with the baby, and so many customers . . ."

"Baby?" His eyebrows lifted.

Of course, he wouldn't have known about Anna's birth. Somehow, he had known of Roberto's passing, for a short note of sympathy had come in the mail. It was signed "Mr. and Mrs. Austin," but she felt sure it was Stewart's handwriting.

"Yes, Anna. She's four months old."

"Ah, a little girl . . . how lovely for you. I always wanted a little girl."

Was the wistful look in his eyes because of the other child, the one that would have been his? She blinked away the thought and let him lead her around to the lively music. "And you, are you happy?"

He looked away. "As happy as I can be, under the circumstances, I suppose."

So nothing was changed; "the circumstances" probably meant his wife was still drinking. Chiara glanced around the hall until she spotted Audrey. Wearing a simple but elegant crimson gown with the new full shoulder pads, she looked vivacious as she spoke to a companion, gesturing with elaborate hand movements. She flicked a lock of hair from her forehead with long, slim fingers.

". . . lovely dresses, all of them," Stewart was saying. "How very talented you are. It must have been a great deal of work. How do you manage it all?"

"It's difficult, mainly because I don't have the room or equipment I need. I have some friends who help, though."

"What you need is more space, a shop of your own. Maybe a bridal salon. Ever thought of that?"

"Yes, lately I've thought of it more and more. Others have mentioned it. But Mike's against it."

His lip quirked slightly; then he nodded, as if he understood fully. "I suppose it would take a great deal of money. I could lend you some, you know. No one would have to know where it came from."

Chiara was touched by his easy generosity. "No, I

couldn't take money from you. Mike would certainly find out and question it. Anyway, that's not the only problem."

Stewart pondered for a moment. "Look, when you get serious about this venture, go to my bank, Detroit Bank and Trust. They're very helpful there. See Mr. Cronin. He'll see that you're well taken care of. Will you do that?"

"I'm afraid a shop is out of the question for now. I've put it completely from my mind." That wasn't quite true. The idea refused to stay buried; it lay on the fringe of her mind, waiting for the right time to resurface.

When the music ended, they clapped politely, then turned toward her table.

Quietly he said, "It would be nice if we could meet sometime, have dinner perhaps, and talk. Just talk. I think about you often."

"No, it's out of the question," she said under her breath. He would never know how often his image filled her mind.

Mike moved his chair back and stood as the couple drew near.

Stewart shook his hand again, saying, "Thank you for the loan of your wife, Mr. Marcassa."

Mike nodded curtly, and as Stewart left, wondered aloud, "Where have I seen that guy before?"

Chiara shrugged.

She tucked away the pleasant memory of dancing with Stewart in her secret cache of reminiscences, to be taken out, like a jewel in a treasure box, for admiring and polishing every now and then.

Stewart's encouragement pervaded her thoughts, and not long after the wedding, Chiara searched the newspapers for rental property. She circled two she considered adequate, one on Woodward and one on Gratiot. When Mike was settled in bed and properly mellowed from his glass of wine, she casually mentioned the shops.

"I wish you and I could go and see what they're like." She buttoned her flannel nightgown and sat on the edge of the bed brushing her hair.

Mike looked at her coldly, incredulously. "I don't want to talk about it."

"Just look at them, that's all I ask . . ."

"Why are you even thinking of opening a shop? You know we can't afford it."

"We're saving a little money."

"That's for a house; you know that."

Chiara could see his anger mounting, but pushed on anyway. "Then we could get a loan from the bank."

"You're dreaming. On what collateral?"

"What is this 'collateral'?"

Mike rolled his eyes heavenward. "You see? How could you run a business when you don't even know what collateral is?"

Chiara sniffed and made a tight mouth. "I know how to make bride dresses; that's all I need to know. Someone else can worry about this collateral. You! You can worry about it. You come to the bank and ask for the money."

"Me? I wouldn't embarrass myself that way. I would need all the facts and figures, the cost of everything down to the last pin! And I know what they'd say. They'd think I was a fool. I want you to forget this business once and for all!" His voice rose steadily. "Women belong at home, not working at some shop."

"Mike, I'm working every day in my house. What's the difference?"

"And that's another thing. I never liked you working day and night."

Chiara's eyes flashed angrily. "I like to work."

"I said forget it."

"You're a stubborn mule!"

Anna's wail startled them both.

"You see? You woke the baby!" Mike jumped out of bed and made for Anna's bedroom. "I'll settle her down this time."

But Chiara couldn't forget the shop. She crawled into bed, pulling the blanket to her chin. There was profit to be made in custom bridal gowns, she was sure of it. The thought of earning large profits ignited her ambition. She could have a sort of production line, the way they did in the factory: one person cutting, another basting, another trimming. She could work out new designs and patterns and pay others to do the simple work, like Dona Isabella did in the old country.

Rich people, she'd found, would pay dearly for something "original." Mike was right when he said she didn't charge enough. But with a proper shop, in the right setting, she could charge more and afford to pay her workers a decent wage. Her shop would have to be in a nice section of the city, to attract the wealthy clients. She would study the window displays of Siegel's and Klein's and Hudson's to make hers as inviting. She began visualizing an elegant little place in ivory and blue, with shimmery curtains at the dressing-room entries. She was willing even to forgo a home of her own for a shop. She heard Mike making cooing noises in Anna's room and her fantasy vaporized and disappeared. How could she go against her husband? He was the boss, the decision maker. Yet didn't her desires count for something? Somehow his opposition only served to strengthen her resolve.

Mike settled Anna down, then sat in the kitchen for a last smoke. His wife exasperated him. She was so naive about business matters; oblivious of all the things that could go wrong. They could lose all their savings; then where would they be? Back to zero, as if they'd just gotten off the boat. No, he had made up his mind. Since returning to work after his dreaded layoff, Mike had guarded his money like a squirrel with a winter's hoard of nuts. Their savings would be a down payment on a house.

He had made a grudging concession when he allowed Chiara to sew at home. He hadn't forgotten it was her money that saved them when he was out of work. Her earnings would help them reach their goal. Chiara deserved a house—a nice cozy place with a large kitchen and roomy yard. That was where women belonged—at home, in the kitchen, taking care of babies.

Family, that was the important thing. They needed more children to have a proper family, but it hadn't happened, and not for lack of trying. He lit a final cigarette and picked up the paper, turning it to the business section. The news regarding the auto industry was encouraging. Sales were on the upswing.

Turning to a back page, he read that near a railroad track in southwest Detroit a body had been found with a bullet hole in the head. Mike recognized the name of the dead man. He remembered seeing him outside the Rouge plant selling *The Daily Worker*. In fact he had spoken to the man and learned he had a wife and an eight-year-old daughter. Mike was incensed by the tone of the article. It implied that because this man was a communist, he deserved to be shot, like a common criminal. And this was the "land of the free." He threw the paper to the floor. So many wrongs to be righted, so much work to accomplish. And he was just an onlooker, sitting on the sidelines, unable to enter the fray the way some of his co-workers were doing by joining a union. He desperately wanted to join, to stand up and be counted. But he knew that to be caught in the union would be the kiss of death for his job.

He stubbed out his cigarette and went to the bedroom. Chiara looked so lovely as she slept, her thick lashes resting on pink cheeks, her fair hair splayed on the pillow, her lips soft and inviting. He would like to make love to her, but he was so sleepy, so tired; his arms and legs felt like lead. They had speeded up the line again. Oh, they did it slowly, a bit at a time, as if the workers would be fooled. But he could barely keep up. Some of the older men couldn't manage it, and out they went. The factory chewed you up and spat you out old and wasted by the time you turned forty. He could hardly keep his eyes open. Tomorrow night, Chiara, he promised silently as he slid into bed. He yawned loudly. After all, he thought, I would like a son, a little replica, a sturdy male to carry on the Marcassa name.

At work, a few weeks later, Mike pushed the button to start the turntable. With gloved hands he worked the rotary resistance welder, which pressed two pieces of steel together between dies to form brake shoes. A current of electricity fused the steel, sparks flying. Each of Mike's hands performed a different job to complete the welding process, while the machine moved at a fixed rate, never pausing, its jaws hungrily closing on the steel. The process required an almost sleight-of-hand dexterity that had defeated many a man before Mike.

The machine's movements had been increased so subtly it was almost indiscernible, but he dared not complain. The foreman would just say, "You don't like it, then leave!" The foreman had a job to do too; a family to support. He was ensnared, like they all were, in a web of helplessness.

When the lunch whistle blew, Mike and Schultz, who

worked on the next machine, unwrapped their sandwiches and devoured them hungrily, washing them down with gulps of strong coffee.

"Yeah, I was one of the lucky ones. They called me back after fifteen months of layoff." Schultz chomped down on a crisp pickle. "But it's going to do me in. You're a young man, Mike; you're smart. You oughta get out of this place, find some other kind of work."

Mike snorted. "Sure, there are all kinds of jobs out there."

"This place'll kill you. Look at me. How old do you think I am?"

Mike glanced at Schultz and said, "Fifty," giving him the advantage of a few years.

"I'm forty-one. I'm an old man, deaf in one ear. I dye my hair with shoe polish so they'll think I'm younger. The factory made me old before my time."

The whistle sounded, ending their conversation, and Mike again proceeded to feed his ravenous machine. He wondered how long until his own hearing would go from the constant bombardment of noises. If he hadn't the family responsibilities, he would try something else, perhaps involve himself in union organizing. In fact, Dino wanted to meet him tonight, to hear someone's union spiel. Maybe he would go, just to listen, see what was going on. He would have to be careful, protect himself from any hint of suspicion. When he recalled the last layoff and his resulting "illness," he shuddered. That was a tortured span of his life he never wanted to repeat. And by God, he would never again allow himself to become so debilitated. Dammit, he wished he could get involved.

At four o'clock, when the whistle shrilled, the line continued its creaking forward movement and the men hurried to leave their work stations so the second shift could move in. Reaching one hand across to the opposite shoulder, Mike massaged an aching muscle. How many more years of this, he wondered, before he was too old to keep up, before he was tossed aside?

Inside the beer garden in Hamtramck, Mike looked around for Dino. The men hunching over their beer mugs seemed vaguely familiar, and he realized that there was a similarity between workingmen everywhere. He listened to the sounds of their good-natured complaining, their teasing insults. The jobs they escaped by coming here were made more bearable as the nickel beer took effect. Some of the conversations were in Polish. Mike recognized a few words of the Polish conversations flowing around him. As he slid onto a stool at the bar, he thought how strange that the Polish living in Hamtramck had remained true to their ethnic origins. That wasn't true of the Italians and other foreign groups in the city, the Germans, Irish, Jews. Though some nationalities had originally congregated in small sections of the city, now they were mostly amalgamated into one large group: laborers. The other exception was the Negroes, who were relegated to their own "Paradise Valley." Still, there was one section that was taboo to many—Grosse Pointe. It was an unwritten credo that only the elite of the population were welcome there. Mike laughed to himself. As if he would ever want to join the upper crust. Still, it rankled. When he was young he had thought there was no caste system. That was what the schools would have you believe. Now he knew better.

His thoughts jumped to the present when he felt a clap on his shoulder.

"Eh, paisano," Dino said, sliding onto the empty stool next to Mike.

As they shook hands, Mike asked, "So, how've you been?"

"Not bad for someone who was out of work for a couple of months."

"Yeah, I heard about the walkout at Briggs." Mike signaled the bartender and pointed toward Dino with his thumb. "The same for my friend."

"It's funny, Mike, but I felt like getting fired was almost worth it. That walkout showed ol' Walter Briggs something. He was vacationing in Florida and didn't even think the strike was serious enough to come back for. Then pretty soon the guys at Murray Body and Hudson Motors and Motor Products followed Briggs's lead and walked out."

Mike leaned his elbows on the water-spotted bar. "Everyone was sure that Mayor Murphy would let 'em have workers from the city employment bureau, but Murphy held out. I give him credit."

Dino said, "Yeah, Murphy wouldn't even let 'em use city trolleys to bring in strikebreakers. Still, that son of a bitch Briggs got his scabs anyway, and never gave in. The other companies agreed to stop the wage cuts, but not him. So there I was, out of a job again."

The bartender slid a beer toward Dino. Hoisting the mug, Dino said, "*Salute.*"

Mike said, "Your troubles don't seem to drag you down, pal. What are you doing now?"

"I was lucky; they needed metal finishers at the Highland Park plant, so I got a job there. Before that I was all set to sign up with Roosevelt's work program, the WPA. They're laying a new road on Grand River. Not much money, but it's better than nothing. At least it's real money, not scrip. My brother works for the city and he gets paid in fake money. Thank God for Roosevelt. He's trying to put people back to work."

"Yeah. One good thing he did was repeal Prohibition." Mike lifted his beer and drank it down in one long guzzle, then threw some coins on the bar. "We'd better get going if we're going to make the meeting. Are you sure you want to do this? It could be dangerous."

"I'm sure. You?"

"Go for broke."

Dino arched an eyebrow. "Aren't you a little scared?"

"Yeah, but dammit, if everyone runs scared, we'll never get organized."

"I hear this union guy is okay."

As they emerged on the street, Mike said, "Yeah, he was pals with Walter Reuther when he worked at Ford in thirty-two. Reuther got fired because he campaigned for the Socialist party, so he and his brother went to Europe and Russia. I'm anxious to hear what happened to them."

"I suppose Bennett's still around, running the service department."

"Ha, that's a laugh—some service. He has crooks and thieves on the payroll, like Chester LaMare of the Black Hand. I think Ford's losing his marbles. He doesn't even trust Bennett completely. Bennett hired a man named Gillespie, and now they say Ford has Gillespie spying on Bennett."

In companionable silence the two men walked down nearly deserted streets to the meeting place in a room above the Polonia Restaurant. Circles of light from the globes sitting atop tall green metal posts illuminated their way and cast long shadows. They lingered outside the restaurant while Dino finished a cigarette.

"Make it snappy," Mike said. "You never know who's watching."

Dino ground the butt under his heel and started up the narrow stairway to the second floor. As Mike made to follow him, he heard a car skidding softly to a halt. Turning, he saw the door of a midnight-black 1930 Ford open and two men emerge. One of the men, a brawny youth wearing a brown fedora pulled down over his forehead, looked familiar.

Mike hesitated a moment, then followed Dino up the stairs. About twenty people, mostly men, filled the room, and two women, pocketbooks clutched in their hands, sat chatting. Big Jim Masterson was at the front conferring with another man, his hand on a sheaf of papers. A light bulb shone under a metal shade of forest green over Jim's head.

He motioned the group to take seats and began talking of the many sins of the giant corporations.

"And Ford's about the worst," Masterson said. "Oh, at Ford you can join a union, all right. When tool and die workers at the Rouge joined the Mechanics Education Society Union, Bennett found out their names in short order. Then he had them transferred, one by one, into one department. Then he abolished the department, thereby putting them out on the street without actually firing them." He paused to let this sink in. "And what about Roosevelt? We thought he would help us with the National Industrial Recovery Act, and found out that NRA stood for National Run-Around. And now that it has bitten the dust, we have the Wagner Act."

A woman called out, "I thought the Wagner Act meant closed shop? What about that?"

Big Jim drew himself up to his full five-foot-three and nodded sarcastically. "Sure, the Wagner Act is supposed to endorse the principle of exclusive representation. You know what that means at the Ford Motor Company? It means now you can join the Ford Brotherhood of America—under the auspices of Henry Ford and Harry Bennett! Brothers, we've got a long way to go, and we've got to start now! What we're after is fair working conditions, decent pay, the end of paying graft to foremen, seniority rights. We're only asking our due as human beings, as citizens of the great U.S. of A."

A white-haired, bent man with a large paunch stood. "It ain't done no good up to now. The craft unions don't stand behind us."

Several people voiced their agreement, a few heads nodded.

Masterson said, "I know you've been distrustful of unions in the past. Who can blame you? Unions weren't always able to help. But the time has finally come when the AFL is forced to stop protecting craft unions. At the last convention a new arm of the AFL was formed, the Committee for Industrial Organization, the CIO—with none other than John L. Lewis, president of the United Mine Workers, as chief." Jim paused and looked over the group. "My friends, a new day is dawning for unionism. The United Auto Workers' Union is organized for all the rank and file, every last one of us." He continued his spiel to a smattering of applause and a few questions from the audience.

"I'm sick of the worker getting shit on," Mike said to Dino. "I've talked about it and thought about it long enough. I'm joining."

"I ain't ready to sign a union card yet," Dino said.

Mike joined a few others at the makeshift table and signed. The paunchy man who had spoken said, "I'm joining too, but with a John Doe. They ain't finding out my name."

As he went back to his seat, Mike glanced toward the fringes of the group. Sitting near the door were the two men who had followed him up the stairs. Mike chanced a closer look at the man wearing the fedora pulled down to shade his eyes. It looked like Jimmy, Penny's husband, but Mike couldn't be sure. He hadn't seen Jimmy in a long time. In fact, Chiara had gone to the afternoon wedding alone because Mike had worked that Saturday. If indeed it was Jimmy, was he interested in joining the union, or was he spying for Bennett?

"What's wrong, Mike? You look jittery," Dino said when Mike returned to his seat.

"I am. Those two guys who walked in behind us are sitting in back."

Dino turned slowly and nodded, "Yeah, so?"

"I think the one with the hat works at Ford. He may be a spy."

"Shit. Does he know who you are?"

"If he's the guy I think he is, he knows me. I'm going to sneak out of here as soon as I get a chance."

"Maybe he didn't recognize you."

Mike didn't answer, but moved from his chair as unobtrusively as possible, keeping his head averted. In his peripheral vision he saw the two men, looking smug, with arms crossed over their chests. Mike ducked out the door and sprinted down the stairs, his adrenaline pumping, not from exertion, but from fear.

By the next day Mike had convinced himself he had overreacted. It was still a free country and *they* couldn't get you just for joining a union. That was un-American. He hurried up the metal steps into his building. As he switched his lunch box from one hand to the other, he was suddenly aware that someone had fallen into step with him. He cranked his head around and saw Jimmy.

"Better try to protect yourself, Marcassa. I tried my best to cover, but my pal, he seen you. He'll try to finger you."

"Thanks for nothing," Mike spat.

Jimmy shrugged. "I don't owe you nothin', but seein' as your wife and mine are friends . . ."

He turned and walked off before Mike could retort.

Inside the building, Mike slipped his time card into the clock and marched to his place. Tugging his work gloves on, he waited nervously for the whistle.

Maybe Jimmy's friend wouldn't discover who he was. Or maybe Jimmy would be successful in diverting suspicion, though that seemed unlikely. His heart thudded inside his heavy cotton work shirt. He should never have gone to the meeting, knowing the danger.

—— 21 ——

Mike started his press and was suddenly aware of the foreman standing next to him.

"You're wanted by the door, Marcassa." The foreman nodded to the relief man to take over Mike's position.

Mike hesitated a moment. "What for?"

"I don't know," the man mumbled, avoiding Mike's eyes.

The relief man nudged Mike out of the way and began the monotonous procedure—reach with the right hand, left hand, bend, toss, begin again—with hardly a ripple in the routine.

Turning, Mike saw the two goons waiting for him at the end of the aisle. He tensed, arms bent upward, hands forming fists. Here it comes, he thought, the moment of reckoning. It had happened before, to men he had known, the swift reprisal for transgressions against Henry Ford; the Henry Ford who insisted that he was a worker, just like them. Surprisingly, as he moved down the aisle, Mike felt no fear, though compared to the two men, huge biceps straining their shirt sleeves, he looked like a child.

"Take it easy, Marcassa, we ain't gonna hurt ya too bad," one of the men, sporting a grimy sailor hat over menacing eyes, chided as he moved behind Mike.

The other, a mountain of a man with a bulldog face and thick black eyebrows, faced Mike, his legs splayed, his fist punching his palm. Sailor grabbed Mike's arms from behind, pinning them, while Bulldog reared his arm back and punched Mike in the solar plexus. Though he had anticipated it, the punch took Mike's breath away as a numbing pain shot through him and he collapsed like a punctured balloon.

"This is just a little lesson, in case some of your buddies gits a notion to join the union." A malevolent grin lit Bulldog's face.

Regaining his breath, Mike sprang forward with a powerful thrust that released his arms from Sailor's stranglehold. He swung a savage right to his attacker's face. Caught off-guard, Bulldog lurched backward, blood spurting from his nose. Sailor grabbed Mike around the neck and wrestled him to the ground.

"Goddamn Bolshevik wop," Sailor hissed, diving on top of Mike. Swinging wildly, Mike landed blows on Sailor's chin and temple, but his assailant had the advantage, and pummeled him mercilessly.

There was a painful pulsing blood-rush to his head. The throbbing beat of it joined with the machinery's crashing racket until it swelled in his head to an unbearable crescendo.

"Let 'im up," Bulldog yelled.

When Sailor lumbered to his feet, Mike twisted and grabbed Bulldog's ankle. It felt like he was yanking a huge tree stump, but Bulldog, caught off-balance, hurtled to the ground.

Mike, on his feet now, traded blows with Sailor, but Bulldog lurched upward and landed a brutish right to Mike's chest, stunning him. His legs buckled and he hit the concrete floor with a thud.

Through a vague mist of pain, Mike saw his attackers lurching over him.

"That's enough," the foreman yelled. "Don't cripple him, for Chrissake." Under his breath he muttered, "They're goddamm animals."

"Yeah," Sailor said, staggering backward, "we wasn't supposed to hurt 'im bad."

The foreman lifted Mike up, supporting him under the arms. Mike shook his head groggily. His eyes wouldn't focus. He wanted to fight, but his leaden arms refused to obey his brain's command. The raucous chords of the conveyor belt rang in his ears, in symphony with the droning motors and the scrape of metal, a shrill machine-age orchestration. The noise combined into one loud scream in his head, obliterating any other thought.

He heard a voice, a faraway echo, saying, "Come on, punk, you're through."

Mike teetered unsteadily and felt his attackers grab his arms, felt himself being dragged away, his feet trolling behind, across the narrow corridor, through the double doors, down a set of stairs. Finally he was tossed outdoors on rubbery legs that barely held him up. The cool morning air revived him somewhat, and he shook his head in an attempt to formulate a coherent thought. He moved past the overpass and gripped the cold rail to keep from falling down the steps. When he swiped at his nose with his sleeve, he noticed a brilliant streak of red. Blinking into the sun, he propelled himself forward, urging one foot to stumble after the other, out past the main gates, beyond the pinnacles of steel that reached the sky, under the clouds of heavy smoke that spewed incessantly from the chimneys, out of the great River Rouge Ford plant, probably, he thought, forever.

Anger, red hot and boiling, gripped at Mike's insides. What was it all about, anyway, the striving and yearning and dreaming? It was about getting a job and keeping it, at all costs; it was about survival. So you worked your ass off your entire life and where did it get you? Your daily bread, a home for the lucky ones, maybe a car. But at what price? Loss of spirit, of individuality, of control. And they were all powerless, all those poor bastards in the plant, impotent, afraid to fight for what they believed in, unwilling to lay their jobs on the line, unable to make the choice for unionism in order to make it better for everyone, afraid of ending up losers.

Well, dammit, *he* wasn't going to run scared any longer.

It had been a long time since he thought of his father, but now Mike recalled the agony of watching him die after the horrible accident which had crushed his leg at Ford's Highland Park plant. With a flash of clarity, it seemed now that Mike had been led to this time and place in some mystical fashion, in order to avenge his father's death. How he would do it, he had no idea.

By the time he reached home his anger had changed direction. By God, they could beat him, but they couldn't defeat him. Now all he felt was a strong determination to get revenge. But not against his attackers—that wouldn't be sufficient. No, his revenge must be against the Ford Motor Company; to be explicit, against Henry Ford. Better yet, against the entire automobile industry. The system was all wrong; it was abominable, demeaning. Rules must be made for all to follow, workers and bosses alike, for mutual profit and protection. The workers should not be at the mercy of a system where the employer was all-powerful.

How often he had returned home so tired that he dropped mindlessly to bed, with hardly the strength to eat. For fifty-two cents an hour!

Union was their only chance for victory in the war between the haves and the have-nots. He would devote himself to that war. There would be danger, physical danger, but suddenly he felt invulnerable. There were battles to be won, and by God, he would be one of the soldiers in the war for human rights.

Chiara screamed when she saw Mike limp into the house, his face bruised, his nose swollen, brown splotches of dried blood marring his shirt front.

Running to him, she cried out, *"Madre di Dio,* what happened?"

"Bennett's bastards beat me up. I'm fired."

Chiara gasped. Fired. The specter of those long and hapless months of discontent when Mike was out of work crossed her thoughts, momentarily negating her concern for his immediate state. *Dear God, don't let it begin again, the depression, the misery. I couldn't take it.*

Mike's groan of pain with each step begged her attention and obliterated all other thoughts.

"Oh, my poor Michele, you look awful." She helped him shed his jacket, cringing when he moaned with each small movement. The area circling his swollen right eye was a deep shade of blue-gray. "Your eye looks bad. Can you see all right? My God, they could have blinded you." A pitiful sob escaped her.

Mike eased himself painfully into a kitchen chair, a grimace flashing across his features.

She was suddenly furious. "Who did this?"

"You never know their names. They can do anything they damn well please."

Chiara hurried to the sink and ran cold water into a basin. She dipped a cloth into the water and wrung it out with a quick twist, then touched it gingerly to his face.

Wincing from the towel's light pressure, Mike said,

"Ouch. Take it easy." He glanced at Chiara's face, all puckered with frowns and wrinkles. "I don't want you to start worrying, Chiara, hear?"

"Ssh, be still. Oh, your poor nose, it looks broken."

He pounded his fist on the table. "By God, they're not going to get away with this! They're going to pay!" His eyes burned with an inner fire.

Now she was truly worried. Would he try to retaliate in some way; perhaps get Fredo and his Black Hand connections to intercede?

"Don't think of doing something foolish, Mike. You can work someplace else. You said yourself that automobile sales are up, and plants are hiring. We have savings. We can manage for a while." She tried to calculate just how long they could last on their meager savings plus her earnings.

Suddenly Mike pulled her onto his lap and hugged her tightly, burying his head between her breasts. Fear again clutched at her heart. They never talked about the "bad time," as she mentally referred to those demoralizing months of his depression. She knew he felt he'd failed her then, and had suffered a loss of manliness, of power, even though he couldn't have foreseen or prevented the forces that thundered along, causing such devastation. *Please, God, she prayed fiercely, don't let it happen again.*

She whispered into his hair, "Things happen for the best. You'll get another job, a better job."

He lifted his head slowly. "Chiara, it's not going to be like . . . like the last time. I'll take care of you. I can handle this. I'm thinking of working for the union."

"No! Don't even say it. I've heard what happens to union men."

"You don't understand. No one will hire me. I'll be blacklisted."

A bile rose in Chiara's throat at the thought of this injustice. "At least try, Mike. Have a little faith."

He sighed. "All right, I'll try. Don't worry, Chiara."

But worry she did. Especially when he returned home each night after a day of constant, tedious job-hunting with no results. Fortunately, Chiara's work was picking up, and Flora and Maria worked almost as hard as she did. Occasionally she even had to call on Rosa's daughters to help. Her earnings at least put food on the table and paid the rent.

At first Mike would saunter in after a day of job-hunting, the paper under his arm, a smile of hopefulness on his face. But by the end of the first week his step was slower, his smile faded.

Near the end of the second week Chiara took heart when, miraculously, Mike gained employment in the tool room of a small job shop. She whispered a prayer of thanks when he told her.

"Don't be too excited about this job," he said. "I'm not sure how long it'll last."

"Praise God. You see? I told you to have faith." Chiara held his face in her hands and brought it down to hers for a kiss.

Three days later he dropped his lunch box on the table and said, "Fired again. The arm of Harry Bennett is long; it reaches out and finds you no matter where you are. The boss said he was sorry. And to give the devil his due, I think he *was* sorry. 'We don't need you anymore,' he said. He wouldn't even look me in the eye. But I expected this. It happens to anyone who's union-connected."

Chiara was in a bad mood to begin with. Anna had been cranky because of teething, and Chiara had held her most of the day. The coat that should have been ready yesterday wasn't finished because in her nervous haste she'd made the lining too large. Now she would have to work late into the night to correct it.

Mike took Anna from her arms and swung her onto his massive shoulders.

Chiara brushed a hand across her forehead. "To think, we left Italy because there was no work there. For what? For this?" She threw her hands up, encompassing the house, the city, the universe. "Mike, let's go back, back home, to the old country. We still have enough money to live nicely until we get situated. My father has more land now, land he bought with his inheritance."

"It's his land, not ours."

"We could buy land," she pleaded.

"Even Carlo won't go back to the land. He's staying in Milano."

"He's a boy, looking for adventure."

"Have you forgotten what happened when you went back?"

A cloud dropped over her features. Her voice was low. "It's better there now. I would boil the water."

Mike moved Anna around his shoulder and slid her gently to the floor, then dropped on one knee to her level, tickling her.

"Anna would have the love and attention of her grandparents. I remember my own *nonna* and *nonno*. We lived with them until they died." Chiara made a sign of the cross. My *nonna* loved me so; she spoiled me, the way my mother would spoil Anna. I could work as a seamstress. Dona Isabella is getting old; she may be ready to give up her business."

"As I remember, Dona Isabella wasn't so old." Mike laughed. "Chiara, your memories are like old family jewels: more precious in the description than in the reality. Your house must have been crowded, with three generations under one roof. There were probably quarrels and misunderstandings. You choose to remember only the good things. I remember crop failures because of no rain, and having only bread with oil and garlic to eat. Maybe once a month we'd have meat. Where would we stay until we had a home of our own? There would be no privacy, no place to talk in peace. Think about it. Would it be so wonderful?"

She hadn't considered that aspect, had only remembered the feeling of being enveloped in a loving household, with many hands to care for the children, to accomplish the homey tasks. "We would manage until . . . until we could build a place of our own."

Mike rubbed a callused hand over his weary eyes. "Maybe," he said, "maybe it wouldn't be so bad."

This was the most encouragement she'd ever had from him. During the next few days, whenever she thought he was in a mellow mood, she again mentioned going home.

It was ironic that a few days later Mike should see O'Malley at the same beer garden where they'd met just before the hunger march. The bar hadn't changed; the calendar on the wall seemed the same, featuring a scantily clad, perfectly formed, pouty-lipped Petty girl—only the year and month printed across the top were different: October 1935; the same smell of booze and stale cigarettes; the same grittiness on the floor and mustiness in the air. The sight of O'Malley brought back painful memories, memories he tried to brush aside.

"O'Malley," he said, taking the empty stool next to his old friend. "How're you doing? Working?"

"Marcassa!" O'Malley swiveled on his stool and pumped Mike's hand. "Nah, I never got work after the big layoff, but my son's at Chrysler now, and the two oldest girls are both working at a cigar factory. So we manage. My ma passed away, God rest her soul. We get by."

"That's all you can hope for these days, to get by."

O'Malley called out to the bartender, "A Stroh's for my pal," then turned to face Mike again. "I had a chance to go back to work. The foreman wanted to take out my oldest daughter—she's a beauty, Colleen is—said if I played my cards right, and she was cooperative, I'd be back workin' steady." His eyes narrowed with cold anger. "I told him what he could do with his goddamm job!"

Mike nodded in sympathy.

O'Malley brightened. "I heard you was back to work, Marcassa."

"Was is right. I got fired a couple of weeks ago. Found another job that lasted three days. I'm blacklisted because I joined the union."

"You never did know enough to keep your mouth shut. Like that Reuther fellow. If you want to work in this town, ya gotta just do your job and collect your pay . . . and don't make no waves." O'Malley waved to a friend's reflection in the mirror.

"O'Malley, don't you understand that a worker should have some rights? You had twenty years in with Ford, yet you got laid off while some kids with only four, five years stayed, because they figured the young ones could work longer and faster."

"That's the system."

"You think it's right what happened about your daughter, that for you to work, she has to be prostituted? You think that's right?"

"It ain't right, but that's the way it is. You nor no one else is gonna change it."

"You're wrong. What would Ford do if everyone in the whole plant struck? Not only the Rouge, but all his plants? And all the shops that supply his plants? He couldn't get enough scabs for all those jobs. He'd have to listen to reason."

"Mike, you're dreamin'. It's been tried before. It don't work."

Mike looked sullenly into his beer. "It could work. If everyone stuck to their guns."

"In 1933 the MESA union struck three GM plants in Flint. My cousin worked there then. It spread to most of the auto plants in Flint, Pontiac, and some in Detroit. Even some small jobbers were struck. Yeah, it hurt sales for a while, but what did GM do? They transferred the work to Toledo and Cleveland, where there wasn't no MESA members." O'Malley swilled the rest of his beer and slid the glass toward the bartender. "And as long as you got your Harry Bennetts—and don't fool yourself, every plant has one—you ain't gonna see no changes."

"Maybe not in your lifetime, O'Malley, but I for one am not going to leave this earth without seeing a giant organization, mark my words."

"Like I said, you're a dreamer. There is an organization, the AFL; but even they back off in front of the big guns."

"Then somebody's gotta take a stand." Mike set his mug down with a smack.

"Ahh," O'Malley said, punching Mike playfully on the arm. His expression reflected what he probably felt: Mike was hopeless.

Mike shook his head. There wasn't much use in talking to O'Malley. He would never see the light. Besides, it was the employed he should be talking to.

O'Malley piped up, "Speakin' of Reuther, I heard he was back in town, still full of piss and vinegar, still trying to organize. Whyn't you join with him if you're so all-fired-up about a union?"

"Yeah," Mike said, "not a bad idea."

That night he made slow, thoughtful love to his wife, savoring her body's gradual awakening, her sensual movements, her sudden clenching stillness.

Afterward Chiara lay contentedly against him, her arm encompassing his waist, her head resting on his chest.

Mike sifted her abundant locks through his fingers, enjoying the clean scent. Her hair was a bit darker now, and he noticed a few strands of gray. She was thirty years old, too young for gray hair. Her face was youthful still, though she'd earned the faint lines on her brow. A well of emotions bubbled in his chest, that old need to shower his beloved with fine things, with a life of ease. So far, he thought sardonically, it hadn't exactly been, like the song, "a bowl of cherries."

Mike lit a cigarette in the gloom and smoked it wordlessly.

Chiara shifted and smiled dreamily at him, then frowned. "What's wrong, Mike?" Sitting up, she plumped a pillow behind her and studied her husband.

He sighed. His wife read him so easily. "Chiara, I can't do it. I can't go back to Italy."

Chiara pursed her lips. Her eyes filmed over. "Why?"

Mike carefully kept his eyes averted from her face, knowing how easy it would be to give in.

"I talked to Walter Reuther today."

"Who is this person?"

"He heads the United Auto Workers and they're getting ready to start a drive for members. They need my help. Chiara, if you could hear him, you'd believe there's a better world out there for the rank and file. I know he's right. I can feel it, I can taste it. I want to be a part of it, part of the machinery that makes it happen." His voice held a fierce determination.

Chiara dropped her head into her hands. "Mike, I want to go home, but that's not the important thing. Your life! That's what's important. The union is dangerous. You were beaten up because of it. Did you forget that? People are killed for it."

Mike's face was stony, his dark eyes intense. "I only know that I've got to stay and fight for the workers' rights. Detroit is my city, America is my country, no matter what."

"I know you love this country. You're more American than Italian." Chiara's voice held the hint of a sneer.

"I was raised here."

She lifted her face to him and there were tears tumbling from her eyes. "Mike, *per che*? Why do you have to do this? Let others fight. You have a family to think about."

"My father died in a senseless factory accident. That sort of thing can't continue. Can't you see that if everyone says let the other guy do it, nothing will get done?"

"Then it won't get done. At least you'll have your life."

Mike reached for her, but she shrank away.

"I thought your dream was a home of our own, a car, a good life for our family," Chiara said. "You can't get all that working for a union. Union work probably doesn't even pay. I'll have to support us."

Mike winced. A bitterness gnawed at his insides. If anything could change his mind, it was knowing that he wouldn't be able to provide for his family, at least not in the near future. He passed his hand over his eyes and said nothing for a moment. Then he gripped Chiara's shoulders. "We'll have it all someday. You have to be willing to postpone a home, along with me. I promise you, all our sacrifices will be worthwhile." He picked up her hand and rubbed his thumb across the back of it.

Chiara drew away from him and got out of bed. She went to the window and stared into the darkness, where the moon made patchy pale sketches on the bare, frost-dusted earth. "How can you promise? Nothing is certain in this life. You just work hard and do the best you can, and even then the fates turn against you."

"That's old-country talk."

"It's true. What have we gained, despite all our efforts?"

Mike didn't answer.

"Mike, *my* dream is going home. It's different for you. You were raised here. Your feet are planted one in the old country and one in the new. This will never be my land. Italy is my home."

"You have one dream. I have another." He would never give in, not now while the fire of determination warmed his soul. "I want you to believe in my dream of a fair deal for workers."

Chiara traced her name in the frosty window. It was impossible to believe in his dream. History proved the working classes would always be wanting. Those with power and money kept both by whatever means. Laws meant nothing, for there were always ways to circumvent them. She wasn't well-educated, but she knew about history from the books in her Uncle Nunzio's library. So many things never changed, down through the ages, and though there were new systems of government—fascism, socialism, communism, capitalism—none of them seemed to actually benefit the common man.

But all her pleading and arguments wouldn't change Mike's mind. He was stubborn as a mule. And as head of the family, his wishes would prevail. No matter her feelings, she must put her own dream aside for a while. Eventually he would recognize the futility of labor unions, hopefully without too much damage. Then maybe he would agree that she was right, that they would be happier in the old country, among their own people.

With the side of her balled-up fist, Chiara wiped away her tracings on the window and returned to bed. She allowed Mike to cuddle around her.

"Chiara." Mike's voice was gruff with emotion. "When we married, I swore I would give you a good life. I know, so far, it hasn't been so wonderful. But I swear it won't be long before the labor movement will turn this country around, and our lives will change. In a few years we'll have the comfortable life I promised you. You have to believe that."

Since Mike's recovery from *the sickness*, Chiara had witnessed the transformation of his spirit and the birth of a formidable determination. He was imbued with an obsession for equality. How could she not give credence and encouragement to his faith, his hope? How could she not offer, at the very least, her support?

A sigh emerged from deep within her. "I believe in you, Mike. You must do what your heart tells you. *Che sera . . .*"

22

Mike shook the warm September rain from his hat as he entered union headquarters on the west side of Detroit. The tiny office across from the Cadillac plant was dusty and cluttered and held a scarred desk, an unsteady card table stacked with leaflets, and an ink-splattered mimeograph machine. An odor of ink and stale smoke pervaded the room.

From behind an ancient Underwood typewriter, Walter Reuther greeted Mike, then poured steaming coffee from a thermos into two mugs.

"You've been a godsend, Mike." Reuther's bland, round face, reddish hair, and slight build gave him a boyish look. But his piercing blue eyes, direct and confident, reflected an iron-willed intelligence. He walked around the desk and handed Mike a mug. "I'm telling you, we're in on the beginning of something big. I wish you could have been at the last convention. That's when the upturn began, when John L. Lewis reared back and took a swing at Bill Hutcheson after Bill called him an SOB. When I saw that, I knew Lewis was our man."

Mike had read about the incident, which had occurred five months ago, in April 1936. He smiled at the image of the bushy-browed, shaggy-maned Lewis, United Mine Workers' president, throwing an angry punch.

"And I wasn't wrong," Reuther continued. "Now that the UAW is under the leadership of Lewis and the CIO, we're going to lick the auto companies in this town."

"We've got a ways to go." Mike straddled a wobbly chair. "Seventy-three men isn't much of a membership."

"We'll grow. And before long, the Big Three will knuckle under."

"When I see Henry Ford knuckle under, that's the day I'm a believer." Mike swilled coffee from the cracked mug. "I don't see it happening in a hurry."

"Believe me, it's going to happen sooner or later. Dillon resigning as president of the UAW was all for the good. I'm hoping for a show of strength from the new president, Homer Martin." Reuther sorted through a pile of cards in a file box. "Have you located a sound truck?"

"Yeah, I found one in pretty good shape. I've arranged to pick it up tomorrow."

"Good."

"At least we've managed to consolidate the scattered small locals on the west side. So what's next?" Mike tapped a Lucky Strike from the packet and automatically offered it to Walter.

Walter waved the cigarette away. "Those things are bad for you—a nail in your coffin." He paced impatiently. "Mike, the Kelsey Hayes plant on McGraw and Livernois is ripe for a sit-down strike."

Mike lifted a butt-filled ashtray from the desk. "Kelsey Hayes? They supply wheels and brakes to the Rouge. But a sit-down? That's a new one on me."

"They've had sit-downs in Europe, successfully too. And there was one in Akron last year. The beauty of a sit-down is that you only need a small group of disciplined men to halt operations from the inside."

"You mean nobody's on the picket line, they're all inside the plant?" Mike looked doubtful.

"Right. The men stay in the plant and refuse to work. That way they can't get scabs in to do the work and you avoid bloody confrontations with the police. When a sit-down gets started in one department, you wouldn't believe how quickly it spreads. But even when the strike's contained in one spot, usually the jobs are so interrelated that if one department is out, nobody else can work."

Mike said, "You'll never get into the plant. You're getting too well-known."

"Yeah, that's the problem." Walter stuffed his hands into his pockets. "My brother Victor managed to get in at Kelsey Hayes as a punch-press operator. He's not as infamous as I am. We've got a few good men there: George Edwards, Stash Kaminski." Reuther stopped pacing and placed his hands on his hips. "Kelsey Hayes is a good place to start because it's not as big and unmanageable as the Rouge, but it's big enough to make a difference."

"And you want me to get hired?"

"Right." Reuther nodded.

"Impossible; I'm blacklisted."

"What about getting fake identification?"

Mike looked pensive. "It's worth a try. But where would I get it?"

"I don't know. Got any ideas?"

"As a matter of fact . . ." Mike thought about Fredo and the large network of "friends" he called on for small favors. At one time Mike might have had compunctions about this sort of illegal monkeyshine, but not any longer. "Consider it done."

"Swell, Mike." Reuther clapped his hand on Mike's back.

The door squeaked as Reuther's red-haired wife, May, nudged it open. She bore a bag full of sandwiches.

"Lunch, fellas. Can't work on an empty stomach." She emptied the bag on the desk. "Ham, cheese, egg salad, take your pick."

May Reuther had taken a leave from her teaching job and now worked every bit as hard as her husband for the union. She took her place behind the typewriter and rolled in a fresh sheet of paper.

"Thanks, May." Mike picked up a sandwich and headed out the door. "I'd better get things started. See you two later." He bit into the sandwich hungrily. So what if this job didn't pay? He had something he'd never had before: a sense of purpose.

What was that name again, the name Stewart had given her? After the wedding Chiara had written it down in her painstaking curlicue script, and put it away for safekeeping. She rummaged through a small enameled jewelry case and finally found the card under a set of holy cards. Cronin. Mr. Frederick J. Cronin of the Detroit Bank and Trust.

Chiara had never before been inside a bank. Mike always took care of business. It was traditionally a man's role, seeing to business transactions, loans, savings. Yet, some women were forced to take over, she supposed, women with no men to protect and guide them. If others could do it, she could too.

The bank building was intimidating, with marble pillars and tall, heavy doors. Inside, a guard stood ramrod straight with hands locked behind him. Chiara's footsteps were noisy on the gleaming tile floor as she headed uncertainly toward a teller's cubicle. What would she say? Already she felt tongue-tied. There were several people in front of her, all seemingly self-assured, little books clutched in their hands. The teller, a ferret-faced man with a sharp nose, was quick and curt, and the line moved speedily. What would Mike think if he knew what she was doing? And if she actually succeeded, what would she tell him?

Her determination was waning the longer she stood there, and she had just decided to leave when she heard, "Thank you. Next. Next!"

With the Hudson's box in one hand and a ledger under her arm, Chiara edged up to the cage. "Please, I want to see Mr. Cronin." She wished she could control the rolling of her R's, knowing it stamped her as a foreigner.

The teller looked annoyed as he jerked his thumb toward a row of doors beyond the line of teller cages, fronted by a receptionist desk "You need an appointment. See Miss Evans."

She backed away. *"Grazie.* Thank you." Of course, she should have known she'd need an appointment. She would probably be told to come back another day and would have to screw up her courage all over again.

Miss Evans, a crisp, efficient-looking young woman, smiled. "Do you have an appointment, Mrs. Marcassa?"

Chiara nervously fingered the widespread white linen collar of her good wool coat. "No, but if he isn't too busy . . . It's about a loan." She swallowed, surprised at her own effrontery. "Mr. Stewart Austin told me to come here. But I can come back another time."

"Mr. Austin? Just a moment, please." Miss Evans stood and disappeared into the nearest office.

Chiara's stomach churned. She had planned her argument, but now her mind went blank and her mouth was dry. She couldn't just baldly ask for a loan.

In a moment Miss Evans was back. "He'll see you, Mrs. Marcassa."

In the meticulous dark-paneled office, large pots of

greenery stood in the corner near a window. At an enormous desk, Mr. Cronin shuffled papers into a file, seemingly oblivious of Chiara's entrance.

When she took hesitant steps forward, he jerked his balding head upward. He looked as if he'd recently been in the sun, with a florid face and deep pink nose. A forced smile appeared and abruptly vanished as he indicated a seat next to the desk. Chiara perched on the edge of the chair, the rectangular box centered across her knees.

"Marcassa, Marcassa?" he said. "Don't I know you from somewhere? The name's familiar."

"No. Mr. Austin told me to come and see you about a loan."

"Mr. Austin, eh? What's old Stew up to, anyway?"

"I . . . I don't know. I don't see him very . . ."

"Ah, wait a minute." He tapped a silver pen on his desk a few times. "Now I remember. Stewart called me a while back . . . yes, yes, it's coming back now—he mentioned you." Mr. Cronin regarded Chiara with frank appraisal.

What was he thinking? Chiara wondered. She sat up a little straighter and smoothed her coat over her knees, then took a deep breath. The words tumbled out quickly.

"I need a loan for a bridal salon. I'm sure I would have lots of business. I make beautiful gowns for wedding parties. Already most of the Italians come to me and I do good work. I have some pictures and a list of what I would need . . . " Catching her breath, she shoved the leather-bound ledger she'd purchased from Kresge's onto his desk. She had carefully penned in every item she could think of: rental, sewing machines, mannequins, fabric, notions, paint, lumber, telephone, even the anticipated electric bills.

Mr. Cronin secured round spectacles behind his ears and drew the ledger toward him. While he scanned the pages, Chiara held her breath, waiting for him to speak.

"Hmm." His thin lips pursed and his brow furrowed with concentration.

Before he could speak, Chiara said in a voice weak with trepidation, "I have some pictures." She stood and placed the Hudson's box before him, removing the cover.

Inside were stacked some of her original sketches and a photograph of the Morrison wedding party.

"Hmm." Mr. Cronin's forehead wrinkled as he glanced through the sketches. "Ah."

Chiara's knees felt weak. She backed away from his desk hoping he couldn't hear the thumping of her heart. She wished desperately she hadn't come here to make a fool of herself.

Mr. Cronin's head snapped up and he said, "Sit down, Mrs. Marcassa. Don't be impatient."

Like an obedient puppy she sat, her hands clenched in her lap, while he sifted through the sketches and peered again at the ledger, then at her, then back at the ledger.

After an eternity, he cleared his throat. "Of course, I'm no judge of fashion, Mrs. Marcassa . . . "

A half-hour later Chiara walked out of the bank in a daze. Clutched in her hand was a check for one thousand dollars. She was bursting to tell Mike and present him with the check, yet dreading his reaction.

That evening, after clearing the dinner table, Chiara placed the check in front of Mike without saying a word.

"What is this?" Slowly he turned the check over in his hands. Frowning, he read aloud, "'Pay to the order of Chiara Marcassa, one thousand dollars.'"

Mike turned it again and scanned the blank side, then looked at his wife questioningly. "Chiara?"

She swallowed hard. "It's a loan. From the bank. For the bridal salon."

Mike sprang up and away from the table, overturning his chair.

"Bridal salon!" His fist pounded the table. "I thought you'd forgotten all that foolishness."

"It's not foolishness. Listen to me, Mike—"

"How did you get this money? Did you hold them up with a gun?"

"No! A man at the bank named Mr. Cronin gave it to me."

"Just like that, he gave it to you?"

"I had all the figures and he liked my drawings, and I told him about working for the Morrisons and the Austins. Oh, Mike, he was so nice."

Mike shook his head in disbelief.

"He said his daughter is getting married and he'll send her to me. She'll be my first customer in the new shop."

Mike glared. "You don't even *have* a shop."

"Maria and I looked at some places last week. There's a nice place on Jefferson, close to Grosse Pointe, and one on Woodward . . . "

"How did you manage to convince the bank? They won't stay in business very long if this is the way they operate."

Chiara's chin puckered, then lifted. She'd hoped Mike would be agreeable. "Mr. Cronin thinks I'll be successful. He believes in me. You're not working; we can use the money."

Mike's mouth tightened. "I have a job with the union."

"A job that doesn't pay," Chiara said quietly.

"It *will* pay!" Mike's eyes glinted in anger. "As soon as things get rolling and we have more members, it'll pay!"

"Mike, listen. You have your dream, a dream to get the workers into a union. I don't like that dream; it's dangerous and stupid to think you can win against the powerful bosses, and—"

"You have no idea of what's—"

"Just let me finish." Chiara stood and placed her hands firmly on the table. "I don't interfere with your dream, because I know how important it is to you, even if I don't like it. Now I have a dream too. I believe in my dream just like you believe in yours."

Mike started to say something, then stopped. He sat down heavily. "I just don't know how you'll manage everything. Having a business takes all your time. The baby . . . who'll take care of her?"

Realizing that Mike was making a halfhearted attempt at acceptance, Chiara hugged him. "I'll manage, don't you worry. Maybe Rosa's girl will help with Anna."

"Chiara . . . " Mike sighed. "This is a big mistake. I only hope you're not disappointed."

A few days later Chiara, Mike, Flora, and Maria, laden with mops and rag-filled pails, stood before the little shop on Woodward Avenue, which was flanked by a five-and-dime and a small office building.

"Well, what do you think?" Chiara asked.

Taking a few steps back, hands on hips, Mike assessed

the place. He shook his head, muttering under his breath, "I can't believe you're doing this."

With her index finger Maria cleared a spot on the dusty glass and peered at the mess inside. Pursing her lips, she made a disparaging sound, then spoke slowly. "I think Mike was right. You *are* crazy." Then she turned to her friend and tossed her head toward the door. *"Andiamo.* We'd better get busy. We have lots of work to do."

With a great flourish, Chiara produced a long brass key and unlocked the door.

Inside, she tugged at Mike's arm and raised questioning eyes to him. She desperately wanted his approval; but with or without it, she was going through with her plans.

Mike cast a frowning glance at the dusty clutter. Cardboard boxes overrun with rubbish were stacked every which way. Paint peeled from the wall, and the embossed metal ceiling had a distinct sag. The open door created a breeze that swirled the dust upward.

Finally Mike grunted. "Maybe it'll be all right."

"It will need more than a broom and a pail," Flora said.

"Much more. Paint and wax and . . . Oh, Mike, just imagine a mannequin in the window, the bride, with a background painting of a church." Chiara almost sang as she gestured grandly. "The bride's stepping out of the church door, and other mannequins, the bridesmaids, are standing to the side, looking at her."

"Dino's good at carpentry; he'll give me a hand with the shelves and partitions. Not that I'm convinced it's a good idea," Mike added hastily. "You can say good-bye to the down payment for our house."

Chiara squeezed his hand. Though he tried to hide it, Mike actually seemed caught up in the excitement.

"Mike, if I can make lots of money, we can go back to the old country and live like kings."

As he paced off a section from the back wall, Mike seemed not to hear her. "Most of the space will have to be for the work area. You'll need dressing rooms. Maybe along this wall." His arm swept upward, toward the left.

"Yes, over there, with curtains of pale blue. The walls will be ivory and we can have blue chairs. Blue and ivory everywhere." Chiara turned and clutched Maria's arm.

"Oh, Maria, tell me, what do you see? Will we be successful?"

With her patient little head waggle, Maria said, "You expect far too much of me. I tell you, I can't know everything." But she closed her eyes in that slow, almost painful way she had. When she opened them, she was smiling. "I see your daughter, Anna, getting married in one of your gowns."

Chiara laughed and hugged her friend. "It isn't much, Maria, but it's something."

The four of them set to work, and by the end of the day the result of their efforts was evident. Chiara almost wept with jubilation when they finally turned the key in the lock and headed for home.

The next night it was Mike's turn for jubilation.

"I have good news," he said, bursting into the house with a November draft of cold damp air. "I got a job with Kelsey Hayes."

"Oh, Mike, that's wonderful." Chiara's cheeks were flushed with pleasure. "Everything's going so well for us."

Mike neglected to tell her that the job had been obtained with false identification and that it would probably end in a firing.

Only a few handpicked union members from the Kelsey Hayes plant attended a meeting in late November. They discussed the Midland Steel plant's successful sit-down strike, after which management finally knuckled under and gave the workers a ten-cents-an-hour raise besides recognizing the UAW as sole bargaining agent.

"The balance of power is shifting," Walter Reuther had declared. "The timing is perfect for a Kelsey Hayes strike."

Mike said, "Tension is running high in Department Forty-nine. The foreman is tough, constantly riding herd on the men. Last week a woman fainted from the speed-up. She's ready to quit, bad as she needs to work. They treat the women poorly—her wage is only twenty-two cents. A man doing the same thing gets thirty-seven."

"Department Forty-nine is the key department. We have plenty of brothers there," Victor Reuther said.

Walter looked up suddenly and tapped his chin with a

pencil. "Wait a minute. It's the perfect setup. Do you think that woman could faint again, on cue?"

Victor hesitated. "Probably."

The three men looked at one another, smiles lighting their faces as the perception dawned. It would be easy to gain sympathy if someone fainted. They began talking all at once, laying strategy, deciding on "brothers" who could be trusted, figuring in unknown factors. Carrying off a successful sit-down strike would be a challenge, Mike knew. They were breaking new ground and there were no rules of order to go by.

On Tuesday, December 8, Mike listened to the whining roar of the machines as he performed his job by rote. His stomach muscles knotting, he envisioned the scene about to take place. Perspiration formed on his brow, caused, he knew, by nerves.

He glanced at his watch, then at the tall, husky Polish girl he'd nicknamed Pinky. Her hair was caught up in a snood and her usually placid face looked tense, with her lower lip caught between her teeth. Her eyes darted to Mike and he smiled reassuringly. He had a fleeting sense of gratitude that his wife didn't have to work in a factory.

He caught Stash Kaminski's eye, then looked significantly at his watch.

Stash's muscles bulged as he worked his machine. A reliable "brother," he wrote union leaflets and distributed them in front of churches on Sunday mornings, and his wife was active in the Housewives Committee Against the High Cost of Living. Mike could count on Stash.

It was time for the shift change, when both shifts would be in the building together for a few short minutes. The second shift began filing in, and Mike's gaze sought out Victor Reuther at the far end of the room. Victor nodded. They both looked in the direction of Pinky. Without warning and precisely on schedule, the Polish girl fell to the floor with a loud thud.

A hue and cry went up from the men around her.

"She's fainted!" someone called out.

Foreman Morrow was at her side instantly, shouting, "Keep it going, men. You, Harley, help me out over here." He slapped at Pinky's hands while, annoyed at the disruption, he kept up a stream of invectives. When he dragged Pinky out of the way, a new man slid into her spot and smoothly assumed the pattern of work. Pinky's eyes fluttered open and she sat upright and began to cry, her face pale and miserable.

She's playing it to the hilt, Mike thought.

Over the din, voices rang out.

"Is someone hurt?"

"What's going on?"

The oblivious conveyor kept its steady, noisy pace, but some of the workers slacked off as they craned their necks to discover the problem. When they realized what had occurred, a babble of voices rose in disgruntled tones.

"The line's too damn fast!"

"We can't keep up!"

"We need a breathing spell!"

"You're killing us with the speed-up!"

It's perfect, Mike thought, a rush of adrenaline pounding through his body. He edged over to the wall, behind the foreman's desk, picking up an iron bar along the way. Reaching upward, he threw the main switch at the power panel. The rumbling machinery ground to a sudden dramatic stop. In the ominous silence, some of the men looked around in confusion, while others, sensing trouble, backed away from their benches with wary eyes.

A foreman from the far end of the room yelled, "What's happening here?"

Another said, "What is it, a power failure?"

Victor made his way to Mike and yelled, "It's a strike!"

Mike's foreman, as confused as the rest, yelled out, "What the hell's going on? Did someone pull the switch?" He turned to see Mike standing before the panel.

"It's a strike," Victor repeated.

"You turn that switch on, Mason!" the foreman yelled, using Mike's assumed name.

"Sit down, brothers!" Mike raised his hands. "This is a sit-down strike."

Morrow started toward Mike. "You heard me, Mason! You got five seconds to pull that switch!"

"We're sitting," Mike shouted as the foreman advanced on him with an angry, menacing expression. Mike raised the iron bar waist-high. "Don't come any farther."

"Are you threatening me?"

"I'm telling you, this is a strike."

"The hell, you say. Turn the power on or your ass is outta here." The foreman's face contorted in an angry snarl.

"Hey, you bastard, get away from him." The deep voice of Clayton, a gigantic black worker, caused the foreman to spin around. With his shirt open to the waist, the black man's massive chest gleamed with perspiration and his arm muscles bulged against the rolled-up shirt sleeves.

"You stay outta this, nigger," Morrow shouted.

"Don't worry," Mike said in a reasonable tone. "This is a peaceful sit-down strike. No one'll get hurt."

"We'll see about who gets hurt," the foreman shouted. "If you men don't get back to work, you're all fired."

The three other foremen had begun walking toward Mike and Victor to see what the ruckus was about. Instantly the workers hefted heavy tools and, glaring menacingly, encircled the foremen. The black man, Clayton, went to Mike's side, saying, "I'm with you, brother."

"Mike, I'll call the switchboard." Victor had a "plant" at the switchboard, who would alert each department. "Brothers" located on each floor were waiting for word of the strike.

"It's just a peaceful sit-down strike," Mike told the foremen, who were being coaxed toward the door. "Tell your superintendent we need to talk."

Morrow made one last attempt. "Get back to work! That's an order!"

No one moved.

"You heard me!" The foreman's gaze swung over the group.

The only response was a menacing stillness. Then the workers slowly edged the four foremen to the exit. With no recourse but to leave, they scurried out through the metal doors, their footsteps sending reverberating echoes from the steel steps.

Victor seized the opportunity and jumped on a crate. "Is this what we're going to put up with for the rest of our lives? Working conditions where people faint from exhaustion? Low wages? Layoffs? It's time to band together—organize. The UAW is behind us one hundred percent! Put down your tools! Sit down!"

The men shouted their agreement.

"Sit down! Sit down!" a hundred voices chanted.

They were caught up in the excitement of the moment, buoyed by the knowledge that at long last they were successfully demonstrating their strength. A few dissenters were afraid of being fired, but Stash and other "brothers" scattered about, encouraging them.

A few minutes later, the metal door swung open and the personnel director bounded in, fury written over his features.

"What the hell is going on?" He marched up to Victor, who calmly continued his spiel from atop the crate.

"It's a strike," Mike said.

The director pulled at Victor's trouser leg. "Goddammit, what do you think you're doing?"

Impatiently shaking his leg, Victor said, "I'm explaining that we need a union to protect ourselves."

"I demand that you get down from there and get these men back to work!"

Victor said, "I tell you, the workers are fed up; they won't work under these conditions."

The director glared. "Someone's got to talk sense to them. Who the hell will they listen to?"

"My brother, Walter Reuther. He's the only one."

"You think your brother can get them back to work?"

"I'm sure he can."

"Who the hell is he?"

"He's the president of our union."

The director ran his hand over his face, muttering, "What the hell . . . okay, how do I reach this guy?"

Mike handed him a card with the phone number and exchanged triumphant looks with Victor. When the director went to the phone, a cheer went up from the workers, and Victor and Mike slapped each other on the back.

Mike shook Victor's hand. "We did it."

"You said it!"

"This is only the beginning. But it *is* a beginning."

Mike sat at the foreman's vacated desk issuing union cards to the eager workers who swarmed around him, while Victor Reuther resumed his spraddle-legged stance atop a large crate, rallying the men.

Within a half-hour the double doors flew open and Walter strode in purposefully, a serious look on his youthful countenance. The personnel director was at Walter's heels. At the sight of his brother, Victor hopped off the makeshift stage and he and Mike gripped Walter's hand in relief. Walter immediately took his brother's place atop the crate and, hardly missing a beat, continued the rallying cry for the union.

"Congratulations," Walter shouted to the assemblage of workers. "This is a historic moment in union history. By striking you've taken the first step on your road toward emancipation. The next step is to join the UAW. The UAW will give you freedom—freedom from speeded-up lines, from working overtime for regular pay, from—"

"Jesus Christ," the director yelled, tugging at Walter's pant leg. "Get down from there! I thought you were going to get them back to work!"

"I will," Walter shot back, "but we can't do anything with them if they're not organized!"

The director stood aside, a bewildered look on his face, while Walter continued his harangue. By now there were about five hundred workers jammed into Department forty-nine, many of them lined up to sign with the union.

Turning on his heel, the director left and returned a few minutes later. He shouted over Walter's words, "The super wants to see you, Reuther—all three of you!"

"You're in charge, Stash, you and Clayton," Mike said, hurrying off with the Reuthers.

As they followed the director, Walter said, "This is the big one, the one we're going to win. Management wasn't expecting it, so the surprise element is in our favor. They're unprepared." He chortled. "It's ironic, isn't it? They wouldn't hire me to work on the line, but now I'm escorted in by a chauffeur-driven car."

Outside the superintendent's office several men appraised the three union men who strode toward them resolutely, proudly. Mike returned their stares with an arrogance befitting a man who had helped shut down an entire plant.

Inside, the super, a heavyset, jowly man, chomped on a long cigar and paced while a large moose-faced man in a dark suit stood beside the door.

As Mike and Victor walked into the office, the super swung around. Yanking the cigar from his mouth and waving it in the air, he said, "What's this bullshit about sitting down?"

"The men want better working conditions," Mike said. "A woman fainted trying to keep up with the speeded-up line."

The superintendent rolled the cigar in his mouth, then walked around his massive desk and sat down. "All right, boys, relax, have a seat." He pointed at the chairs across from his desk.

None of them stirred.

The superintendent's angry scowl disappeared. He leaned back in his chair and directed a smile at Walter. "You're Reuther, eh, head of the local?"

"Right."

The super turned his head, and using dulcet tones, directed his remarks to Mike and Victor. "Ah, now, boys, you've been working here awhile and we been treating you real good. Let's be reasonable. This strike business will get you nowhere. Just tell the men to get back to work, and nobody'll be fired. You'll still have your jobs."

"They won't listen," Victor said. "They're hot now, and getting hotter. The longer this goes on, the madder they'll get."

Jumping from his seat, the superintendent stood and leaned on his desk, his weight centered on his stiffened arms, his face contorted with anger. He looked from one to the other. "What the hell are you after?"

"Better working conditions, decent wages, job security. That's for starters," Walter said. "They're willing to negotiate."

"Negotiate! Negotiate, my ass. Either they go back to work or they're fired!"

"They won't leave the building," Mike said. "This is a sit-down strike."

"Sit-down strike, eh?" he said in a sarcastic voice. "We'll see about that! I'm calling the police, and you'll all be hauled out on your asses!"

Mike crossed his arms on his chest. "There aren't enough police in the city to carry out all five thousand workers. Besides, we're not here illegally. We belong here."

The super's face was slowly turning crimson. "Listen to me! You bastards go back and tell them to get to work! That's an order. Now, get the hell out of my sight!"

The three men made no move to leave. The super switched the cigar from one corner of his mouth to the other and growled, "All right. I gotta have this plant running again in short order. Every minute we're shut down, I'm losing money."

Walter smiled and leaned over the desk until he was almost nose to nose with the super. "I want formal negotiations to begin tomorrow morning, nine o'clock, with representatives from all departments of both plants. Then maybe, just maybe, we can get this plant operating again."

The super sputtered for a moment, then fell back into his chair. In a tight voice he said. "All right. Nine o'clock."

23

Outside the office Walter said, "This is the big one, the one we're going to win. But there's lots to do now. You stay on the inside, Mike, while Victor and I mobilize the other locals. We'll have to begin operating the sound truck." Walter looked hastily at some scribbled notes. "Management has to get production moving again to complete a brake order for Ford. If they can't get the orders filled, Ford will go to another supplier. They're in a bind, and we know it, and they know we know it."

"Do you think the police'll try to force us out?" Mike asked.

"I doubt it. Technically you're not here illegally," Walter said. "And I don't think Mayor Couzens will fight us on this."

Mike looked doubtful. "But management will try to get strikebreakers in. I know the tactics. They'll try to provoke us to violence, then get the police to throw us out."

"There won't be any violence, no matter what happens. It's up to you to see that tempers don't flare up inside, and we'll take care of any picketers outside. I've already alerted some of the other locals. They'll picket the entrances. But I've given them the word: no violence." Walter's face expressed the urgency they all felt.

Back in Department Forty-nine, Mike listened to fragments of conversations and detected a slight shift of attitude. Now that the consequences of their actions had become clear, the men's words held overtones of apprehension. They understood they were breaking new ground and they were fearful. Mike understood that fear.

A thin young man named Connor, newly married, with a pregnant wife, cornered Mike. "I hope you know what you're doing, Mike. Sure, I believe in the union, but let's face facts. The union ain't done shit for nobody so far. Management always gets the upper hand."

Mike put his hand on Connor's shoulder. "This time it's us who have the upper hand."

"I can't go home and face my wife if I get fired."

"Trust me, Connor, we're going to win." As he said it, Mike formulated a prayer of supplication. It *has* to work. It *can't* fail. Too much is riding on this. The livelihood of too many desperate human beings is hanging in the balance.

Mike easily empathized with the feelings of the workers. On the one hand, they wanted to believe; on the other, history was against them. The laboring masses were always the victims.

He listened again, trying to pick up threads of different conversations. Though they were fearful of defying management, they had no choice but to place their bets on the side of the union. Many were union, but more were not. By God, their faith had better be justified, Mike thought.

Then he heard a hopeful sound, a musical sound. Clayton, in his full, resonant voice began singing.

When they tie the can to a union man,
Sit down, Sit down.

Others joined in:

When they give him the sack, they'll take him back,
Sit down, Sit down.

When the speed-up comes, just twiddle your thumbs,
Sit down, Sit down.
When the boss won't talk, don't take a walk,
Sit down, Sit down."

After the last notes died down, Clayton and Stash joined Mike. "What do you think, Mike? Will we be home by Christmas?" Stash asked.

Mike closed his eyes and said fervently, "I hope so, guys, I sure hope so."

Hearing a commotion from outside the plant, Mike hurried to the window. He was cheered to see pickets, some barring the entrances, other patrolling outside the plant with bold-lettered signs raised high above them. But his hope turned to alarm when he saw another group approaching the building. He recognized several foremen among them. Strikebreakers! The foremen were trying to get scabs inside the plant. Mike had a few anxious moments, wondering if the pickets would attack. They had their instructions to avoid a fight, but when men reached the limit of their patience, they could easily react with violence. As the strikebreakers approached the doorways, the picketers stood firmly together in an attempt to halt their progress, but they were outnumbered by the powerful scabs, who easily shunted them aside.

Mike hurriedly gathered a large group together and led them to the front door, where they met the scabs head-on. With menacing scowls, the workers pushed the strikebreakers toward the infirmary. Frightened, the scabs dashed inside the relative safety of the clinic, and Mike immediately positioned workers to block the exit and keep the scabs from going out into the work areas.

Cranking open a window, Mike felt his hopes rise anew as more picketers arrived. Their voices swelled with the chant, "Throw the scabs out, throw the scabs out!" The cry was picked up by the strikers inside, and soon the sounds reverberated throughout the plant.

Inside the infirmary the rattled strikebreakers, fearing for their lives, finally surrendered and left the plant under police escort.

Relieved, Mike returned to his department. Rubbing his arms, he realized with surprise that he was getting cold. So that was management's new tactic—turning off the heat. The other strikers were beginning to notice it too. Before long they all felt the cold December wind through the drafty walls and their breath was exhaled in steamy clouds. One worker picked up a tool and began banging on the machinery. In moments, others followed suit.

Mike yelled, "Don't do any damage; just let them think you might." He felt sure management wouldn't risk the destruction of expensive equipment. He was right. Within minutes the heat was turned on again.

Mike moved through the men, giving encouragement, telling a joke, shaking a hand. Someone produced a deck of cards, and a lively game of gin ensued, with plenty of kibitzers standing around. Others stood or sat in small groups, talking about sports or the movies, trying to divert their minds from the serious nature of their actions.

At the sound of banging on the glass, Mike rushed to the window. Christ, what now? he thought. A group of picketers stood outside, laden with food and hot coffee. A matronly woman Mike recognized as the wife of one of the part-time organizers said, "May says, 'Keep it up, guys.' "

"I figured May Reuther would come through," Mike said, gripping the woman's free hand.

"Yeah, she got the woman's auxiliary together for sandwiches and coffee. We ain't gonna let you starve."

After the food had been dispensed and devoured, Mike leaned wearily against the wall. Yawning, he realized he was exhausted. Day one was winding down. Men bundled in coats searched for relatively clean spots on which to lie. Soon a quiet fell on the plant and someone began a soulful singing of the Solidarity song to the tune of "The Battle Hymn of the Republic." Others joined in, and soon the sound rang out in deep heartfelt tones, reflecting the hope that stirred in their hearts.

When the union's inspiration through the workers' blood shall run,
There can be no power greater anywhere beneath the sun.
Yet what force on earth is weaker than the feeble strength of one?
But the union makes us strong.

Solidarity forever!
Solidarity forever!
Solidarity forever!
For the union makes us strong.

By midnight a restive peace had settled on the plant. Mike lay on the concrete floor, his head on his rolled-up coat, and tried to sleep. The buzz of conversation mingled with the sound of light snoring and deep breathing. Soon even the talk died away. But sleep eluded Mike.

His thoughts went to Chiara and Anna. His wife must be beside herself with worry. Since he had come home beaten and bloody, she had considered, rightly, the union dangerous, and tried to talk him out of joining as an organizer. She had no clear concept of the importance of his work, and thought only in personal and immediate terms. Mike was sorry he had told her so many horror stories of maimed and mutilated unionists.

Soon it would be Christmas. He had planned to shop on Christmas Eve, in the hopes that he could find bargains then. Now there might not even be a Christmas celebration; this impasse could easily continue into the new year.

His heart had been set on buying Chiara something special, a brooch perhaps, or a necklace. She had few treasures, yet she never complained. Her life was one of hard work, most of it self-imposed. The bridal salon took much of her time and effort, but surprisingly, she seemed to thrive on it. He supposed her work was going well enough, though he had been too busy to really take an interest. Whenever he asked her, she said business was good. She had plenty of customers. Still, when he saw her pen moving slowly across the ledger, her face pinched in a frown, he wasn't sure she'd done the right thing. He knew she wouldn't easily admit defeat. Stubborn. She had been determined to have her shop, no matter how he tried to dissuade her. If things weren't going well, she would be reluctant to tell him. Maybe she would soon get it out of her system, and stay home and take care of the family. At that moment he envisioned her waiting for him, brushing her abundant silky hair, her fleshy lower lip in a slight pout, her eyes shiny blue, and he longed for her, ached to crush her against him, to kiss her sweet face. He tried to dispel the appealing, yet disquieting image. He twisted to his side to relieve the ache of his back against the cold hard floor, but his thoughts churned on and on until the smoky gray light of daybreak swept over the wide, soot-darkened factory windows.

The stalemate continued the next day and the next, with the Reuthers and Mike hammering out their demands with management. The workers interrupted their interminable card games and impromptu songfests to cheer their leaders on, their courage never flagging.

As the strike dragged on, management attempted to move some of the tools and dies to the Rouge plant. When word of the company's plan got out, the sit-in workers halted the operation by barring the exits with huge dollies filled with all sorts of heavy auto parts.

By the second week, morale was low. The strikers confided to Mike their fear that Christmas would be spent without their families. Christmas decorations and gifts began to appear inside the plant, from generous donations of outside supporters. On December 23, Walter Reuther appeared, haggard but jubilant, before the crowd that had assembled in one large area.

"Management has finally caved in!" he shouted.

A great roar rose up from the crowd. "We've won! We've won!"

"They've signed a truce agreement," Reuther screamed over the roar of the jubilant group. "The minimum wage has been raised to seventy-five cents an hour starting immediately for both men and women, and they've tentatively agreed to premium pay for overtime, seniority rules to protect job security, and a twenty-percent reduction in the speed of the assembly line."

He could hardly be heard over the joyous shouts of the men. They hugged each other and did little jigs. Mike saw an old man weep unashamedly.

Reuther gathered his leaders and said, "They were pushed to the wall after Ford threatened to go to another supplier. It's ironic that Ford, who abhors unions, should be the catalyst that sent Kelsey Hayes into the UAW's waiting arms."

Some two thousand supporters and a union band greeted the weary sit-downers as they jubilantly marched out of the plant. Cheers went up as though they were soldiers returning from a valiant and victorious battle. And indeed, they were.

It was the night before Christmas Eve. Mike burst through the doors into the cold, biting air, and Stash, striding alongside him, said, "By God, there is a Santa Claus."

It was an amazing victory for men who had been dehumanized to the point that they were identified and called by management, prisonerlike, not by name but by number.

"This is only the beginning, Stash. You're going to see sit-downs all over the city. And in the end, the big three will capitulate." Mike paused and faced Stash. "Henry Ford. I want to see Henry Ford brought to his knees."

When Chiara opened the door and saw her exhausted husband, she threw herself into his arms with a cry of joy and scattered kisses over his face.

"Thank God you're home." She pulled him inside. "I haven't slept since this started."

Mike reached behind him and dragged in a fresh-smelling balsam. "I had to stop for a Christmas tree. Come on, let's wake Anna."

Chiara reached up and patted his stubbled cheek. "You'll frighten her with this beard."

Together they woke up the slumbering child, and Mike cradled her against his chest with one arm while hugging his wife with the other.

"Mike, I missed you so. Promise you'll never do this again." Chiara pulled closer to Mike, reveling in the feeling of security his muscular arm provided.

Mike said nothing, but settled the sleepy-eyed child back in her bed, covering her gently to her chin with the pink blanket.

"We won't talk about that now." Mike scooped Chiara up into his arms and carried her to bed. Pressing his face against her breast, he said, "Later. We'll talk later."

The next day, Chiara unwrapped the delicate ornaments she had put away from last Christmas. She delighted in the American customs—the glitter and glow of a tree, the gifts, the enchanting shops filled with toys and decorated in red, green, silver, and gold. In Italy San Nicola's day was celebrated early in December, with small treats left in shoes waiting by the door.

Mike handed Anna a shiny blue globe and the curly-headed toddler stretched on tiptoes to place it on a tree branch, then hurried back to be cuddled and praised by her father. When Mike began singing an Italian song to his daughter, it warmed Chiara's heart. There was no mistaking they were father and daughter, with the thick jet hair and matching eyes, though Mike's eyes, she noticed, were still ringed with dark circles.

"A man came by yesterday and dropped off a package for us," Chiara said. "There were clothes inside, underwear, and mittens, and even a doll for Anna. He said it was from the Goodfellows. I thought it was a mistake."

Mike exploded. "It *was* a mistake. That's a charitable organization. They give to needy people. We're not in need."

"You don't have to get so mad. It's nice warm clothing."

"I want you to give it back. Or else give it to someone else who needs it far worse than we do. Understand?"

"All right. It's Christmas, Mike. Try not to get so mad about little things like that." She had no idea where to return the package, and after all, they could use the clothing for Anna. Mike was so preoccupied, he would forget all about it anyway. He was overly sensitive when it came to accepting charity.

Mike plugged in the lights and the room was suffused immediately in a warm glow. The shabbiness of the furniture was disguised in the blurred light.

Chiara poured two small glasses of anisette, and sat next to Mike, basking in the quiet, enjoying the feel of him, the musky scent of him.

"I missed you, Mike. So did Anna." Her only contact with him had been a hastily scribbled message delivered by one of the pickets.

"I missed you too." Mike's arm tightened about her, and his lips nuzzled her hair. "I wanted to call you, but without a telephone . . . Dammit, I'm getting us a telephone."

"Every night I would read the paper and cry, especially when I saw pictures of the pickets and the police."

"You shouldn't have worried. We agreed there would be no violence."

She tugged at his arm. "This won't happen again, will it?"

Mike shifted uneasily.

"Mike, it won't, will it?"

"There are some problems in Flint. I may have to go."

She had read something about a strike, but why did Mike have to be involved?

"Flint? Flint must be a hundred miles away! Why?"

"There's a sit-down strike in progress right now at the Fisher Body Plant Number Two. It started in Cleveland, when the plant officials refused to meet with the union."

Chiara pulled away from his arms and turned to look at him. "You don't have to go. Let the others do it."

"Either I'm in this or I'm not. It's my job." He leaned forward with his hands hanging loosely between his legs. "It's come at a bad time for the union. The CIO has its hands full trying to organize the steel industry, which means John L. Lewis is occupied. This certainly wasn't planned."

Chiara moaned, wagging her head in a defeated gesture. "When will all this end? It's as if you're a soldier going to war."

"Chiara, think of what this means. If we play our cards right, we can unionize the entire General Motors organization." Mike's voice reflected his excitement. "Think of it! General Motors in Flint has fifty thousand workers. If we sign them, the other big companies will probably follow. It'll revolutionize the labor industry."

"I don't know about all that, and I don't even care," Chiara said with a little sob. "I only know it keeps you away from us."

Mike stood and paced the small room, made even smaller by the Christmas tree. He punched a fist into his palm. "I have to do this. It's not just for me, it's for our children and our children's children. Can't you see that?"

"No. I can only see that your child hardly knows you."

Mike was silent for a moment. He plucked Anna up from the floor, where she was stacking wooden blocks, and tickled her under the chin. "I'll make it up to her, and to you, Chiara. I promise you that. But some things can't wait. We have to move when the time is right, and now it's right."

A few days later Chiara gave Mike a kiss and a blessing as he prepared to leave for Flint.

At the door, he pulled her roughly to him. "Don't worry about me."

"Of course I'll worry." For several moments they clung together; then Chiara handed Mike his lunch box filled with hearty sandwiches and Christmas delicacies.

She watched him leave with a jaunty step and obvious anticipation. *He's happy doing this,* she thought with a mixture of exasperation and pride. In the face of Mike's hope and courage, her own doubts were beginning to diminish.

What a way to begin the new year, Mike thought as he arrived in Flint on January 1. He was met at General Motors Plant Number Two by Victor Reuther, who had rigged up speakers on the roof of a black Chevrolet sedan.

"Walter stayed behind to meet with GM's Detroit workers," Victor said as Mike took his place at the wheel.

The sound of pickets singing the solidarity song was encouraging. "I hear GM's president, Knudsen, refuses to talk until the plants are vacated."

"The strikers won't leave. We're at an impasse."

Mike snapped the key in the ignition and the car roared and sputtered before it moved slowly forward. "I only hope they can hold fast. If GM gives in to the union, it'll be the greatest victory in the history of labor."

"With each side so determined, I'm afraid this may go on for weeks." Victor picked up the microphone in his gloved hand. "The court may rule that sit-downs are illegal. Then we're in for real trouble."

Victor began talking into the microphone, spewing his special brand of inspiration. Pickets cheered and waved their signs in the direction of the car.

Mike circled the buildings while Victor's voice boomed over the loudspeakers. The man was good. Mike hoped Reuther was wrong and the strike would be over soon. By the second week, Mike knew they were in for a long one. The strike dragged on, with small skirmishes but no clear victories for either side. On January 11, in sixteen-degree weather, Mike and Victor took a circuitous route to the plant and found a grim and silent picket line.

A youthful picket wearing a woolen hat pulled down over his forehead rushed over to report, "Management has turned off the heat. They think they can starve and freeze them out."

Police at each gate barred entrance into the plant. The men inside, Mike thought, must be bitter and angry. He sent music through the loudspeakers and selected a committee to confront the guards at the front gates.

"We're going to demand that they open the gate," Mike told the small assembled group. "It's a long shot, I know, but the guards are workers too, and most of them have friends inside. They may be sympathetic."

The group managed to open up an alley where food could be brought in and then approached the gate.

Mike yelled, "Let the food inside, or we'll force our way in."

To his relief, the guards quietly moved aside to allow the food bearers in. From inside the building a great cheer went up at the sight of food. The plant guards were obviously in sympathy. They did their duty, but reluctantly.

When he returned to the car, Mike heard shouts of "The police!" From beyond the railroad track came the burst of tear-gas shells and over the bridge came a phalanx of police, wearing gas masks and carrying stubby-muzzled guns. As the uniformed men approached, they lobbed tear-gas shells at some of the pickets and through the windows of Fisher Two.

Victor immediately got on the microphone and called on the workers to stand fast. "Don't allow GM to drive you into submission by police power!" His voice was an inexhaustible stream, pouring courage into them. There were about a thousand onlookers by now, and Victor urged them to come in and help the pickets. Mike's faith was renewed when thirty or so men hurried forward.

From inside, the workers sent a barrage of homemade weapons into the police. When pickets charged from all directions, the men in blue were momentarily overwhelmed. But Mike's hope was short-lived when, minutes later, police reinforcements arrived. They charged the gate, but were met by freezing jets of water from a fire hose that the strikers inside aimed from a second-story window. The police again retreated, then returned to attack again, this time shooting into the picket lines with long-range tear gas missiles. Pickets, choking and wheezing, staggered to the fringes of battle, trying to get fresh air. Mike helped move wounded men out of range, and as soon as he could, returned to the sound car with Victor. Fumes seeped up through the floorboards.

"The bastards must have fired a tear-gas bomb under the car," Mike said, choking on the words.

Victor soaked a handkerchief in his thermos of coffee and pressed it against his nose and, undaunted, kept on preaching. The random shelling continued until past midnight. After a half-hour of relative quiet, Mike waited fearfully for the next barrage. A few minutes later, one of the pickets reported that the police had run out of ammunition.

It was six A.M., before Mike and Victor left the car. In the tenebrous light of dawn, Chevrolet Avenue looked like an industrial-age battlefield, with overturned and smashed vehicles, shattered glass, pieces of iron pipe and metal scrap, bolts, hinges, and spent tear-gas canisters. The skirmish was over, but what of the next battle, and the next? Could the men endure? Would they become battle-weary and give in? Would frustration overwhelm them when they could no longer feed their families? They were losing money every day. Local business extended credit and the union supplied a few dollars, but it was a pittance, hardly enough for sustenance.

Victor's voice cut into Mike's thoughts. "The Battle of the Running Bulls, they're calling it. And, damn, the cops did finally take off running."

Weary to the point of exhaustion, Mike ran a cold, rough hand over his face. His stubble of beard was scratchy; his eyes burned. He needed nourishment and a shave.

"Let's get some food, Victor."

At the diner, the coffee was hot and strong and the eggs soft and fluffy.

"Where do we go from here?" Mike asked. "This is hardly what you'd call a victory."

"We're not defeated yet. The point is, the strikers are still in the buildings. That *is* a victory of sorts."

Mike spread jam on his toast. "But how much longer will they hold out?"

"As long as it takes." Victor stirred his coffee.

"I hope you're right." Mike ate the last of his toast. "I've got to call my wife. She's in the shop by now. I'm sure she's heard the news and is having a fit." She'd cry, he knew, and beg him to come home.

"I can't even get hold of Sophie," Victor said. "She's in Anderson, Indiana, working with the Guide Lamp and Delco people there. I'm worried about her. That town's dead set against unions."

"I suppose it's hard for the women, whether they're working union or home worrying."

The two men exchanged looks that spoke volumes. Mike finally said the words they were both thinking.

"Victor, are we doing the right thing? What about our families? Will they always come second after the union? Is this the way it's going to be?"

Victor was silent a moment, then said, "Mike, don't go soft now."

Mike dropped his eyes and stirred his coffee. "What the hell. If we don't do this, who will, right?"

Victor nodded his agreement, but neither spoke again, and Mike left the diner fighting a sense of futility.

Chiara jumped each time the phone rang in her office. She'd heard from Mike only once since he left Detroit for Flint. Was he in the thick of the fray, getting beaten up? He'd said he'd be safe behind the wheel of a sound car, but knowing his brashness, his determination to see justice done, she was sure he'd be in the thick of battle.

She'd hardly gotten her coat off when the phone jangled.

"It's me, Chiara." Mike's voice sounded far away and weary.

"Mike! I read about the mess in Flint. Are you all right?"

"I'm fine. Don't worry."

"Don't worry! Of course I worry. I want you to come home. Today!"

"Look, I'm okay. The papers exaggerate everything . . ."

"I see pictures, Mike. Pictures don't lie. I'll bet you're not getting any sleep."

"I'm sleeping at a brother's house when I can manage it. Listen, I think the strike's almost over," he lied. "A few days, maybe. The strikers are holding fast. I've never seen such courage and determination."

Chiara couldn't keep the sob from her voice. "You're going to get killed, or arrested."

"I won't get killed." Mike's low laugh was uneasy. "I have to go now, Chiara. I love you. I'll call in a few days."

Mike noticed that Victor's voice was getting hoarse. "I'll take over for a while. You'd better rest that throat."

Victor seemed grateful for the respite. The men took turns sending a barrage of encouraging words to the strikers and pickets. But the long hours combined with the frigid weather were taking their toll. Mike developed a hacking cough and yearned for the comfort of his own bed and his loving wife.

Mike's cold worsened as January dragged on and February appeared and still the strike continued. A judge ordered the plant emptied, but when it was discovered he owned General Motors stock, his decision was deemed unlawful.

A few days later, Mike drove to the site to find it barred by the National Guard. He hopped from the car and confronted a fresh-faced guardsman.

"We got our orders," the youth said, a rifle held chest-high. "Governor Murphy wants an eight-acre area sealed off. Better leave peaceful."

Mike sputtered and turned toward the car. Before he could reach it, two guardsmen jumped inside.

"Hey, what the hell are you doing?" Mike yelled, rushing to the driver's-side window.

"Sorry, buddy, orders," Mike heard through the glass. The motor purred and the car backed slowly away.

The young guardsman with the gun said, almost apologetically, "You'll get it back when the strike is over."

Mike swore softly to himself, completely frustrated. But as he walked away, he knew Governor Murphy had made the right decision by sending in the guard. The situation was ripe for bloodshed. He soon learned the governor had also intervened to prevent the eviction of strikers in the three plants. They were at an impasse. It was an uneasy respite at best.

When another injunction against the strikers was issued by an impartial judge, Mike and the other union men urged the workers to ignore it. The strikers stayed. There were now 125,000 workers idled in 117 plants.

Finally President Roosevelt himself ordered John L.

Lewis of the CIO-UAW to meet with General Motors' William Knudsen, who had steadfastly refused to cooperate. It took a solid week of constant negotiations, with Governor Murphy running interference between the two, but finally an agreement was reached. It spelled the end of the longest sit-down strike in history, forty-four days.

The Goliath of General Motors had been conquered by the David of UAW.

—— 24 ——

Chiara placed a beret atop her thick hair and adjusted her coat. The long mirror in her shop revealed a look of anxiety. She adjusted her face into the semblance of a smile and squared her shoulders.

There was always something to worry about. At least the problem of leaving Anna was solved when Flora, unhappy working in the shop, asked if she could care for Anna while Chiara worked. Flora preferred being a nursemaid to being a seamstress any day. She doted on the energetic two-year-old, often bringing her to the shop, where she ran about picking up scraps of material and begging attention from her "aunt" Maria and from Nina, Rosa's girl, who had taken Flora's place. But even that caused Chiara worry. Would Anna begin thinking Flora was her mother?

On top of everything else, Chiara had missed her period. As badly as she wanted another child, this didn't seem like a good time.

Now that Mike was safely home again, Chiara forced herself to make some decisions. Though slow at first, her business was increasing to the point where she would have to consider hiring another woman. But the problem that she hadn't foreseen was that she wasn't making any money. Not yet. Despite the growing clientele, her receipts didn't keep up with her debits. The bulk of her bills weren't collected until after the work was completed, and even then, when people asked for a delay, Chiara cheerfully acquiesced. Meanwhile the electric bill hadn't been paid, the time payments on the three new electric sewing machines were late, Flora and Maria agreed to take only half their wages, and still Chiara couldn't meet her loan payment, though Mr. Cronin had agreed to delay it twice.

Mike was right: she was a greenhorn. How could she have imagined it would be so easy? Why hadn't she foreseen the problems, the hidden costs, like a plumber for the leaky lavatory, and an electrician for more outlets?

She wanted Mike's advice, but was reluctant to burden him with her problems. Not now, when he had so much on his mind. Besides, she couldn't bear admitting defeat. She dreaded hearing those wounding words: *I told you so.*

Since Mike had returned from Flint, sit-down strikes were springing up everywhere, like clover in a meadow. One newspaper commented that "Sitting down has replaced baseball as a national pastime, and sitter-downers clutter up the landscape in every direction." Poor Mike hurried from one spot to another, helping to mediate problems, often working late into the night.

Chiara squared her shoulders and forced her mouth into the semblance of a smile. In spite of the problems, she was never so happy as when she was working. She found delight in consulting with the happy young brides-to-be.

So many of them wanted a gown "just like the one in the window," but Chiara would say, "No, no, for you something special, something original. Now, if I just lower the line in front, maybe a sweatheart neckline, and instead of lace . . . " Each bride felt special, *was* special.

But Chiara could worry about only one problem at a time. Now she would have to go to the bank and convince Mr. Cronin to give her more time. Failing that, she would be forced to speak to Mike about going to his friends for a loan. Perhaps Fredo could be persuaded to help. He seemed to have an abundance of money. If *that* plan was unsuccessful, and next month didn't produce more revenues, Chiara would have to admit defeat and close the shop. She shuddered at the thought.

The bank's imposing walls seemed taller than they had the last time Chiara had been there. She had trouble keeping her lower lip from trembling as she approached Miss Evans' desk.

"You may make your payments directly at the teller's window, Mrs. Marcassa," Miss Evans said kindly. "Any window will do."

"No, I have to see Mr. Cronin, please."

In a moment she was again facing Mr. Cronin, who, intent on a large ledger, kept his balding head lowered.

The room seemed larger than before. A draft from the open door stirred the long green tenacles of the Boston fern on its wooden stand in the corner.

Mr. Cronin finally looked up, adjusted his spectacles, then stood and extended a welcoming hand. "Ah, Mrs. Marcassa. My daughter is very impressed with you and your shop. You did a fine job."

Chiara accepted the warm handshake from the soft manicured hand and sat stiffly on the chair he indicated, across from him. "Your daughter is a lovely young lady. For her I made something special."

Mr. Cronin nodded with pleasure, his double chin bobbing above the blue bow tie.

He glanced at Chiara's hands clasped tightly in her lap. "Come, come, Mrs. Marcassa, don't look so nervous. I won't bite. What's the problem?"

"I . . . I don't have the money. I have lots of business, but people don't pay until they have the finished gowns, so that takes time. And everything was more expensive than I thought, and there are payments and wages." Her voice rose shrilly with each word, and now she brought it down an octave. "And there was the electrician and the plumber and—"

Mr. Cronin interrupted, "Is that all?" He came around the desk and took her hand. "My dear Mrs. Marcassa. It's quite all right, you know. You can pay double next time. Or if you don't quite have it then, why, we'll just have to make your payments a bit more manageable, won't we? I have every confidence in you, my dear, especially after my daughter spoke so glowingly of your work."

Chiara was stunned. She had heard so many horror stories about cruel, whip-cracking bankers, and here was kindly Mr. Cronin treating her like a good friend or a member of the family who owed him a small favor. His willingness to bend for her made her want to throw her arms around him and kiss his cheek.

But instead she rose and pumped his hand nervously. "Thank you, thank you. You are a very kind man. I will surely have the money to pay you next month. God bless you."

Back on the street, Chiara breathed in the crisp March air and almost sang with relief and renewed hope. The worst would soon be over, she was sure. In a month the receipts would be rolling in, the shop would begin showing a profit, and she would be caught up with her payments. Already her desk was stacked up with orders for June wedding gowns. She had to consider hiring another woman.

Reaching the shop, she paused to admire the display, a sense of joy engulfing her. The sign, "Chiara's Bridal Salon, Custom Designs," lettered in pale blue script and encased in a sculptured ivory frame, always gave her a surge of pride. A mannequin dressed in bridal finery stepped out from the painted backdrop of a church door and was surrounded by four bridesmaids in pale pink. The shop was painted inside and out in ivory, with a blue-and-ivory-striped awning shading the scrupulously clean front window. It was all just as she had envisioned it.

Chiara turned at the sound of an automobile pulling up to the curb. She released her hand from the doorknob, momentarily flustered as she recognized Stewart's black Lincoln, shiny and sleek. Stewart emerged and tipped his hat while Chiara took a few steps toward him.

He stood a moment gazing at her, then said, "How are you, Chiara?"

She composed herself and extended her hand. "I'm well, thank you. And you?"

"Fine."

Stewart looked fit and dapper. She thought he'd regained the self-possession he'd lost in those *bad* days.

He motioned to the shop. "I understand you're doing a lot of business."

Chiara's eyebrows raised slightly. How would he know how she was doing?

"It's going well enough, but I expect to do better in the next few months."

He nodded toward the shop. "It's nice. You've made it very appealing." His gaze returned to Chaira. "Classy."

"Thank you." Her smile was pleased, self-contained.

Stewart said, "Look, let me buy you some lunch."

"Oh, no, I've eaten," she demurred.

"Oh, come on, coffee, then. We'll go someplace very public."

When Chiara hesitated, he pressed his advantage and took her arm, urging her toward his car.

Chiara allowed him to ease her into the automobile. She inhaled the new-leather smell that permeated the plush interior of the latest-model Lincoln.

Stewart drove a few miles up Woodward and stopped at a small restaurant.

"You're a marvel," he said after they'd ordered coffee and pie. "A few years ago you could hardly speak the language, and now look at you. You're an enterprising businesswoman."

"Oh, no, only a seamstress."

"A seamstress, eh?" He smiled. "I'll always remember when I first saw you, sitting in the sewing room, singing to yourself like a happy and carefree bird . . . ." He had a faraway look as the sentence trailed away.

"It does seem a long time ago." Chiara's smile mellowed as she recalled the warmth of the sewing room, the charm of the gentleman of the manse, and the magnetism between them that she attempted to shrug off uneasily.

Directing her thoughts back to the present, she said, "I'm not doing so well, really. I haven't been able to make my payments."

Stewart didn't look surprised at this admission. "Don't let old Cronin frighten you. He'll wait for your money."

She nibbled on the apple pie. Stewart must have talked to Mr. Cronin. Had the two of them discussed her shop, her loan? Did Mr. Cronin tell Stewart about her problems?

Chiara gave Stewart a level look, then changed the subject. "How is your family? Your wife and son."

His forthright gray eyes looked into hers.

"Audrey's . . . well, thank you." He brightened. "And

Sonny's growing tall and handsome. He's eight now, in third grade. Smart as a whip, but sometimes a bit of a problem. He doesn't always behave as he should. High-strung, his teacher tells me. I think he simply has too much energy."

"And your wife, she's still . . . the same?"

"Yes, nothing changes. We plod along. I'm afraid there's no hope for Audrey. Sometimes I shudder at the thought of the two of us growing old together this way." He shook his head in a resigned fashion. "I think about getting a divorce, but . . . well, there's Sonny; we both adore him."

Chiara toyed with her fork. "I think you still love your wife, don't you?"

Stewart didn't answer immediately. "I don't know. I suppose there's something there. I know I can't abandon her." He looked down uneasily at his plate, then glanced up again with a falsely bright smile. "And what about you? And Mike."

"Mike's good to me." Chiara placed her fork down and pushed the plate away. "He isn't with Ford any longer. He was beaten up and fired for signing with the union."

Stewart raked his fingers through his thinning hair. "I heard about it later, much later. It's barbaric, the way the men are treated. I can't tell you how sorry I was about that, but there wouldn't have been anything I could do. Bennett's in charge, and I have little influence. I think old man Ford's senile, but he won't give up and let his son Edsel take over."

"It's wrong, what they're doing. Mike says the workers are underpaid, they have no seniority, no protection." Chiara bristled. "It should be against the law to fire someone just because he joins the union."

"It *is* against the law. But the law is circumvented, or unenforced. I don't think we'll ever see unionism take hold. It would take a totally united front, and too many workers won't risk their jobs. They have my sympathy. It's hard to believe what so many have to endure. Something should be done about it."

"If you feel that way why don't you talk to Henry Ford, convince him? You're an important man, close to Ford. Mike told me so."

Stewart laughed. "You don't understand. No one can convince Henry Ford. Not even Edsel. Edsel sees the writing on the wall, but he doesn't have his father's ear."

Chiara made a bitter mouth. "When I first came to America, I thought Henry Ford was a saint. Mike told me how he raised the wages to five dollars a day, how people came from all over the country and even across the ocean for jobs. He was good to the workers then. He had stores selling good merchandise at low prices and a social department to help people manage better. He even had English classes for foreigners. But he changed."

Stewart nodded. "Yes, he changed. The company is too vast now. And power and wealth change people."

"Well, Mike's working for the union now. He works long hours, for little pay, and I worry about him, but he's happier than I've ever seen him. It's because he's working for something he believes in."

"A union will never take hold at Ford. Henry will never let that happen."

Chiara pushed away the unfinished pie. "I must get back now. I've hours of work to finish."

Stewart put his hand over hers. "Actually, I came to ask if you'd do some new draperies for the house. I told Audrey I'd stop to see you about it. Why don't you come by the house and take some measurements?" His gaze rested on her eyes, caressing them. Very softly he added, "No one's home now."

Chiara caught her breath. Her neck grew warm, and her skin tingled from the warmth of his hand. She flushed, remembering the heady thrill of his mouth upon hers.

Quickly she drew her hand away and put on her gloves. "No, I . . . I must get back now. There's so much to do. And I don't have time to do draperies any longer."

She pushed her chair back and walked toward the door, feeling light-headed.

Stewart tossed coins on the table and hurried after her.

Neither spoke on the short ride back.

When he pulled up at the shop, Stewart touched Chiara's gloved hand, saying, "I'd like to see the shop."

She allowed his hand to linger for a moment on hers, then moved away. "Come in, then."

The bell jingled as the door opened, and from the back room Flora greeted them with little Anna in tow. Chiara turned to hang her coat on the white iron coat tree, then held her arms out to her child.

"She needed some fresh air, and wanted to visit her Mama," Flora explained.

Anna ran into her mother's arms, while Stewart looked on.

His eyes looked sad, Chiara thought. Was he wondering, as she so often had, what their child would have looked like? Would their baby have had round inquisitive eyes and heavy dark hair, like Anna's? A ready smile from rosebud lips?

"Hello, little one. You're a sweetheart, aren't you?" Stewart stooped down and chucked Anna under the chin.

Anna swayed on sturdy legs and favored him with a flirtatious smile.

"Do you know who I am? I'm your uncle Stew."

Anna giggled, then turned and ran to the back, while Chiara introduced Stewart to Flora. "Mr. Austin's wife was my first client. You remember, Flora, we went there together." She laughed. "How nervous I was!"

"*Sì.*" Flora nodded, looking intrigued, then hurried after Anna.

"Anna's beautiful, Chiara. Like you," Stewart said.

"Really, she looks more like Mike."

"I hope I see you again soon. And remember, don't let old Cronin give you the runaround."

In a sudden flash of intuition it became clear to Chiara why Mr. Cronin had been so understanding about the loan payments. She gave Stewart a penetrating look. "Are you guaranteeing my payments to the bank?"

Stewart looked flustered. "I've only assured him that you're good for the money, that's all."

"No, banks don't work that way."

"They're lucky to have such an enterprising woman as a client. I told Cronin that. And he realizes it too. Look, I must be going now."

Chiara lowered her eyelids slowly. "Thank you, Stewart."

A cool March wind blew in from the river and whistled through the downtown streets, whipping Mike's coat about his legs. As he hurried up the wide City Hall steps with his union brother Ed Hall, he felt a twinge of pessimism.

Under the umbrella of the UAW and AFL, the workers had banded together for a rally to protest the cruel treatment and arrests of nonviolent picketers. Mike and Ed were charged with the task of obtaining a permit.

"It's fitting, isn't it?" Ed asked. "A march in the month of March."

"If we get permission, that is."

Ed jabbed Mike with his elbow. "Hey, have a little faith."

It took only a few minutes for the Detroit City Council to refuse the request.

"We don't give a good whoop in hell about a permit," Ed Hall said as they left the building. "We'll be there anyhow."

Though Mike agreed they should proceed with the march, he nonetheless felt anxious. The sanction of the council would have at least provided some protection.

Thankfully, at the last moment Mayor Couzins who, Mike thought, was motivated by political considerations, gave his informal approval, and plans for the demonstration proceeded.

Mike arranged for the fifty-piece UAW band and gassed up the sound truck. At three-thirty all the downtown department stores closed as fourteen hundred police deployed in the Cadillac Square area. From as far away as Ohio, some two thousand marchers met in front of the Michigan Central Railroad Station and proceeded down Michigan Avenue toward the square. All told, over one hundred thousand demonstrators crowded the downtown streets. Passions ran high as Walter Reuther led cheers from atop the truck, and Ed Hall promised, "For every eviction there will be ten sit downs."

The unity, the power, inspired Mike, reviving again his hope and determination.

"At least it was peaceful," Chiara said afterward. "I always expect you to come home with a black eye."

"It was a great demonstration. It showed our unity." Mike stirred a pot of lentil soup gently simmering on the stove while Chiara set the table. He made it a point to help his wife with supper, though tonight he was more tired than usual. His energies were directed toward the Chrysler strike. After General Motors struck, sit downs sprouted around Detroit like crabgrass in a vacant field, and Mike was kept busy extinguishing the small fires of discontent.

Their success with General Motors had paved the way for a Chrysler strike, and finally the Chrysler workers, obeying a court order, evacuated the factories on March 25 with bands playing and the Stars and Stripes flying high alongside the UAW flag. But it wasn't until April 6 that a compromise was reached between Walter Chrysler and John L. Lewis. Chrysler agreed to negotiate with the UAW, but only for UAW members, not for all workers, a disappointment for the more militant members at Chrysler. At the urging of Governor Murphy, Walter Chrysler finally signed the pact.

Mike considered it a victory. The second of the big three had fallen. Flush from the recent victories over General Motors and Chrysler, Walter Reuther made plans for a giant drive at the Rouge plant. Now, Mike thought, two down and one to go—the toughest one of all—Ford.

Tasting the soup, Mike said, "Ah, perfect."

Chiara handed him a bowl and he ladled the thick soup into it and set it before three-year-old Anna, who sat impatiently tapping her spoon, a napkin tied under her chin.

"Look how far we've come from *la via vecchia*. My wife works, and I cook." Mike served Chiara and himself and sat at the head of the table.

"I wonder what my mother would say," Chiara mused. "I've written her about the shop, but she doesn't realize how much of my time is spent there. I suppose she thinks we've become 'Americanized.' " Chiara buttered a slice of bread for Anna. "Everyone is striking; it's a disease. I went downtown today, to Crowley Milner's. I forgot they were striking."

Mike ate with gusto. "Were there pickets out front?"

"Yes, and when I passed the store I heard loud music from inside. One of the pickets said that the Detroit Federation of Musicians sent a dance band to entertain the strikers. Isn't that nice?"

"It's wonderful. It just goes to show you how everyone's cooperating in this fight."

"I wish you wouldn't use the word '*fight*.' It's like a war."

Mike refrained from stating the obvious: it *was* a war.

Lives were on the line as each faction battled for its ideals, sure it was right. Instead he said, "Tomorrow we go to my old plant to pass out leaflets."

Chiara slammed her fork down on her plate. "To the Rouge? Why do you have to put yourself into danger? Haven't you been abused enough?"

"There isn't going to be any confrontation. We're just passing out literature to the workers. Believe me, there's no danger. We have a permit from the Dearborn City Council. I went and got it myself."

She shook her head in a resigned fashion that told Mike she knew the futility of arguing. But he noticed the worry lines around her eyes and mouth, and the sprinkling of gray hair mixed among the golden-brown ones. Still, she was beautiful, as lovely as the day they met, with the same youthful verve and a mixture of fragility and strength. Today she looked a bit pale. He should pay more attention to her, listen to her, take her to a movie. So immersed was he in his own work that he didn't even talk to her about the bridal salon. Certainly she must have worries. He hadn't had time to stop at the shop in over a month. As soon as things let up a bit, he would look in and check out the troublesome plumbing.

But for now there were more urgent matters to consume his thoughts. When Mike entered the union office the next day, several people were already assembled. As he rattled a folding chair open, he sensed an uneasiness among the aggregation circling Walter's desk, especially from Ed Hall.

"What's the problem, Ed?" Mike asked.

"I'm not sure we should go through with this. I got a phone call from John Gillespie, former police commissioner, who works for Ford now. He said he doesn't want to see me get hurt. He wouldn't say anything more than that. I have a feeling something's going to happen. I told him I have a license to carry a revolver, and I won't hesitate to use it."

Walter ran his hands through his hair. "It does sound like trouble. This may not be as easy as we thought."

Ardith, a young and eager unionist, declared, "Let us ladies pass out the handbills. Surely they'll leave the women alone. Even a rat like Bennett won't stoop to beating up the women."

"You don't know these guys. Some of them would attack their own mothers," Mike said.

Reuther nodded, toying with the watch chain draped across his vest.

"We should be safe with a permit," Ardith declared. "I'm game."

The leaders finally agreed and decided to proceed with the plans.

Hall, Frankensteen, a fellow organizer, and Reuther went ahead in an automobile while Mike stayed behind with last-minute instructions for the workers. He distributed the pamphlets and shepherded the group onto the streetcar.

As they came in sight of the Rouge, Mike, sensing danger, said, "I want you all to stay in your seats until I tell you to move."

The streetcar ground to a halt. Through the windows Mike saw several burly men loitering about outside. He recognized one of them—Angelo Caruso, head of the Downriver gang. They've recruited some tough bastards, he thought. As the door slid open with a grating metallic sound, Mike moved to the exit.

Two men blocked the door from outside, shouting, "Nobody's getting off! Get this trolley out of here." One of the men jumped aboard, and before Mike could stop him, ripped leaflets from the hands of several of the women.

Furious, Mike swung at the man blocking the doorway and landed an uppercut to his jaw.

"You women stay put," Mike yelled as he jumped from the streetcar. He flailed his arms against other attackers who swarmed around the trolley. Darting between them, twisting and sidestepping, he made it to the overpass, where a burly seviceman guarded the stairs.

"This bridge is private property," he yelled. "Don't try nothing, Mac."

Frustrated, Mike turned away in time to see several Ford attackers forcefully pushing two women. One of the women fell to the ground, while a mounted policeman watched indifferently.

"Do something!" Mike screamed.

The policeman looked blankly at him, unconcerned, then reined his horse away. Mike sputtered angrily. Christ, they were unfeeling beasts.

On the bridge up ahead, two men, hats yanked low over their eyes, advanced toward Frankensteen and Reuther, who seemed unconcerned. Mike didn't like the look of them. Suddenly one of the strangers sprang forward and pulled Frankensteen's coat over his head, locking him as if in a straitjacket, while the other caught Walter by surprise with a stunning blow to the head. Crouching on the ground, Walter tried to shield his blood-stained face. The goons struck both men repeatedly in the chest and groin.

Mike tried to run to their defense, but powerful hands grabbed him from behind. He grappled ineffectively with his huge attacker and was easily shunted aside.

Enraged and helpless, he watched as his friends on the bridge were pummeled and kicked again and again. Once more Mike made a dash toward the stairs. Hunching down, he rushed like a football blocker, into the waiting goon, butting against the man's knees with his head and shoulders. The man toppled and Mike managed to stagger upright, but another serviceman lunged against him, throwing him back to the ground. When the man attempted to kick him in the stomach, Mike jackknifed and put his arms over his head for protection, but a blow struck his temple. Before blacking out, his last thought was: I hope there's no blood; blood will frighten Chiara.

He came to in an automobile. Someone was slapping at his hands and calling his name.

"You okay, Mike?"

Mike's lids lifted heavily, slowly. He recognized a reporter for the Detroit *Free Press*, a man he'd spoken to several times. "Yeah, I'm great," he said, his words slurring as if he were drunk. He lifted his hand to his temple and felt a thick, sticky stubstance. Blood. "Some show they put on, eh?"

"You're lucky we were there," the reporter said. "Those animals could've killed you. But we got pictures of them throwing Reuther and Frankensteen down the steps. We're taking you to the hospital."

"No, take me home. My wife'll be worried." He hated to face Chiara after all her dire warnings, but the hospital was a worse alternative. It seemed he was always coming home beaten and bloody, like some trouble-prone kid.

At home, Flora, who was caring for Anna, cried out in

alarm at the sight of Mike. With an ice pick she chipped ice from the fifty-pound block, then wrapped it in a washcloth and laid it against the bruise on the side of his face, mumbling her disapproval.

Anna, her little face pinched into a worried frown, asked, "Do you have a boo-boo, Papa?"

Mike lifted her into his arms. "Papa's fine, Anna. Come, little one, lie next to your daddy, and I'll tell you a story." He felt like a jackhammer was at work on his skull.

Chiara stole into the room where Mike slept fitfully. At the sight of his bruised face she shrieked, and he bolted upright,

"Oh, Mike! Look at you! One of these days—"

"I'm all right, Chiara." Mike moved to make room for her on the bed. "I'm just a little sore. Believe it or not, this hurt Ford more than it hurt us. There were photographers there and they got pictures of Bennett and his goons attacking us. Tomorrow it'll be in all the papers. The whole world will see how the Ford Motor Company operates."

Chiara placed her hand gently against the swollen, purplish flesh at his temple, then traced her finger around his split lip. He flinched and she burst into tears.

Mike drew her to him on the bed. "Cara, I told you, I'm not hurt."

Chiara sniffed, resisting his pull. "When will it end?"

"When the Ford Motor Company goes union." Mike's voice was flat and hard.

"So you'll let them kill you?"

"They won't kill me. Listen, Chiara, I'm not giving up the fight."

She collapsed against him and whimpered at his chest.

"Come on, it's not that bad."

"It's not just that. I'm . . . I'm going to have a baby."

"A baby! Chiara, that's wonderful." He pulled her tighter against him. "Why are you crying?"

"I . . . I don't know. I worry about you all the time and there's so much to do, with the shop and everything . . . When will I have time for another little one?"

"You have no choice but to make time. You'll have to sell the business."

With a horrified look Chiara pushed away from Mike. "Sell the business? After all I've put into it? Never!"

Mike sighed in exasperation. "We can decide about that later. Did you just find out about the baby?"

"I've known for a few weeks."

"Why didn't you tell me sooner?"

"At first I wasn't sure; then I didn't want to worry you. You have so much on your mind."

Mike massaged the nape of her neck. "Worry? I'm happy about it. A boy. We'll have a little boy this time."

She laid her head on his shoulder while he patted her back. How would she manage it all, the children and the shop? Somehow she'd do it; she'd find the energy to do it all. She had worked too hard on the business to give it up, especially now that it was beginning to turn a profit.

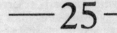

—— 25 ——

With each week that went by, Chiara's little shop crept further out of debt, until finally it was operating in the black. If it weren't for her constant worry over Mike's work, she could be quite content. As Mike had predicted, the "battle of the overpass," as the newspapers had dubbed the atrocious attack by Harry Bennett and his henchmen against defenseless union men, gained sympathy for the union.

Toward the end of Chiara's pregnancy, she and Mike searched for a house. Unsuccessful in finding one they could afford, they decided instead to rent a larger flat in a neat east side neighborhood. It would be ready for occupancy in two weeks.

Mike had impetuously spent some of their savings for an automobile. From the time he brought it home, the used 1933 DeSoto was a source of conflict. Chiara was dismayed to see the carefully hoarded dollars that had half-filled the cigar box disappear so quickly. With the contents so greatly reduced, her sense of security was threatened. The specter of their poverty through the depression hovered ever near.

Even though the shop made money, and Mike received a somewhat regular paycheck, Chiara worried about expenses. The new flat would be more expensive, and there were other bills, like the gas stove and refrigerator they'd ordered. The hospital stay would cost a pretty penny too. All necessary expenses, she knew, but the money for a new house wasn't accumulating as fast as she would have liked.

Still, she had to admit grudgingly, having their own automobile was a great convenience. Gradually she adjusted to the car and even suggested that Mike teach her to drive. She should have known better. To Mike, a woman in the driver's seat was akin to a woman playing cards or smoking; activities properly reserved for men. Because of her pregnancy, Mike drove her to work and back. Over her protestations, he insisted she quit working in her sixth month. She cajoled until he let her "just look things over" every few days. After she began showing, she stayed in the back, out of sight.

Although the new flat looked spotless to Mike, Chiara insisted on going there the day before moving, to make sure everything was scrupulously clean.

She was delighted with the neighborhood. St. Margaret Mary Church was within walking distance, and there was a grocery store on the corner run by a *paisano* named Giovanni, as well as a fresh-fish market and Italian bakery close by. The yard was spacious. At the back door stood a lilac bush that the landlord, Mr. Ferguson, assured them was covered with aromatic blooms each spring. Now, in December, the branches were weighed down with thick, wet snow. A garage opened out to an alley, and next to it was plenty of room for a vegetable garden.

As Mike, laden with boxes, led the way upstairs, he was full of apologies. "I promised you a home of your own, and all I can afford is an upper flat."

A home of their own had become more Mike's dream than her own, a symbol of prosperity. Chiara felt in some subtle way that owning a home would tie her irrevocably to the United States, and she still harbored the notion that someday, some way, they would return again to the peace and security of Italy.

She sought to minimize Mike's self-reproach. Her earnings, which now exceeded Mike's, constituted the bulk of their savings. That fact vexed him, she knew, though they never talked about it.

"I like this flat, Mike." Chiara tugged at Anna's hand, urging her little feet upward. "The church is close and Mr. Ferguson said there are lots of Italians in the neighborhood. We've waited this long for a house, we can wait a little longer."

With Anna following like a small shadow, Mike went to the front room to install hardware for the new curtains Chiara had sewn. Chiara scrubbed the linoleum in the kitchen with a bar of Fels Naphtha soap and a stiff brush. The linoleum was almost new, a far cry from the worn and faded one in the old flat. After a few minutes she stopped the circular motions and rested on her heels. Her back had been aching lately. After they moved in tomorrow she could relax and wait for the baby, due in three weeks. Everything was in readiness, all the little baby clothes washed and ironed, new tiny underthings and flannel diapers placed neatly in a fresh, newspaper-lined drawer. Yesterday was her last day at the shop, and she had gone over everything with Maria. She felt confident that the shop would be in good hands.

Chiara moaned as a pain flamed briefly, then receded. She pressed both hands at the small of her back, then resumed her work. The next pain, ten minutes later, was stronger, starting at the bottom of her abdominal mound and working upward.

"Oh, no, it's too early; I have too much to do," she wailed.

Mike, hearing her, dropped a rod to the floor and rushed in, with Anna trailing behind.

"Is it starting?" He helped her to her feet and onto a kitchen chair.

"Yes, I think so."

"It's early. You see? I told you you were doing too much. I warned you about trying to wash the floor. Didn't I tell you I'd do it? You worked too long at the shop."

Chiara waved away his concern. "Babies come when they're ready."

"Mama?" Anna's eyes were wide with questions; she knew something of importance was happening.

Chiara motioned for Mike to lift the child onto her lap. Pulling Anna close, Chiara said, "Mama's going away for a little while, Anna. Then she's coming home with a new baby."

Anna tucked her head on her mother's comfortable soft breast and put her thumb in her mouth. "Baby," she said in a cheerless voice.

"We'd better get going." Mike lifted Anna from her mother's arms. "Now, aren't you glad I bought the car?"

"No." Chiara's mouth was pinched. "I'd rather have the money saved. We could call a taxi just as well."

"Ah," he said, shaking his head in mock disgust.

St. Mary's Hospital was antiseptic and orderly. The sheets smelled of bleach and felt stiff and scratchy against her skin. Starched, serene nurses announced their entrances and exits on squeaking shoes. Chiara missed the smell of coffee brewing in the kitchen, the kindly eyes and gentle hands of the midwife Sophia. But this was the modern way to have babies, and one must move with the times, she supposed, staring at the gaudy picture of the Virgin Mary in a flowing robe, holding the Christ Child. Her mother would like that picture, she thought.

Chiara felt the thrum of her heartbeat, experienced the excitement that came with having a baby. She had longed for that all-encompassing emotion, that feeling of total unity when she held a little one against her breast.

She thought of her Michele waiting outside, chain-smoking and pacing. The hospital was a new experience for him too, the wait in a public room, among strangers. In many ways Mike was so strong, in other ways so fragile.

Outside the tall window, a powdery snow drifted down, blanketing the sill. She moaned as the pressure increased. Soon the moments between pains evaporated and she felt one continuous tormenting agony.

"It's time, Mrs. Marcassa," said the nun in a starched wide-winged cap.

The stark whiteness of the delivery room was forbidding. A nurse clamped something over her mouth, and in no time she was in a vague dream state, feeling the tugging of her insides, knowing her child was fighting to emerge, but feeling clearly distanced from the process. When the pains reached a steady crescendo, she revived and gave several mighty, muscle-straining pushes. When she heard, as if from a distance, a loud wail, she knew it was over. The smiling nun nudged her. "Look, Mrs. Marcassa, you have a beautiful girl."

Chiara raised her head to see the tiny bundle, pink and plump, with eyes that were open under puffy, hairless lids. "Let me have her," she said.

"Later, when we've cleaned you up." The nun whisked the baby away, leaving Chiara feeling bereft.

"Is everything all right?"

"Hunky-dory."

Chiara whispered a prayer of thanks.

"What will you name her?" a disembodied voice asked.

"Luisa. That's my mother's name." Inexplicably, Chiara began to cry. Would her family in Italy ever see her two children? Mike said someday soon, but she knew there would never be enough money or time for a trip to the old country. Something urgent always seemed to take their hard-earned cash. Mike said first they'd buy a home. After that, maybe, maybe . . . She would have to try to put more money aside from the shop's earnings . . . hide it . . . maybe put it in Mr. Cronin's bank . . . maybe if they had a house . . . Where was Mike? He should be here . . . He must see his new child . . ..

She drifted off to sleep, and when she awakened, Mike was beside her, holding her hand.

A tear slipped from Chiara's eye. "I'm sorry it's not a boy. You wanted a boy."

"No, this is a beautiful child. I just saw her."

"Is she beautiful? As beautiful as Anna?"

"Yes, but this one looks like you." Mike kissed her cheek. "We'll have a boy the next time."

Mike was late. The baby was dressed and sucking her thumb, and Chiara sat primly on the bed, waiting for Mike to take them home to the new flat. He had corralled his friends into helping with the move the day after Luisa was born.

When Dino entered the room, Chiara looked up in surprise.

"Mike had to go to Ohio. Union work." Dino smiled apologetically. "I came to take you home."

Chiara's mouth puckered despite her attempt at composure. Union again, she thought bitterly. Mike was in a strange Ohio town, when he should be taking his wife and new baby home. Damn the union! It was ruining their lives. A tear slipped from her eye and Dino, embarrassed, looked away.

In the lobby, a youthful group of carolers sang "Silent Night" and "The First Noel" accompanied by jingling bells. It was three days before Christmas 1937, and Chiara felt anything but merry.

When Luisa was just two months old, Chiara went back to work for a few hours a day, much to Mike's annoyance. She took both little ones along, for she was nursing the baby, and couldn't bear to leave Anna behind. The "big sister" was so obviously resentful of time Chiara spent with Luisa.

Mike gave up trying to talk sense to his wife and grudgingly partitioned off a section in her office, which was small enough to begin with, for a cradle.

Anna would pull up on tiptoes, peer into the cradle, and make disparaging remarks. "She's a lot of trouble, isn't she? Why does she cry like that? It makes her face ugly." To her three-year-old mind, this tiny interloper was usurping her own place of honor in the family.

Somehow Chiara took it all in her stride, managing with a minimum of nervous tension. *By the third one, you finally know how to do it*, she told Flora, who admonished her to take it easy.

A strange mixture you are, cara bambina, Chiara thought as she nursed the baby amid the clutter of her office. In truth, other than her dark, thick-lashed eyes, Luisa resembled Chiara, with fair, downy hair and docile temperament. *Your grandmother, your namesake, would love to see you. Someday, please God, someday.*

On a brisk spring evening in 1938, Chiara fidgeted from one foot to the other while Mike pushed the doorbell of Walter and May Reuther's apartment. Chiara was a recalcitrant guest and had tried to beg off by insisting she didn't feel well, which wasn't totally untrue. She was still nursing Luisa and hated to leave her for any length of time. But Mike insisted she come to the birthday party for Victor's wife, Sophie.

"You're always curious about the people I work with—now here's your chance to meet them," he'd said. "They're regular guys. You'll like Sophie. May too—they're both swell ladies."

"You know I hate your union work, and everything connected with it."

Mike ignored Chiara's remark. "We'll have a fine time; you'll see."

She knew there was no point in arguing further. Mike's friends were *American* and she was never quite at ease with Americans, with the exception of Penny and Stewart. Oh, she dealt with Americans in her work, but tonight was different. This meeting was purely social. She knew the Reuther women worked right along with their husbands for the union. She imagined big strong women, tough-talking, like their men.

Now Mike gave her arm an encouraging squeeze.

The woman who answered the door was pretty and young-looking, with red hair and a ready smile. "Hello, Mike. Come on in," she said, ushering them inside. Her hand reached out to Chiara. "You must be Chiara. I'm May Reuther."

"Nice to meet you," Chiara said shyly.

The small living room was filled with people, and the furnishings were comfortable but not elaborate. Chiara tried to remember the names that flew from May's lips, but only Sophie, Walter, and Victor—people Mike mentioned often—made an impression. Walter looked young, too young to have such an important position, and none of the guests looked tough.

Sophie, dark-haired, curious, was perched on the arm of Victor's chair, asking questions about Chiara's shop.

"I've passed your shop, but of course I've never been inside. It looks marvelous, so elegant. And you have how many workers?"

"Only four, but I may need more soon." Chiara was charmed by both women, who seemed to be trying to make her welcome. "You must come in someday. I'll show you what we do."

"You've a lovely accent."

"Oh, no. I try hard to talk like an American, but . . . " Chiara shrugged, her hands aloft.

"My own parents are from Russia," Sophie said.

"I'm ordering food," Walter yelled to the crowd in general. "How does Chinese sound?" After genial agreement he phoned a Chinese restaurant for delivery.

Chiara had never eaten Chinese food. She hoped it wouldn't be too unusual. She listened to the conversation flowing around her. All of the guests were unionists and the talk was naturally about their activities. There were jokes she didn't understand and words with which she was unfamiliar. But for the most part they seemed nice people, good people, polite and considerate. Although they were intense about their work, they obviously loved and believed in it. Chiara began to relax and enjoy herself.

When the knock sounded, Victor yelled, "Soup's on," and opened the door.

Victor's gasp claimed Chiara's attention. In the doorway, instead of the delivery boy, stood two men with drawn revolvers.

"Okay, against the wall!" One gunman, wearing a snap-brim black hat, pushed into the room.

Terror-stricken, Chiara shrank back into the chair. One of the women screamed.

"Move it!" With a wave of his revolver, the gangster directed everyone standing to move toward the wall. The other hoodlum put his gun in its holster and drew an enormous blackjack from the rear pocket of his black suit. At first some of the men snickered, as if they thought it was a joke, and indeed it looked almost staged, like an elaborate gangster movie.

"Okay, Red, you're coming with us," said the black-suited man. He moved menacingly toward Walter, who had backed into a corner. While everyone watched trance-like, the man with the blackjack grabbed a glass floor lamp and broke it over Walter's head. Walter, red-faced and furious, began kicking and flailing his arms to fend off the blows from the blackjack. He managed to grab the weapon and wrench it free from its leather thong.

"Kill the son of a bitch," the larger thug yelled.

Chiara noticed one of the guests, Al King, had slouched out of the room and into the kitchen during the commotion. Now she heard his screams for help from outside the apartment. He must have jumped out the window, Chiara thought.

The thugs, surprised by this turn of events, began backing toward the door, and to Chiara's dismay, Mike started toward them, fire in his eye. Suddenly a pickle bottle whizzed through the air, striking the triggerman in the head. The two bruisers, apparently frightened and confused by the commotion, escaped through the door before anyone could stop them.

Mike and the others gathered around Walter to assess his injuries. Other than cuts and bruises on his face, he seemed unharmed. Suddenly everyone collapsed into giddy laughter, all but Chiara, who sat hugging herself, still terror-stricken. Mike hurried to her side, pulling her upright, patting her back. "It's all right now, it's all over."

"Please. Take me home, Mike."

It was several hours before Chiara stopped shivering. When would someone actually be killed? When would it be Mike's turn? And for what? For an ideal; a union. It was all crazy. It didn't make sense. When would Mike realize how futile it all was?

Chiara realized that her objections fell on deaf ears, that Mike had an altruistic vision of the union's role. Obviously there were rewards in unionism for Mike, although he complained bitterly about battles for power between parent organizations, the CIO and the AFL. Within the UAW itself, there was infighting, fostered by the president, Homer Martin, who had labeled his opponents as communists.

Although over a year had gone by since the attempted kidnapping, the menace of that night never quite left Chiara's thoughts. She sat in her office, a letter in her hand, the humming of the sewing machines providing background music for her musings. She took solace by rereading letters from home, which were less frequent now, since Chiara's father had suffered a stroke a year ago, in 1938. This letter was from Gabriella—Chiara's mother had never learned to read and write. Chiara spread photographs from the letter on the desk. A deep sadness engulfed her as she examined them one by one. Her brother Carlo was twenty-six years old, a man now, so proud and handsome in his uniform. He remained in the army, and was serving in Africa, but talked of leaving the military and going to Argentina. Thank God, we're not involved in a war, Mike had said, with Mussolini and Hitler holding hands. Who knew what the strutting, pompous dictator Mussolini would do next?

And her sisters! They had blossomed into young women. In the snapshots their arms were entwined and their heads tilted toward each other with coy smiles. And "little" Dino, little no longer, but towering over his father. Emilio wore spectacles now, and his hairline had receded at the temples. If Chiara's brothers and sisters were to walk in the front door she wouldn't even recognize them. Her mother looked the same, only a bit fatter, with hair almost totally gray. Thinking of them made Chiara's face pucker with sadness. She wiped away a tear. She would have to send more pictures of her girls, now five and almost two.

Ever since she'd had a miscarriage two months ago, she'd been prone to crying spells. Some days she didn't even want to get out of bed. Melancholia, Dr. Catrone had said. Her depression wasn't unusual, and she would gradually begin to feel better.

She was three months when she had miscarried. *That* one might have been the boy that Michele wanted so badly. Perhaps it was a judgment from God.

At the sound of footsteps she turned to see Maria enter. She looked over Chiara's shoulder, admiring the sepia-toned pictures. "What beautiful youngsters. Chiara. You're still not feeling well?"

"I feel like crying all the time." Chiara rested her forehead in her hand.

Maria put her hand on her friend's shoulder. "Everything happens for the best. Losing the baby was God's will."

"Why is it that God's will and mine never match?"

"That's just the way it is. You learn to accept what life hands you."

Acknowledging her friend's concern by placing her

own hand over Maria's, Chiara said, "I'm still homesick. After all these years."

Maria gave her shoulder a reassuring shake. "Don't worry, you'll go back home one day."

Chiara tilted her face to look into Maria's eyes. "Are you certain, Maria?"

"Yes." Maria's heavy eyelids dropped slowly and she nodded. After a moment she said, "I see you on your own soil, with your loved ones around you."

Chiara squeezed her eyes shut, desperately wishing for the same vision. A tear escaped beneath her eyelid and she wiped it away impatiently. Grabbing Maria's hand, she said, "Thank you, my friend. *Speranza*. One hopes."

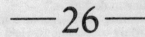

— 26 —

Mike maneuvered the DeSoto through narrow streets lined with parked cars as he made his way toward Eastern Market with Flora and the girls. The warmth of the April day had brought a hint of summer. Spiky tips of hyacinths and tulips were spearing through the soil toward the sun, and the trees sprouted caps of pale green. His daughters delighted in the strange sounds and smells that emanated from the noisy, bustling market. They stared in fascination at the chickens that clucked with irritation in their wire cages, listened raptly as their father harangued with the merchants for a better price on the vegetables.

"Come along with us, Flora," Mike said after the shopping was completed. "We're picking up Chiara and going for a drive in the country."

"No, thanks, I want to make *gnocchi*, and do some baking. I'll bring some over when I come. The girls love my homemade pasta."

"You're good to them, Flora."

Flora, in the back seat, hugged both girls and said, as if it weren't a well-known fact, "I love them. You go and enjoy. And make your wife relax a little. I'm worried about her."

"I'm worried about her too. She shouldn't be working on a Saturday morning, but you know how she is." Since the miscarriage, she hadn't seemed to regain her old energy. Often, at home, she would sit and stare into space. He had wanted her to stay home for a few months after the trouble, but she said there was too much to do, and insisted on going to work in three weeks. He should put his foot down, *demand* that she work less. "Maybe if she hadn't been so overworked in the first place the trouble could have been avoided."

Flora shook her head. "Dr. Catrone said her working probably had nothing to do with it."

If only he were earning more, then he could order her to quit. She was overly conscientious. He'd told her so, but she declared she could handle the work and pointed out that he was just as diligent, just as dedicated. But of course that was different; he was a man, doing his duty. It was another matter for a woman. The awful paradox was that they depended now on her earnings, so his objections had no teeth. Of course, neither of them mentioned the fact that she was the major moneymaker in their family.

Money. It was always a problem. Occasionally, through Fredo, who seemed to have connections with everyone in the city, Mike would get odd jobs—carpentry, car repair, janitorial work—but they barely supplied cigarette money.

After he dropped Flora off, he thought about the last few years. His pay when he first started as an organizer with the UAW had been little or nothing, depending on the union coffers. At least now he received a reasonable, if irregular, paycheck. Though the union membership kept increasing, men were often out of work and unable to pay dues.

He suppressed the occasional twinges of uneasiness caused by his inadequate earnings, with the knowledge that he was fighting for the rights of the common man; rights that would be won, *must* be won. Eventually he would be recompensed, of that he was sure. Meanwhile his faith was further sustained by his certainty that God and time were on the side of the UAW.

He swerved onto Woodward Avenue and cranked the window down for a breath of spring air.

"Are we there yet?" Anna's voice piped up impatiently from the back seat, and she hopped up and down with excitement.

"In a few minutes." Mike shot another glance to the back. "Watch your little sister; don't let her fall."

His thoughts shifted back to his work. So much had been accomplished, but there was much left to do. It was 1939 already. Where had the years gone?

Since the breakthrough at Kelsey Hayes he'd kept busy putting out the small brushfires of strikes and working for the release of union agents who'd been arrested for passing out leaflets. In one month alone, 352 union members were arrested.

The UAW had come a long way, but they seemed to take one step forward and two steps back. There were twenty thousand UAW members last year, but the majority were unemployed.

After the General Motors sit-down, Chrysler workers followed suit with a well-organized strike involving all nine Detroit factories. It was a revolution, joined by the laborers of practically every industry in the city, including parts plants, hotels, department stores, cigar plants, almost any establishment employing more than a couple of dozen people. Over 125 businesses were occupied and held from several hours to several weeks.

At one point, daily "box scores" were published in the newspapers.

But now, at long last, it seemed that the wave of sit-down strikes was gradually subsiding.

Mike's musings were interrupted by Luisa's wail.

"Papa, hurry, Luisa's getting crabby," Anna called out over her little sister's sporadic yells.

"Play peekaboo or something," Mike answered impatiently. "We'll be there soon."

He drove past a neighborhood beer garden. When he had gone there recently, former pals from his Rouge days told him the situation at Ford was worse than ever. The reign of terror of Harry Bennett continued, with over eight hundred underworld characters actually employed in the service department and nearly nine thousand others, who worked with the rank and file but were actually stoolies for Bennett. The speed-up and the stretch-out continued as well, forcing men to work beyond their normal endurance, breaking them both mentally and physically. They raged in frustration against the machines and against the bosses who drove them with no regard for human dignity.

The surrender of General Motors and Chrysler to the UAW-CIO was a glorious victory, but for Mike, bringing Ford to its knees would be the ultimate triumph, for he had seen firsthand what the forces of power and greed could do to the common man; had felt the debilitating effects of dehumanization from the hands of Harry Bennett; had heard the men crying out in silent agony with their eyes, with their bent backs and fearful faces.

Any day now the union would be ready for the big push at Ford.

"Papa, we're here!" Anna's shout jarred his thoughts.

He parked in an empty space near the bridal salon, lifted Anna from the back seat of the DeSoto and onto the sidewalk, and hefted Luisa. Anna hurried to the door and pulled the knob. When Mike tried to assist her, she elbowed his arm impatiently. "I can do it. I'm five now."

Mike stood aside and let her tug at the heavy door, a frown of effort creasing her forehead. Stubborn. Just like her mother. She might look like him, with that halo of dark curly hair, but she had her mother's determination.

The bell jingled as Anna succeeded in opening the door. Mike set Luisa on her feet to toddle to the back, toward the work area. Anna, flushed with excitement from the day's activities, was full of importance as she hurried to the back, taking her sister's hand and guiding her along.

Mike smiled endearingly at Anna. She loved going into the sewing area, where the workers indulged her by making fancy doll clothes from the scraps lying about and fashioning necklaces of sequins and bracelets of lace.

Mike felt as out of place as an ape in an aviary. He was amazed each time he stepped into his wife's domain. His once-unassuming and shy little Chiara hustled about giving instructions, going over orders, signing checks—and doing it all with aplomb, as if she'd done it all her life.

Business looked brisk, as evidenced by the four women working diligently at their machines and by the two customers at the counter.

Chiara glanced up from a sheaf of sketches on her desk, then opened her arms and let her children scramble up onto her lap. She hugged them tightly, pressing her face in their hair.

When they scampered away, Chiara rose wearily, pushing a stray lock from her forehead. "I'm almost finished," she said, kissing Mike's cheek.

Mike looked about nervously at the staff, then whispered to Chiara, "I hope you're paying them overtime."

Chiara patted his cheek. "Of course. But if you're here to sign them up for the union, you can leave right now."

Mike laughed. "You're small potatoes. We're still after Henry Ford. When we get him, then we'll go after you."

Chiara rolled her eyes and shook her head. "Isn't Flora with you?"

"No, you know Flora. She went home to cook."

Chiara felt a little pull of envy toward Flora, and a twinge of nostalgia for the days when the two of them, heads covered with clean cloths and knuckle-deep in dough, would cook and bake and reminisce about their childhood in the old country. Now there was no time for those simple pleasures. She was also bothered by the strong attachment the girls had formed to Flora. *Zia Flora says this, Zia Flora says that.* Both girls adored their aunt; and why shouldn't they? She spoiled them terribly.

"Don't give them their way all the time," Chiara had scolded Flora. "They think they're Princess Elizabeth and Princess Margaret Rose."

Flora shrugged her shoulders. "They are my princesses. Anyway, babies are for spoiling."

And after all, how could Chiara fault her? Flora was like a mother to them; the only person Chiara would trust with her children other than her own mother. She'd made the decision to be a "businesswoman" and so had to accept all that went with it, which included relegating the raising of her children to someone else. Truly, she had the best possible situation for a woman who worked: a loving replacement.

Che sera, sera. One makes choices, then must live with them.

If only she weren't so tired from the miscarriage.

Mike pried the girls away from their mother's desk, where they rummaged through drawers looking for hidden treats. "Hurry, Chiara, I have a surprise for you."

She looked suspicious. "What is it?"

"We're going for a ride. You look too pale. You need some fresh air, country air."

Chiara found two lollipops in the back of a drawer and handed them to the girls. "I have work to do at home."

"That can wait. I'll help you tomorrow."

Anna tugged at her mother's hand. "Please, please, we want to go to the lake, Mama. Papa brought bread and salami and cheese. Wine and cookies too."

"Get your sweater, we're leaving," Mike commanded. "Let Maria close up."

"It's too cold for the shore; the girls will catch cold."

"No, it's beautiful and sunny. They have sweaters. They need to get out of the city once in a while." He took Chiara's sweater from the rack and shook it impatiently. "We'll go north on Gratiot, past Mount Clemens, maybe to Port Huron."

Chiara obediently shrugged into her sweater, and with last-minute instructions to Maria, followed the others out and into the car.

Mike sped through the city, and as they neared the water, he rolled the window down. "Ah, smell that air."

"I can smell the water!" Anna called out. "I can hear it!"

Mike parked the car on the edge of a dirt road. The girls darted ahead over a grassy knoll, to the beach.

On the sand, Mike spread out a blanket and urged Chiara to sit, then brought the provisions from the car. Chiara dropped to the blanket and shivered. Ever since the miscarriage she'd been cold. Now the sun-heated sand began to warm her. She breathed deeply of the sweet, clean air. The whitecaps on Lake Huron rolled to the shore with a soothing whoosh. A sandpiper hurried furiously toward the water's edge, making tiny indentations in the sand.

Chiara lay back with a sigh. "If I close my eyes, I imagine I'm home again, beside the Adriatic Sea."

Mike patted her hand.

"Come on, we'll find shells," Anna called to her sister as she ran along the shore.

Luisa hurried after her, stumbling in her attempt to keep up.

"Don't go too far," Mike yelled.

Their happy cries faded away as they darted about, snatching up tiny shells and stones. Chiara dozed for a while. When Anna dropped a handful of her treasures into her mother's lap, Chiara started. Luisa, always mimicking her sister, added to the hoard. The sound of the shells clinking against one another, the sun warming her cheek, the gulls swooping and calling—all recalled another time, another day. Scooping up a handful of the shells, Chiara brought them close, scrutinized their crusty cream outsides and peach satin insides.

With crystal clarity Chiara envisioned the turquoise of the Adriatic, smelled the aquatic aroma, felt the sunwarmed Italian sand against her legs, heard melodious Italian voices in playful argument, and in the background, the tinkling strains of a mandolin.

Suddenly seized with a nostalgia so great it took her breath away, she bent forward, lowering her face into her hands, and sobbed. She rocked in rhythm with the waves, wailing with the water.

"What is it? Chiara, what's wrong?" Mike hurried to her and pulled her hands from her face.

She couldn't catch her breath long enough to speak.

"Please, Chiara, tell me!" He shook her shoulders.

"I . . . I . . . want . . . to . . . go . . . home."

Mike stretched his hands out with a questioning gesture. "Are you sick?"

Chiara took a handkerchief from the sleeve of her sweater and snuffled into it. "No. I want to go home."

"All right, then. Come on." Mike looked frightened as he tugged her upward. "We'll go home. I'll get the girls."

She stood, but her head hung low and her shoulders hunched forward, the sweater hanging loosely from them. Swaying unsteadily toward Mike, she grabbed his arms. "No, I mean *really home*. Back to Italy."

Mike stared at her, bewildered.

Chiara's eyes pleaded with him. *"Home, Michele. Home."*

"How can we go to Italy? We both have our work. The girls are too young to travel that far—"

"I want to go home." Her voice cracked.

Mike pulled her roughly to him and caressed her hair. "Chiara, Chiara. What do you want of me?"

"I want to go home."

"All right." Mike swallowed. "All right. We'll go back to Italy."

She began crying again, softly this time. "Do you mean it?"

"Yes, I mean it."

"Grazie, grazie, Michele." The words were muffled against his chest.

When Mike was asleep, Chiara rose wearily from her bed and took the old black leather purse from her top drawer. The clasp was stubborn but she forced it open and pulled out the dark green bankbook. Five hundred dollars. Plenty of money for a trip home. There would have been more, but they'd been sending money to her parents, twenty dollars last month alone. Her mother and father never asked for it, but the crop had failed last year because of bad weather. Chiara recalled the deprivations of village life, realized that since her father's stroke, the family needed help more than ever.

There was money in the cigar box too. Maybe a hundred dollars.

She replaced the bankbook and, slipping back into bed, curled up against Mike's warm back. The lines left her brow, and a smile played across her lips. She fell asleep and dreamed happy dreams of home.

Planning a trip home was just the catharsis she needed. The next day, her optimism restored, she hummed at her job. Mike needed time to plan and organize for his absence from work. They could probably leave at the end of September. Of course Chiara, too, had to plan for the shop, though with Maria in charge, she could relax on that score.

Home. They were going home, she thought, pausing in her paperwork to smile. She hated this chore especially, because the only time to accomplish it was the quiet hours after the shop closed.

A light tapping brought her attention from the jumble

of numbers that danced on the ledger page. She went hesitantly to the front and peeped through the small square of glass. Stewart Austin's serious angular face grinned at her.

He occasionally dropped in for a short chat when he saw the light on after hours. They would sit in her office and talk over a cup of coffee, hot and strong from the pot that sat forever warming on the hot plate. Rarely were words of a personal nature spoken between them, though in the warm smiles Stewart showered on her and the pressure of his hand when he took her own, Chiara read the passion that was submerged under his civilized manner. She was loath to examine her own tightly controlled emotions. Stewart was a friend, a good friend. Nothing more. Or so she tried to tell herself.

He sat next to her desk now, peering down at the numbers marching in neat rows down the lined ledger sheet.

Chiara pushed a wayward strand of hair from her eyes. "I'm almost finished."

"See here, you shouldn't have to worry over the books." Stewart frowned, watching her fierce concentration as she penned in figures. "For one thing, I'm not even sure you know what you're doing."

Chiara bristled. "I know what I'm doing. It takes me so long because I hate doing it. I'm always thinking about getting back to the designing and sewing, the work I enjoy."

"I'm going to send you a good man from my department, a qualified accountant. Save your receipts and bills, and he'll do the books every couple of weeks."

Chiara cried out with delight. "Oh, that would be wonderful." She'd gladly give up the dreaded chore of totting up figures from her box of receipts and canceled checks.

She closed the ledger and patted it, as if to signal that things would work out fine, then poured coffee from the aluminum pot.

"How are things going for you?" She passed a china cup and saucer to Stewart.

"There's trouble brewing at Ford. The tension mounts daily. The uneasiness from the laborers has infiltrated to management."

Chiara said nothing. She knew he liked to talk. It seemed to be therapy for him, even though she didn't always understand.

Stewart continued, "Something has to be done about Bennett. At first he simply controlled the laborers, but now he's reached into supervision. He's eliminated two of my best men; just came through and told them they were fired. Then he promoted one of his pals into a critical position. If only Edsel could get through to his father."

"Surely Henry Ford will listen to his own son, his own flesh and blood."

"No, he only listens to Bennett. He's even worse since he had the stroke, suspicious of everyone, frightened and wary. It's a far cry from the era of the five-dollar day, when Ford was the champion of the workingman."

"Mike says things will change."

"Are they planning a major strike?"

"I don't know. He doesn't tell me everything."

"The Rouge would be a tough place to get a strike going. There are ninety-three separate structures." He picked up his cup and paced around the tiny office. "Yes, indeed, old Henry has changed. His star has definitely fallen. He accepted Hitler's second-highest decoration, the Grand Cross of the German Eagle. It's an embarrassment for the entire Ford Motor Company. I suppose the award was because Ford and Hitler are of the same mind concerning Jews. Ford has always blamed his problems on Jews and the Wall Street bankers."

He poured more coffee and stirred it absentmindedly. "Hitler offered Ford a partnership in the new Volkswagen firm, but of course there's no future in that sort of automobile, and Henry wisely declined." He paused and looked at Chiara with warmth. Touching her shoulder, he said, "Enough business talk. It only serves to aggravate me. I must say you're looking better than the last time I saw you."

"I'm feeling better. Much better. We're going back to the old country for a month's visit. Maybe even a little longer. We leave next week."

"Why, that's wonderful. So that's what put the bloom back into your cheeks. Lucky you."

"Yes, lucky me. But somehow I have the feeling that

something will go wrong, because this trip means so much to me."

"Nothing will." Stewart looked at his watch. "Do you have time for a quick bite of supper?"

The invitation was tempting, but of course it was out of the question. Her family would be waiting for her. "I've too much work right now."

Stewart cradled her hand in his. "Well, I suppose I won't see you again until you return." A note of sadness crept into his voice and clouded his eyes. "I'm sure you'll have a wonderful time." He kissed her cheek and left.

Chiara sang as she made lists and preliminary preparations for the trip. She resolved she'd begin speaking Italian exclusively to the girls. Her family would be disappointed if they couldn't communicate. Lately she found she spoke English more often than not.

She wished Mike were more excited about the trip. He seemed reluctant to leave his work now that the union was finally making progress, but she reminded him that they'd never had a real vacation, that he needed the respite as much as she.

"Right after the first of September I'll get the tickets," he promised.

But on September 1, 1939, the devastating news sounded throughout the world. Hitler had marched his troops into Poland.

"There'll be no trips for a while," Mike told her. "This may mean a world war."

The next day, when Chiara unpacked the gifts she had bought for her family, large tears fell freely, splotching the tissue wrappings. She stored the gifts away in a closet. Making the sign of the cross, she prayed, "Just keep my family safe, *Madre di Dio*." The gifts would wait. So would the trip. Someday, she vowed, before I die, I'll go home again.

The frigid January air stung Mike's cheeks. He wished he'd worn a sweater under his coat, had forgotten how the wind could whip around you at the Rouge. He shifted the sack of leaflets to his other hand. At least there was no longer the fear of arrest. Last October they'd celebrated a major victory when a City of Dearborn court bucked the Ford political machine by declaring the ordinance against distributing leaflets unconstitutional. Since then, every two weeks Mike and his workers distributed fifty-thousand copies of the UAW's *Ford Facts* to the workers under the hateful glares of Bennett's henchmen, who were unable to stop them.

Despite that victory, Mike felt increasingly frustrated as 1941 dawned and still the Ford Motor Company resisted unionization. He thought that part of the problem was the union infighting. When the UAW president, Homer Martin, instituted secret negotiations with Bennett, there was a hue and cry. Though Martin was ousted from the UAW-CIO, he marched his followers into the American Federation of Labor. That sort of inner strife weakened the union position, made them look foolish. Now, with Windham Mortimer at the helm, Mike's optimism was restored.

His companion, Tom, an apple-cheeked young man, interrupted his thoughts. "Do you think we're doing any good?"

"Sure. We're getting the word out to the workers." Mike paused to light his cigarette with a Zippo lighter. "We've tried everything to get to the workers, even hired a plane. We circled the Rouge, shouting slogans from a loudspeaker. Unfortunately, at that altitude no one on the ground could hear a word." Mike laughed.

Tom laughed along with him. "Yeah, I heard that one. How about when our wives and friends went on the tour of the Rouge plant? Once they were inside, they pulled on UAW caps and unfurled signs that said 'Get wise. Organize.' There ain't nothing we won't try."

"Yeah, we've tried it all. I spoke on the radio a couple of times, on *The Italian Hour*." Mike drew his muffler close around his chin. "For some reason, the Italians are reluctant to come out for the union. I think it's social conditioning against 'organizations.' " He blew on his frigid fingers. "But the toughest fence to hurdle is selling the UAW to the coloreds. If we could get the backing of the Negro workers at Ford, it would tip the scales."

Tom hunched his shoulders and blew on his free hand. "They're just not buying it, are they? What're they so scared of?"

"They're suspicious of being used. Besides, the Negro ministers won't approve of the UAW for fear Ford won't hire men from their congregation. And good ol' Harry Bennett comes along with fists full of money for those churches that support Ford's views. They think he's a saint."

"It can get pretty discouraging, can't it?"

Mike shrugged. "Yeah, but you have to have faith."

A tall thin man dressed in a houndstooth overcoat strode through the Rouge main gate. At the sight of Mike, the man paused, then nodded in greeting. A flash of recognition tickled Mike's memory.

"Hey, Tom, do you know that guy?" he asked his companion.

"Yeah, I think so. Austin's his name. He's one of Ford's top people."

"Yeah, that's it. Stewart Austin," Mike said. Austin had been responsible for Mike's job at Ford. Probably he should be grateful to Austin, but he only felt resentment. Come to think of it, if it hadn't been for Austin, he might not have worked at Ford, would never have been fired, never have mustered the anger necessary to work for the union. Yes, as a matter of fact, he *was* grateful to Austin.

"Hey, Mike, wake up, here comes the next shift."

Mike returned to the task at hand, and once again yelled slogans and thrust leaflets into the hands of un-smiling workers who filed through the gates.

When the last of the leaflets had been distributed, Mike hurried back to the office to prepare the speech he would give that night. Each week he spoke at one meeting or another, sometimes in large halls, more often in private homes with only seven or eight workers present. The private meetings were the safest, because spies weren't likely to show up in someone's living room.

At home, he ate a rushed meal under Chiara's disapproving eye. He hardly blamed her silent reproaches. He was so caught up in his work, he had little time for his family. Little Luisa was a bright, curious three-year-old now, and he'd missed practically her entire babyhood. Anna was almost seven, determined and clever, with a dozen questions a day, questions he hardly had time to answer. He'd make it up to them, just as soon as the push at Ford was over.

Chiara broke into his thoughts. "What kind of meeting is it tonight?"

"Oh, the same thing. Campaigning for more members. I won't be gone long."

Mike had told her little of his activities, ever since the debacle at the Reuthers'. To this day no one had been arrested for that attempted kidnapping they called the "Chop Suey Incident," even though there had been over a dozen eyewitnesses. Even the police were in the pocket of Henry Ford.

That night Mike glanced approvingly over the large mixed group of men and women, white and Negro, at Eastern High School. His gaze hesitated over three men in the audience he recognized as "spotters." When would the spying end? Not until the UAW was officially sanctioned at Ford, he supposed.

Mike began his speech by praising the workers for turning out in spite of Harry Bennett's underhanded tactics. Pointedly he paused, glared directly at the informers, who stirred uncomfortably in their seats, and continued.

"The National Labor Relations Board has commanded the Ford Motor Company, time after time, to cease and desist its efforts to keep the union out of the plant, and to reinstate the fired union people. Ford has refused and now has appealed to the Supreme Court. But I'm telling you, Henry Ford cannot win. The laws of the land are on our side."

Afterward, only a few stalwarts signed up, though he could tell by their reactions that the majority were solidly with him. Some of them, he knew, would manage to get signed up through friends of friends, and their dues would come in through the mail.

When the auditorium had emptied, Mike gathered papers into his briefcase and hurried outside. The meeting had gone well, he thought; he'd felt the audience's empathy. He paused on the steps to light a cigarette and snapped the brim of his hat down against the wind. As he walked toward the car, parked just beyond an alley, the darkness seemed to thicken and envelop him. A single streetlight barely illuminated the dark alley where exaggerated shadows loomed. Mike was aware of nocturnal sounds coming from the black abyss—the tinkling of a wind-tossed tin can, a dog's growl. A battered garbage can cast an elongated shadow, and Mike started when a mouse scurried past his feet.

"Hey, Marcassa!" The voice, obviously from a black man, sent adrenaline rushing through Mike's veins.

"Over here!" The command came from the alley. Mike heard footsteps coming toward him. Automatically his muscles tensed and his fist curled tightly around the handle of the briefcase. Hefting the heavy case, he wondered if it could fell a man with one blow. He wished now he had heeded Fredo's offer of a gun.

The outline of a huge man was discernible now as it moved toward him. Mike doubled his fist and pulled back, ready to connect.

A black hand appeared out of the darkness as the figure became visible.

"It's Mortimer. I was your neighbor on Chene Street, remember?"

Mike swallowed hard and let out a low whistle. He gripped the man's hand. "You scared the shit out of me."

"Sorry. I didn't want nobody to see me inside. I want to join."

Mike clapped Mortimer on the shoulder. "Good man!"

"Some of my friends, they want to join too. But the

churches preach against it, 'cause Henry Ford he donate to the church.''

"I know, and I can't blame them too much. Bennett hires Negroes from the congregations that support him. The preachers have to knuckle under in order to get jobs for their people."

"That's so. But my preacher, he don't abide by that no more. But when he spoke up for the union, a hundred men got up and left. Sure, ol' Henry, he always hired us, that's true. But he put us in the baddest jobs, like me, in the foundry where my friends be dying from lung sickness. There's soot so thick I can wet my finger an' write my name on my arm."

"I know. I've seen it." Mike remembered his own experience, years ago, in a foundry. "The UAW plans to change all that—we'll have equality, and seniority rights—"

"I know, I been readin' 'bout this UAW. I be your man. I get the others to join, don't you worry. I ain't scared no more. We gots to take a stand." He thrust a bill at Mike. "Sign me up, Marcassa."

"You won't regret this, Mortimer."

The two men clapped each other on the shoulder and Mortimer quickly disappeared into the shadows. Mike slammed his key in the ignition and pulled the choke. When the engine sputtered and sparked to life, he sped toward home. Mortimer's vote of confidence was an omen. The tide was turning. Surely Ford would fall.

But despite their best efforts, several weeks passed before the union made any gains.

On a crackling cold winter day in mid-February Mike cranked out leaflets on the inky, noisy mimeograph machine while May Reuther folded and stacked them. Walter manned the ever-ringing phones.

Even over the roar of the machine, Mike heard Walter's excited whoop of joy.

"I just got the word," Walter yelled, slamming down the phone. "The Supreme Court upheld the ruling of the National Labor Relations Board."

Mike punched his fist in the air with a victorious shout. He switched off the machine and wiped his ink-spotted hands. He grabbed May and Walter and they hugged and did a little dance.

"Now we'll see things happen," Mike said with smug satisfaction. "Ford will give in."

"What, exactly, is the ruling?" May wanted to know.

"The Ford Motor Company must cease their opposition to the UAW and they've been ordered to rehire the union workers they fired illegally," Walter said.

A few weeks later, in a typical Harry Bennett maneuver, the president of the Rouge local was reinstated and then fired again. The rank and file, in an angry mood, threatened a sit-down strike unless he was brought back. Mike had to talk tough to convince the workers that the timing was poor for a strike.

Sit-downs were now illegal, and the union needed public sentiment on their side. Though the company yielded and rehired the president, Henry Ford declared he would never submit to the union. The Wall Street group and the Jews were behind the union, he claimed, and they were out to get him.

When Mike answered the phone at UAW headquarters on April Fool's Day, he expected another prank call. He'd had a couple of jokes played on him already. But this call jerked him upright. This was no joke.

He slammed down the phone and told the others, "Trouble at the Rouge. There are twelve hundred men outside the superintendent's office at the rolling mill. Several union men have been fired."

Soon they were deluged with calls reporting work stoppage.

"A-Building has shut down."

"Rubber plant's been closed by the company."

"The axle-plant men walked out."

In short order practically the entire Rouge complex was paralyzed. Only a few units like the foundry, where the UAW had never gained a foothold, were still operating.

Although Mike and Reuther had worked for months behind the scenes to avoid a bloody confrontation, it looked like they were in for one now.

Mike grabbed his coat. "We'd better get down there in a hurry. They can't pull a sit-down now. The government won't back us if we pull an illegal strike."

"You go ahead. I have to make calls to the other locals." Walter was already dialing.

Mike rushed out as May called, "Be careful."

At Gate Four, the same gate where the bloody "battle of the overpass" had taken place, several servicemen met Mike's car.

"You can't go in there." The steely-eyed guard recognized him. "Management won't meet with you."

A man hurried to Mike's car and leaned against the door. Breathing hard, he said, "I work at the mill. I'm a brother, Joe Serra. I know who you are." He stuck his hand through the open window and shook Mike's hand. "I managed to sneak away. It's spreading like wildfire. I figure there are over fifty thousand men refusing to work. They're hot for a strike."

"Get in the car," Mike said. "We may need you."

A few minutes later, Walter's car pulled up behind Mike's.

Walter hurried toward Mike, glancing at the angry, belching smokestacks in the distance. "I hope the workers keep cool. A wildcat strike would mean bloodshed. Bennett would love that."

Mike nodded. "The service department would have a field day trouncing the workers. With this overpass layout, they could easily plant machine guns on the roofs."

But Mike knew the spontaneous demand for justice by the workers couldn't be denied. "If management won't even talk to us, where do we go from here? We can't very well tell the men to go back to work."

A dark sedan pulled up and Michael Widman hurried out with a companion. Widman, who'd successfully helped organize the United Mine Workers, had recently been sent to Detroit to oversee the Ford campaign. The four men shook hands.

"It's a strike, whether we like it or not. How can we stop fifty thousand men?" Widman said. "First we'll have to get the executive board together in a hurry to vote on this. Once we've got a vote for the strike, the best strategy is to order them out of the plant. Mike, I want you to organize a blockage of the five highways leading into the Rouge, so the next shift can't get in."

Walter said, "I've got the battle plan in operation. We've got support lined up from the other locals. The pickets should be here any minute. I've got union men taking control of the switches along the railroad tracks and on the drawbridge across the river, so there won't be any shipments by rail or water."

Mike pushed his hat back on his head. "Too bad Edsel's in Florida. He's the only one we can talk sense to."

"Edsel will be back soon enough, when he hears what's going on," Walter said.

Widman snorted. "What good will Edsel do? Henry only listens to Bennett."

"He still has a little influence. It's due to him we've been able to keep the lid on so far." Mike flicked a cigarette butt to the road and ground it out with his shoe. "We'd better get started."

Mike quickly commandeered brothers from other locals and organized barricades of cars, railroad ties, telephone poles, and whatever junk they could manage to find to block every road leading to the plant.

Just after midnight Mike sent word to the workers that they were officially on strike.

The next day the rank and file threw down their tools and marched out. The Ford servicemen stood watching, not daring to say a word or to stop them. Spellbound, Mike beheld fifty thousand workers pour out of Gate Four. They marched across the infamous overpass, where Mike and his brothers had been beaten, and into the ebony night, singing "Old Hank Ford, he ain't what he used to be." Wave upon wave of men rolled out, their heads held high. New songs broke out as they marched four abreast to union headquarters a mile away: "Solidarity Forever," and "We don't give a damn for the A.F. of L."

The strike was in full swing, and no official of the Ford Motor Company dared to intervene. Hope surged in Mike's chest. This time they would do it. They would outfox Henry Ford and Harry Bennett.

As Mike drove his car around the complex, he stared out into the inky blackness toward the administration building. Silhouetted in an upper window were two figures; a stocky man and an upright, rigid one, whose white hair caught a faint light. Mike gripped the smooth round knob of the gearshift and muttered, "I hope you're getting worried, you bastards." Gunning the motor, he sped away.

The next morning the problems they had anticipated became reality. In an effort to get inside, Negro foundry workers loyal to Henry Ford attacked the pickets with iron bars.

Despite Mike's constant admonition to avoid violence, the pickets had no choice but to defend themselves.

"The Negroes inside can't be reasoned with," Mike reported to Walter when they met outside Gate Four. "Maybe we can convince the NAACP to talk sense to them."

Reuther said, "Good thinking. Try to get Walter White, the executive secretary, out here. They'll listen to him. Tell him he can use the sound truck." Reuther pushed aside his coat and shoved his hands in his rear pockets. "The word is that Edsel's back in town, and his father told him 'hands off.' He wants Bennett to handle things."

"Bennett's a jackass. We're in for a hell of a battle," Mike said as they walked along behind the pickets. "I hear he wants to use tear gas."

"The good news is, we've run out of union buttons. They're signing up as though their lives depended on it. And maybe that's so."

Mike turned when he heard his name called out. A burly Negro hurried toward him.

"Mortimer!" Mike greeted his old friend.

"Mike, if I can get back in there, I can maybe convince my brothers in the foundry to come out."

"I don't know, Mortimer. They're in a foul mood. They may turn on you."

"They be scared. Inside, Bennett's men be telling them the pickets'll beat them up 'cause they scabs. An' they think they be fired if they join the strike."

"Tell them Ford can't fire ten thousand men. Tell them . . . well, you know what to tell them, Mortimer. We'll get you past the picket line."

Mike and Walter paced nervously while Mortimer delivered his message. The time stretched from minutes to hours. Finally they saw a few scattered blacks marching out onto the overpass. Leading them was Mortimer. Several more followed; then a burst of men paraded through the doors. There were over three hundred Negroes, some with uncertain expressions, others looking jubilant.

Mike moved through the tight line of cheering pickets.

"This is it, Walter, the turning point. There can't be many men left inside now."

Reaching Mortimer, Mike extended his hand. Mortimer grabbed it and said, "Brother!" In that moment Mike felt as close to Mortimer as if he were kin. Their eyes met and held in an intense moment of profound comradeship.

"Brother," Mike echoed.

In the next few days Mike saw Bennett use every trick at his disposal to instigate city, state, and federal intervention, but a "hands-off" policy seemed to prevail, from city officials all the way up to President Roosevelt himself. But still Bennett steadfastly refused to negotiate. After another week of the stalemate, with tensions running high and violence barely kept under control, Bennett summoned Walter and the other leaders for talks.

After several long, intense sessions, Walter reported, "We talk and talk, but there's no progress."

The impasse served to make the pickets more restive than ever and Mike thought it would take very little for them to erupt into violence. They shuffled along in locked steps, their signs propped on their bent shoulders, their anger seething just below the surface.

On April 10 Mike and Victor stood at the building entrance discussing strategy.

"There's a chance the talks will fall apart," Mike said.

"Maybe," Victor said, "but the word is that Henry's wife, Clara, and Edsel are pushing him to settle this thing."

"Henry's stubborn as a mule." Mike turned to see Walter and Widman emerge from the building with several others from the union, deep in conversation. Their faces were inscrutable. A muscle jumped in Mike's forehead. Bad news, he thought as the men strode toward them.

When the group drew near, Walter looked up and said, "Well, don't just stand there! Let's celebrate! Ford's capitulated!"

Mike could hardly believe it. After years of working and praying toward this end, the reality of it was hard to grasp.

As news of the victory spread, men shouted and stamped their feet and cheers swelled up in waves.

"Hallelujah "
"We done it!"

Solidarity forever
Solidarity forever
Solidarity forever
And the union makes us strong.

Mike saw several men cry and thought it would take very little for him to do likewise.

Walter explained that Ford had agreed to allow the workers to vote for their choice of union representation and promised to negotiate a contract after that. Mike tried to shrug off a sliver of doubt. Would Ford actually keep his word?

The next day, over twenty-five thousand Ford workers packed the Fair Grounds Auditorium to ratify the settlement.

Once again, on April 13, the smokestacks belched clouds of gray smoke into the air and the belts creaked and groaned as they made their endless circles through the factories.

Mike, the two Reuthers, Michael Widman, and a dozen volunteers waited at union headquarters for the outcome of the election. For once the mimeo was silent, as were the men. A blue smoke haze hung over the office. Someone's foot tapped impatiently.

Mike stopped his pacing and broke the silence. "Ford is sure they'll vote 'no union.' "

Walter played a tattoo on the desk with a yellow pencil. "Not a chance. With the campaign we waged, they *have* to vote UAW-CIO."

"Don't forget the campaign Bennett had going, calling us communists. Plenty of people bought that propaganda. And don't forget that Homer Martin and the AFL still have a following."

"We'll know soon enough." Walter snapped the pencil in two.

When the phone rang, Walter jumped to attention and picked it up. The others hung over his desk, watching his face for the reaction that would tell them the results.

"Yeah. Yeah. Yeah." Walter's expression was noncommittal. He slammed the phone down as his face settled into a look of dejection.

"Well? Tell us, dammit!" Mike shouted.

Walter's face burst into an ear-splitting smile. "We did it! Almost seventy percent voted for the UAW! Only 2.7 percent voted for no union, and 27.4 percent for the AFL!"

Mike was speechless, overcome with the enormity of what he had helped put into motion.

Back home, he pulled Chiara to him in a great bear hug.

"Mike, what's wrong? Are you crying?"

Mike choked out the words. "After all these years of struggle, we've beaten Henry Ford. Detroit has become a *union town!*"

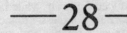

—— 28 ——

"It's nice to have a car on days like this, eh?" Mike hustled the girls from the back seat.

"Hurry into the house." Chiara held her scarf across her mouth. "Don't let the cold air in."

"Mass was too long. I don't know why Father has a half-hour sermon," Mike complained. "You girls help your mother with breakfast and I'll take you to that Abbott-and-Costello movie at the Rivola later."

While Chiara laid bacon in the pan, the girls set the table. Mike loved the quiet domesticity of Sundays. He lit his ritual weekend cigar and took short puffs to get it going.

In the living room he twisted the radio dial and heard a newscaster's excited yet solemn tones. Crouching before the radio, he tuned in WJR.

Pearl Harbor . . . Japanese . . . a bombing.

Could he be hearing correctly? *The Japanese have bombed an American base at Pearl Harbor on the Hawaiian island of Oahu.*

Chiara appeared at the doorway, wiping her hands on a towel. "Mike, what does it mean? What is this Pearl Harbor?"

"Shh, let me hear it!"

They listened intently, their eyes fastened on the radio as if reading the words, their faces drawn, while in the background Anna and Luisa bickered.

After a few moments Mike straightened and said, "It means war with Japan.

Chiara covered her mouth with her hands and gave a little scream. "War!"

Anna brought Mike the world atlas from the buffet drawer, and Mike pointed out a series of dots somewhere in the Pacific Ocean. Hawaii.

Soon neighbors were shouting the news through windows open to the frigid December air, while radios blasted out the shocking report in ceaseless broadcasts. Later, Franklin Delano Roosevelt's somber and resonant voice declared that because of the *dastardly and unprovoked attack,* the United States would go to war. *A day that would live in infamy. December 7, 1941.*

Mike thought it ironic that just as the UAW began to press out the creases in the collective-bargaining process, the urgency of war took precedence, diminishing the union's power. In the following weeks, union struggles were all but forgotten as Detroit rose to the challenge of war, turning over their factories, expertise, and manpower to defense work.

At least his wife needn't worry over his involvement in strikes and what she called "union foolishness." Because the workers were required to take a no-strike pledge for the duration of the war, workplace disputes would be arbitrated by the War Labor Board. Mike was still involved in enough union business to keep busy, but the intensity, the urgency, had lifted.

Chiara began noticing the slack in her trade. Often women opted for simple street dresses and men wore business suits in a hurried ceremony preceding the groom's induction into the armed forces. Chiara lamented the lack of romance and tradition in the speedy ceremonies.

She was forced to discharge a worker, Lois, because of the dearth of work. But Lois promptly found a job in a factory for a higher wage. "And," she explained, "you can really make the bucks in overtime. Getting fired was a lucky break for me."

While Chiara rearranged small boxes of buttons, snaps, and other "notions," she and Maria bemoaned the decline in their patronage. The bell's jangle brought them to the sales area, where Penny was striding in with her son, Patrick. The small freckle-faced youngster resembled his mother.

Penny, thinner than ever, looked world-weary. Gone was the joy that used to shine from her eyes, the light-hearted gaiety that had drawn Chiara to this American girl. Her auburn hair was caught up in a snood, and she wore navy-blue slacks. When Chiara's gaze went to a grayish bruise on Penny's cheek, Penny's hand flew up, touching it.

"Would ya believe it, I walked into a door. Talk about clumsy." Her eyes darted about uneasily.

Chiara pulled the boy toward her and hugged him tightly. *Che bello masco*. He's beautiful, Penny."

"He's nine." Penny tousled his head. "He's shy."

The boy, irritated, shrugged her hand away.

"Come to the back. I have some cookies."

In the workroom Chiara handed the child a *biscotto* from a tin by the coffeepot. Patrick took the hard doughnut-shaped cookie with a shy grin and bit down on it.

"Say thank you, hon." Penny moved about, touching bolts of material, fingering a partly finished rainbow-hued gown draped on a hanger. "So pretty. It's been ages since I wore something pretty."

"How's Jimmy?"

"He's okay. He just got drafted." Her smile was pleased.

Chiara's hand went to her mouth. "Oh, how terrible."

"It ain't so terrible. I'm glad." Her hand moved to her bruised cheek. "The truth is, I didn't walk into a door at all."

Chiara shook her head, understanding. She touched Penny's arm, saying *sotto voce*, "Did he ever suspect about the boy? Is that what makes him so mean?"

Penny shrugged. "Who knows? Sometimes I think so. We just don't talk about it. He ain't home much anyway. We hardly see each other. I'm on the graveyard shift. Rosie the Riveter, that's me." She gave a mirthless laugh. "He's either working or at the beer garden. Anyway, he leaves next week for Camp Custer." She faced Chiara with a determined lift of her chin. "I been thinking about getting a divorce."

"Penny, how can you? You're a Catholic."

Penny looked down. "Well, hell, Chiara, what am I supposed to do? Hang around from one blowup to the next, waitin' for things to get better?" Her chin lifted. "Of course I won't do it now that he's going in the service. But if things don't change when he comes back, Catholic or not, I'm ditching him."

Everything changes, almost daily everything changes. What about the old values? Marriage to one person forever? Yet confronted with abuse, what alternatives were there? What would her mother think of the new way?

As Chiara saw Penny to the door, another customer walked in. Maria began serving the woman, but moments later asked Chiara to take over and hurried to the back. The woman had been in earlier, browsing, and introduced herself as Gina Fontini. A plain, birdlike little thing, about thirty years old, she was second-generation Italian, the daughter of a prominent doctor. By Italian standards she was considered an old maid. At a time when most eligible men were in the service, Chiara thought Gina fortunate to find a husband at all. The woman settled on a simple design in ivory satin, without a fussy train.

Afterward Chiara questioned Maria. "What's wrong? You just turned your back and walked away from her. We don't need the business anymore?"

Maria, always so self-contained, looked distressed. "I don't know what came over me. Like a cold wind passing over."

Now Chiara was solicitous. "You're not sick or anything, are you?"

"No, it's . . . I don't know what."

Chiara looked pensive. "One of your visions?"

Maria gulped from a glass of water. "Maybe. I don't understand these things myself. It's very confusing."

Once, long ago, Maria had said, "It's true that often I get a small vision of the future. It's also true that often, when I try, I see nothing. But I'll tell you, some people look for good fortune, expect it. It's in the set of their shoulders, in the determination of their faces. And when they expect it, then they get it. And I tell them that. Others? They expect bad fortune, and then I just shake my head. So often you get what you expect in life."

When Gina returned a few weeks later for the completed gown, she gushed over it and explained, "My fiancé, Mr. Gabriel, is paying for this. He's picking me up. He should be here any minute." She looked nervously at her watch. "I told him about this place. It's nice to see Italians succeed so well . . . Ah, here he is."

Gina greeted the dapper man with a kiss on the cheek. He looked self-possessed as he bestowed an adoring smile, the thin mustache over his lip twitching.

After introductions, he pulled out a wallet and counted out the bills. While Chiara made out a receipt, Maria, finished for the day, entered the showroom. When Maria cast a passing glance at the trio standing at the counter, she stopped suddenly and gasped, poised in a frozen position.

Gina, bewildered, turned her head at the sound, while Mr. Gabriel, following her gaze, stopped talking in midsentence and stared, eyes wide.

"Tony!" Maria spat out.

Chiara dropped the pen she held, and hurried to Maria's side. Not Tony, Maria's missing husband; it couldn't be! Not the husband who had left Italy and disappeared!

Maria repeated the name. "Tony!"

For a moment Mr. Gabriel seemed confused; then he swallowed and composed himself. *"Signora?* I'm afraid I'm at a disadvantage." His speech was clipped, accented.

Maria moved toward him. Her voice was low. "Yes. Yes, it is a disadvantage."

He took a step backward as Maria advanced. "I . . . I don't believe I know you."

"You know me!" Maria's eyes bored into his.

He stepped back again, pressing against the wall, his eyes darting about like those of a cornered rodent. Gina looked from Maria to Tony in bafflement as she watched the scene unfold.

"I'm your wife, Maria, the wife you left in Italy, the one who traveled halfway around the world to find you."

Mr. Gabriel tugged at his collar as if it had grown suddenly tight. "I . . . I'm not married. I have no wife. As you see, I'm engaged . . . engaged to—"

"You are married!" Maria shouted. "To me! Tony Gabriel? Gabriel? You're Tony Gabriani!" Her voice had risen in a crescendo.

The man sputtered, licked his lips, and suddenly, swinging his arms as if clearing a path, he pushed past Maria, past Gina, out of the shop.

Gina stood staring after him for a moment, eyes wide in disbelief. For a moment Chiara thought she might faint. Then she seemed to collect herself. She stumbled outside, but Tony's car had screeched away from the curb, leaving a curtain of exhaust smoke behind.

Rushing back into the shop, she pointed at Maria and screamed, "You! Filthy liar!" Then she crumpled onto the blue velvet chair and buried her face in her hands.

Now completely composed, Maria laid her hand on the woman's head. "*Signorina*, I am truly sorry for you. He is my husband. My father was right all along. He is an adventurer, a gigolo."

Gina cried out an anguished, "No, no."

"My father's money brought him to the United States. I suppose he planned all along to forget about me once he arrived."

Dragging her hands from a tearstained face, Gina said, "But I love him."

Chiara pressed a glass of water into Gina's hands, but the distraught woman pushed it away and stood unsteadily, then rushed from the shop.

Maria, strong, composed Maria, laid her head on Chiara's shoulder and sobbed.

When Gina returned several days later she went directly to Maria. "Tony's gone. He's taken all his belongings and disappeared."

"You're better off without him," Maria said in a bitter monotone.

Gina's eyes beseeched her. "Where could he be?"

Maria shrugged. "Who knows? Looking for another victim, I suppose. Forget him. He's no good."

"I wish it were that easy." Her shadowed eyes were awash in tears. "I think of him all the time."

"I know. All these years I thought I wanted him, thought he was the love of my life. I wouldn't face reality. If it makes you feel better, I will get a divorce if he should return." Maria's tone implied she didn't think it likely.

By the time Gina left, she and Maria were friends, bonded by the knowledge that they had both been duped.

Chiara told Mike the sad tale, and Mike in turn told some of his old friends, Fredo included. Fredo, who had always claimed a fondness for plucky Maria, was incensed. "I'll take care of that swine," he swore.

When Chiara told Maria of Fredo's reaction, Maria said, "No, tell Fredo it's all right. For so many years I thought that's all I wanted, my Tony. That's all I lived for, to find him. But the fire had been dying in me little by little. Now that I know the truth, I feel no hatred."

Though Maria, in her stolid way, vowed to put her woes behind her, Chiara knew she was suffering. Chiara invited her to join the family on a picnic at Belle Isle, to distract her.

June 20, 1943, promised to be a scorcher. Only ten o'clock Sunday morning and already the temperature had climbed into the eighties. Even at early Mass the heat and humidity had made the girls cranky.

Chiara crammed food into the oilcloth-lined bushel basket, saying, "Maybe we shouldn't go. The island will be packed on a day like this. It's hard to even find a picnic table anymore."

Mike said, "So we'll spread it on the ground."

The girls, excited about going to the park, hopped around underfoot until Mike loaded them into the car. When they picked up Maria, she echoed Chiara's sentiments. "Maybe we should stay home. There's a heaviness in the air."

Mike gave an exasperated snort. "You women, you're always whining."

As Chiara had predicted, a steady stream of cars crossed the bridge at East Grand Boulevard and Jefferson. Swarms of pedestrians paraded past on the walkway.

"Since this damn war the city's bursting its seams from

all the defense workers," Mike grumbled. "There aren't enough parks."

"I want to rent a bicycle," Anna said.

Chiara said, "Oh, I don't know, Anna—"

"Let her, Chiara," Mike interrupted. "She's old enough; nine years old. If you want to stand in the long line, Anna, go ahead."

As the car inched along, Chiara craned her neck to observe the throngs of people bumping and shoving for a turn to rent canoes or bicycles. "This is the biggest crowd I've ever seen."

The same situation existed at entrances to the zoo, aquarium, greenhouse, and bathhouses. Young people jostled one another, and minor squalls erupted.

"There are more Negroes than whites now," Maria remarked, smoothing the skirt of her patterned Sears, Roebuck housedress.

"The city's full of them, and there's not enough housing," Mike said. "They can't build projects fast enough, and when they do get them finished, they're mostly for whites. There's going to be trouble if we don't take care."

"What kind of trouble?"

"Revolt. Fighting in the streets, black against white. Even *Life* magazine had an article saying 'Detroit Is Dynamite.' There've been flare-ups already, riots at Northwestern High School and Eastwood Park. The union's always trying to settle fights in the factories. Lots of whites don't want to work alongside coloreds. Southerners, especially, aren't used to seeing Negroes treated fairly. They hate it if a Negro's sitting on a bus while they're standing."

"The only Negroes I know are Laurelia and Mortimer," Chiara said. "They're good people. I was frightened of Laurelia at first. I'd never seen colored people in Italy. I'll always remember when we first moved to Chene Street, how she brought over a sweet-potato pie. She was nice to me, even though I could hardly understand her."

"Yes, good people," Mike mused as he shifted into reverse and maneuvered into a parking spot. "Detroit is the 'Arsenal of Democracy.' We make the weapons to fight fascism. Yet in the plants we still have the 'nigger' jobs and the 'white' jobs. Plenty of whites hate the union because we refuse to discriminate. They booed the president, R. J. Thomas, right out of the hall when he defended the upgrading of Negroes.

"It seems like people always need someone to hate," Maria said. "If it's not blacks, it's Jews, Japanese, Polish, Italians, Germans. When will the hating end?"

Mike finally found a parking spot and edged the car in.

The girls scrambled out and shed their outer clothing to expose bathing suits underneath. They ran to the edge of the river, sparkling in the sun, and squealed as the water lapped at their toes.

"Come on, baby." Anna tugged at her little sister's hand.

"Don't call me baby!"

Anna smacked at the water, splashing her sister. Wailing, Luisa chased Anna, but her little legs weren't fast enough to catch up.

They are both babies, Chiara thought, watching the girls' playful squabbling. Nine years old and five. It won't be long until Anna embarks on womanhood. Oh, if only they could stay babies a little longer.

"What beauties we've produced," Mike said, looking after them lovingly. "Luisa looks more and more like you."

"She reminds me of my sister Gabriella."

Mike sprinted after the girls, yelling, "Today I'm going to teach you to float."

"Do I have to get my face wet?" Anna asked.

"Of course, silly."

Maria went for a solitary walk while Chiara settled against a tree. Birds twittered in the thick green foliage that formed a shady respite from the sun, while from the river sounds of children's delighted laughter filled the air. If it weren't for the war and the unrest in the city, she could feel quite peaceful, Chiara thought as she opened a book. A bookmark fell out, a holy card centered on a snowflake design that Anna had made. It was signed *Anna*. Chiara smiled with contentment.

Mike called out, "Chiara, come on, get your suit on. You need to get wet." He ran to her and drew her to her feet.

"No, Mike, I just want to read." She pulled back, but he picked her up in his strong arms and brought her to the edge of the water, while she shrieked at him. Laughing, he set her down. "At least get your feet wet. It'll cool you off."

She shed her shoes and anklets and they waded hand in hand in the warm river, filled with bathers. Chiara scanned the sea of bodies for the girls and saw them playing with two Negro children. Moments later a young dark woman went to the edge of the water and shouted for the youngsters, who trudged to her reluctantly. Though Chiara couldn't hear her words, she recognized a scolding, and noticed that the children didn't return to play with Anna and Luisa.

By late afternoon, though she knew the heat would be even more unbearable in the city, Chiara wanted to go home. The girls, grumbling, helped gather their belongings and shuffled to the car. As they made their way back out of the park, Chiara saw a group of black and white youths scuffling near the casino, with a circle of spectators egging them on.

Maria fanned herself with a folded newspaper. "I don't like this," she said when, further along, the same sort of scene was repeated.

The oppressive heat cast an air of frenzy into the atmosphere. Buses lined up along the curb, loaded, and rattled off. Passengers with perspiration-soaked hair plastered to their foreheads hung out of the windows.

"I don't like it either." Mike steered the car onto the bridge, joining a long procession that inched its way along. "The heat doesn't help. It must be close to one hundred degrees. This place is a tinderbox."

Chiara grew more uneasy by the minute. "I wish we could go faster."

"How? I'm wedged in." His voice was tense.

Maria rubbed her temples with both hands.

Chiara knew the gesture. Maria *saw* something. "What?"

"Nothing." Maria turned away. She mumbled, "This is not a gift, it's a curse."

Chiara sighed in exasperation, knowing Maria couldn't be persuaded to reveal her thoughts.

The pedestrians making their way back home to the city seemed tense, many pushing and shoving, with eyes sullen and angry. By the time Mike's DeSoto crossed the bridge, scores of sailors from the naval armory on the corner of Jefferson were moving toward the bridge.

"There's trouble brewing," Mike said. "And I wish we were home."

Chiara watched the long twilight settle on the Detroit River, illuminating the buildings in Windsor across the way. An ominous shudder passed through her.

Despite Mike's efforts, with traffic moving so slowly, another hour passed before they made it home. The wet spots of perspiration on her husband's shirt weren't only from the heat.

By the time darkness descended, even on their usually quiet street rumors ran rampant: a white woman with a baby had been thrown off the Belle Isle Bridge. Then the story changed: a black woman with a baby had been thrown. When they tuned the radio dial to the news late that night, they heard of unrest in the city, and dire warnings not to venture out toward Woodward and Paradise Valley.

The next morning they heard of riots, burning, and looting along Woodward and in the black ghetto. Chiara made the sign of the cross.

"Don't even think of going to work today," Mike told his wife. "Things will get worse before they get better."

"Then you'd better stay home too."

"No, I have to see what the damage is."

"Mike! There you go again, rushing into danger."

He waved away her concern and hurried off. He returned home that afternoon with a small gash over his temple.

"As I passed Hastings, they threw rocks at the car. The side window is smashed and there are dents all over it." Mike shuddered. "It's like a war zone: fires, gunshots, looting."

"My God, you could've been killed. You never learn, do you? Here, let me see." Chiara gingerly touched a spot of dried blood at Mike's temple.

"It's just a scratch. I'm all right." He moved her hand away. "I finally got to Woodward, and it was bedlam there. The whites were in an ugly mood, moving toward Hastings. The police aren't helping; they seem like part of the mob. I couldn't get away fast enough." Mike took her hand and held it tightly. "There's something else . . ."

Chiara tensed, frightened by the tone of his voice.

He sat her in a chair. "I tried to get to your shop, but the police had cordoned off the area. Finally I convinced them to let me through." He swallowed and wet his lips.

"Yes? Yes?" Chiara's words were tortured.

"It's gone."

"Gone?" She tried to absorb the information. Where could it have gone?

Mike wrung his hands helplessly. "Burned to the ground. There's almost nothing left. Charred and twisted machinery, plumbing fixtures, some shelving . . ."

"Burned to the ground?" She repeated the words as though in a trance, trying to understand their meaning. *Burned to the ground.* But, no, it couldn't be true. No, the blue-and-ivory salon, the sewing machines, the fabrics, the gilt-framed pictures of lovely brides, *her* brides . . . She jumped up, running to the door. "We have to go."

Mike grabbed her hand. "No, it's not safe. The cops said, 'If you know what's good for you, you'll stay away from here.' There's nothing we can do anyway."

She sat down heavily. "Burned to the ground."

A few days later, Mike parked in front of what had once been the bridal salon and helped Chiara out of the car. Head high and dry-eyed, she held on to Mike's arm and stared at the wreckage. Around them, small puffs of smoke rose from piles of gray ashes.

She hadn't cried, not a drop. Even now, faced with the reality, she couldn't believe it, the sheer hatred that must have swelled and burst, like a water-filled balloon, to wreak this havoc. The walls were barely standing. A quick wind would blow them down. She moved forward, the acrid smell of stale smoke in her nostrils.

The sewing machines were twisted metal. The hand of a mannequin, charred and gray, beckoned with one uplifted finger. Stepping further into the ruins, she saw a glimmer of something silver. She reached down into the rubble and lifted out a pair of scissors, miraculously intact.

"Look, Mike, the scissors I brought with me from Italy." Her mouth turned down at the corners. "This is what I started with and this is what I end up with."

That was when she cried, her face crumpling, her shoulders sagging. She leaned weakly against Mike, sobbing as though her heart would break.

Mike held her close. He had no words of comfort.

After President Roosevelt authorized the use of federal forces, the streets were finally cleaned up and the city restored to an uneasy order. Twenty-five blacks and nine whites were dead.

Whenever she used her scissors, Chiara would think about the useless destruction and realize she couldn't return the hatred. She could almost understand the frustration and anger that had caused it.

It was several days before she could think clearly and try to make plans. "We'll get the insurance money, then find another place, a better one."

Mike looked at her in disbelief. "Chiara, don't you know what's going on? There are no shops to rent. Any vacant spot in the city is filled with people. Every cubbyhole, some no bigger than a telephone booth, has a family living in it."

Yes, she'd even seen once-empty stores now filled with families, sheets strung across the plate-glass windows to keep out curious eyes.

Perhaps it was just as well. She was exhausted, business had been down, and—she consulted the calendar—her period was late. Her heart quickened at the thought. She'd wanted more children but had resigned herself to the fact that it wasn't to be. Mike rarely talked about it, but she knew he still harbored the hope of having a son. She prayed it was so, even though she was no longer young, thirty-seven. Her hands went to her hair, where a few silver strands sparkled among the dark gold ones, then down her body, from chest to hips. She was still firm, there was no excess fat, and she felt fine. No, she wasn't too old.

Che sera, sera.

When Chiara announced to Maria and the other workers that she had no plans to reopen her shop, the atmosphere was funereal.

Chiara tried to console them. "At least there are plenty of factory jobs available, and at better pay, too."

It was even harder to break the news to Flora, who

had become more like a member of the family. Now that Chiara planned to resume her role as mother and house-keeper, Flora's services were no longer needed.

"I'll still need your help part of the time," Chiara said. "I'm going to do some sewing out of the house." But she knew full well there was no kitchen big enough for two women, not on a regular basis.

Flora wrung her hands. "What will I do?"

"After the war, I'll start again, Flora. This damnable war can't last forever." She touched her cousin's arm reassuringly.

Flora shook her head helplessly.

"Besides," Chiara said, "I'll need you. I think I'm pregnant."

A few weeks later Chiara walked out of Dr. Catrone's office and into the outer room, where Mike waited with a questioning look.

She smiled and nodded then whispered in his ear, "The doctor said yes. I'm pregnant."

Mike squeezed her hand.

In the front seat of the run-down, rust-spotted DeSoto, Mike pulled her close. "We'll have a boy this time."

—— 29 ——

The metal handle of the Red Flyer wagon dug into Anna's mittened palm. Metal scrap of all kinds—rusty tools, old pots, tin cans that had been stomped flat after their ends were removed—filled the wagon. She and her best friend, Agnes, had gone door to door collecting scrap and the used grease that went into making nitroglycerin. She wasn't even sure what nitroglycerin was, only that it was important to war. The war was rather an adventure, but a remote one, something she saw unfolding on the news-reels at the movies each Saturday.

"It feels good to do this for the war effort," Agnes said, grinning righteously as she pushed the wagon from behind at a steady trot. Puffs of steam accompanied her words.

"Not when the handle is cutting your hand. You pull for a while." Anna traded places with Agnes. "I wish this dumb war was over. Do you remember Gerald VanDerwegh?"

"Yes, your neighbor. He was nice." Anges strained as she tugged the loaded wagon up a curb.

Anna nodded and remembered Gerald, home on furlough last year, looking dashing, his army cap tipped over his eye. She had written him a letter once, and tried to be clever, opening with, "What's buzzin', cousin?" She said, "Mrs. VanDerwegh came over to tell my mother Gerald was wounded. She was crying. He lost an arm at the shoulder and part of his leg."

"Oh, how awful!"

It seemed to Anna they couldn't get away from the signs of war. When the war had begun in 1941, she was just seven years old, and now she was ten. She turned to glance at the barbershop window as she passed, where a poster of Uncle Sam with stern, demanding countenance and pointed finger stared at her under the words, "Uncle Sam wants YOU!" And on the side of a building a poster read, "Loose lips sink ships."

Even the Saturday matinee at the Rivola was usually about war, with planes spinning downward in spirals of flame and smoke. The heroes wore brave lopsided smiles, proud to go into battle, to die if necessary, while strains of patriotic songs blared in the background—*There they go, into the wild blue yonder* . . . *Anchors aweigh, my boys, anchors aweigh* . . . *And those caissons go rolling along* . . . At the end, the American flag would unfurl in the breeze, and her heart surged with pride and patriotism. And before the cartoons they had to sit through Pathé news, with film of the actual battles. She always scanned the soldiers closely, looking for a familiar face.

The girls reached the playground and unloaded their scrap, then stayed to help others. Soon there was a mountain of twisted metal remnants, much of it unrecognizable. There was an air of gaiety as they sang: *Whistle while you work, Hitler is a jerk, Mussolini is a sheeny, whistle while you work.*

The sun had disappeared in a leaden sky when the girls ran home, towing the empty wagon.

Pungent cooking smells warmed Anna as she entered the house. Zia Flora, at the stove, turned to greet her. "Your mother isn't feeling so good, so I came after work. I'm making pasta. The government says it's meatless Tuesday. What's the difference, meat or no meat? I'm used to skimping; it's the way we were raised."

The family didn't see nearly as much of Flora since the fire. Because Mama was home all day now, she didn't need Flora's help. No one expected it when Flora got a job at Willow Run making B-24 bombers! She told Anna the plant was one mile long and a quarter-mile wide, and called it Willit Run, because their quota of one bomber every day was never met, due to all the problems. After she began working, Aunt Flora was different. She used makeup and began smoking cigarettes; she wore slacks and a snood. Slacks were an abomination, Papa said.

Flora hugged Anna and fished in her purse for some bills. "Here's two dollars for you. And Luisa gets the same. Save it for a rainy day." She was generous with the overtime money she made.

"Bring this to your mother. It'll settle her stomach," Zia said, handing Anna a glass of Vernor's ginger ale. "Then come back and mix the margarine." It was Anna's job to squeeze and mix a blob of yellow coloring into a lardy mixture that was supposed to taste like butter, but didn't. Mama always saved a little real butter for Papa.

The bubbles from the Vernor's tickled Anna's nose as she took it to the living room, where her mother sat with a letter in her lap. Her feet, looking swollen, were on a footrest.

"I got a letter from home," Mama said. "My poor brothers. Carlo in Africa, and Dino; Dino, he's just a baby and they've put him in a uniform. This terrible war." Her mother hated the thought of Italy as the *enemy*.

Anna kissed her mother's cheek.

"I have to tell you something, Anna," Mama said, making room for her on the footrest. She looked so serious and a little flustered.

"What?"

"I . . . I'm going to have a baby."

"A baby?"

"Yes." Her mother pulled her close and hugged her. "Are you glad?"

"Gee whiz." Anna, stunned, didn't know what to say. She had thought there was something going on, thought Mama was "tired" a lot. "When?"

"In a few weeks."

Anna swallowed. "Gosh."

"Well, you'll have to help me more now. You're the oldest. I have to rely on you."

"I'll help you, Mama. I'll help you a lot." Anna squeezed her mother's arm, then backed away. She began piecing together seemingly unrelated happenings—the laundering of stored baby clothing, new, loose-fitting housedresses her mother had sewn, whispered adult conversations, suddenly hushed when the children came into earshot.

That night her father was late because his car-pool driver had to work overtime. Gas was rationed, along with practically everything else, even shoes. They had books of ration stamps, but with or without stamps, some items were hard to come by, like silk stockings and bobby pins and anything metal. They'd barely finished dinner when the eerie siren sounded, its wail beginning low and soft and getting ever higher and louder. Anna put her fingers in her ears. It was scary and exciting at the same time. Papa, wearing his air-raid helmet, hefted his big flashlight and left. As an air-raid warden, it was his job to inspect the neighborhood during a drill.

"Close the black blinds and turn out the lights," Mama said. Luisa and Anna scampered to do Mama's bidding.

That night, Anna couldn't sleep. She'd been barely old enough to remember when Luisa was born, a baby was a new experience. She hugged her arms to herself, then hopped out of bed and drew her old doll from a box in the tiny closet. The doll, with its cloth body, rubbery face and limbs, and stiff, sparse hair, was hardly a replica of the real thing. But she hugged the doll, called Gabriella after her aunt, close to her heart and hummed "Rock-a-bye Baby," imagining it was alive. She was going to love the new baby.

Hearing her parents' voices, she squeezed her eyes shut and strained to hear their words.

Anna will be a big help, Mama was saying. Anna's heart swelled. *But she's a dreamer, like you, Mike. I put a needle and thread in her hand and it takes her a week to embroider a little doily.*

Leave her alone. She's a thinker.

Thinker! She should be a doer. Idle hands are the devil's workshop.

Anna shook her head. Mama's so *Italian!*

Her mother's voice softened. *But she's a good girl. I want her to go into the business with me when she's older, but I just don't know if she has the head for it. Now, Luisa's different. She likes to sew and never complains. She takes Communion every day and never forgets to kneel by her bed and say her prayers.*

I worry more about Luisa. She's shy.

Yes, but she'll outgrow that.

Anna snuggled down under the covers, her doll fast in her arms, and fell asleep.

One night a few weeks later Anna awakened with a start. It couldn't be morning—it was pitch dark. Papa came toward her and put his finger to his lips. "I'm taking Mama to the hospital now."

Mama came in behind him, breathing heavily, her face flushed. She kissed Anna and cuddled her for a moment.

"Listen to your Aunt Flora and don't fight with Luisa."

Anna nodded, but was too overcome to say anything. When they left she lay awake thinking for a long time.

Did it hurt? Why did a birth take so long? Would the baby be a boy or girl? What would it look like? Was Mama scared?

The sun was coming up when Anna heard Papa's key scratching in the lock.

He burst into their room and said, "It's a girl!" He took Anna and Luisa into his arms. "She's beautiful, just like my other girls." Anna suspected Papa had wanted a boy. "Mama says you and Luisa have to help find a name."

"I like the name Christine," Anna said promptly. "It's American. Do you like it, Luisa?"

Luisa was nodding off against Papa's chest and didn't answer.

"That's a good name," Papa said, tucking them back into bed.

When Mama came home she started calling the baby Cristina or Tina, so it sounded Italian anyway. Anna felt overwhelmed with love for the little one and often coaxed her mother to let her hold the infant.

Anna studied herself in the mirror for a long time, front view, side view, and, craning her neck, rear view. Things were definitely changing. She was eleven years old and her breasts strained against the cotton undershirt Mama insisted she wear. So many things were happening that she felt confused and . . . not exactly *sad*, but certainly not happy. She cried for almost no reason, like last week, when she discovered the awful red stains spotting her undies. *You're a woman now,* Mama said and Anna cried as though her heart would break. For of course, she wasn't a woman. She was a little girl; she always had scabs on her knees, she loved dolls and roller skates and Deanna Durbin cutouts and playing seven-up and jacks. Women didn't do that. Mama hugged her and rocked with her and made that comforting, sympathetic clucking sound with her tongue.

It all seemed so *momentous*. There had to be more to this, something Mama wasn't telling.

The following Saturday, Anna and Agnes walked to the Rivola for the double feature. When a heavyset woman strolled toward them, Agnes whispered, "See that lady? She's having a baby."

"How do you know?"

"She's fat." Agnes took a few steps and said smugly, "I know how she got that way."

"How?"

Agnes pointed dramatically downward, below her waist. She acted so superior sometimes.

Anna shrugged. "So?"

"My sister told me about it. I saw my brother naked once." Her voice dropped to a whisper. "The man puts his *thing* down there, and that's how it happens."

Anna nonchalantly acted as if this was no surprise, of no importance. But her heart raced. So that was the secret. The *thing*.

"But you can't have a baby until you get the curse. I wonder if I'll ever get the curse." Agnes looked crestfallen. "You have it, don't you?"

The curse? "You mean the bleeding? Yes, I have it." It was Anna's turn to be superior. "You'll probably get it soon."

Everything was coming clear now. That was what made her a woman—the fact that she could have a baby. A thought struck her. This meant that Mama and Papa did it. With the *thing*. No, it was just not imaginable.

Yet facts were facts.

Anna loved babies, especially Tina, but she would never have one if it involved the *thing*.

Spring seemed to arrive suddenly. The dirt-crusted snow that just last week had lain in mounds along the lawn edges was now reduced to small puddles. Anna walked home from school alone, because Agnes was sick.

Tom Reilly and a gang of boys walked behind, and every once in a while one of them ran up and tried to trip her. "Cooties, cooties," they yelled.

Anna lifted her chin further into the air and pretended she didn't hear them. Tom liked her; that was why he tried to get her attention in that nasty way.

After Anna passed the Lutheran church on Warren Avenue and turned the corner to her street, Tom ran to catch up with her. His friends continued on Warren. If they knew Tom was walking with Anna, he'd be teased unmercifully.

Anna ignored Tom, but he walked doggedly beside her. She liked walking the long arrow-straight street lined with Dutch elms just now budding out, liked the neat, solid homes with their lace-curtained windows and their friendly and familiar inhabitants.

White-haired Mrs. Grant rocked and knit on the porch, though it was a mite cool, and called out a smiling hello.

Finally Tom said, "What do you want to be when you grow up? A nun?"

"I used to think I wanted to be a missionary nun, a Maryknoll, and save Chinese babies," Anna mused. "But I hate those long habits they have to wear. And they shave their heads too."

"I always see you praying in church."

"We *have* to pray in church. What else would you do in church besides pray?"

"Well, I just think a lot." He punched his fist into the leather mitt on his left hand.

"Maybe Luisa should be a nun. She's always so good." Anna's last words had a sarcastic edge.

"What will you be, then? A secretary, I suppose."

"No, not that either. Maybe a teacher. Or a nurse. Somebody important."

"You have to go to college for that."

They strolled in matching measured steps past Tom's house, but he didn't turn up his walk. She was pleased that he wanted to walk her home, even if she didn't *really* like him.

Anna skipped over a crack in the sidewalk. "My father'll never let me go to college. Maybe I'll just get married." She loved her father, but sometimes he exasperated her. He liked to act as though he were mean, saying he'd give his girls "a licking," but it was all talk. She saw through his act, could crumble it so easily, just by hugging him. He was too softhearted, she knew, ever to lay a hand on her, even when he was provoked. Her mother was more likely to give her a whack with the ever-handy wooden spoon, but that didn't happen very often either.

She wished her parents weren't so overprotective. They seemed to be in constant fear that some terrible disaster would befall her. Sometimes she felt suffocated. And sometimes they embarrassed her with their old-country ways. Her mother said she wouldn't be allowed to wear lipstick until she was sixteen, if then. And Anna was sure she wouldn't be able to date until she was eighteen, though she didn't dare broach *that* subject.

Her mother always said she should be proud of her Italian heritage. In many ways she *was* proud. But she wanted even more to be "American," like the people on the radio, in *Stella Dallas* and *One Man's Family*.

"My mother wants me to go into the bridal-gown business with her, but I won't. I hate sewing!"

"My mother wants me to be a priest, but I don't think I will. You have to be smart and know Latin."

"You're pretty smart."

"Not that smart."

"My parents expect me to be the smartest girl in my class, but once I mentioned college and they laughed. 'What does a girl need an education for?' my father said. 'The education you need for running a house you can learn from your mother and your Aunt Flora.' "

"What does your dad do, anyway?"

"He's a union organizer."

"What's that?"

She wasn't sure exactly what it was. "I don't know. I guess he gets people to join the union." She switched her books from one arm to the other. "He's always talking about how the workingman gets a raw deal."

"Oh." Tom leapt upward to whack at a tree branch. "Why is your dad so strict?"

"I guess because he's Italian."

Tom seemed to consider this for a moment. "Are you going to the movies on Saturday? The Flash Gordon serial is on."

"I suppose so, if I have enough allowance left. I have to bring Luisa, though. She's such a pest. And a scaredy-cat. She always screams when Flash Gordon gets into bad trouble." She knew Tom would try to sit next to her at the movies, even at the risk of his friends' taunts.

Anna was sorry when they reached her house. Even though she acted like she didn't like Tom, she really thought he was pretty nice.

"Hang your coat up and don't leave your books on the dining-room table," her mother said when Anna walked in. "Who is that boy who walks with you?"

"Tom Reilly."

"Reilly? That's not an Italian name."

Anna rolled her eyes skyward. Although she adored her mother, lately she resented her questions, her disapproval. Her mother expected Anna to know what went on in the world, but didn't want her out in it, tried to shelter her from it. All boys were suspect.

Anna watched her mother now as she cut up potatoes for the soup. Anna wished she looked like her mother instead of her father. Her mother's eyes were the brightest blue, and held depths of emotion—love and anger. And her hair was a golden brown, shiny and waving into a soft pageboy on her shoulders.

"Don't stand around. Do your homework, then set the table," Mama said.

"It's Luisa's turn," Anna said, perversely dropping her books on the dining-room table.

As soon as dinner was over that night, her mother slipped the letter from her apron pocket and began to read. Anna fell silent. She enjoyed hearing news from the old country, loved the graceful, melodic phrases.

Her attention was drawn to the wall where her grandparents, aunts, and uncles smiled down from sepia photographs, as if in benediction. The pictures and the letters gave her a small sense of connection with that part of her family she would probably never see.

She already knew what the letter would say. The first page would tell of how pleased and happy her grandparents were to receive the last letter and how they wished they could see their beautiful children and grandchildren. The second page would report news of the village, births, illnesses, and deaths. And the final page would be filled with flowery phrases of love and the hope that the family would all be together someday. At the very end they would send embraces and *bacci,* kisses, to all.

After her mother read the news of the family, she paused and said, "Now, this is the exciting part. 'Dr. Ariella, who has finally given up the practice of medicine, paid us a visit. You would be surprised at how he has aged, but I suppose I could say that of many of the villagers, almost all of whom are old. The young people are either in the army or off to the north looking for work. The doctor had news of interest to you. He told us that his grandson is a prisoner of war in a camp in Detroit. He asks that you try to find him and pay a visit. It would please Dr. Ariella so, to know someone is looking after his Franco.'

"Well, what do you think of that?" her mother asked. "We must go there tomorrow. How will we do it, Mike? Who can we talk to? I'll make some pasta and amarettis and—"

"Hold on. We'll do better than visit. I heard of Italian families who invite the prisoners home for a day. I'll find out what we have to do."

Anna's eyes opened wide. "A prisoner? In our house? Will he have chains and handcuffs?" She remembered cartoons she'd seen of shackled convicts in striped suits.

Her father looked amused. "No, he won't have chains."

"Where is the camp, Papa?" Luisa wanted to know.

"There's one at the Michigan State Fairground, over on Woodward and Eight Mile Road. All the prisoners are Italian. I've been by there and seen Italian soldiers pressed against the wire-mesh fence, trying to make connections with the girls."

"Wow, a prison camp right here in Detroit," Anna said.

"There are camps all over Michigan, even in the Upper Peninsula," her father said. "Some are old Civilian Conservation Corps camps. The prisoners work on farms or do logging."

Mama said, "Well, let's do it right away; call someone. I remember the doctor's grandson, even though he was just a youngster when I was home."

The visit was arranged for the following Sunday and Mama made the girls clean and even wax the furniture and the floor, just like spring cleaning.

When Franco arrived with Papa, Anna and Luisa just stared, not knowing what to say. He seemed an intense young man with piercing, almost black eyes, and at first appeared uneasy. But he loosened up soon enough when Mama asked questions about everyone in the village. Mama's eyes misted when he mentioned her family.

For dinner they had fresh tomatoes drenched in olive oil, basil, and vinegar, the way Anna loved them, green peppers and tiny bland cucumbers, all from the "victory garden," and pasta and meatballs made with lots of garlic and herbs.

Franco, smacking his lips, kept telling Mama what a wonderful cook she was. "It's like my mother used to make." It was obviously his highest praise.

By the time they'd finished the meal, the adults were talking and laughing all at once. Anna and Luisa listened intently, chins resting in their hands, trying to absorb all the Italian words.

"Don't you speak Italian?" Franco asked Anna.

"A little," she answered in Italian, a bit embarrassed.

"I suppose they're more American," Franco remarked sadly.

Afterward, Franco, taken with little Tina, jostled her on his knee, which endeared him even more to Mama.

"You must come again next week," Mama said when they all hugged good-bye.

Anna couldn't wait to tell Agnes all about the visit. Nothing like this had ever happened in Agnes' family.

When Franco came the following Sunday he asked if he could bring along a friend. "His name is Dante Ravenna and when I told him about your family, he was very interested. He comes from Campania, like you, *signore,* and said the name Marcassa is familiar to him."

"Of course," Papa replied. "Bring him next Sunday. I'll arrange for the pass."

The next Sunday, after their father left to pick up the prisoners, Anna and Luisa waited at the window for a first glimpse of the men.

"They're here, they're here," Luisa squealed when two uniformed men exited her father's car.

At first sight of the young man accompanying Franco, Anna was startled by his good looks and by something in his face and his mannerisms—something familiar and compelling. She had the strange feeling that she'd seen him before. She hung back a bit as Franco introduced his friend Dante.

"Come, say hello, Anna." Her mother gave her a small shove forward. Dante shook her hand as if she were an adult, then winked at her.

Quickly she pulled her hand away. He was so handsome it almost hurt her eyes to look at him.

All during dinner she never said a word, but could hardly keep her gaze from straying to Dante. He had large velvety dark eyes that were serious, then crinkled into narrow slits when he laughed. He was as tall as Papa, and very polite.

Dante smiled across the table at her, his grin forming deep creases in his cheeks. Whenever he looked at her, Anna's heart jumped inside her chest and her cheeks grew warm. She would like to touch his face and run her hand over the thick thatch of dark, waving hair, combed so neatly. She wanted to ask him questions, but her mouth was dry and the words stuck in her throat.

"Dante's father has a vineyard in Campania." Franco speared a black olive.

"When I return, I'll help my father run the vineyard," Dante said. "I have many ideas about expanding and exporting."

"You're only forty-fifty miles from my village," Papa said. "Ah, it's beautiful there, the winding streams, the mountains, the piazza and fountain." Papa's eyes got dreamy.

"Yes, that entire area is lovely," Dante said. "The name Marcassa is one I've heard before. Perhaps you have relatives in my village?"

"No, I don't believe so." Papa poured more wine.

"Drink up. I'll bet you don't get meals like this at the camp."

"It seems I've heard my aunt say that name. Maybe she knows some of your family."

Papa shrugged and passed the *ensalada* to Franco. *"Mangia,"* he commanded. "Everyone, eat! My wife doesn't like leftovers."

Dante said, "When this ugly war is over, you must come to visit. My parents would welcome you to our home. I'll give you the best wine you ever tasted." Then, as though remembering his manners, he lifted his wineglass and amended, "Next to this wine, of course. It's excellent."

"Do they treat you well at the camp?" her mother asked.

Franco said, "I have no complaints. Americans are not mean by nature. Since I was captured at Salerno, I've met many kind people. This is a war many Italians are not in sympathy with. Historically, we have never been friendly with Germany. We are undertrained, underarmed, and undernourished. Many of the Italian villagers are aiding the Americans." He laughed. "Every Italian has relatives in America."

"Yes, it's true," Papa agreed.

"Do you think you'll ever go back to Italy?" Franco asked.

Papa shook his head. "America is my home."

Very quietly Mama said, "My heart is in Italy."

Papa reached over and patted her hand.

As the adults talked through the meal, Anna absorbed every word. She imagined Dante, his hands above his head, being pushed at gunpoint by American soldiers.

"Anna!" Her mother's voice cut through her reverie. "This is the third time I've called you. Help clear off the table and serve the dessert."

Anna pushed her chair back clumsily, stacked the dinner dishes, and hurried to the kitchen. Luisa followed her with the bread and butter.

"What's wrong with you?" her mother hissed at Anna. "You're in a dream. Wake up." She handed Luisa a plate of cookies and Anna the pot of espresso.

Anna poured the hot liquid into Dante's cup, forcing

her hand to steady. When he said *grazie* in that melting voice, Anna thought she would swoon.

Later the adults played cards and then Papa sent Luisa to fetch his guitar and they all sang *"Torna a Sorrento,"* and then Papa strummed and sang Anna's favorite, *"La June in Arizona."* Afterward Dante smiled, reflecting. "That's an Italian song I've never heard."

Papa said, "No wonder; it's an Italian cowboy song, probably the only one ever written."

When the young men said their good-byes, Dante again winked at Anna. Her heart jumped when she heard Papa promise to pick them up again the following week. She gathered the remaining wineglasses and coffee cups from the table. Swishing soapsuds into hot water, she began washing the dishes.

"You're dreaming again, Anna," her mother said. "You've been washing the same cup for five minutes. Move, I'll wash and you dry, or we'll be here till tomorrow morning."

"She's mooning over Dante," Luisa said with a little snicker.

"No, I'm not." Anna's retort was delivered with a hateful stare.

The visits became a Sunday ritual. Franco and Dante would come for dinner and spend the better part of the day. Sometimes Papa picked them up early enough for Mass, which was even better. On those days, with a long, lazy Sunday ahead, Dante taught Anna to play chess, and she helped him learn English. He was brilliant, and so patient, the way Papa was sometimes.

During one of their chess games Mama interrupted, as she always did, calling Anna to help with dinner. Anna tore herself away to make the salad.

Mama gave her a sidewise, knowing glance. "He's nice, *non è vero?*

"Who?" Anna pretended she didn't know.

"Dante. You've become like a little sister to him."

Little sister! No, he was her Errol Flynn, her Tyrone Power, her Robert Taylor, all rolled into one.

Her mother sighed. "We'll miss them when the war ends and they go back home."

Anna hadn't wanted to dwell on that possibility. She

hoped the war would last another five years. By that time she would be old enough to date.

"Maybe Dante—and Franco too—could stay here."

Mama clicked her tongue in exasperation. "They're prisoners! They have to go back."

Anna was crestfallen. Their lovely Sundays had been magical, enchanted. If only it could last forever. "Maybe Papa could do something, talk to important people."

"*Figlia,* they want to go home to their families. Italy is home to them, just as the United States is home to you. If you were in a foreign country, wouldn't you long to go home?"

I would long to be where Dante is, she thought.

But Anna was learning that everything changes, like the seasons, like her own body, which was taking on surprising curves.

On April 12, 1945, Franklin Delano Roosevelt died. Everyone cried, even her father, who *never* cried. Since before Anna was born, Roosevelt had been President, and she'd had the vague belief that it would always be so. She'd heard his resonant voice come through the speaker on the Sunday-night "Fireside Chats."

"My friends," he would intone in that intimate way. She'd seen his broad smiling face in countless newsreels.

Had he lived a few months longer, he would have seen Germany surrender. The peace that came in June was a partial one; the United States was still at war with Japan.

At church everyone prayed for peace. And finally their prayers were answered, but in a horrible and shocking way. They heard about it on the radio and saw pictures in the papers and in newsreels. It was called the atom bomb; a huge mushroom-shaped cloud of destruction. When Japan surrendered, there was happy, crazy rioting in the streets, but there was a sadness too.

The United States had won the war. But what did we win? Anna wondered. She supposed it meant they could buy real butter and shoes and gas. The war hadn't been real to her anyway. War had been a film that unfolded in black and white every Saturday at the movies. It was just a newsreel.

When Anna realized that the war's end meant Dante and Franco would be going back to Italy, she felt disheartened. The prisoners continued their visits through the humid summer, joining the family for picnics or swimming at crowded Murray Beach. Autumn came, crisp and colorful, with an occasional long ride on carefully hoarded gas, northwest as far as Orchard Lake. It was almost as though the men were members of the family.

That October Anna had learned to knit, and began work on a Christmas present for Dante. It was a muffler of soft pale green wool, which she hid under her bed for fear of teasing from Luisa.

On a cold Sunday afternoon in early November, Franco and Dante burst in the door in high spirits.

"We're going home!" Franco shouted. "Home!"

"In two weeks we leave for Savannah, Georgia, then on to a troop ship back to Italy." Dante's smile almost split his face.

Anna's mouth went suddenly dry. She turned and slipped away to her bedroom, afraid they would see the tremble in her chin.

After dinner her father hustled everyone into their coats and outside for pictures. He arranged them on the steps and clicked and turned the knob on the box Kodak Brownie.

"I hope these pictures turn out. The sun is so hazy. One more, now."

"You get in, Mike, and I'll take one," Mama insisted. "Move in closer to Dante, Anna."

"This is our last visit, little one." Dante put his arm around Anna's shoulder. "I'll miss you. Who will play chess with me?"

He would miss her! Oh, if only she could put her arms around him and tell him how completely devastated she felt. Each Sunday would be dry and cheerless without his pleasant face, his patient instruction across the chessboard.

At the last moment, both men hugged her mother and pressed cheeks with her father, with effusive thanks for all their kindness. Dante kissed Anna's forehead and ran his index finger from her cheek to her chin. "Will you write to me, Anna?"

Anna's heart thrummed in her chest. "Yes," she breathed.

Afterward she ran to her room and pulled the shoe box

with her knitting from under the bed. She would mail the muffler to Dante for Christmas. Pressing the soft bundle to her cheek, she watched as dark wet spots, made by her tears, spread on the soft wool.

Chiara knocked on Anna's door and entered without waiting for an answer. Frank Sinatra's mellow voice flooded the room with the strains of "This Love of Mine." He sang well enough, but why didn't the girls listen to opera? Anna sat on the pink-and-white-striped spread, her head resting on knees drawn up to her chin. She had picked out the material for the spread and matching curtains, displaying a flair for style and color, but much to Chiara's disappointment, she had absolutely no interest in sewing.

Chiara turned the radio's volume down and Anna gave her a disgruntled look.

"Leave it, Ma, it's Jack the Bell Boy."

"What is this Bell Boy?" Chiara lifted pursed fingers toward her daughter.

Anna looked exasperated. "He's a deejay."

Chiara, puzzled, ignored the answer. The children seemed to have their own secret speech these days, and she wasn't interested in learning yet another language.

"Have you done your homework?"

"Not yet."

"Well, you'd better get it done."

When Anna didn't move, Chiara sat beside her. "What's the matter, Anna?"

"I hate school. I hate homework."

"You used to like school. What about all your friends?"

Anna shrugged, hardly altering her position. "I miss Agnes since she moved away."

Agnes' family had left, as others had, because of rumors that Negroes were moving into the area. What did it matter, black or white? Chiara had said. But Mike explained it mattered because people were afraid property values would go down and a poorer element would come in and neglect the property. Everything was complicated, nothing simple.

"You can invite Agnes here sometime, you know."

"It's a long way. Anyhow, now she has new friends."

Chiara patted her daughter's arm. Friends seemed so important, too important to Anna. "I left my entire family when I came to America. I survived. You will too." Suddenly remembering, she said, "Ah! I have something that will cheer you up. A letter from Dante."

Anna was suddenly lively. "To me?"

"To the family, but also a note for you."

"Let me have it."

"At dinner. That's letter time." Chiara hadn't missed the excitement in Anna's face, the pink blush that spread over her cheeks whenever they spoke of Dante, the animation in her eyes. The child was certainly taken with the handsome young man.

"Come, Anna, and entertain the baby while I get dinner."

Anna swung her legs off the bed. "Why do I always have to watch Tina? She's not a baby, she's two years old—and spoiled."

Chiara left the room, ignoring her daughter's complaint.

They'd barely finished dinner when Anna said, "Ma, the letter."

"Let's get the coffee first." Chiara rose and put a hand on Mike's shoulder. "A letter fron Dante."

"Good. I've been thinking of that lad. He's a fine young man, a credit to his family." He brushed crumbs into a circle on the white cloth. "You know, I still miss those visits from Franco and Dante. Doesn't seem like six months have passed."

Chiara wiped Tina's chin while the toddler squirmed in annoyance.

"Go on, Ma, read the letter," Anna said impatiently.

Mike winked conspiratorially at Chiara. "I think Anna's sweet on Dante."

Anna blushed furiously. "I am not.

"She has a crush on him," Luisa said.

Anna reached across the table to smack her sister, but Luisa darted out of range.

"Enough!" Chiara gave both girls a steely glare.

The cream-colored parchment crackled as Chiara slipped the paper from its envelope. She held the page aloft so they could all see the crest embossed at the top. A picture slipped out and Chiara passed it along. It was of Dante in a debonair pose, one leg bent across the other, leaning against a snappy sports car. In the background was a large villa with enormous double doors.

Mike whistled. "That's an Alfa Romeo. It cost a few lire."

Chiara read the letter, in which Dante thanked the family profusely for their kindness during his internment in Detroit. He was overjoyed to be back home once again, and extended, from his parents, an invitation to come and visit someday. He wished them good fortune in the future and assured them he would have them always in his thoughts.

"And here's a special note and small package for Anna," Chiara said, extending the note across the table. "Anna? Do you want to read it to us?"

Anna's fingers trembled as she unfolded the note. She cleared her throat and read, " 'Cara Anna, a thousand thanks for the beautiful scarf, which warms my heart as well as my neck, especially knowing it came from your own hands.' " Anna swallowed and continued. " 'I have sent a small token, partly in gratitude for your gift, but mostly in gratitude for your friendship. Perhaps someday we can play chess again, and I'll allow you to win!' "

The family laughed while Anna drew in her breath and carefully removed the folds of tissue to reveal a slender gold chain on which hung a pendant etched with the same crest that appeared on the letterhead, along with a curved horn, a symbol that warded off evil spirits.

"Oh," she breathed.

"That's a very expensive gift, Anna," Mike said. "You must take good care of it, cherish it."

"Oh, I will, of course I will." Anna reached around

her neck to clasp the chain. "It's beautiful. Isn't it beautiful?"

She was so young. Twelve. But already her bosom and hips had rounded out, her waist nipped inward. Her hair, dark and thick like her father's, hung in soft waves to her shoulders. Her lower lip was full, her smile wide and easy. Yes, Chiara could easily see how someone could be attracted to her, even though she was a child. But Dante was a man, with a man's appetites, and Chiara was relieved he was an ocean away. Anna would soon become interested in boys her own age. She would bear careful watching.

"I'll write to Dante and send the picture of all of us, the one we took on his last day," Anna said.

"Be sure to sign it 'With love,' " Luisa teased.

The next day, as she sat at her sewing machine in a cramped corner of her bedroom, Chiara's thoughts were of Anna. She would make Anna a plaid skirt in wool, accordion-pleated all around. At Hudson's she had seen such skirts, decorated with oversize safety pins. That ought to cheer Anna up and maybe take her thoughts off Dante. Chiara enjoyed having the leisure to sew for her children, though she still had a clientele for her special designs. In truth, she turned away work. Her old workers had moved on to defense jobs during the war, and now she wasn't sure what they were doing. She made a mental note to call them, see how they were faring. Perhaps they would be willing to work for her again. She drew out a notebook from her spool drawer, where she had jotted calculations in a haphazard fashion. It wouldn't take too much capital to open a bridal salon. Mr. Cronin would surely help her again. She itched to be working, really working again. Her business had been gratifying. She dealt with people at the most joyous time of their lives.

Mike, of course, would be a problem. He loved the status quo, having his wife always at home, caring for her husband and children. Still, maybe he wouldn't object too strenuously to her just looking around. He wouldn't even have to know she was looking.

"No!" Mike shouted when Chiara brought up the subject. Little Tina, who sat on the floor stacking lettered blocks, stared up at her father, startled.

"No. Again you say no before you even hear me out!" Chiara waved her hands wildly.

"I don't have to hear you. I know how that mind works. First you make all the plans, then you tell me! You think I don't know you?"

Chiara saw she would have to change her tactics. Her tone was dulcet. "I haven't made plans. I want you to help me."

Mike jabbed his finger at the official letter on the kitchen table. "Right here it says 'bank loan.' You've already talked to Cronin, haven't you?"

Chiara shrugged. "So, I called him up, just to say hello, and—"

Mike snorted. "Sure, you're two good friends who just like to chat."

Luisa and Anna peeked into the kitchen, curiosity written on their faces. Chiara shook a warning finger at them, and they scurried away.

"Better leave them alone when they're fighting," Anna said in a stage whisper.

"I wouldn't have to work every day. Maria needs a job; she could help run things, and Flora lost her job. She'd be happy if we had her help at home."

Mike grabbed his cap and headed for the door. "I said no, and that's my final word!" The door slammed behind him.

Anna returned, looking concerned. "Is Pa mad?"

"No, he's just out thinking things over. I'm not worried; he'll see things my way."

Chiara had argued and cajoled, and finally, in a weak moment, Mike had given in. Chiara lost no time in getting the wheels in motion, and though Mike had reservations, he knew there was no stopping her once she made up her mind. Knowing he was beaten, he made a graceful turnaround, and in the end it was his idea to have a champagne party for the bridal-salon opening.

Keyed up, Chiara flitted about at the last moments, rearranging plates of canapés, adjusting folds on the skirt of a mannequin, twirling champagne bottles in their beds of ice.

She straightened Mike's tie and brushed at a speck on his navy suit. He looked distinguished, *successful.*

Mike took her hand, stilling it. "Calm down," he said.

She couldn't relax. She was as nervous as an actress on opening night. Her heels sank into the plush sky-blue carpet. Glancing around at the small marble-topped table and Queen Anne chairs, the graceful mannequins, the looped brocade draperies pulled back with gilt tassels, she felt pleased. Other than the ivory-and-blue color scheme, there was little to remind her of her former salon. On Mack Avenue, close to the Pointes, this shop was larger than her former one, with plenty of room for her workers in back and an ample, well-furnished office for herself. Mike had surprised her with a sturdy oak desk sporting elaborate brass pulls.

The first guests arrived, new friends and old, and paraded by, gushing with enthusiasm, pressing her hand with warm good wishes.

Here was Mrs. Morrison reminding Chiara, as if she needed reminding, that she had been the first customer at her first salon. Her youngest daughter was newly engaged, and now, to carry on the tradition, she would again be the first customer at the new shop.

Here were Dino and Rosa. Rosa, with her silky hair pulled back severely into a bun, still battled the English language and in Italian exclaimed over the elegance of the establishment.

Here was Mr. Cronin, the banker, his pate now totally devoid of hair, pumping her hand. "You did it before, Mrs. Marcassa, and you can do it again."

Here was Penny, Chiara's first "American" friend, a lively, pert girl-woman when they'd met. Her figure was girlish still but her eyes, faded and slightly weary, contradicted the youthful image. Everything had looked so promising for Penny in those early years. What had happened? Life, the world, had intervened, she supposed.

The two women hugged.

"And how are you, my friend?" Chiara said when they pulled apart.

Penny shrugged. "Jimmy came home." There was a bitter quirk to her mouth.

"Is he all right?"

"No injuries that you can see. But he ain't the same. Battle fatigue. He don't care about anything, just follows me around, eats when I tell him, goes to bed when I tell him." With an almost imperceptible lift of her chin she added, "But we get along fine."

Chiara's first thought was that Jimmy had received his just rewards for the way he'd treated Penny. But no, she wished evil on no one, not even Jimmy. And it was Penny who suffered as well. But Penny, like the willow, would bend with the wind. As Penny turned away, the auburn hair bobbing on her shoulder seemed, somehow, a symbol of her courage.

A few of the guests were leaving when Stewart Austin appeared. Chiara's heart jumped at the sight of him. Though he looked, as always, every inch the gentleman, he'd aged in the several years since she'd seen him. His hair had thinned and was peppered with gray and his brow had permanent ridges.

Stewart pumped Mike's hand. "I have a great deal of admiration for you, for what the union's done, even though we're on different sides of the fence."

Mike acknowledged the compliment with a smile and a nod. "I know you've been helpful."

The small group surrounding Chiara began dispersing as Stewart moved toward her. He took her hand and brushed her cheek with a kiss, saying, so softly only she heard, "You're quite a woman. And still as lovely as ever."

Chiara flushed. Dear Stewart. He would always have her abiding gratitude for his aid and encouragement in the opening of her first bridal salon. For decorum's sake, she restrained the urge to hug him.

"So good to see you again, Stewart. And how is your family? Your wife and child?"

"All well. Sonny's back home. It didn't work out for him at Yale." His smile was replaced with a small frown. "He may go to Wayne University, but for now he's just . . . well, he's doing nothing, actually."

Others moved close and she hadn't the opportunity to draw forth more information. How was Stewart *really*? When the last guest left, Chiara sank into a chair and watched Mike as he moved about picking up glasses, tossing out crumbs from the canapés. He was still handsome, she thought with pride. The dark hair had wings of white at the temples and the planes of his face were set; rock hard. She remembered the soft lips he had pressed on her hand the first time they met, the line-free face, the tender eyes. So much had happened since then. They were both older and wiser. At age forty-six, Mike had hardened. He'd always met life head-on, careless of its dangers, and it had toughened him. She went to stand beside him.

Beaming, he put his arm around her, pulling her close. "It was a great party, don't you think?"

He had put up a gallant fight against the shop, but given in gracefully when he'd realized he was beaten.

"It was wonderful." Chiara returned Mike's hug; then he reached down and kissed her fully on the mouth. They stood entwined for several moments, each engrossed in his own thoughts.

Finally Mike whispered, "Let's go home. It's time to put the proper ending on this celebration."

At home Mike poured champagne from the bottle he'd salvaged at the party, and toasted his wife. Chiara downed two glasses of champagne and collapsed wearily against Mike. She giggled softly against his chest, light-headed and exhausted, as he swept her into his arms and up the stairs. His lovemaking was unhurried and fulfilling, and afterwards she fell asleep in his arms.

The next day Chiara poured coffee for herself and Flora and set a plate of sponge cookies on the table.

"Who would have thought, Chiara, when we were children playing with dolls made from rolled-up towels, that someday you would be a businesswoman? *Madonna!*"

Chiara turned the flame low under the silver pot and settled down at the table. "God must have directed me. I found the perfect store to rent, the workmen moved swiftly, the shipments came in on time. And you, Flora. Once again you've come through to help with the children. It means a great deal to know they're well-cared-for."

"Ahh, they seem as much my children as yours. I love them as well as you do." Flora patted her heart. "But I would have stayed at the plant if they hadn't fired me to make room for the returning soldiers. I suppose it's fair. I'd signed an agreement that the job was only for the duration of the war."

"It's fair for the soldiers, but what about you and all the others who have come to depend on the earnings? What about you?"

"It's a man's world. Woman's place is in the home; that's the way it is."

"There are some women who like working a man's job and getting a man's pay. They've proved they can do it. And what about widows? They need paychecks as much as any man."

Flora shrugged. "What can you do? Nothing. That's just the way it is."

"Well, it's not right. Even Mike's attitude has changed. He said that as long as women do the same job as men, they should be paid the same. The union fights for women's rights. During the war he helped set up a women's bureau in the UAW. They tried to get equal pay and child-care centers near the plants." Chiara brushed crumbs from her skirt. "At General Motors they paid women inspectors half what the men they replaced made. Mike tried to get seniority rights for war workers like you, too. He says 'right is right; fair is fair.' "

"Mike surely has changed. I remember how he hated it when you first went to work. For me it works out fine." Flora dipped a cookie in her coffee. "If only Eduardo had lived." Tears welled in her eyes as she placed her hand on top of Chiara's. "I'm grateful to you, my friend."

"No, I'm the one who's grateful."

The door slammed and Anna yelled, "Ma, did you see the sign in front?"

"Don't holler. Yes, I saw it. For Sale. Our landlord is selling the house."

"Does that mean we have to move?" Luisa dropped her books on the table and her trench coat on a chair.

"I'm hoping we can still rent."

When the landlord, Mr. Ferguson, came to visit a week later, Mike was pleased to see him. After having worked in auto factories for forty years, the old man had retired six years ago. He was still interested in union business, always contrasting the "old days" with the present. But Mike suspected it was as much for the home-brewed zinfandel as for the talk that the old man came knocking on his door.

The square-jawed Scotsman removed his Detroit Tigers baseball cap and eased himself gingerly into a kitchen chair. "I hear they finally settled the big strike at GM. A hundred and thirteen days, wasn't it?"

Mike nodded as he wiggled the cork from a fresh bottle of wine. "It was the longest strike in auto history. Reuther wanted a wage increase of thirty percent, but mainly he wanted an agreement not to increase car prices. What good is it if they get the raise, then can't improve their standard of living because all the prices are upped?"

"Yep, he's got a point there. But I knew he'd never get it. Reuther always asks for the moon."

"He came close. President Truman was a help. He agreed that GM's ability to pay should be considered in the settlement. Of course in the end Reuther had to drop that fight in favor of wages. He settled for eighteen cents an hour."

"I see prices going up all over." Ferguson hunkered down into his chair, getting comfortable.

Mike tore the cellophane from a pack of Luckies. "Better days are coming. Reuther says down the road we'll see company-financed pension plans, sick pay, life insurance, paid vacations, disability coverage, even medical and health plans."

"Mr. Reuther's either a genius or a fool. It's a utopian dream." Mr. Ferguson drained his glass and lifted it for a refill.

Mike hesitated a moment, then poured more wine. "Why shouldn't the workers have the same benefits many of the white-collar workers have? The big bosses call it 'socialistic meddling,' but it's coming, bit by bit." Mike pointed his finger for emphasis. "In another month Reuther will be president of the UAW. Mark my words."

"He deserves it, hard as he's worked." Mr. Ferguson wagged his head. "I was a Ford man, myself, back in the early days." His eyes took on the look of reminiscence. "Worst thing that ever happened to the Ford Motor Company was Edsel's death in forty-three. It was old Henry's fault, too. Edsel got undulant fever from the unpasteurized milk of Henry's cows. Ulcers finally got him. Good thing they got young Henry out of the Navy to run things. Before that, Harry Bennett was in charge, with his thugs and ex-convicts."

Mike had heard his friend's ruminations many times. "Ford's not the problem now. It's General Motors. Remember when it was the Big Three? Now it's the Big One: GM. The war set the union back ten years because of the no-strike pledges."

"The War Labor Board was supposed to solve problems. Ha! I know how fast the government works. But it's better than in the twenties, let me tell you." Mr. Ferguson heaved a sigh and fell silent for a moment. "Well, enough about the factories and the government. I get going and don't know when to stop. I really came with news, Mike." He looked apologetic. "I sold the house. Sold it just like that." He snapped his fingers.

"Already? The sign's only been up a few days."

He picked up his baseball cap and turned it around in his hands. "I put off telling you, because I kinda hate to leave. I'll be moving to Florida with my daughter. I been in this house forty years. Seen a lot of changes." The old man looked as though he might cry. "I can't take the cold weather no more."

"We'll miss you, my friend," Mike said.

Chiara had slipped into the kitchen in time to hear Mr. Ferguson's last remarks. She touched his shoulder. "I'll hate to see you go. You've been a good friend. Have you talked to the new owners about us?"

"That's the other news. They want to rent the flat to relatives. I'm afraid you have one month, then you'll have to move."

"Oh, no." Chiara had loved this old, settled neighborhood where she'd felt welcome from the first day they'd moved in. She felt sheltered and nourished, warmed in a community spirit of trust and cooperation. There were stores within walking distance and buses on the corner. On summer evenings she could look straight through dozens of porches almost to the end of the block. Children played in the street, their shrill voices singing "Red Rover, Red Rover, let Mary cross over." Sometimes several youngsters would gather for croquet in a grassy yard, or they'd race through the street, the metal rasp of roller skates ringing through the evening air.

Chiara's regret extended to the church, the focal point of the family and of the children's activities. Anna and

Luisa attended the Catholic school, where they heard Mass each morning and were drilled in the Baltimore catechism. Chiara was a member of the Altar Society and Mike ushered on Sunday mornings. It was almost as if the parish were a small village.

After Mr. Ferguson shuffled off, settling the cap over his thin white hair, Mike said, "What's bothering you? We've always wanted a house. Now is as good a time as any to buy." He popped the cork back into the mouth of the wine jug. "I tell you, Chiara, it's probably a good thing. I've seen young toughs hanging around a pool hall on Warren Avenue. We should look for a better neighborhood for the girls' sake."

"This is a good neighborhood."

"It's changing; I've been noticing it."

"Where will we go?"

"There's construction going on all over, past Eight Mile Road, pushing against the boundaries of the city. They can't build houses fast enough. I'll talk to a real-estate agent. At least now we have enough money. We're in good shape."

Mike had saved quite a bit during the past few years, and the earnings from the bridal salon, since opening six months ago, were remarkably good.

"We should make sure there's money left for a trip to the old country." It had been a long time since she'd thought about going home. During the war years she had relegated that dream to the very corners of her mind and allowed it to resurface only in rare moments when she was disheartened or overworked.

Mike frowned. "Have you applied for citizenship like I told you?"

"No, I've been too busy."

"Make time, then."

A few days after Mr. Ferguson's visit, Chiara saw the house she wanted. Just thinking about the house gave her a warm, cozy feeling. Although it was in Grosse Pointe, it was unpretentious, not like the large homes around Lake Shore Drive. The house, in an ordinary neighborhood, was rather small, constructed of red brick. Black shutters framed the windows, including the two dormers on the second story. A flagstone walk led to a small porch surrounded by a neat curved border of sweet-faced pansies.

When Mike picked her up from work, she said, "I saw it today, Mike, the house I want."

Absently he said, "You did, eh? Where?"

"Mrs. Morrison's daughter came by. You remember her; I did her gown not long ago. I told her we were looking for a house and she told me about one for sale not far from hers."

"Where?"

"In Grosse Pointe."

"We can't afford Grosse Pointe. You're getting fancy ideas from working with those rich people."

"I work with all kinds of people, Mike, rich and not so rich. What's wrong with wanting to live in a nicer neighborhood?"

"Money, that's the problem. We'll find something in Detroit."

"No, I want that house."

"I told you we can't afford it."

"At least look at it. Can't you do that?"

"No, I don't want to look at it, and that's my final word."

Chiara decided to bide her time. Mike had no idea how much money she'd saved in the past few years. Because she made regular trips to the bank for her business, their financial responsibilities fell to her. Long ago she had given up saving her money in the cigar box and had opened a separate account for her "house savings." Mike was too engrossed in union affairs to notice that there should be more money in their regular bankbook, the one he looked at occasionally.

After dinner the girls scampered off to the front room, where Anna turned on the radio to *The Lone Ranger*. Chiara poured Mike a cup of coffee and handed him the small forest-green book. He opened it and thumbed to the page with the last entry. Eleven hundred dollars. She saw the frown leave his face.

"I had no idea." He closed the book and dropped it in his lap. "You did it, Chiara. It was all your doing."

"It was both of us."

"My earnings are almost nothing. All I get from my work is . . . What? Satisfaction, I suppose. If satisfaction were dollars, we'd be millionaires." His shoulders heaved in a resigned shrug.

"You're doing what you believe in, Mike. That's important too." Chiara moved his arm and sat on his lap. "Can we buy the house?"

"We can look at it."

Mike piled the family into the car on Saturday morning and headed for Grosse Pointe.

It wouldn't hurt to take a drive and check out the Grosse Pointe house before talking to a Detroit realtor. Actually, it was nice to see Chiara so excited. It occurred to him that she hadn't been this enthusiastic in a long time.

"Pipe down," Mike said as the girls began arguing in the back seat.

Anna said, "I wish we had a radio. Betty Ann's father has a radio in his car."

"Quiet, or I'll take you back home. Don't you want to see this house?"

"No." Anna sulked. "I finally have a new best friend. Why do we have to move?"

"You know why. The house is sold. We'll have a better place in a good neighborhood."

"I'll hate it. I don't want to move."

"Don't talk back to your father. And hold Tina so she doesn't fall." Under her breath Chiara said to Mike, "She's at that age."

"I want to move," Luisa said. She hadn't as many friends as her sister. It sometimes worried Mike that outside the family she seemed so shy.

"Slow down, Mike, there it is." Chiara pointed to the tidy dwelling surrounded by a well-tended lawn.

Mike parked the car and pushed his hat back on his head.

"Well?" Chiara nudged Mike with her elbow. "Isn't it beautiful?"

Mike assessed the house in silence. It was just Chiara's sort of house, neat and tidy, Mike thought. Two silver maples and a blue spruce shaded the front. There was even a garage, solid-looking, though it needed a coat of paint.

"Mike?" Chiara persisted, tugging at his arm. "Do you like it?"

He turned the key in the ignition and said, "Let's go see the real-estate people."

In the tiny wood-paneled office the real-estate agent nodded patiently, his small pointy chin bobbing, as Mike described the house.

"I don't believe I have anything on that street you'd be interested in. But see here, there's a great little house, an English tudor style, near Chandler Park Drive. It has four bedrooms, all upstairs. There's even an extra lavatory in the basement. Neat as a pin."

"No, my wife has her heart set on this one in Grosse Pointe. She has lots of clients from that area."

Mr. Emerson tapped his head with his index finger. "Ah, I know just the place for you. Not far from Grosse Pointe, either. It's a bungalow, but the upstairs has been made into a nice big bedroom, and—"

"You didn't hear me." Mike's eyes were getting steely. "I told you which house I want."

Chiara balanced the squirming Tina on her lap, while Anna and Luisa bickered as they squashed themselves into a chair. Chiara reached over and tapped Luisa's thigh and put her finger to her lips.

Mr. Emerson cleared his throat. "Maybe you should consider other areas, Mr. Marcassa."

Mike's jaw firmed and a little gray vein jumped on his temple.

Threads of a frown pulled together on Chiara forehead.

Mr. Emerson nodded slowly. "Well . . . ah, I'll see what I can find for you. Meanwhile, I wish you would look at this great little place—"

"I said Grosse Pointe." Mike enunciated each word as if it were a a complete sentence.

Mr. Emerson's lips clamped together, while his eyes evaded Mike's and slid to Chiara's in an appeal. She fixed a stare on him.

"Well, say," Emerson said finally, "I'll see what I can find and call you."

Mike stood abruptly and leaned across the desk. He jabbed his index finger into Mr. Emerson's chest. "No. Don't call me, Emerson. You just missed a nice commission. Because I'm going to live in a house in Grosse Pointe whether you like it or not. And you're not the guy that's going to sell it." Mike turned and scooped Tina up from Chiara's arms, jerking his head toward the door. Chiara pushed the two girls ahead of her. When he'd herded them out, Mike slammed the door behind them.

In the car, Chiara said, "Mike, I don't understand. Why didn't he want to sell us the house? I know there are plenty of houses for sale. I've seen the signs in front."

"Bah, he's just a stupid bastard." Mike took his anger out on the gears, shifting fiercely.

"But why was he acting that way?"

"He's a bigot, that's why."

"What do you mean, bigot?"

"He doesn't want to sell to Italians."

Chiara looked offended. "But why? I keep my house as clean as any on the block. My children too."

"It hasn't got anything to do with being clean. It's just prejudice. Blind prejudice."

"Well, if they don't want us, I don't want them." Chiara's mouth tightened. "We'll live someplace else."

"Not on your life!" Mike shouted angrily. "You want Grosse Pointe, you'll get Grosse Pointe!"

"But if they won't sell to us—"

"Don't you worry. They'll sell. I'll talk to Fredo. He has connections." Mike had that look in his eyes that said no one had better cross him.

——31——

Chiara was surprised when Mike dropped into the shop a few days later. As usual, he looked out of place in the feminine trappings.

Shunning the delicate Queen Anne chair next to her desk, he dropped heavily onto the cot he'd insisted Chiara have for "rest periods."

"Fredo's sick," he said sadly. "Rheumatism. I didn't have the heart to ask him a favor."

Chiara tacked a sketch on the board behind her desk. "What favor?"

"The house in Grosse Pointe."

Chiara was pleased. She didn't want Fredo pulling strings, exerting pressure; didn't want to *owe* him for favors.

"It's a sign, Mike. We mustn't pursue this house. Even Maria says so."

Mike leaned toward Chiara, pointing his finger. "I don't care what Maria says. You want to live in Grosse Pointe and I'm going to see that you do just that."

Mike had been challenged and wouldn't give up easily. Chiara sighed. At one time she had thought a home in Grosse Pointe would be the ultimate dream. But now it mattered little. Life was difficult enough without living where her children might be looked down upon. The irony was that she and Mike had reversed their positions.

"Mike, I changed my mind. I don't care where I live."

"You're the one who wanted to live in Grosse Pointe; now you say you don't care." He gave an exasperated grunt.

"I know. But I don't want to live where I'm not welcome." Chiara moved around her desk and faced Mike with a pleased smile. "Listen, I saw a beautiful house in Detroit today. Nicer than the other one, and not so expensive."

"Jesus Christ! Why can't you make up your mind? First it's one thing, then another . . ."

Chiara narrowed her eyes. "If Fredo does you this favor, then you owe him. That bothers me. I don't like owing people."

"Ah, Fredo's okay, he'd never ask something impossible."

"You never know." Chiara's voice turned dulcet. "You were right in the first place, absolutely right. Why spend all that money when we can get just as nice a place in Detroit? I was wrong to push you about the Grosse Pointe house."

By the time Mike saw the Detroit house, his ire had cooled and he reluctantly agreed to the purchase.

But for Chiara, though she wanted a home of her own, the move wasn't an easy one. They'd made good friends in the old neighborhood, and the flat held many memories, happy and sad.

She stifled a tear as she shooed the others out ahead of her.

"Good-bye, old house," she whispered just before she closed the door and hurried down the steps.

At the sight of the new house, Chiara's heart quickened. A flagstone walk led to a small porch surrounded by purple and white alyssum, and the door and window trim sparkled with new white paint.

They were barely in the front door when the girls began fighting over which bedroom to take. They chased upstairs, staking their claims to two of the four bedrooms. Chiara bustled about the kitchen, unloading boxes on the modern tile sink. She burrowed in a carton for the old metal coffeepot. In minutes the familiar clucking sounded as water danced through the pot's glass bubble. Chiara made Mike pause a moment in between carting furniture to have coffee at the breakfast nook, where three windows overlooked a spacious yard.

She found a cookie tin and pried it open. Handing a cookie to Mike, she said, "The girls are happy, especially Anna. Agnes lives just a few blocks away." She chewed thoughtfully. "I like this house, Mike."

"If you like it, then I like it." He pulled her close in a hug and they remained that way for several moments.

Later Chiara placed framed pictures of her family on the carved eggshell-colored mantel over the fireplace. She recalled her childhood and the fireplace that was the heart of the home and essential for cooking and heating. This one was mainly decorative. What would her mother think of this lovely place?

Dino and Rosa visited the next day and brought a sturdy young fig tree. Mike wasted no time in planting the sapling. When he'd anchored it with rope and stakes, he tamped down the last bit of earth.

A neighbor sauntered by their corner lot with a leashed Labrador reluctantly following. The dog stopped to watch the little tree-planting ceremony, and his master indulged him.

"Welcome to the neighborhood," the stroller said with a wave.

Chiara's heart warmed. This will be a good place for my family, she thought as she shaded her eyes and gazed toward the sun. A strong sense of peace and well-being engulfed her. In the year of our Lord, 1947, life was good.

She gave the tree a silent blessing and whispered a prayer of thanks to God.

After the staff had gone for the day, Chiara sent Maria on her way too. This was the time Chiara enjoyed most—after working hours when the hustle-bustle had ended, the women's chattering had ceased, the buzz and clatter of the sewing machines halted. She sat quietly for a few moments, letting her thoughts wander, going over the events of the day.

The modern, well-lighted space was a far cry from the cramped quarters of her earlier office, which had housed a scarred secondhand desk and wooden file cabinet with sticky drawers. She ran her hand appreciatively over the smooth surface of the new desk, then opened the top drawer. In an open velvet-lined box lay the silver scissors that had miraculously survived the fire. They were her talisman.

Chiara allowed herself a smile of contentment. Business was increasing steadily. The move had gone well, though she hadn't had time to meet many neighbors. The girls were adjusted to their new school, especially Anna, who had made friends and joined, of all things, a basketball team. She seemed to have an abundance of energy. Luisa hadn't fared quite as well, but then, she had always been a little shy with anyone other than family. Tina seemed happy wherever she was put. Chiara smiled to herself. They were good girls, all three of them. She wondered what the future held for her daughters. They would graduate from high school and get office jobs, with the city or federal government probably; something secure. Then marriage. That was the way of things.

She had hoped that Anna would take an interest in sewing and join her in running the shop, but no, Anna had no head for the work. Anna was more like her father, in looks and personality. Now, Luisa was different. She reminded Chiara of herself at the same age; her fair hair and blue eyes, the slenderness, the love of reading, especially poetry. She liked sewing well enough, but had no great interest in fashion. Still, if Anna wouldn't succeed Chiara in the sewing business, perhaps Luisa would. Even as a youngster she cut and sewed clothing for her doll, unlike Anna, who hadn't the patience for sewing and gave up when her stitches looked crooked or she lost her thread.

The little one, Tina, who could tell? She was a delight, and unfortunately a bit spoiled by all of them.

Chiara reached for a bag lying on a nearby chair and drew out a length of pale yellow cotton. She would begin on the curtains for Luisa's bedroom tomorrow. She folded the material and slipped it into a drawer. It was time she went home. The family would be waiting. Thank God for Flora. She needn't worry over the children as long as she knew Flora was with them. She slid orders into a file and kneed the drawer closed, then banded receipts together and placed them in a large envelope.

When Mike came to pick her up, as he often did, she hugged him, clinging for a moment.

"What's this for?" he asked.

"I just feel good today. Everything's going so well."

A few days later, when Chiara had finished measuring a matron for a mother-of-the-bride gown, Maria summoned her to the phone. "It's Flora and she sounds worried."

Flora's voice was flustered. "Luisa's sick. I think you should come home. Everything hurts her and she has a fever." When nervous, Flora spoke in shrill Italian.

Chiara felt a pinprick of anxiety. "What's her temperature?" she asked, fingering the tape measure that hung around her neck.

"One hundred and three."

"I'm coming." Chiara hung up and told Maria to take over.

The bus took forever, each stop and start a sluggish crawl. Yesterday Luisa had complained she wasn't feeling well, which was unusual. Though thin, she was blessed with good health.

When Ciara entered the bedroom, Luisa said, "My throat hurts."

"Open up. Let me see." There was no redness or spots. Chiara felt her daughter's warm cheek and placed a thermometer in her mouth.

The mercury reached one hundred and two.

Chiara snapped the thin rod a few times and wiped it with alcohol.

"Don't you want a little soup?" she urged, taking a bowl from the table next to Luisa's bed and pressing the spoon to her mouth.

Luisa turned her head. "I'm not hungry. My back's sore; my legs too."

A nameless fear clutched at Chiara. She replaced the spoon and stood upright, pressing her cool hand against Luisa's hot forehead.

It was just the flu. The flu did that to children, made them achy. She went from Luisa's room to her own, where she lit a votive candle before the statue of the Virgin Mary on her dresser.

"Ave Maria," she prayed, while her brain sifted through the symptoms. Sore throat, fever, aching limbs and back. She'd heard those symptoms often enough. The newspaper articles, the warnings, swam before her: keep your children away from crowds, from movies and beaches. When last they'd gone to Chandler Park, the wading pool, devoid of water, looked strangely empty. The enemy was the same one that had felled Franklin Delano Roosevelt in his prime. Infantile paralysis. Poliomyelitis. Polio. Ultimately it led to paralysis.

Seconds later she phoned the doctor.

Mike and the doctor arrived together.

Dr. Catrone listened with deep concentration as he positioned the stethoscope at different places on Luisa's chest and back. His breathing was audible—measured and comforting. When he finished, there was the barest frown on his wide pink brow. He pressed large, competent hands over Luisa's body.

"Does this hurt? Does this?"

Luisa winced in pain.

He lifted her leg and she groaned. Assisting her into an upright position, he said, "Put your chin to your chest."

She did as she was told and sank back to a reclining position.

Chiara clutched Mike's arm as they both hovered at the end of the bed, leaning forward. Dr. Catrone pulled the bedcovers over Luisa and patted her cheek.

In the kitchen the doctor stirred his coffee. Chiara and Mike watched his benign expression in silence, waiting for him to speak.

"Try to keep the fever down with sponge baths and have her touch her chin to her chest every few hours."

"What does she have?" Mike asked.

"I'm not sure yet. Let's see how she is tomorrow." He stared into his coffee cup, evading their eyes. "Call me in the morning."

He didn't say the dread word, and Chiara couldn't bring herself to utter it. Her fear was palpable, a large lump in her stomach, a bile in her throat.

Several times through the night Chiara woke Luisa to check on her. The next morning, when Chiara brought a tray in with toast and milk, she thought Luisa looked a bit better, more rested.

Chiara set the tray on the nightstand. "Come on, sit up, *figlia.*" She supported Luisa under the arms and plumped the pillows behind her head. "Now, touch your chest with your chin."

Luisa strained with the effort. Her eyes widened with fear. "I . . . I can't."

Mike sat beside Chiara and stubbed his cigarette out in

the metal stand. The hospital waiting room seats were filled with a variety of people, most of them enveloped in a private misery. Maria and Flora, wearing similar stricken looks, sat across the room.

Chiara clutched Mike's arm. "They should be finished with the examination by now. Why are they taking so long?"

Mike patted her shoulder absently.

Dr. Catrone had ushered them outside the room over an hour ago, while he and a gaunt hollow-cheeked man he'd introduced as Dr. Enright examined Luisa.

After what seemed an eternity, a nurse beckoned to Chiara and Mike and led them to a small office.

"It's as we feared. Infantile paralysis." Dr. Enright spoke in hushed tones. He had a slight twitch in his left eye.

Chiara's knees felt weak. She clutched her heart and took a deep breath. Mike's grip on her shoulder tightened.

"Already her left leg is becoming rigid," the doctor continued. "The treatment we recommend is immobility. We'll put her legs in casts."

"How bad is it, Doctor? How long will it last?" Mike's voice was low.

"It's hard to say at this point. Perhaps she'll recover and be left with only a limp. But, again . . ." He shrugged. "We'll do the best we can."

"I have to see her." Chiara hurried out into the corridor, Mike close behind.

In Luisa's room, she hugged her daughter. "The doctor says you're going to get better."

Luisa's pale face was turned to the wall. "He told me, Ma. Polio."

"But you'll be well in no time." Chiara straightened the sheet, tucking it under the mattress.

Luisa turned tear-filled eyes to her mother.

Chiara swallowed hard. "The doctor is very hopeful. You need lots of rest." She lowered the blind, darkening the room.

"Bring my rosary when you come tomorrow."

"Yes, we'll pray together. The Blessed Virgin will help us. You'll get well."

Mike entered the room and patted his daughter's hand and silently bent to kiss her forehead.

Dr. Catrone had followed Mike in. "Better let her rest now."

Back in the waiting room, Chiara collapsed against Mike in a vale of tears. Maria and Flora whispered, with heads together and faces drawn.

Chiara sat heavily next to Flora. "My poor baby, my daughter. It's what we thought, polio. *Dio, Dio,* why has this happened? What shall I do?" She turned imploringly to her friends.

Maria clutched Chiara's hand, then suddenly looked into the distance, her eyes glazing over. She placed her fingertips on her temples and lowered her eyelids.

With her finger to her lips, Flora nudged Chiara. "Maria sees something."

Both women watched Maria intently.

Presently Maria opened her eyes, leaned back in her chair with a great expulsion of breath, and said, "Get Sophia. She'll know what to do."

Flora said, "Sophia's a midwife. She doesn't know about infantile paralysis."

"Get her."

Chiara clutched Maria's arm. "What do you see, Maria?"

"I see Sophia helping Luisa."

Sophia, her plump cheeks dimpling, smiled at Luisa. "Don't look so sad, little one, you're going to be all right." She met Chiara's questioning eyes over the limp figure of Luisa on the bed and tipped her head toward the door.

"We must bring her home," Sophia whispered when they met in the hallway. "They're giving her the wrong treatment."

"Sophia, what are you saying? I trust Dr. Catrone. He's always taken care of us."

Sophia's hands wagged, shoulder-high. "They think they are doing the right thing, but they are not. I remember seeing my mother treat a child with these very same symptoms—they had no idea what it was in those days. There was no doctor in our town, so she did what she could, used old-country wisdom. She placed hot compresses on the child's legs, and after a few days she slowly and gently massaged the tightened muscles. She nursed several children with the same disease, and I would help her place the hot cloths on their sore bodies. Several months ago my cousin Vittorio's son got infantile paralysis. His feet were bent, one downward and one up. They had no money for the hospital, so I treated him at home. He's fine now. Doesn't even have a limp."

Mike shook his head with a frown. "But, Sophia, the doctors say she must have a plaster cast; she'll be crippled if she's not placed in a cast."

"And I'm telling you they're wrong. The doctors don't know everything. I also read of the hot-compress treatment in *The Reader's Digest* a few years ago. An Australian nurse, Sister Kenny, began doing it and saved many patients from being crippled. I saved the article because it impressed me."

"Sophia, I read about this Sister Kenney in the paper too. Some say she's a fake, a charlatan." Mike raked his fingers through his hair. "No, we must trust Dr. Catrone."

Chiara tugged at Mike's elbow. "Mike, don't say no; we have to talk about this more."

Sophia hugged them both. "Let God guide you. I must be going now, but call me if you need me."

When the grilled elevator doors closed on Sophia, Chiara turned to Mike. "I trust Maria. She says let Sophia do it."

Mike thrust his hands in his pockets and marched to the window at the end of the hall.

Chiara followed him and tugged at his elbow. "Mike?"

"Chiara, you're like a child, you believe everything Maria says."

"Yes," Chiara hissed, "because she is always right."

Mike's hands flew in the air. "Sometimes she guesses right! This is too important to leave to a fortune-teller."

Sobs tore from Chiara's throat as she flung herself into his arms. "*Dio, Dio*, what will we do? God has deserted us. What have we done to deserve such heartache?"

Mike held her close. "Sh, sh. Don't, Chiara. Don't cry."

He patted her head as it rested on his shoulder, until her sobs subsided. "All right, we'll let Sophia try with her. I pray to God we're not making a mistake."

The next morning the two doctors stood at the foot of Luisa's bed. "Listen to reason, Mike," Dr. Catrone said.

"This child belongs in the hospital. We've treated many cases like this."

"And they end up crippled."

"Not always."

Chiara spoke up, her jaw set. "We've made up our minds, Doctor. We know you want to help, but this isn't the proper treatment for Luisa."

Dr. Catrone steered Mike out of the room and Chiara heard them arguing. Mike was wavering. She slumped into a chair. Even she wasn't sure they were doing the right thing. What if they were wrong? Their child's life depended on their making the correct decision. She dropped her head into her hands, too tired to think any longer.

Mike reentered the room with resolute steps. At Luisa's bed he inched his hands underneath her. Gently he lifted Luisa, and her frail arms encircled his neck.

Dr. Catrone looked defeated, while Dr. Enright, standing beyond the doorway, shook his head in disgust. As they left, Chiara heard him mutter, "Let them use their snake oil and see where it gets them."

Back home, Sophia tore strips from an old woolen blanket. "Wool retains the heat. We'll soak these in hot water."

Chiara hurried to the basement and pressed the wet, steaming strips through the wringer and watched them snake, curling, to the basket below.

Luisa's pathetic whimpers of pain cut Chiara like a knife. Dear God, she prayed, why Luisa? She's so young, so good. What has she done to deserve this punishment?

"Does it hurt here?" the midwife asked, touching her gently beneath the knee.

"Yes." Luisa drew in her breath. "But it's okay. I'll offer it up."

"For now we'll just use the heat," Sophia said to Chiara, who hovered over the bed, her hands linked in a tight knot. "The muscle is in spasm. I'll try again tomorrow to massage."

During the long night, Chiara murmured endless prayers as she exchanged the damp, cooling strips for warm ones. The night darkness lifted, giving way to a gray dawn, when Chiara felt Mike's arms lift her up against his chest.

She had fallen asleep in the chair beside her daughter's bed.

Struggling against Mike's firm grip, she forced her heavy lids open. "No, I must change the compresses."

"I'll take over until it's time to leave for work. You sleep until then."

In the morning, Sophia returned and began in earnest to treat her charge.

"The muscles are still in spasm," she explained, examining her patient.

It was several days before she could begin to massage Luisa's limbs. With competent fingers she stroked the hollow beneath Luisa's knee, coaxing, "Feel that muscle? Think about how it can move. Force it to move. It's almost forgotten how. You can move it if you try."

Perspiration dotted Luisa's brow. Frowning with concentration, she said, "I . . . I'm trying."

After a few moments Sophia shook her head sadly. *"Niente."* Lifting and lowering the leg manually, she said, "We try again tomorrow."

Tomorrow. Yes, Luisa would be better tomorrow. Chiara swallowed hard. It was difficult to keep from crying in front of Luisa, but she must put on a cheerful face.

In the days that followed, a path was worn from the basement, where the wringer stood, to the upstairs bedroom, where Luisa bore the ministrations with a minimum of complaint. When she wasn't at school, Anna minded Tina and tried to help in any way she could. The girls were not allowed into the bedroom for fear of contagion.

"Mama, put a votive candle on my dresser in front of the Virgin," Luisa said.

Chiara complied, murmuring a short prayer as she dusted off the small plaster statue of the Virgin Mary. It had been two weeks. Surely Luisa's flaccid muscles would begin to work soon. If they did not . . . She dared not think of the consequences.

Luisa's fingers slid over the glass rosary beads in her hand while her lips moved continually, mouthing the words, "Hail Mary, full of grace, the Lord is with thee . . ."

Anna called from outside the bedroom, "Here are

some books I got you from the library, Luisa . . . *Little Women* and *Eight Cousins*."

"Yes, maybe you can read a little," Chiara said. "You don't have to pray all day. God understands if you take a rest from it."

"I have to pray that I get well. I know God will answer my prayers."

Chiara turned and walked swiftly from the room. It was difficult to keep the look of despair from her face. Surely Luisa was right and God would answer all their prayers. It wasn't fair, her beautiful daughter so afflicted. But her years of living had taught her that "fair" did not always enter into the scheme of things. God's will did not always align with hers.

Her thoughts were interrupted by the doorbell. Chiara let Sophia in and followed her up the stairs.

"What do you think, Sophia? She won't be . . . paralyzed, will she?" Chiara finally uttered the dread word.

"My friend, it's in God's hands." Sophia's attempt at a smile failed.

Even Sophia is losing faith, Chiara thought as they entered the bedroom.

—— **32** ——

Sun filtered through the lace curtains in Luisa's room, forming shadowy patterns on the bedspread. When Chiara entered with Sophia, she saw her daughter sliding a rosary beneath the pillow.

"How are you today, little one?" Sophia chirped.

"Better, I think." Luisa's blue eyes were rimmed with red and shadowed with gray.

Gently Sophia lifted the warm compresses from her patient's limbs. Her hands arched beneath the knee and worked down to the calf, palms and fingers kneading the lifeless flesh, her face intent.

"Yes, yes, there's something there, some movement. I can feel it," Sophia said, almost to herself. "Can you feel it, child? Can you feel that pulse?"

Chiara held her breath as she intently watched her daughter's face for a sign.

Luisa's cheeks were pink with effort for several minutes. "It's no use," she cried, "I can't feel anything."

Sophia's voice was stern. "Try!"

Chiara thought the child would cry. Her mouth puckered and her chin quivered, but she took a deep breath and squeezed her eyes shut with determined effort. Beads of perspiration formed over her lip. Slowly her mouth quirked in a minuscule smile and her eyes opened wide. "Yes," she whispered, "I can feel it."

"Now, you must move that muscle," Sophia commanded. "Push it. Make it work."

For several moments Luisa's wan face contorted with effort. Finally she burst into tears. "I can't."

Sophia drew in her breath, then let it out in a long sigh. Her hands dropped to her sides. *"Basta,"* she said, meeting Chiara's eyes across the bed.

Choking back a tear, Chiara patted Luisa's hand. "Courage, *figlia."*

Later, in the kitchen, Sophia said, "I don't want to discourage her." She placed a comforting hand on Chiara's shoulder. "You, my friend, you don't look well."

Chiara put her hands over her face and cried. She realized suddenly how utterly exhausted she was. Her days and nights were filled with nursing Luisa. Nothing was more important than bringing her daughter back to health, helping her maintain the use of her legs. The niggling fear that perhaps Luisa wouldn't recover nipped at her consciousness. No, she mustn't let herself give up hope. She must trust in God.

She lifted her head and dried her eyes on the edge of the tablecloth. "I'm tired, that's all."

"Your daughter will recover. I wasn't so confident before, but this is the first sign."

"Are you sure?"

"Almost sure."

"Thank you, my friend." Chiara hugged Sophia. "Why don't you stay for supper?"

Before Sophia could answer, they heard Luisa calling, "Mama, Mama, come here."

The women raced up the stairs and into the bedroom. Luisa's leg was dropped over the side of the bed.

"I can move it! Honest, I can, I can!"

While the two women watched, Luisa, her bottom lip caught between her teeth, inched her leg forward so slightly as to be almost indiscernible. But Chiara saw it. She saw Luisa's leg move!

Throwing her arms around Luisa, Chiara sobbed, "Thank God." Mother and daughter, locked in an embrace for several moments, didn't even hear Sophia leave.

Chiara sat in the breakfast nook a few weeks later, absorbing the last rays of afternoon sun. Louise was on the mend, slowly but surely, though nursing her still took hours of Chiara's time. Three-year-old Tina, dragging a large rag doll by the leg, ran and laid her head on her mother's lap.

"I wish I was sick." Her thumb found its way into her mouth.

Chiara's heart thumped. She took the child by the shoulders and shook her. "Don't ever say such a thing!"

As Tina's little mouth puckered, then opened in a wail, Chiara grabbed her and pressed her close. In a flash of understanding, Chiara realized she'd been neglecting her other children. It wasn't so terrible for Anna, because she understood and she had friends and school to occupy her, but not so her baby, her Tina. True, Flora had been a constant presense, ministering to the family, but Flora was not their mother.

Burying her head against Tina's neck, Chiara said, "Poor little one. I've forgotten about you, haven't I? Well, things are going to change around here, now that Luisa's mending." She picked Tina up and carried her into the living room. Collapsing into a rocking chair, she said, "Shall I tell you a story?"

Tina purred contentedly in the warmth of her mother's arms, and was asleep before the story was finished.

Chiara laid her gently on her bed, and fought back a sick feeling that she suddenly realized had been recurring lately. She'd ignored the fact that her period was late, and dismissed the symptoms of nausea and fatigue, sure that they were due to distress and lack of eating proper meals. Her hands fluttered over her abdomen. It wasn't a good time for a baby, after all she'd been through with Luisa. At forty-one she was too old for another child. Still, it would be nice to hold a little bundle in her arms again. And this time, maybe it would be a boy. *God's will be done.*

When she told Sophia, that knowing woman passed a practiced eye over Chiara. "I thought so. You're still healthy. Maybe you'll have a boy this time." She tipped her head, saying quietly, "I'll always remember your first."

Chiara's eyes misted and she made the sign of the cross.

"I know, it still upsets you." Sophia rose painstakingly to her feet. "My days of delivering babies are over. Everyone goes to the hospital now. No one needs a midwife any longer. Everything changes." Her lids lowered slowly over sad eyes.

In the next few months, Chiara, Mike, and Flora took turns massaging Luisa's legs, and she gradually gained strength, but she seemed more introverted than ever. Once a week, a visiting teacher came by with assignments, which Luisa completed with Anna's help.

Winter's gloom gave way to a sunny spring, and Chiara and Michele looked forward to the birth of their child in May.

"Now that things are almost normal again, I'm going to spend more time at the shop," Chiara told Mike as he carried Luisa down the stairs and set her on her feet.

"No, don't go to work, Ma," Luisa begged, hobbling to the kitchen with her father's arm as support.

Mike said, "Let Maria manage. You stay home with the children. They need you now, especially Luisa."

Chiara spooned a string of spaghetti from the boiling pot and tasted it. "I'll go in for only a few hours. Flora feels lost when she doesn't come here every day. She needs the work too."

Chiara beamed affectionately at her brood, finally all together again at the table, the girls sniping at one another, Mike yelling for quiet. She served the pasta and dolloped on ladles of extra sauce. "Two meatballs, Anna," she cautioned. That girl's stomach was a bottomless pit. But why worry over how many meatballs they ate? There was plenty now to go around. The old habits of restraint and frugality still hobbled her. Her childhood, she thought, shadowed her always.

Life was good again. Mike, though always dissatisfied with the slow progress of the union, was at least in no immediate danger, the way he had been in the old days. Or, anyway, none that she was aware of. He spoke little of his work lately. She supposed it was to spare her worry.

"Mike," she said, an idea striking her suddenly. "Why don't you play your guitar for us tonight?"

"No, I haven't played that old thing for so long, my fingers won't know what to do."

"Yeah, Pa, play for us," Anna begged.

"Do it, Pa. Like you used to do in the old days. Play 'O Sole Mio.'"

When they'd finished their dessert of lemon ice, Anna ran upstairs for her father's guitar. Mike pushed his chair back and plucked at the strings. When he'd tuned it to his satisfaction, he began strumming randomly.

"Eh, it comes back," he said, smiling nostalgically. " 'O sole mio, sta 'n front a te . . .'. Come on, Anna, you know the words, Luisa too. Sing!"

Anna knew the Italian words and Luisa followed along pretty well, but Tina comprehended very little. More and more Chiara spoke English at home. She must remember to use her native language to the children more often, to renew a sense of their heritage. Poor waifs, they had no grandparents, no aunts or uncles in their lives to encourage an understanding of their motherland. Or was she mistaken? Was America their motherland?

At the very least they should see their kin, the place where their parents were born, feast their eyes on the aquamarine hues of the Adriatic, the ancient church of San Nicola di Bari, taste the succulent *frutti del mare*. She dabbed at the tear that formed in the corner of her eye. Ah, she was feeling sentimental tonight. That song always did that to her.

*   *   *

A few days later, Chiara shuffled through the mail in her pleasant little office. She opened a note addressed in a cramped, quick handwriting. It was from Stewart. "Since you never seem to be in when I come by, thought I'd drop you a line. I've seen the perfect little place for a shop. It's in the boondocks, Royal Oak, near Eleven Mile Road. The rent is reasonable, but it will go fast. Talk to Ron Forster if you're interested." There was a number and a scrawled signature. The last time she had seen Stewart, he encouraged her to think about opening a branch in the suburbs of Detroit.

Somehow, he was often in the background of her life, offering her encouragement and friendship. He had no idea of the trauma she had suffered during the past few months. Though they had shared much, they were still intimate strangers, intruding occasionally into each other's lives. She stared at the note for a long moment, then crumpled it and threw it in the wastebasket.

Back in the workroom, she said, "I had a note from Mr. Austin, telling about a shop to rent in Royal Oak."

"You talked about opening another shop before all this trouble happened. Have you given up that idea?" Maria talked around the pins in her mouth. She removed one and expertly placed a tuck in the rose nylon dress that clung to a padded, matronly form.

Chiara lifted her hands and shoulders in a characteristic shrug. "Luisa's going to be fine, but with another baby coming, I can't think of another shop. It's just too much work. You'd have to manage this one, and I would take over the new one. Unless I found someone as good as you to help me, I would have to be there all the time. No, it's impossible." She mused a moment. "But when Anna graduates, that's when I'll think about it again. Anna could manage a store. I'd train her. She's a smart girl, my Anna, she catches on quickly."

"She's smart, all right, but she doesn't like this business. She never did."

"She's young. She'll change her mind."

"Chiara, you only see what you want to see. Anna wants to go to college. She told me so."

"It's just a foolish notion. What good is college for a girl? She'll only get married. I'll convince her to do what's right." Chiara smoothed her hand over the bodice of a partially completed gown. It was one of the designs she had worked on at home. "It needs a larger shoulder pad, don't you think?"

Maria stepped back. "Hm. Maybe."

Chiara pressed the small of her back and sighed.

"Your back is bothering you, isn't it? You don't have to come in, you know," Maria said. "I can handle things."

"I know that. You manage very well. Lately, it's more your shop than mine," Chiara grumbled. "But I especially want to convert some of our old designs into the 'new look.' "

"The new look," Maria echoed. "Nothing is new in fashion. It just makes a circle and comes round again."

"I like the new styles. After having to skimp on fabric all through the war, it's nice to have designs with fullness, and plenty of material to work with."

"Yes, look at this suit for a trousseau." Maria pulled a hanger from the rack. The suit had a full, mid-calf skirt and roomy jacket. "It's nice, *non è vero?*"

Chiara agreed and shuffled her hand over the clothing hanging on the rack. It was almost discouraging to see how well everything ran without her. She sighed.

"You must be tired," Maria said. "You look bigger than the other times."

"I think I am bigger. I've got three weeks left. I'm sick every morning and my ankles are swollen."

"Sit, then." Maria urged Chiara into a chair and moved an empty box under her. "Put your feet up."

Chiara did as she was told. "Well, Maria, what do you think, is it a boy?"

Annoyed, Maria threw her hands up. "You ought to know by now that I can't see everything."

"Mike wants a boy. I'm calling him little Michele." Chiara stroked her stomach. "This pregnancy is so different from the others."

Maria closed her eyes slowly, painfully, then, opening them, averted her head.

Leaning forward in her seat, Chiara said, "You see something. What is it?"

"No, it's nothing." Maria energetically moved the padded form into a corner of the workroom, then returned to rest her hand on Chiara's shoulder. "Go home now. Go home and rest."

Chiara knew it would be futile to question her further.

At three o'clock in the morning the first contractions began. Chiara roused, and dressed. She tidied up the bathroom and made a cup of weak tea. By the first tender lifting of darkness, the contractions had intensified. Chiara shook Mike's arm.

He slowly came to. "What . . . what's happening?"

"The labor's starting. I'm all packed and I called Flora. You go and pick her up."

She tiptoed into the girls' rooms and kissed them as they slept. Gently she shook Anna's shoulder. "I'm going now. To have the baby." She wondered what Anna knew of babies and how they came to be. She supposed she should talk to her fifteen-year-old daughter about these things, but it was so difficult to begin that sort of conversation. Once when she tried, her words were so awkward that she gave up and changed the subject.

Now Anna, half-asleep, forced her eyes open and tried to absorb her mother's words. When she finally understood, Anna looked a bit frightened. "Are you okay, Ma?"

"Yes." Chiara took her daughter's face into both her hands and kissed her. The dear face, so like Michele's, with the deep-set, intense dark eyes. When a contraction began, Chiara straightened with a groan. Anna grabbed her mother's hand and started crying.

"I'm fine. It's just a little early, but I'm fine." In truth, she hadn't felt fine. It seemed the baby had hardly moved in the past week. But she hadn't mentioned it to anyone.

"It's a boy, I know it is," she said to Mike as he bundled her into the car for the ride to the hospital.

"It's too early." Mike's concern was masked by a gruff manner. "Maybe it's false labor. I've heard of that."

"It feels real to me," Chiara said, arching her back against the seat.

In the hospital she was efficiently settled in a labor room, but the pain had become excruciating. A nurse prepared and then examined her, not once but several times, looking anxious. She injected something into Chiara's arm, and the pain gradually lessened. Finally Dr. Catrone arrived and repeated the examination, first with the cold metal stethoscope against her huge white mound of a belly, his brow furrowing, then pushing her knees up to continue the examination in unsettling silence.

His glance toward the nurse seemed secretly significant and sent a vague buzz of alarm through Chiara's aching head.

"Get her into the delivery room," the doctor instructed.

Someone put a mask over her mouth and nose. White globes of light, blinding light, the smell of alcohol, a nurse's face over her own, pressing her eyelid upward. *Mrs. Marcassa? Mrs. Marcassa? Push now, dear, a little harder.* She dozed in between contractions. What had they given her that made her so drowsy? The dulled pain was continuous now, but nothing seemed to be happening. Then all at once, an eruption, an agonizing and compelling force downward, and the baby pushed through. But she didn't hear a cry and no one was talking. The room was unnaturally quiet. Then, when someone spoke, the voice was hushed. There was movement. Then urgent whispers. *Where is my baby? Where is the familiar newborn wail? Why is no one speaking? Where are Dr. Catrone's booming laugh and hearty congratulations? Why is the nurse's face above me so sad? Why is she patting my hand?* The haze dulling Chiara's brain began lifting, and the realization struck her. Something was wrong, very wrong.

"My baby!" she heard herself shriek. "What's wrong with my baby?"

The doctor's face loomed above her, puckered in a frown. *"Chiara, il bambino è morto."*

Dead. Her baby was born dead. Chiara's wail bounced against the sterile walls and filled the room with sound.

"A boy; a big one," she heard a nurse's sad voice. "Nine pounds."

She grabbed the doctor's hand, her nails digging into his wrist. "Why? Why did my baby die?"

"Signora, these things happen. He was dead in the womb. No one knows why."

She was so tired, so defeated. You work and strive and cope and hope and pray, and still things go wrong. This was the boy they had both wanted so desperately. Why had God abandoned her?

While she lay like a corpse, half-awake, half-asleep, they did things to her body—stitched her, washed her, pulled her arms into a stiff, fresh gown. She felt herself being shuffled onto a gurney and wheeled out of the delivery room and into another room.

When she opened her eyes, Mike was beside her, squeezing her hand.

"We have all the family we need." His smile seemed forced. "I have my harem of girls to do my bidding. What more could I want?"

She turned her face to the wall. She had failed him.

—— 33 ——

June 1951 and graduation came too quickly. At seventeen, Anna felt some apprehension and wasn't quite prepared to enter that other world, the working world, where women passed the time until Mr. Right came along. Her high-school years had been a time of fulfillment. An apt student, she'd learned the joy and gratification of stretching her intellectual limits.

She envied Agnes and the friends who would go to Wayne University or the University of Detroit or Marygrove College. Those college-bound few were the exception rather than the rule. The others would work at Edison's or Michigan Bell, or some lucky ones in the offices of the Big Three.

Anna wished she could postpone working for a little while, but with almost no discussion and before she could formulate plans, her father pulled strings to get her a job in the City-County Building. Before Anna knew it, she had exchanged bobby sox and loafers for pumps and suits, and had reluctantly entered a new arena.

She tried gallantly to make the best of her new job, tried to do everything correctly, but it wasn't easy. There were strange names and terms to remember, a recalcitrant, error-prone typewriter, and personnel, all her seniors by at least ten years, who were not overly friendly.

When her supervisor called her into the office, Anna wasn't surprised. Miss Jensen, with her little beak nose and thin hair, looked a bit pompous sitting at her orderly desk, tapping her silver pen. At thirty-seven, she was head of the general-office department, and the epitome of an old maid.

Pursing her lips, Miss Jensen said, "Anna, you've been here two weeks."

Anna nodded.

"Don't you like it here?"

Anna wished she could tell the truth, but that was out of the question. "I like it okay." Her voice, she knew, did not sound convincing.

The supervisor paused. "Your typing, Anna, is not very good."

Anna reddened and dropped her gaze. She could say nothing in her defense. Her typing was awful.

"Anna." Miss Jensen's pointed little chin went up, then down. "If you had your choice of any job, what would it be?"

Anna gained a tad more confidence. "It wouldn't be office work."

"What, then?"

"I don't know. I'd like to go to college, then decide."

Leaning back in her chair, Miss Jensen asked, "What's holding you back?"

"My parents. Money."

A kindly smile appeared on the supervisor's face. "Where there's a will, there's a way." She stood, terminating their talk. "Meanwhile, practice your typing."

Miss Jensen wasn't so bad, after all.

Eight pairs of inquisitive eyes glanced her way as Anna made her way past the bank of identical desks. With little enthusiasm she rolled a fresh sheet of paper with five carbons into her Underwood and silently begged her fingers to punch the correct keys.

That night at the dinner table, when her mother asked how the job was going, Anna risked a complaint. "I don't like it, Ma."

"You don't like it, eh? You wouldn't listen to me and work in the shop, no, you don't like that either."

Anna mumbled, "Luisa can work for you. She likes that kind of stuff."

"Your father says a government job is the best you can get; it's secure."

"I hate office work."

Her mother, hands on hips, observed Anna. "Mike, what are we going to do with this girl? She has a nice job in a nice office and she hates it."

Reaching for a chunk of bread, her father remarked absently, "It's still new. She'll get used to it."

Anna's mouth formed a pout. "Agnes is going to Wayne University. Her parents *want* her to go." Her friend fairly gushed with excitement when she talked about college. She had already chosen her classes and planned on trying out for the cheerleading squad. But with less and less in common, the girls seemed to be drifting gradually apart, much to Anna's chagrin.

Luisa, who always hated to hear arguments, said, "Did you see you got a letter, Ma, from Italy? It's on the hall table."

"Ah, good. It's been a while since I've had news. Run and get it, Tina."

Her mother's eyes misted over, as usual, even before she opened the letter. She scanned the contents, and this time she didn't begin reading aloud. Her hands, holding the letter, dropped heavily into her lap, and her face crumbled.

"What's wrong, Ma?" Anna let her fork clank against the plate.

"My father had a stroke." Ma hugged her arms to herself, tears dribbling from her eyes, and rocked back and forth in her chair, not saying a word.

Pa went to her and held her shoulders. He picked up the letter and read it quickly. "He's paralyzed on the left side, but the doctor thinks he'll recover."

Ma wiped her eyes on a napkin. "I want to see him, Mike. What if he dies?" Her mouth was set in that determined line. "We're going home."

Home. Italy. That fairy-tale land that Anna had heard so much about; that sunny, paradoxical place of both richness and poverty.

They would all go, her father decided. And when Anna timidly mentioned visiting Dante, Pa said, yes, of course, as long as we're there, we'll visit Dante. Her heart thrummed. Dante had never completely left her thoughts; Dante, a shadowy figure in the corner of her consciousness, who enriched her fantasies and sparked romance in her soul. He was her Valentino, her John Wayne, her Tyrone Power.

At last she would see Dante again.

They flew from Willow Run Airport to La Guardia in New York. The trip from New York to Rome seemed a circuitous one, Chiara thought, with stops for refueling in Newfoundland and the Azores before finally landing in Rome. The children begged to stay a few days in the city, and extracted a promise from Mike that they would do so on their way back to America.

On the train bound for Bari, Chiara's excitement heightened with each mile that brought them closer to home. Scenes flowed past, a moving travelogue of sleepy towns and rugged hills, straw-hatted toilers bending over hoes on their small plots of earth, tethered goats idling in the shade, placid sheep grazing, glimpses of concrete row houses topped with rusty-hued tile roofs in half-hidden valleys.

When they neared their destination, Chiara gave Anna a stern look. "Better take off the lipstick. Your grandmother would be shocked at that red mouth." She tapped Luisa's shoulder. "Comb your hair." She wet a tissue to wipe Tina's face and gave the impatient seven-year-old a little shake when she tried to wrench free. "Quit wiggling. It's the next stop."

The train had hardly ground to a halt when Chiara nudged the three girls ahead down the metal steps. Mike brought up the rear, his arms loaded with luggage. At the top step Chiara's hand went involuntarily upward to shade her eyes against the bright sun as she searched the small crowd for a familiar face.

"There!" she shouted. "There's Mama!"

Tears streaming from her eyes, her short legs pumping furiously, Chiara's mother hurried toward them. She caught Chiara in a tight embrace while they both cried with joy, then moved her aside to draw each grandchild into the circle of her arms. Anna and Luisa, though not so tall themselves, towered over their little grandmother.

Murmuring their names over and over again, "Anna and Luisa and Tina," their *nonna* went from one to the other, scattering moist kisses over their faces. Pushing them an arm's length away, she studied each one with awe and delight, then began the cycle of kisses all over again.

She looks so much older, Chiara thought, smaller, rounder, more bent. But her hair was still thick, with wide wings of white at the temples, worn, as always, in a tight bun.

Mike, observing the scene with an indulgent smile, finally came into his share of hugging too. Chiara noticed a tall, handsome young man who had come up behind her mother and now stood patiently aside, watching with amusement.

With sudden recognition, Chiara realized the grinning youth was her brother.

"Dino!" she burst out, grabbing him tightly round the neck. "My baby brother."

"Not a baby," Dino said, lifting her easily off the ground.

"You look so much like Papa," Chiara said, noting the blue eyes and reddish hair, the set of the jaw. But with his white shoes and tight jacket, he had the appearance of a dandy.

When they finished with all the greetings, Dino said, "*Avanti.* The others are home waiting, preparing a feast. I've borrowed a car for the ride home." He hoisted two bags and herded them along to the car. "You'll meet my new wife, Ninetta." An unmistakable note of pride crept into his voice.

How had the years slid by so quickly? Chiara wondered as Dino stashed their luggage in the trunk of the car. Her brother had been frozen in her memory as a toddler, despite the occasional photographs depicting a young man. Now he was practically a stranger. She remembered the way his thumb had sneaked up to his mouth when she sang him to sleep. But of course, he wouldn't remember that.

Her father was not up to the trip to Bari, her mother explained after they all crammed into the ancient Chrysler.

As they drove along the road by the sea, the Lungomare, a whiff of tangy salt air wafted into the open window.

Chiara turned her gaze toward her beloved Adriatic, as brilliant as she'd always remembered.

"You see? What did I tell you about the sea? It's beautiful, *non è vero?* Sometimes you can see Yugoslavia."

The car nosed west and made its uneven way toward rolling green hills.

"Look, look," Chiara commanded after they'd bounced along for almost an hour. Ahead, the village spread out like a colorful painting—the piazza with its ornate statuary and fountain; small shops with patrons lolling in their doorways; rows of stone houses wedged together; a naked toddler playing in the road.

"Ah, time has almost stood still." Chiara craned her neck in all directions. "It looks much the same, just a bit smaller and shabier."

As Dino maneuvered the car through narrow passages, Chiara pointed to several three-story structures. "What are those new buildings?"

"Apartments," Dino said. "Government-built. And we have sewers, water pipes, and electricity now."

"Eh, sometimes it all works; more times, it doesn't," her mother said with the well-remembered little sneer of contempt for "government" projects.

When the car pulled up to their house, her father shuffled out, leaning heavily on a cane.

Papa looked a bit thinner now, but the blue eyes that dominated his face were still sharp. His gaunt leathery face was capped by a thatch of totally white hair. He hugged the girls all at once in his bearlike arms, kissed Mike on each cheek, then pulled Chiara to him, enfolding her gently with mewling noises, too overcome to speak.

Inside, her sisters Gabriella and Tonina waited their turn. Gabriella hugged them all and introduced first her husband, then the seven beautiful children who stood in a row like stair steps.

The last time Chiara had seen Gabriella, she'd looked vibrant and beautiful, but now the beauty had faded, and she appeared simply weary. Her husband seemed much older than she, a squat, complacent man with a perpetual smile. They lived in a government apartment, she said. It was small and cramped, but what could one do? It was shelter.

Acceptance, Chiara thought, the family trademark and its strength, or so she had always believed. Now she wondered. Could blind acceptance be detrimental, could it hold one back?

Tonina had twins and expected another child in three months. She lived with her parents while her husband worked in Milan. He managed to come home every two or three months.

Dino's wife, Ninetta, shook hands shyly. She was very young, slim and fashionable, and, Chiara noted, wore bright red lipstick.

Missing was Carlo, who with his wife and three children lived in Argentina now, and apparently made a good living.

After the effusive greetings, Chiara looked around her. It was all much the same. She had the strange sensation that time had stood still. The south of Italy had once been described as the "land that time forgot." Perhaps it was truer than she would like to believe.

Yet there were some changes. A room had been added to the back of the little house, and some of the older furniture had been replaced. The dining table, newer, longer, but otherwise hardly distinguishable from the old one, almost groaned with the weight of food. In the place of honor on the wall was a picture of San Nicola di Bari surrounded by photographs of the family, mostly the Marcassa children in various stages of growth.

Veal, linguini, fresh vegetables, and a ricotta pie were set out on the table. The dinner conversation was at first self-conscious and halting. We are related, Chiara thought, yet at this moment strangers to one another; even Mama and Papa, who are blood of my blood, heart of my heart, seem distant, unfamiliar.

At the end of the meal, when they lingered over the last of the *vino*, Chiara had a fleeting sensation of the child she had been, felt again a comforting envelopment in her parents' love, the delicious security of being a beloved child. But she wasn't a child, and her parents were not the same people she'd left as a young bride. It had seemed then that her family and her village and its inhabitants would always remain the same, like scenes in a book, but she could see that the attitudes were changing, the religiosity not so pervasive, modern ways more accepted. Even her siblings hadn't been nearly so restricted as she. Yes, there were changes, subtle ones. The world turns, and everything with it.

Ninetta, close in age to Anna, quickly lost her shyness and became friendly and talkative, though the conversation between the younger people proceeded slowly and erratically, with laughing translations between phrases.

"Did you bring magazines?" Ninetta asked. "I love American magazines."

"No, but I'll mail some when we get back home," Anna assured her.

"Your clothes are so lovely; like some I've seen in the cinema. Have you ever seen a cinema star?"

Anna smiled and shook her head. "Hollywood is a long way from Detroit."

Youth are alike the world over, Chiara thought.

After draining his wineglass, her father excused himself and went to bed. He tired easily now, Dino explained. Chiara signaled to Anna and Luisa with her eyes to help Ninetta wash the dishes.

Chiara heard Ninetta tell the girls with candor, "Your *nonna* has been saving to buy the best food for your visit. You know, with Emilio's small pension, there's not too much left. Tonina's husband sends back money from Milan, but . . ." She shrugged, leaving the obvious unsaid. So things were not so good after all, Chiara thought. Her parents wouldn't take money, she felt certain, but perhaps Mike could arrange to deposit some cash and have the bank inform her parents after the Marcassas returned to America.

Dusk was descending when Chiara and her daughters crowded onto the little balcony.

"This is where I always said my morning prayers." Chiara's smile was nostalgic.

"So this is the balcony you always talked about," Luisa said. "I used to think it was like in *Romeo and Juliet*."

Chiara laughed. "This was my private place, where I dreamed my silly dreams." She must have been Luisa's age when she had entertained visions of . . . What? She couldn't even remember now. Of love, she supposed, and a family, and a home of her own. And now she had all that, and she had no more dreams. Was that a sign that she was growing old? She was forty-five—not so old.

Almost imperceptibly her shoulders straightened. She would have to thwart the aging process, and begin dreaming again.

Her hand reached out to stroke Luisa's fair hair. Sweet, docile Luisa, fourteen years old. What sort of dreams did she have? Did she yearn for a sweetheart? She never spoke of boys the way Anna and other girls did. But she had always been the quiet one; her dreams were secret ones. Chiara drew Luisa to her in an affectionate hug. Touching and hugging, she realized, became less frequent as her children grew older.

Luisa dropped her head on her mother's shoulder with a contented sigh. "It's so peaceful here."

Chiara yawned, realizing how tired she was. "It's late now. We've had a tiring journey. Better get to bed."

Pallets were made up for the girls, and Chiara and Mike retired to her old room.

"This place seems strange—different, *foreign* somehow," Chiara admitted, slipping into bed beside her husband. "Did I forget the way it used to be, Mike?"

Mike slipped his arm under her shoulder. "The memory plays tricks. You remember things the way they were when you were a child. You think everything will remain the same. But everything changes, not only the physical things, like young parents becoming old, children becoming adults, new buildings. Other things change too—society, attitudes, governments."

Chiara was silent for a few moments, digesting Mike's words. "When I was a little girl we would wash dishes with the water we used to boil pasta. We had oil lamps, made our own bread and clothing." Chiara's hand found Mike's and she wound her fingers through his. "Home always seemed like a special place. Now it doesn't seem so special."

"Everything changes." Mike yawned. "Go to sleep now, my dear Chiara."

When she finally nodded off, Chiara's dreams were scattered and strange, of a long-ago childhood and a little girl who was a stranger to the woman she had become.

Chiara, her finger to her lips for quiet, woke Mike early the next morning while the children slept. Neither spoke on their stroll to the church where they'd been married. A warm breeze frisked through Chiara's hair as she took Mike's arm and entered through the battered wooden doors of the simple stone edifice. Kneeling with her husband beside her at the linen-covered altar, Chiara had no prayers to offer, no thanks to give, no supplications. Her heart felt heavy, her mind filled with images of Roberto. He would have been twenty-two years old.

When Mike nudged her shoulder, she arose heavily and they left through a side door. The graveyard was silent except for a pair of birds trilling in a cypress tree. A few wilted flowers bowed their heads at neglected graves. After so many years, Chiara had thought the wound would be healed. But the sight of the small headstone, with ROBERTO MARCASSA inscribed, brought back memories of that last misbegotten trip home. Clearly she saw his sweet face, remembered, with a visceral stab, his limp body lying inert in her arms.

She remained immobile while tears streamed down her face. When she looked at Mike, she saw his tears too, and reached her hand to him.

"Our son," Mike said. He turned and gathered Chiara into his arms, squeezing tightly, and they remained that way for several moments. No other words were spoken. They needed none. The scar would always remain on their hearts.

Luisa always felt at home in a church, be it a chapel or a basilica, like the one they approached later that afternoon in Bari. A bride and groom emerged from the wide doors of the basilica of San Nicola di Bari. Well-wishers kissed the smiling couple and others took pictures as the entourage moved to the horse-drawn carriage decorated with fresh flowers.

Her mother, Luisa noticed, scrutinized the wedding gown, probably taking mental notes for some future design. Chiara sighed with pleasure. "You girls will be beautiful brides someday, like that one."

Luisa felt a niggling worm of discomfort, as she often did when her mother alluded to marriage. Was it ordained that all women be married? What if she wasn't interested in men and marriage? Even Comare Maria had said that she didn't see a wedding in Luisa's future.

"I don't know if I want to get married," Luisa said.

Chiara dismissed her remark as they proceeded past the tall doors of the basilica. "Of course you'll get married."

They wandered through the cavernous church and stopped to pray at an altar.

"This church was built before Christ. The remains of Saint Nicholas, Santa Claus, are buried here," Mike informed them as he scanned a brochure.

"So Santa Claus is Italian," Tina murmured.

"He was a bishop in Asia Minor. Many years after he died, his bones were stolen from Asia by Italian sailors and brought to rest here."

Anna looked around her. "Where are the pews?"

"There aren't any pews. People stand for Mass or rent a folding chair," Mike answered, tugging a recalcitrant Tina along. "One more reason why you don't see many men in church." He continued reading, then reported, "This was the first church to be built in Apulia, in the ninth century."

"It's lovely, but so big and . . . and impersonal," Luisa said.

"I always thought that too," Chiara said. "I know the sort of place you'd like. Tomorrow I'll take you to my favorite spot, the grotto of the Blessed Virgin. It's small and simple, about a mile out in the country, just a place to stop for a little prayer."

While the others were still asleep the next morning, Luisa stole to her mother's room and reminded her of her promise. As they trudged down the dusty road, the sun warming their backs, Chiara said, "I used to stop often at the grotto to rest awhile. What a sweet feeling of peace I'd get. They say many young women feel the call to a vocation when they pray there."

"Did you ever want to join the convent?" Luisa asked.

Chiara gave a short laugh. "No, I hated the idea. To me the convent represented a prison, a place for women who had lost all hope of getting married—old maids. I was so afraid I'd be one of them. But your father saved me."

"Ma, it's not a prison, not at our school. The sisters have some freedom."

"Well, it's different in America. Maybe it's different here now too."

Daisies grew wild along the path to the grotto, and

stones impeded their steps. The grotto itself, a natural indentation in the hillside, held a statue of the Blessed Virgin, her feet upon a globe, her arms holding the infant Jesus. Nearby, the crystal-clear water of a mountain stream burbled pleasantly.

"It's not a work of art." Her mother touched the hem and her face relaxed and settled into contentment. "The mantle used to be blue, but now it's a faded gray. Still, it takes me back to when I was a child."

Luisa was entranced with the beatific smile, the thin webbed lines on the Virgin's toes, the delicate turn of her hand. "She's lovely. I almost feel like I've been here before."

Kneeling, she made the sign of the cross, her eyes fixed on the statue. A feeling of tranquillity settled over her and she closed her eyes and let her mind empty of all thought. She had learned to pray, to really use prayer as a communication with God, during those devastating and lonely months when she was ill with polio. Left alone for long periods, she had battled with the despair that comes from fear. At first her prayers were desperate pleas, but later she simply surrendered to his will. Her trust had turned the tide. Trust that she would indeed recover, trust that he wouldn't give her a greater cross than she could bear. When Dr. Catrone had seen her progress a year later, he called it a miracle. Perhaps it was.

She knelt for a long while, transfixed, until her mother finally tapped her shoulder, saying softly, "We should get back now."

Luisa roused herself and floated back to reality. For a moment she had forgotten where she was.

"You were off in another world," her mother said, her eyes narrowing. "I had to almost shake you."

Reaching out, Luisa touched her mother's cheek. "I *was* in another world."

They walked back to the village arm in arm, not speaking, enveloped in a cloak of serenity.

The next morning Luisa awakened before daybreak and stole away to the grotto by herself. She felt pulled, involuntarily, by invisible threads, down the narrow steps, out the door, through the sleeping village.

The sun was almost directly overhead when she returned. Her mother waited at the door with an angry scowl.

"Luisa, where were you?"

Very softly Luisa said, "I had to go to the grotto again."

She walked to the courtyard in back, and her mother followed her, shaking a fist. "You should have told me. I worried. Your father is out looking for you."

Unperturbed by her mother's anger, Luisa plucked a pink oleander from the bush that grew at the edge of the courtyard and buried her face in its petals. Nothing could mar her happiness at that moment.

"Mother, I've made a decision. I want to be a nun."

Her mother's eyes opened wide. "You what?"

"I have a vocation. I always thought so, and yesterday at the grotto, I felt it so strongly . . . then today, I thought it would disappear, that feeling, but no, it was still there. I want to be a nun."

"A nun!"

"Yes. Why are you so shocked? I've often thought about it. Now I'm certain. The Blessed Virgin is calling to me."

"A nun!" Her mother, who had words for every occasion, could only repeat those two words with a bewildered look on her face.

Luisa put her arms around her mother. "Aren't you happy? Please be happy for me."

"Well, I . . . I don't know what to think. Yes, of course. Yes, I'm happy." Her mother suddenly burst into tears.

"Ma, don't cry."

"It's just that it's so . . . so sudden. You're young, just fourteen!" Her mother sniffed. "I thought you would go into the bridal business with me."

"It's really not so sudden. I did a lot of praying when I had polio, and decided God had saved me from crippling for a reason."

Her mother sat heavily on a backless chair. "Yes, I remember how you would lie in bed, always with a rosary, rolling one bead after another in your small dry hands."

Luisa patted her mother's head. "Don't say anything just yet to Anna and Tina. I want to tell them myself, after we get back home."

"I won't say anything." Her mother looked stricken. "You may change your mind."

"I thought you'd be pleased."

"I am pleased." Her mother drew her into a hug, but her words sounded hollow. "This is a big decision. You're not sure about it."

"I'm sure."

Later, Chiara tried to sort out her contradictory feelings. Certainly she *should* be pleased for Luisa, happy and thankful that one of her children had a calling. Then why was she dismayed? Wouldn't any mother be proud to have a religious in the family? But Luisa, her sweet Luisa, her good, obedient daughter, the one she thought would grow up to help her manage the bridal salon . . .

When everyone was asleep, Chiara beckoned Mike to the courtyard, where she told him Luisa's decision. "I should have guessed, Mike. Why, just to look at Luisa's face, you can tell there's a sort of *goodness* there."

Mike was just as bewildered as Chiara had been. "Well, maybe we'll have a little pull in heaven, when the time comes," he said finally, with an uneasy laugh.

"It was the polio that did it." Chiara pulled a dying geranium blossom from its stem and watched the faded petals scatter. "The sickness made her too withdrawn, too somber. We were always thankful that she wasn't interested in boys and parties, but now I wonder. Maybe it wasn't natural. Even on Saturdays, Luisa always goes to church. The others would rather sleep in. Luisa *is* different."

"I would think you'd be happy," Mike said.

"I should be, shouldn't I? But it's like . . . like we're losing her."

"Yes, it *is* like that. Our girl wants to leave us." Mike's voice cracked.

Perhaps when they returned home, Luisa would change her mind. But it didn't seem likely.

Chiara would have to pray once again for acceptance.

—— 34 ——

The bus's erratic movements, its spurious starts and stops, did nothing to settle Anna's already uneasy stomach. Now that they were finally on their way to Dante's villa, her insides fairly quivered with anticipation. At last she would see him again. Dante. Closing her eyes, she imagined his face, the direct eyes of liquid velvet, the unruly black hair, the appealing cleft she remembered wanting to press her finger to.

Since the trip had begun taking shape, her thoughts of Dante were charged with excitement. But it was seven years since she'd last seen him. A lot could happen in that time. He could have a girlfriend, could even be engaged. But, no, surely he would have mentioned a fiancée in his most recent letter, the one urging them to visit.

It was foolish rainbow-chasing, she knew, to feel this way about a romantic figure from her past. But her reckless, eager heart seemed unable to reason.

Did he think about her? If he did, was it as a "little sister"? She *had* been a child then, a silly, awkward girl. His attitude during those visits had been a bit playful, like that of a brother. His letters, the few she'd received (hidden in an empty heart-shaped red-satin candy box), were warm and teasingly affectionate, the way one would behave toward a favorite sister.

Well, that was all right. She could change his perception. She was attractive, she knew. But she had only three days. And the ever-watchful eyes of her parents would be on her. Oh, if only she could be alone with Dante, even for a few precious moments.

The bus lurched, jarring her forward in her seat.

Her father tapped her shoulder. "Almost there," he said.

Anna craned her neck to peer out the dusty window. Her eyes scanned the faces of the few people loitering about, waiting for the passengers to disembark. Dante wasn't among them. Had he forgotten? Had there been an accident?

As they exited the bus, a squarely built, beady-eyed man wearing an old, unpressed suit approached them. "Marcassa?" he asked, squinting up at her father.

"Yes."

"Signor Ravenna apologizes for not coming himself, but there was some business . . ." He picked up the larger pieces of luggage. "I'm Salvatore. Come along." His chin pointed to a vintage American Packard. He tossed their luggage into the trunk and settled the group in the car.

As Salvatore squashed his cap firmly on his head, he explained, "There was a problem with some of the workers. Everyone wants more money, eh? No one is satisfied. Not the pickers or the winemakers. For me, I shut my mouth and do my job. You like the motorcar? It's one of several belonging to Don Ravenna, Dante's father. He likes American cars, but for me, they are too big. I like to drive a Fiat; it's small and quick."

As he navigated through the narrow streets of the town, he kept up a commentary, not waiting for responses. "I and my father before me worked for the Ravennas. A fine family. Have you ever tasted the Ravenna wine? No? Then you will soon see how fine it is."

When he turned the car northward, he pointed to lush vineyards as far as the eye could see. "Ravenna grapes. All this belongs to the Ravenna family." His arm made a sweeping arc over the verdant landscape. Anna's eyes widened at the vast acres of grape vines. Dante's family must be very well-off indeed.

Presently they came to a concrete wall, gleaming white in the sunlight, which curved around to a huge dark green wrought-iron gate. Salvatore stopped the car and tugged open the gate, muttering at its resistance, then resettled in the seat and drove up a gravel drive that stretched to a lovely pink villa as large as a small hotel.

Stone statuary, chipped in places, lined the drive, while cypress and pine trees dotted the parklike garden. Salvatore parked at the entrance and opened the doors for his passengers. Brilliant geraniums sprang profusely from huge clay pots on the portico. It was breathtaking, Anna thought, like a picture postcard.

The door opened and Dante walked out, his arms wide in welcome. He was not quite as Anna remembered him. He had filled out, his broad shoulders almost straining the fabric of his sporty tweed jacket, his thighs powerful against knife-pressed trousers. Dark hair appeared at the V of his open-collared shirt. Anna's memories had imprisoned him in a time and place, in his prisoner's garb of dark green. The flesh-and-blood Dante glowed with a self-confident maturity.

Anna stood back as Dante ran down the steps to greet them. Though his face was a bit fuller, the vivid, well-remembered features stood out: dark straight eyebrows over intense, almost black eyes, prominent cheekbones, a surprisingly tender-looking mouth, ebony hair, thick and curly. First he touched cheeks with her mother and father, then made a big fuss over Tina and how she'd grown. Luisa came to his attention next. He was pleased, he said, to see her looking so healthy after her ordeal. She had turned into a lovely young lady. Finally his gaze fell on Anna.

"Ah, Anna." His eyes narrowed a bit. "You've grown to be a beauty, as I knew you would."

Anna's heart thumped at his frank admiration.

"Yes, all my girls are beautiful, *non è vero?*" her father said.

Dante's hand shot out to slap her father's shoulder in friendly camaraderie. "All of them," he agreed, "including their mother."

The woman who met them at the door wore a single strand of pearls at her long, graceful neck, and an elegantly simple navy-blue dress. Her graying hair was swept into deep side waves and gathered into a chignon at the back. "This is my mother," Dante said, introducing everyone.

Signora Ravenna repeated their names with a gracious smile. "Dante has spoken of you so many times. It's a great pleasure to welcome you. Our home is your home."

"You will meet my father at supper," Dante said, showing them into the large drawing room.

The house was like a museum, only homier, and radiated a serenity that spoke of money and privilege. Anna, awestruck at the richness that surrounded them, gazed about her at the tapestries and carved wood and marble-topped tables on gently curving legs and colorful carpets that didn't quite hide the exquisite floor tiles arranged in unique designs.

They were offered sweet bread, fruit, and coffee, then taken on a tour of the house. One room led to another and another. One could easily become lost in this place, Anna thought. They exited through a double door in the rear and found themselves on a lovely garden terrace encircled by a wall of shrubbery. Beyond flat stone steps, exotic flowers with enchanting scents nodded in the light breeze.

Signora Ravenna spoke of the history of the house—a portrait of an ancestor, a voluptuous contessa, hung in the dining room—and occasionally directed a remark to Anna and her sisters in British-accented English.

Afterward they were shown to their rooms. Her parents had one bedroom, Luisa and Tina shared another, and Anna had her own. Heavy mauve brocade draperies matched the spread and the chaise. Twin armoires, side by side, were intricately carved in a flower-and-vine design.

"The plumbing is sometimes erratic," Dante apologized. "If you have a problem, or need something, ring for the servant." He indicated the long embroidered pull next to the bed. "Dinner is at seven. I'll be on the terrace."

Did his eyes hold an invitation? Did he mean he wanted her to come to him there?

She bathed quickly. Her red dress—yes, she looked good in red . . . the belt nipped in her already tiny waist— her hair pulled back, *his* necklace at her throat, a bit of lipstick and mascara, and down the stairs. Now, if she could only find the proper door. Ah, this way, through a hallway and past the dining room.

Dante, pacing, turned when he heard her footsteps. He smiled as she approached, and stubbed out a cigarette in a potted plant. He held his hands out to her, then pulled her close in a light embrace. He moved back, assessing her as if she were a bauble he was considering buying.

"You are lovely, my dear Anna. Have you any idea how many times I've thought of you? Your letters were so delightful. They made me smile."

He enjoyed them, then, the letters she scribbled over and over until they met with her approval.

She felt a blush rising to betray her lack of sophistication. "Oh, I'm sure they were silly schoolgirl notes."

"Not at all." He led her to a secluded grove, where thick shrubbery circled a white wrought-iron settee. "Come, sit and tell me what you've been doing with your life."

How easily the words tumbled from her. Some in Italian, most in English. He stopped her at unfamiliar words, asking for explanation, then nodded encouragement. His gaze invited confidence, his warm hand on hers was reassuring, as she told him of her unhappy job experience, of her desire to go to college, of her vague discontent.

"But why would you want to spend time in a university, poring over books?" he asked. "It's tedious; I know because I've done it." He jostled her hand lightly in his own. "No, Anna, you should be a rich man's wife, and bear children as sweet as yourself. You should live in a fine villa and have servants to do your bidding." He kissed her hand and lifted his eyes to hers, holding her in a spell. Tipping her chin upward with his thumb, he drew toward her slowly, so slowly. When his lips reached hers, she was enthralled at his gentle, sweet kiss.

Oh, it was delicious, his mouth moving against hers, his hand wandering lazily over her shoulders and her neck.

Somewhere, far off, a bell tinkled a tune, intruding into the enchantment. Hesitantly Dante pulled away and then gently kissed her neck below her ear. "The dinner summons. We must go in now. But later . . ."

The words were left unsaid as his mother passed the door and called out to them. "Ah, there you are. And Anna too. Come, Dante, you know your father likes his meal on time."

Don Pietro Ravenna was not an imposing man, as Anna had supposed he would be. He was small and dapper, with a thin mustache, not at all like his son.

Dante didn't resemble his mother either, Anna thought, wondering where he got his height.

Dante's mother yanked a tasseled pull and a servant appeared. She ladled soup from a steaming tureen into their bowls. The soup had a delicate fish flavor and herbs Anna couldn't identify.

Don Pietro addressed her father. "I understand you make your own wine, also, *signore.*"

"Yes, but it doesn't compare to this." Raising his goblet to the light, Mike assessed the claret liquid. "I only make a barrel or two each year for myself and my friends."

"Don't be modest. Your wine was excellent, as I recall," Dante said. "My father is thinking of exporting his product to the United States. What do you think, Michele, is there a market?"

"I don't profess to be an expert on the subject, but yes, I should think wine like this would sell."

Dante proposed a toast to both their families and to their continued friendship. He looked directly at Anna as he drew out the word "friendship."

Tina, sitting next to Anna, fidgeted in her chair until Anna nudged her and gave her a warning look.

The conversation had shifted to Dante.

"We don't know what to do with him. He doesn't want to settle down, no, he wants to be a playboy." His mother laughed indulgently. "I tell him, 'It's time, Dante, for some grandchildren,' but he doesn't want to hear that. It's not for lack of girlfriends, I can tell you."

Dante merely rolled his eyes at his mother's lament, while his father said indulgently, "In due time, my dear."

When Dante caught Anna's eye, he winked conspiratorially.

Anna observed the Ravenna family during the leisurely dinner. Both parents seemed to dote on Dante. And why not? He appeared to be a good and dutiful son and had obviously become a valuable partner to his father in the wine business. Dante seemed to adore them too. As the only child, he would inherit this magnificent estate and a lucrative business. There was a catch at Anna's heart when she glanced at that handsome, aristocratic face. All the boys back home paled by comparison. And when he looked at her with those large liquid eyes, she could hardly keep from trembling. He had hinted at their meeting later. If only she could escape her parents for a little while tonight . . .

The meal stretched on, with talk and laughter, and after a dessert of raspberry ice, Dante and his father led Mike into the library for more wine and cigars, while Dona Adela, as Dante's mother preferred to be called, showed the women into one of the parlors and offered Anna and Chiara a sweet liqueur. To Anna's surprise, her mother said nothing when Anna took the brandy glass.

The two older women talked about raising children, about the havoc wreaked by the war, about fashions, but Anna hardly heard the words swirling around her. She wondered what the men were talking about, and if Dante were thinking of her, as she was of him. He had glanced at her often across the table, his eyes approving, his smile inviting. Would he be waiting on the terrace for her later, when the others had all gone to bed?

When her mother noticed Tina yawning, she caught Anna's eye. "Anna, look, your sister's tired. Take her up to bed."

Luisa rescued her. "I'll do it, Ma. I'm tired too."

The two younger girls kissed their mother good night and thanked Dona Adela for the fine supper while Anna wondered if they would find their way through the labyrinthine halls.

Dona Adela drew Anna out, asking what her school had been like, what sort of hobbies she had. Anna had difficulty focusing her attention on the conversation and away from thoughts of Dante.

"My own hobbies are a little gardening and some painting. My life," Dona Adela admitted, "is centered around my two men. I suppose I've spoiled them. But now, I'm sure you are both tired after your long bus ride. Don't let me hold you back if you'd like to retire."

To Anna's relief, her mother admitted, "I am a little weary."

Dona Adela rose. "Then get your rest and we'll visit the city tomorrow. There's the basilica, and interesting old shops and the piazza."

In her bedroom, Anna recombed her hair, wishing it were longer, instead of the "cap" cut that was fashionable. Still, it was becoming, thick and shiny. She freshened her lipstick, then, pressing her ear to the door, listened for sounds. Stealthily she opened the door and tiptoed down the hall, mentally preparing an excuse should anyone see her. *Oh, please, please let him be there.* She fairly flew down the steps and through dimly lit halls to the terrace. The terrace doors were slightly ajar and she stepped through, halting after a few steps.

When her eyes adjusted to the blackness, she made out furniture scattered here and there, a low table, settees and chairs. But no Dante. Her disappointment was palpable.

A single night bird's song trilled in the heavy, flower-fragrant air. The only light came from the moon, gleaming as if whitewashed.

"Here, Anna."

Her heart stopped as she turned toward Dante's voice. She vaguely discerned his silhouette outlined in a chair at the far end of the terrace. As she glided toward him, his expression came alive, though he sat still as a statue. He watched her with amusement and beckoned her closer. His knees spread and he took her hands and drew her to him. She inhaled the faint smell of wine, the tobacco clinging to his clothes. His head tilted up to her, eyes half-closed, seductive, inviting.

"I watched you all through dinner, did you notice?" he whispered.

"Yes. I watched you too."

"I wanted to reach out and touch you. You're very beautiful, you know." Gently his hands touched her shoulders and pressed her downward, to her knees. Taking her face in his hands, he leaned toward her until his mouth was above her own. She made the small movement forward to kiss his waiting lips. Anna was immediately engulfed in a floating sensation, light-headed and buoyant. *Oh, please, let this kiss last forever.*

Dante's mouth moved insistently against Anna's. His hand grazed her breast, stirring unnamed passions in her young, maidenly body. A rapturous awakening, a budding sensuality, enveloped her. She was vaguely aware of the sultry perfume of unfamiliar flowers and a serenade from a chorus of cicadas.

Abruptly Dante released her. "What am I doing? I'm sorry, Anna," he murmured. "Too much wine."

Anna, longing for his mouth to return to hers, yearned toward him. "No, I let you. And I didn't have too much wine."

Dante, his hands on her shoulders, held her steadily, and smiled. "Anna, I can't betray your parents' friendship, their trust." He pulled her gently upright. "We'll talk again tomorrow."

He steered her toward the door, his hand on her arm.

"Oh, please, Dante, let's stay out here awhile longer."

He turned her toward him. "Listen to me, Anna. I don't trust myself alone with you, not now. You're too . . . young, too innocent."

"Well, I wish I weren't!"

His laugh echoed on the darkened terrace as he took her arm and led her indoors. At her bedroom door he brushed his lips across her cheek. "Good night, sweet Anna."

"Good night, Dante." But Anna made no move to go inside.

With a rueful grin, Dante opened her door and gently pushed her into the moon-washed room.

For a long time Anna lay on her bed, fully clothed, reliving the emotion of his kiss. She was in love with Dante. She had been since she was eleven years old. And he loved her too. He hadn't said so, but he would. His kiss expressed far more than words ever could. Before she left, she would extract from him a declaration of love, she was sure of it.

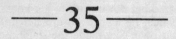

—— 35 ——

Mike awakened to the cock's crow early the next morning and stole to the window. Breathing deeply, he thumped his chest, engulfed in a feeling of well-being.

The view was spectacular. Immediately below his window an expanse of grass and trees rolled toward the unending vineyards. In the distance a road wound to the mountain, where, half-hidden, a brown fortresslike building peeped from the surrounding greenery like brushstrokes in a painting. This was the enchanted Italy of his dreams.

As he hastily dressed, he glanced at Chiara. She stirred and lifted one sleepy lid.

"It's early," he whispered. "Go back to sleep." The trip had been tiring for her, and the visit to the graveyard emotional for them both.

Old memories stirred again, of his adored son, Roberto, whose short life had been snuffed out by a disease that was now almost nonexistent. He'd had such plans for the boy; plans to help him achieve the American dream that was there for the grabbing. Under his father's tutelage, Roberto would have been hardworking, dedicated, and tenacious. He would have been tough but fair, strong but kind. He might have followed in his father's footsteps, a union man. Mike had always hoped they'd have another son. That the family name would die with Mike would always be a source of regret.

Chiara turned with a fluttery sigh. Mike dropped a kiss on her forehead and left, closing the door softly behind him.

He must content himself with his girls. They were reward enough, all three bright as well as beautiful.

Mike hadn't realized how much he needed a vacation. He was fifty-three years old and had been working since he was a child. In Detroit, day and night he was plagued with union troubles; problems such as mediating strikes, dealing with communist infiltration, fighting for a pension plan, and any number of other issues, major and minor.

There was union progress, nonetheless. Walter Reuther had risen to the presidency of the UAW, and under his brilliant direction, gains had been achieved that in the thirties had been only outrageous dreams. And yet, each victory was a battle in itself, and each skirmish took its toll. Mike realized he'd become battle-fatigued in the never-ending union war.

Fortunately, employment was up, but it was because of the Korean conflict. The paradox of war being the catalyst that provided work and profit vexed Mike.

During the past week he had gradually shed the weighty responsibilities of his job and had begun to enjoy himself—not difficult in this paradise. Chiara used to say she wanted to retire in the old country, and he had ridiculed her. But now, surrounded by such elegance and grace, it didn't seem like such a bad idea.

Closing the door quietly behind him, he encountered the keen aroma of freshly brewed coffee, a smell that never failed to quicken his senses. He followed it into the kitchen and saw Dante at the table, laughing with the cook while he ate a hearty breakfast.

"*Ah, buona mattina, Michele,*" Dante said, wiping his mouth with a large napkin. "Let Minna make you some breakfast."

"I'd like just coffee, please."

"My father regrets he can't be here to show you around. He doesn't take much time away from his work. Even though he could leave things to his manager, he likes to make sure everything is working smoothly."

"I can understand that." Michele sipped the strong brew Minna had set before him and munched on a thick slice of dark bread awash with pale yellow butter.

"I'd like to take you for a drive around the countryside. Finish your coffee and we'll take the new Lancia Aurelia. It's a beauty.

The spotless garage housed four cars. Besides the Packard that had ferried them from the bus yesterday and the gleaming white Lancia, there were an Alfa Romeo and a Fiat, all shining with a waxy luster.

Michele climbed into the Lancia beside Dante. Looking very much at home behind the wheel, Dante tapped the accelerator, bringing the engine to life. The powerful machine, humming with vigor, nosed forward and onto the dusty road.

"What is that building high on the hill?" Mike pointed to the turreted rectangle jutting into the clouds. "I noticed it from my bedroom window. It looks like an abbey."

"It is an abbey, or what you might call a convent. My aunt is a nun there. It's a magnificent structure, *non è vero?* Over four centuries old." Dante took a curve with wild abandon, demonstrating his impressive mastery of the vehicle.

"Take it easy," Mike said, trying to keep from sliding onto Dante's side.

Grinning at Mike's reaction, Dante slowed slightly. His air of supreme confidence amused Mike.

Throwing his head back, Mike inhaled the fresh mountain air. "Ah, this countryside is wonderful." The atmosphere was redolent with the smells of his boyhood: the grape vines and olive trees, the oleanders and rhododendron. It reminded him of his village. He thought of his parents, and his childhood. Other memories came back in a sudden searing flash, another face. Concetta, as a child, as his bride, a wounded bird, introverted and forever fearful. What had become of her? Had she wandered, alone and afraid, down just such a lane? Had she missed her step and fallen down one of the steep embankments like the one they were now passing? Mike shook his head to clear away the unbidden thoughts. Why now, those painful memories, when he'd gone so long without their nagging taunts? He had thought, foolishly, that he'd successfully excised them from his life. But no, inside one's mind there are no hiding places, only shadowy recesses where ghosts tarry to reappear uninvited, unexpected.

Dante's voice interrupted Mike's musings. "Would you like to see the convent up close? We could visit my aunt. She would be delighted to meet you."

Mike was pulled back to the present. "What?"

"The convent. Would you like to go there?"

"Sure, I'd like that."

"I try to visit my aunt every week or so. She's old and frail, and is so pleased when I show up."

The road narrowed to a single lane. Only the purr of the motor and the chirping of the birds were heard in the serene countryside.

Dante slowed, then speeded up, looping around the upward spiral.

"Almost there, Michele. Lovely, isn't it? Built to last, in the sixteenth century. You won't see anything like this convent in America." The dark stone structure loomed high above them, its narrow bell tower outlined against the vivid blue sky.

"We'll have to park here and walk the rest of the way. The lane *dei nani,* 'of the dwarfs,' is too narrow for a car."

Lined with tall weeds and wild shrubbery, the road led them past a meadow of brilliant red poppies. Mike stopped, hands on hips, and turned slowly, absorbing the untamed beauty, the serenity. But despite nature's splendor, a cloud passed his thoughts, a fleeting uneasiness.

When they arrived at the wide iron gate, Dante pulled the bell cord. Presently an angelic-faced nun proceeded slowly to the entrance, her hands tucked into the sleeves of her black habit. Dante greeted the nun, who smiled benignly with friendly recognition. Silently she opened the gate with a key fished from her deep pocket. Behind them, the gate clanged as it swung closed.

Inside the dark, musty-smelling vestibule the nun indicated tall narrow chairs grouped around a small wooden table. The men sat and waited in silence until they heard slow, uneven footsteps coming from the spectral hall. When his aunt appeared, Dante rose and walked toward her with outstretched arms. He bent to the old nun, who hugged him tightly with palsied hands. He murmured to her and pointed toward Michele, while she smiled and nodded. When they approached, Michele stood.

"Zi Teresa, this is the friend I told you about—Michele, the man who befriended me when I was a prisoner in America."

She clasped Mike's hands into her shaking ones. "Dante has told me of your kindness, and indeed, of the kindness of all your family. God blesses such charity." There was gratitude in the nun's sunken round eyes.

"Having Dante was our pleasure. He brought us many stories of the old country."

She lowered herself gingerly into a chair, and the men did likewise. "He has also told me of your beautiful daughter. Anna, is it?"

"Yes, Anna, my eldest daughter."

"She is here with you also?"

Mike nodded. "All my family is visiting. We leave tomorrow morning."

The woman, Michele thought, looked over eighty years old. Her nut-brown face was a network of fine crisscrossing lines, of valleys and planes, but her eyes were bright and alert.

"So, you are an American now. But your parents, are they from these parts?"

"Not too far away, the village of Ramolita."

Her eyebrows shot up. "I know of Ramolita." She

coughed behind her small hand. "You were born here, yet you speak with an accent."

"I was just six years old when my parents took me to America. I returned to Italy nine years later, after my father died. But after a few years, I went back to America. The last time I was here was when I married in 1928."

Suora Teresa fingered the brown beads that hung at her waist. "Ah, and you have relatives in Ramolita?"

"Only some distant cousins. We've been visiting my wife's family near Bari. We stopped here on our way to Rome, where we leave for home."

"You're leaving too soon. You must take time to visit all the wonderful sights, *Signore* . . ." She appeared perplexed. "I don't recall your surname."

"It's Marcassa," Dante supplied.

The nun's smile faded and she looked momentarily puzzled. "Marcassa? Marcassa, you say?" She leaned forward, peering at Mike closely through narrowed eyes.

"Sì, Michele Marcassa."

As her lips mouthed the word "Marcassa," she blanched, then shrank back into the chair.

Reaching deep into her pocket, she drew out a handkerchief. With trembling hands she patted her brow and neck.

Clearly, Suora Teresa was agitated. Had he said something to upset her? Mike frowned with confusion.

Dante looked concerned. "Are you all right, Zia? Do you want something? Some water, perhaps?"

Suora Teresa put her hand on Dante's arm. "Yes, water. Please go into the kitchen, Dante, and bring a pitcher of water."

When Dante left, the nun leaned toward Michele. "When were you in your village last?"

Why was the woman so curious? "In 1928, before I got married. Before that, it was 1921."

The old woman's eyes darted about, telling clearly of her consternation. Her tongue darted out, moistening her dry lips. Finally she whispered in a crackling voice, "There is something I must tell you."

What could this woman possibly have to tell him? She was acting so strangely that he wondered if she was perhaps a bit demented.

Suora Teresa closed her eyes and spoke in a soft monotone. "Many years ago a young woman came to the
convent doors, seeking refuge. She was disheveled and
incoherent, but still a lovely thing, hardly more than a
girl. After we took her in, we discovered she was with
child. Poor waif, she spoke hardly at all, and wouldn't
give her name. Still, she was likable, and comely, and
was given light kitchen duties, which she performed without complaint."

The nun leaned back with a deep breath. Her eyes
closed and her breath became shallow. Mike thought she
had fallen asleep.

"Suora . . ."

She raised a trembling hand in a gesture that silenced
him. "The woman soon gave birth to a strapping boy, but
sadly, there were complications. The unfortunate woman
died soon afterward. It was March in the year 1922. I
remember it so clearly, as though it were yesterday."

Pausing, she took a deep breath and stared out the
window.

Although Mike wondered why the nun was telling him
this story, he was reluctant to interrupt her reverie.

In a few moments she continued. "I cared for the little
one in the days following, and fell in love with him. So
sunny he was, so dear. All the nuns lavished attention on
the infant." She paused, obviously lost in memories of
the past, a small smile creasing her cheeks. "When my
sister, who was barren, came to visit, she was also taken
with the little one. It was arranged for my sister to adopt
the baby." She paused and took a deep breath, her
eyelids dropping slowly. "Dante was that child."

Mike, aware that he'd been holding his breath, released it with a smile. So her story had a point to it after
all.

Dante returned bearing a silver pitcher and three glasses
on a tray. "Have I missed something?" He poured water
and handed the glass to his aunt. "You look as though
you're having a serious conversation."

"Dante," she said, "I am suddenly cold. Please go
back and ask Suora Renata for the loan of her shawl."

Dante shrugged, giving Mike an exasperated lift of his
eyebrows, but turned to do her bidding.

Leaning back in his chair, Mike said, "This is an interesting story, Suora, but why are you telling me all this?"

The nun drank thirstily, and with shaking hands returned the glass to the tray. "When I cared for Dante's mother, I prodded her for her name. Just before she died, she told me. She also told me her husband's name."

Suora Teresa's fingers sought the rosary hanging from her waist, and moved the beads along with her thumb. "Her name was Concetta. Her husband's name was Michele Marcassa."

Mike's eyes opened wide. "What are you saying?" His brain was a confusion of thoughts. He calculated quickly. He had been in Italy in June 1921. The nun said Dante was born in March 1922. Nine months exactly.

His mouth went dry and his mind reeled. As the reality crept over him, his heart did an erratic dance in his chest. The words formed in his mind.

Dante was his son.

Her voice barely above a whisper, Suora Teresa said, "I am old and may die soon. Dante has no idea he is adopted. I made a solemn promise to my sister that I would never tell the boy that he is not her son. I will honor that oath. But when I heard your name, somehow I knew I must unburden myself of the secret I've kept all these years. Perhaps it is wrong of me, but somehow, I think you must know about this . . . know that you have a son." She shrank into the chair, her face ashen. "Now you are armed with the truth. What you do with it is your choice. I will never speak of this again."

Mike hardly noticed when Dante returned with a shawl and placed it gently about the nun's shoulders. "I hope you're not ill, Zi," Dante said, kissing her atop the head.

Now Mike turned and stared openly at Dante as if seeing him for the first time. *This young man is my son. I can see the unmistakable likeness across the brow and eyes; the cleft in his chin like my father's; the hair, like my own and Anna's, thick and dark.*

How had the resemblance escaped Chiara's quick, knowing eyes? Fool, why would anyone ever think of connecting us? When Mike stood, the nun rose unsteadily and stretched on tiptoes to reach frail arms around his neck. She hugged him tightly, her eyes wet with tears.

Somehow, he said good-bye and stumbled to the car alongside his son. He turned and stared at Dante. *His son.*

Dante was chattering on and on, about how his aunt seemed to be getting addled in her old age, how she was unwell, but Mike hardly heard. This youth sitting next to him, driving with expertise, speaking intelligent words, this young man who had the world in the palm of his hand, this young man—smart, successful, confident—this man was his son.

Dante was staring at Mike. "You're lost in thought, Michele. I asked if it were something very important my aunt discussed with you, to take your concentration so fully."

Mike blurted the first thing that came into his head. "No, no, she thought she knew of some of my relatives." He wiped the perspiration from his brow. "Some old skeletons in the closet, as we say in America. But it must have been another branch of the Marcassa family."

Dante glanced at Mike curiously. "I'm sorry if she's upset you, my friend."

Mike didn't reply. He turned to look out the open window at the blooming fields and grassy meadows. His son's country.

His son.

No, not his son. Had he watched Dante grow, had he inspected his first tooth, urged him to take a first step? Had he helped him with his sums and his history? Had he watched his soccer games? Had he cuddled him and kissed him; chastised him when he was bad, rewarded him when he was good? Had he watched him grow, given him small toys, then larger ones? Had he directed his mind, his body?

No . . . no . . . no . . . no. . . .

Someone else had done all of that. Someone who loved him dearly.

Now that you are armed with the truth, it is your responsibility, Suora Teresa had said. Why had she told him? Near the end of her life, had this knowledge, this thirty-year secret, troubled her conscience?

He must tell Dante the truth.

But what was the truth? His seed had been implanted,

mindlessly, with no plan or intention and certainly with no knowledge. A seed that grew strong and healthy, despite its weak and unhealthy vessel.

Yes, Dante must know the truth.

But what impact could this information have on Dante's life? And on Mike's life? Ah, but that was only the beginning; what about Chiara and the girls? He had never been able to tell Chiara of his first marriage; it was too painful, and would have served no purpose. How would his family take such traumatic information now?

And what of the Ravennas? For whatever reasons, they had chosen to let Dante think he was their natural child. How would this revelation change their lives, their attitudes? It wasn't as though, by assuming his fatherly role, Mike could take Dante under his wing, bring him to America, give him a better life. No, Dante had everything he could wish for right here.

Dante was his natural son. But could Mike begin now, after all these years, to behave like a real father? Mike rubbed his hand over his face. His thoughts veered. He imagined Concetta, frail and malnourished, walking, walking, sleeping in stables and caves until, exhausted, she found herself at the convent doors. He thought of her in childbirth, probably confused and unaware of what was unfolding, with no family to sustain and nurture her. Thank God she'd found kindness and solace with the nuns. Mike's eyes stung with suppressed tears.

The rich resonant tones of the Angeles bells rent the stillness of the noon air. Mike turned to gaze at Dante, who, with eyes straight ahead on the winding road, had been speaking. Mike tried to focus his concentration on the words.

". . . and certainly I've had girlfriends in the past, many of them, in fact. I'm known as a 'good catch.' " His tone was cocky, but his laugh was self-deprecating. "Yet none of them have caught my fancy. None. And none could be as sweet, as charming, as lovely, as Anna. I must confess to you"—he cleared his throat and went on nervously—"she captured my heart when I came to your home in Detroit. Oh, she was young, true, a child, really, but her sweetness, her goodness, shone through. And I realize that she is young still. A twelve-year age difference. But that's not so unusual for Italians. I've felt the urge increasingly the past year or so, the urge to settle, to"—his chin jutted upward—"to have children."

What were all these words Dante spoke? The words made no sense. Or did they? Mike was suddenly aware that Dante was speaking of Anna, *his* Anna. He stared in astonishment. Anna was Dante's half-sister!

Oblivious of Mike's horror, Dante went on. "Yes, we stole a few moments yesterday, we talked quite a lot, actually. Of course, I've said nothing about an engagement, knowing I must speak to you first, but well, you can appreciate my feelings, can't you?" His short laugh was self-conscious. "I'm a man in love and I think Anna has feelings for me too. Of course, she would have to make the final decision, but I'm sure she could grow to love me."

Mike put his fingers to his temples to ease the throbbing that had begun. This nightmare couldn't be happening. With all this information thrown into his face at once, it was impossible to think. Why didn't Dante just stop talking?

Dante turned the car onto the circular gravel drive and pulled up to the main door of the villa. He lifted his hand from the steering wheel and reached across to grip Mike's shoulder. "Well? You haven't said anything, Michele. Do I have your blessing? That is, if Anna feels the same way?"

Mike felt ill. Here was the sort of young man he'd always wanted for his daughter, a man of confidence, of stature. But the man was his son; blood of his blood. Just yesterday Mike would have been wildly happy at this turn of events. But now . . .

"No!"

Dante reared back, startled. "No?"

Mike jerked the door handle and sprang out of the car. "No!"

Dante followed him up the wide steps and faced him at the door. "Why?" he pleaded. "Because she would leave America? I assure you, her life with me would be—"

"No! And that's all I'm going to say about it."

A manservant appeared at the door, opening it with a courteous bow.

"Signore." Dante's shoulders lifted in bafflement as he strode beside Mike. "Surely you have a reason . . ."

Mike stopped at the bottom of the staircase and asked the servant in rapid Italian, "Have the women returned from their shopping trip?"

"No, signore."

"As soon as they're back, ask my wife to see me in our room."

"Sì, signore."

"Michele . . ." Dante began, grabbing Mike's arm.

Mike shrugged him away and climbed the steps with heavy legs, feeling Dante's bewildered gaze following him. Inside the bedroom Mike leaned against the closed door for a moment, then sat, incongruously large on a small woman's chair. He lowered his head into his hands and cried, his body shuddering with emotion. Finally, his tears spent, he stared out at the deep blue expanse of sky unmarred by even one cloud, and waited, unmoving, for Chiara's return.

Chiara found Mike sitting as still as the furniture around him, and as silent. Her hand went to her heart at the sight of his gaunt, saddened features.

"Mike, what's wrong?" She hurried to his side and shook his shoulder, but he didn't move. His eyes were red, as though he'd been crying. She stared in wonder for a moment as memories, old memories, tumbled forth, of Mike during the depression, when he had the sickness. No, it couldn't be happening again. Their lives were happy and secure now. He had his family, a good job. There was no reason to be depressed.

Kneeling in front of him, she took his hands and looked into his face. "Michele?"

He seemed not to hear as he continued staring out the window. She put her hands on either side of his face and turned him toward her. "Mike, talk to me."

Turning his gaze to her, he focused on her face. His hand went to her hair, smoothing its errant wisps.

"Are you all right, Mike?"

He nodded, then stood abruptly, saying, "Get the girls packed up. We're leaving."

"What do you mean, leaving? We're staying another day. What's happened?"

"Nothing happened. I just have a headache, that's all. A terrible headache."

Chiara rummaged through her purse until she found a small metal case. "Here are two aspirin," she said, shaking them out into her palm. She poured water from the etched-glass pitcher on the chest and handed it to him.

He pushed her hand away, causing the aspirin to tumble to the floor. "Get the girls packed up. We're going home."

"But, Mike, be sensible. The Ravennas are having a dinner party for us tonight, and tomorrow morning—"

"I said we're leaving." He reached for the suitcase and flipped it open.

"Be reasonable. What will we tell them? We can't be so impolite as to—"

"*Basta!*" His steely glare silenced her. She knew better than to pursue it. Whatever the problem was, he apparently wasn't willing to divulge it now.

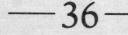

— 36 —

The long trip back to America was an uneasy one. Angry and perplexed, Chiara demanded an explanation, but Mike evaded, refusing to comment except to say that he'd felt ill. After a while, Chiara's questions were met with a stony stare and she knew it was futile to pursue the matter.

Something had happened that morning Mike spent with Dante. Had they argued? About what? When they said good-bye to the Ravennas Chiara could tell Mike was making an attempt to appear normal, but he seemed . . . What? Hurt? Sad? Miserable? All of that and more. Dante had looked merely bewildered, and his parents, though kind and gracious, seemed mystified as well.

Luisa, in her own world, was unperturbed by their hasty departure and Tina was hardly aware of the circumstances. But Anna was devastated. Chiara had noticed the looks that passed between Dante and her daughter, and attempted to talk to her, but Anna, upset and angry, was curt with Chiara and hateful toward her father.

Fearful of pressing Mike too hard, of precipitating a depression, Chiara finally gave up, and battled a depression of her own, born of confusion and an inability to communicate with her husband.

Chiara was happy to be back in her shop. Work had a way of distancing her from her problems. When she told Maria of their last day in Italy, that good woman had no insights whatsoever.

"Don't you *see* anything, Maria?"

"I'm sorry, Chiara, but I see nothing. Maybe I'm getting old." She folded a length of dove-gray satin and stored it on a shelf. "If Mike won't talk about it, better you forget it. Don't torture yourself. Time heals."

Chiara sighed. "He does seem better now. It's been two weeks."

Maria picked up her purse, saying, "Don't stay too long. The work will wait for you. Go to your family."

Chiara tidied her desk and watered the philodrendon that trailed vines down her filing cabinet.

"Always busy," said a voice behind her.

As she turned, a glow of pleasure spread over her. "Stewart. I didn't even hear the door." She hadn't seen him in almost a year. Rising, she extended her hand. "It's nice to see you again."

He held her hand between his own. For a moment neither said anything. Chiara felt the small crackle of electricity, could even acknowledge it now, though the reasons for that invisible steel cord that seemed to connect them were unfathomable.

"I just wanted to check up on you, my dear," he said, finally releasing her hand. "Looks like you're doing very well."

"Yes, business is good. Maria's been a godsend. She takes over for me whenever one of the children is sick or if I have things to do at home."

"And the family is well?"

"Yes, all well and growing. We've moved, into a home of our own." She nodded proudly. "We just returned from a trip to Italy."

"How wonderful. Was it all as you'd remembered?"

Chiara gave a rueful laugh. "Not exactly. But it was wonderful to see my parents and brother and sisters. And how is your family?"

He shrugged. "My wife and I live in the same house. We rarely communicate. In fact we hardly see each other. Yes, she still drinks, if you're wondering. But she's a very civilized sort of drunk, if there is such a thing." He drummed his fingers on the edge of the desk. "And Sonny . . . well, he's dropped out of school. But I think he'll straighten up soon enough."

"I hope so." Chiara thought his optimistic words hid an edge of despair. Her eye fastened on her ledger, and to change the subject she said, "I'm using your accountant. He's very good."

"Yes, I know. I spoke to him recently. He's the one who told me you're making an excellent profit. He thinks you ought to open a branch on the west side, maybe Birmingham or Royal Oak."

Chiara looked up in surprise. "I couldn't possibly do that. I have far too much work right here. How would I manage it all?"

"Let Maria manage this one. She could handle it, couldn't she?"

"I suppose so. It's just that . . . well, I never thought about opening another shop."

"Think big. Remember, Henry Ford started with just one automobile."

She laughed. "This is just a little different, isn't it?"

"Not really. Every journey begins with but one step. I think Confucius said that."

Chiara looked off into space. "Hmm. Maybe. Maybe I could do it." Then she frowned and shook her head. "Mike wouldn't like it."

"Tell you what. I'll scout out some places for you."

His eyes fell to the pictures on her shelf. "You've a lovely family. What beautiful girls. I remember seeing the two older girls when they were so high." He gestured with his hand at knee level. "Who are the others in the picture, relatives?"

"No, they were both prisoners of war and spent time with us when they were imprisoned here. Franco is from my home town, and this one, Dante, is from Campania."

Stewart peered at the picture. "Dante could be a member of the family. He has the same dark looks of your husband."

Chiara drew closer to study the picture. "Yes, I suppose he does. They come from the same region."

"How quickly our children grow up. Girls must be easier to raise than boys. Sonny's been, well, rather a problem. He was bounced out of Yale." Stewart raked his hand through thinning hair. "He seems so unhappy."

"They're all hard to raise. Still, mine haven't given me too many heartaches. Not yet, anyway. But the day may come, especially with Anna. She's very headstrong sometimes, that one."

Stewart cocked his head to one side, observing Chiara. "She comes by it honestly, you know. That's not such a bad trait, determination. Especially if it's properly directed."

Chiara conceded with a nod, then consulted her watch. "I must be going. My family is waiting."

"The family always comes first, doesn't it?" He moved toward her until their arms touched. Reaching up, he traced his finger along her cheek.

She arched her head away and his hand dropped.

"You're never far from my thoughts, you know. You're very dear to me." He encircled her with his arms.

Chiara wanted to wriggle free, but his arms thwarted her brief struggle. With a sigh, she laid her head against his shoulder, surrendering to the comforting warmth, feeling his breath across her eyelids. They stood that way for several moments; then he tipped her chin up and kissed her gently. With his body pressed against hers, she experienced again the wondrous awakening of her senses. She had wanted to deny the yearning she felt toward Stewart; wanted to believe their relationship, since that one carnal act, was based solely on friendship. But her responding desire refuted that idea.

As Stewart's fingers roamed over her back, she knew she must move away. Now. Before it was too late; before the old hunger stirred fully in her center, potent, compelling; before the needs of the flesh could trap and betray her.

"Chiara," he whispered into her hair. "You feel the same as I do. You can't deny that."

She steeled herself and moved away, loosening his grasp. "I won't deny it. For so many years you've been my friend, my protector, even. But we mustn't repeat mistakes of the past, and I can't . . . I must not . . . weaken what I have with my husband."

Stewart released his hold and clasped both her hands, kissing the fingertips.

She dropped her head, her voice a whisper. "Mike and I . . . we love each other."

His arms enfolded her again, warm and protective. *"I* love you too." His voice was wistful.

Chiara shook her head slowly, sadly.

"So be it," Stewart said. "We go on as before. At least let me visit you now and again. I promise I'll behave."

"Of course you must visit. I would be hurt if you didn't. I need . . . want your friendship." She nestled against him for a moment, reluctant to break away.

In the far recesses of her mind Chiara thought she heard the front door opening. The sound of hurried footsteps was just registering when she heard Luisa's voice calling out, "Ma? Are you in back?"

Chiara jerked her hands away from Stewart and twisted a wayward lock of hair behind her ear just as her daughter burst through the door.

"Pa's waiting in . . ." The sentence splintered off as Luisa gazed at the two of them. "Oh. I didn't know anyone was here." Her eyes were questioning.

"Luisa. I was just closing up." Chiara tried to control her breathlessness. Had her daughter seen them in an embrace? Chiara's back had been turned, so she couldn't be sure they'd pulled apart in time. She thought they had. Surely they had. *Please, God.*

"I was just leaving, young lady." Stewart moved to the door. "Paying a bill, an overdue bill. Good evening to you both."

"I didn't know your father was picking me up." Chiara lifted her coat from the rack and shoved her arms clumsily through the openings. "He should have called. I might have been on the bus by now."

Louisa watched as Stewart made his hasty exit. "Who was that, Ma?"

Was her voice accusing? "Just a customer." Chiara tried to sound easy, offhand. "I'll turn out the lights. You go on ahead."

Luisa looked at her mother for a moment before starting through the door. Was that suspicion clouding her eyes? Did she think something was amiss? No, Luisa hadn't seen anything. It was just her own conscience reacting. She had been startled, hadn't composed herself. She hoped her agitation wasn't evident. Chiara looked around the room one last time, replaying the scene. Their backs had been to the door. Chiara felt her heart pounding, felt the clutching in her abdomen. Luisa had seen nothing, intuited nothing. She was just a child. Yet young people were so aware these days, with explicit talk of affairs and divorces in the movies and newspapers.

As she slipped into the car beside Mike, he asked, "Who was that just leaving? He looks familiar."

"Oh, the husband of a customer, paying a bill." Chiara jammed her hands into her coat pockets so Mike wouldn't see their trembling. How easily the lie comes to my lips, she thought.

She dredged up the old memories of herself and Stewart on that fateful day, so long ago. For many years she had steadfastly refused to dissect and analyze that fall from grace, but now, with the passage of time blunting the sharpness of her old self-accusations, she realized that the act of love, in itself, had not been so evil. Even the result of that first act, in the context of those dreary, unhappy days, had been forgivable. The Bible said God would forgive. If he could forgive her, why couldn't she forgive herself? What was done could never be undone. And now, why did she feel again that she was being punished for that one act of desperation?

Luisa didn't speak of the incident, but Chiara thought of it often in the next few days, and wondered whether it was that or her newfound godliness that caused her daughter's aloofness.

Anna adjusted her wide-brimmed straw hat against the dazzling afternoon sun as she waited for Agnes at Detroit's favorite meeting place. She had heard that if you waited long enough under the clock at Kern's Department Store, you'd see everyone in the city. When she spotted her friend, Anna pushed away from the crush of people. Though she had made several tearful phone calls to Agnes, this would be their first meeting since *the Italian fiasco*.

The two girls squealed as they hugged one another.

"Agnes, you look great!"

"Annie, my God, you've lost weight! What did that trip do to you?"

Anna's quick glance in a display window confirmed Agnes' observation. The new tailored Handmacher suit hung loosely from her shoulders. Still, she knew she looked good, with her hair in a neat cap cut and new sling pumps enhancing her slim, curved limbs.

She squeezed Agnes' arm. "Let's splurge at Frame's. My treat." With her fifty-dollar-a-week salary, Anna could afford it, though she gave her mother part of her earnings.

At Frame's they sat near the huge crosshatched windows and, relying on Agnes' fake birth certificates, chanced an order of frozen daiquiris, while Anna recounted, for the third time, the entire episode at the Ravenna villa. Though Agnes had heard it all before, she devoured every word.

"Oh, if you could see Dante, Agnes. He is so handsome, so sharp." Anna's eyes rolled heavenward. "He has this positively dreamy car, and money too. I mean, really rich."

"Oh, man." Agnes' eyes rolled back. "It all sounds so romantic."

"It was, until my father spoiled it all, and literally dragged us out of the villa and on to Rome. I didn't even have a chance to say good-bye to Dante. If you could've seen the Ravennas' faces, Agnes. They all looked so confused. I'm sure something happened, something with Dante. My father was mad at him . . . or not mad, actually, but he wouldn't talk to him or even look at him." She glanced at the menu. "Let's just get a sandwich. I'm not even hungry."

"Okay." Folding her menu, Agnes leaned forward, her

expression urging Anna to continue. "What about your mother? Didn't she know what happened?"

"No, she was as bewildered as the rest of us. She was afraid, too. She told me that during the depression my father had a nervous breakdown and she thought that was happening all over again. I never knew that about my father." Her eyes were wide, wondering. "It just goes to show you how little you really know about your parents. So, anyway, Ma just went along with whatever Pa wanted."

"I can't imagine your father ever having a nervous breakdown, can you? He's so . . . so strong and domineering."

"Sometimes he's domineering, but usually my mother can get her way." Anna stirred her drink, looking thoughtful. "Honestly, Agnes, I've never been so mad at my father. I didn't speak to him for days, and thought of stowing away on a ship back to Italy."

"Oh, sure."

"Or I could spend the rest of my life like Miss Havisham in *Great Expectations*, waiting in her wedding gown, beside the cobwebbed wedding cake, for her true love." Anna's voice held humorous cynicism.

"Well, at least you can laugh. I guess you're getting over it." Agnes nibbled at the lacy lettuce edging her sandwich.

"I'll never get over it." Anna's face darkened. " 'Everything works out for the best,' my mother keeps saying in that annoying way she has of *accepting* whatever comes along. Well, that might be all right for Italians, but I'm American; I don't have to constantly *accept.*"

"Well, I'll tell you, Annie. From what you've said, Dante may be handsome and everything, but he sounds like a big flirt to me. I mean, you told me even his mother said he had a string of girlfriends. Just because he kissed you! Big deal." Agnes chomped down on her sandwich.

Anna's lips thinned. Obviously Agnes had never been in love, really in love. "Agnes, believe me, it wasn't just a kiss."

Agnes shrugged. "And besides," she continued, "would you actually want to live in Italy? You said yourself everything's different there, that Dante's mother is bored with her life and dotes on her husband and son. She'd probably be the world's worst mother-in-law. That is, if Dante were actually thinking of marriage. And you don't know that. Maybe he thought you'd just have a little fling—you know . . ." Agnes' left eyebrow raised with unsubtle significance.

Anna reddened. "Agnes!"

"Well, you don't really know. I think you've blown this whole thing out of proportion."

Agnes was no help at all. But she hadn't been there. She hadn't seen Dante, felt his hands on her body, his lips on hers. Anna shuddered with the memory.

"I just wish you could go to Wayne University with me," Agnes said around a mouthful of bread. "That would take your mind off this Valentino."

Anna grimaced. "Whenever I mention college, my father has an absolute fit. He won't even discuss it." Anna pushed her plate away. "Agnes, I forgot to tell you about Luisa. You'll never believe this, but she decided to become a nun! Can you believe it? She was at this grotto and had this sort of religious experience, a *calling*."

Agnes opened her mouth in surprise, then clamped it. "Well, it doesn't surprise me that much. She was always in another world, you know? I guess your mother's pleased."

"No, that's the funny part. My mother always thought Lou would go into the business with her. She gave up on me, but Lou's like Ma—she likes to sew. Now Ma's decided Tina will be the one to join her. Ha! Tina's so spoiled she'll do just what she wants."

"Gee, everything's changing. It must be strange between you and Lou."

"Not really. She's just real patient and doesn't want to argue. It's not much fun."

When the girls finished their lunch, they hugged and went their separate ways. Anna felt an emptiness spread through her as she watched Agnes walk away. Agnes' path was stretching toward the adventure of learning, while she faced a bleak future in a crowded office and a job she hated.

A week later, Anna glanced around the dinner table. Everyone was so predictable: her mother fussing to make sure everything was in order, the food properly seasoned and hot, the bread sliced just so; her father ranting about the union and about injustices; Tina whining about having to eat her peas; and Luisa looking peaceful and distant, her body here but her mind elsewhere.

"How's the job, Anna?" her father asked. "How is Jensen treating you these days?"

"We get along. She transferred me to the purchasing department."

"Is it a promotion?"

"No, more like they're getting rid of me in general office."

Her father glared at her, his eyebrows knitting. "What do you mean? You're not doing a good job?"

"I wouldn't exactly put it that way. Actually, Miss Jensen said she thought I'd be happier working in purchasing. Would you please pass the potatoes, Tina?"

Her father carefully set down his fork and knife. Here it comes, she thought. The lecture.

"What's the problem, Anna? A daughter of mine can't do a good job of office work?"

Anna heaped mashed potatoes on her plate and made a well for gravy. "I do a good job."

"That's not what it sounds like."

"Pa, I just don't like it. I'm bored. Miss Jensen knows it; that's why she transferred me."

"You're bored." He gave that irritating little snort.

"Does anyone want coffee now?" Luisa, as usual, tried to avert an argument. "I made oatmeal cookies for dessert."

Anna ignored her. "Yes, Pa, I'm bored. I do the same dumb things over and over. I *hate* filing and I never could type very well either. I'm going to look for another job."

"No you won't, young lady. You've got a perfectly good job, a secure job with decent pay. Where do you think you can get a better job?"

"Do I have to eat my peas?" Tina grumbled. No one answered.

"Well, I could probably get a better job if I had a degree," Anna said in a rush. "What I really want is to go to college. Is that such a sin?" She hadn't intended for her voice to edge upward like that.

Her father banged his fist on the table. "College! For what? To marry and have babies? And where would the money come for your fancy ideas?"

Her mother turned sympathetic eyes toward Anna, then said to her father, "Mike, settle down. You don't have to yell."

He turned to Chiara with his eyebrows raised in a look that shut her up, but Anna wouldn't give up without a struggle.

"I could save what I earn instead of giving most of it to Ma. I would work part-time while I went to school, and full-time summers."

"You're not going to college, and that's final."

"You always said you could have done better if you'd had an education. So many times I've heard you say that."

"That's different. I'm a man. If you were a boy, then I'd think about it."

He shoved away from the table and stomped out to the living room, shouting, "The subject is closed."

Luisa started to clear away the dishes and Tina took the opportunity to escape the table and her peas.

Anna followed her father into the living room and glared at his back, so angry she could only sputter. Her father snapped on the brand-new Philco television and swore when it flashed a pattern of zigzag lines. He adjusted knobs until a snowy picture flashed on, of Buffalo Bob, Howdy Doody, and Princess Summer-Fall-Winter-Spring. Swearing, he flipped the dial until he found a news program, then sprawled in a chair in front of it, his face as serious as a wooden Indian's.

Anna would have gone on with the battle, but her mother took her arm, leading her to the kitchen. "Come on, Anna, help with the dishes."

Anna banged pots as she rinsed and stacked them, and dropped her head, trying to hide the angry tears that rushed to her eyes.

Her mother touched her shoulder. "Is this really so important to you?"

Anna nodded.

"You've had a bad time, haven't you? This thing with *Dante* . . ." Her mother tipped her head . . . her eyes sad.

"Don't be too upset with your father. That's the way it is, *la via vecchia,* the old way. We thought college was for the upper classes, or a chosen few."

The old way. It was a familiar refrain. "This is not Italy, it's America." Anna's voice was punctuated with sarcasm.

"We were taught that the old way is the best way; it's safe. And we were taught not to question things, always to obey our parents, even after we were grown, and that the man had to make the decisions, even when the women knew the decisions were bad ones. That's the way it was." Her mother's eyelids slowly lowered in that resigned way she had. "But now, I don't know, everything's different, the world's changing . . ."

Her parents were impossible; so rigid in their thinking, so unreasonable. Anna ran hot water and sprinkled soap flakes over the dishes. "I can't believe how old-fashioned you two are! You might as well be back in Italy." Hot tears dropped into the sudsy water. "You'd think parents would be proud to have a college graduate in the family."

Her mother's sigh came from deep in her chest. "You know, it might be nice to have a nurse in the family, or a teacher. It would be an honor. My uncle Nunzio was a professor," she mused, as if talking to herself. "Ah, how I loved that man. You would have loved him too, Anna. I remember, years ago, before I was married, he said, 'Don't forget to dream, Chiara.' "

Anna turned to her and said softly, "Ma, *I* have a dream. Doesn't my dream count? Just because it's not the way things were done in your day, in Italy . . ."

Her mother frowned with a characteristic tightening of her mouth. "Yes, *cara,* your dream counts." Chiara stood abruptly, and squared her small shoulders in a combative way. "Your father's stubborn, but maybe I can talk to him. This isn't the old country, it's America. In America all dreams are possible."

Anna had no words. Ma seemed to be on her side, after all. She grabbed her mother's hand in gratitude, but the glimmer of light at the edge of her rainbow suddenly faded. "Pa will never listen to reason."

"Never mind. We'll see what happens."

*　　*　　*

Mike, settled in bed, was winding the clock when Chiara entered the room.

Sitting on the bed, she slipped her shoes off and let them drop to the floor. "Mike, Anna's very unhappy."

"I know she's unhappy. Life's not always a bed of roses." He reset the hands carefully, and, satisfied, replaced the clock on the bedside stand.

"I don't like to go against you, but I'm going to say my piece."

Mike sighed. Why didn't she let it rest? "Listen, Chiara, we've been all through this college thing, and . . ."

"It isn't only that, Mike. I know something happened in Italy; something you won't talk about."

Mike's jaw tightened, and he raised his hand in a gesture meant to silence her. He didn't want to think about Italy and Dante. He'd handled things badly, rushing them out of Italy like he did. In his state of shock, he hadn't thought things through, hadn't invented a reasonable explanation.

"All right," Chiara said, looking exasperated. "So you won't tell me. But think about Anna. Do you realize how you upset her, dragging us all away like you did? I think she was in love with Dante. I'm not blind, even if you are. I saw the looks, back and forth, between them."

Mike winced. "She'll fall in love many times."

Chiara moved close to him on the bed. "Oh, nothing would have come of it, probably, but she's miserable just the same."

Softly Mike asked, "You think she was really in love with . . . with the boy?" He couldn't bear to say his name.

"Yes, I think so."

Mike shook his head sadly. "I just didn't think about her feelings." It was true; he hadn't even considered the effect his rash actions would have on the family, especially on Anna. It was upsetting to realize he'd caused her misery. "I guess I only thought about myself."

"Yourself?"

Mike closed his eyes tightly, willing away thoughts of his son, afraid of saying too much.

Finally he said, "Do you think Anna hates me?"

"No, she doesn't hate you. She's just very unhappy, after this business with Dante, and now a job she doesn't like."

"I care about her, I worry about how she feels."

"If that's true, at least think about sending her to college. Just think about it."

Mike's heart would always ache for the son he could never acknowledge. But what about the children he could claim? Didn't they deserve a chance at a better future? Didn't he owe Anna something?

"Mike, are you listening to me?" Chiara touched Mike's cheek.

He picked up her hand and put it to his lips. "You're right, Anna deserves a chance. I'll think about it." He pulled Chiara close. "You're a good woman, Chiara." He pulled her roughly on top of him and kissed her long and lovingly.

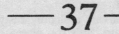

— 37 —

Anna loved the smell of the library—musty leather and paper—and the sound of it, hushed and almost reverent.

She found the book she sought, on Italian art, and settled at a scarred table. The book fell open to an illustration of a villa faintly reminiscent of Dante's. Her eyes closed as the memory of Dante filtered through her mind, hardly faded by the passage of time.

It was 1955, almost four years since the trip that had ended in unhappiness and confusion. To this day it wasn't clear why her father had dragged her away from the romance and enchantment of the villa and what she had felt sure was the beginning of a love affair. From a lofty maturity, Anna smiled at the immature girl she had been.

When she finished her research, she glanced around the Wayne University library. In two months she would graduate, and so would Martin. She rose and searched the tables until she found him. Martin sat in his usual spot in a corner, deep in concentration, his head bent over his book, tan hair dropping forward. When she sat beside him, he looked up and smiled. Her thigh rested lightly against his and she could sense his pulse quickening.

"No point in trying to study now," he whispered, gathering up his books and papers.

Outside, in the fresh March air, he turned and kissed her lips, a tease of a kiss, then took her hand. Just the feel of his warm fingers squeezing hers left her tingly. She studied Martin—the forthright gray eyes, so somber, the fair complexion, the neatly creased chino pants. He was often withdrawn, sometimes not even tuned in to what went on around him, not like the boys she had gravitated to in high school, boys with a quick quip, jokers. She pondered the reasons for the strong attraction, but her intellect, her powers of reasoning, seemed blunted in the presence of so powerful a physical pull. She only knew she needed to be near him, to feel the warmth of his flesh against hers, to absorb the wonder of his adoration and need.

Helping her into his car, a slightly rusty white 1947 Ford coupé, Martin said, "It's too nice a day to waste studying." He consulted his watch. "We've got an hour. Let's go to Belle Isle."

A few minutes later, Anna snuggled in the crook of Martin's arm under the restful bower of a willow tree. They looked across a narrow canal where the earth, underneath the newspapers Martin had provided, felt spongy and damp.

The air, untouched by fumes and gases in the secluded spot, teemed with the signs of spring: new buds bursting from shrubs and trees, pale green shoots listing toward the sun, noisy birds calling among themselves.

Although Anna had dated Martin only a few months, it was obvious theirs was a special relationship. She wished they could have more time together, but Martin worked nights and weekends and Anna helped out at the bridal salon on Saturdays and caught up on bookkeeping for her mother on Sundays. Anna's "dates" with Martin consisted of meeting briefly before or after classes, and sometimes, when each had a free afternoon, a drive or a quick snack together. They would sit close and talk of all manner of things, piecing together the fabric of each other's lives. *What were you like when you were ten? And twelve? And fifteen?* Anna would ask, storing away his answers.

Anna wondered again how two such diverse personalities could be so attracted. Martin was reasonable, even-tempered, in contrast to her own excitable nature. He was analytical and logical while she was emotional. He was fair, with faint freckles emerging from the sun's pale wash, and had changeable eyes, sometimes green, sometimes gray. What sort of children would they have? she wondered idly. Would they have blue-black hair and wide dark eyes like hers? Would they be spare and gangling boys, like Martin? She slipped her hand into his.

"Umm, it's so nice here. So peaceful, I could stay here forever." Anna hugged her knees and raised her face to the sun.

Martin eased his arm around Anna's waist. "We should probably go for a walk. You don't exercise enough."

"Neither do you."

"I exercise every morning in front of an open window," Martin said.

"Every morning?."

Martin nodded. "Rain or shine, winter or summer."

"What if you get up late?"

He looked askance.

"I mean, if the alarm didn't go off or something."

"That wouldn't happen. Anyway, I always wake up before the alarm."

Anna was amazed. "That's so . . . so *predictable*."

"I guess I'm a predictable guy." He nibbled her ear, then trailed his mouth across her cheek to her lips in a lingering kiss. When he released her he asked, "Is this predictable?"

She cupped his cheek and snuggled close, purring.

Screeching tires intruded and a car full of teenagers emptied out close by.

"Let's get back," he said, swinging upright and offering his hand.

Back in the car Martin pulled her close to him. "Anna, have you ever been in love before?"

"Hmm, well, yes." She sighed as the memory of Dante flitted across her mind. "But it was just puppy love."

He kissed her nose. "Tell me about it."

"Oh, someday I'll tell you. I was only seventeen." She sighed. How could she tell him? Dante had been an obsession, a romantic illusion. "I get sentimental when I think of it."

She laughed, and Martin covered the laugh with his mouth. Usually she held back, but today she felt reckless. His kisses grew more and more impassioned as his hands wandered to forbidden places, and Anna, absorbed in the mounting pleasure, couldn't bring herself to stop him. Finally she pushed away, afraid of the precarious unknown that lurked, she was sure, just seconds away. "We have to stop this, Martin." She wriggled from his grasp.

He groaned and threw his head back against the seat.

Anna tugged her skirt down. "Not until we're married. I told you that." They had necked and petted before, and each time she'd stopped him short. In all other matters he showed remarkable control.

"Annie, Annie. What's the difference? No one will know."

"I'll know. Besides, it's not safe."

"I'll use something."

"No."

Martin slapped the steering wheel with the heel of his hand. "You always do that to me."

With splayed fingers she arranged her hair. "You're so reasonable about everything else, why can't you be reasonable about this?"

"You're the one who's unreasonable." He shoved his shirt into his pants and switched on the radio. Rosemary Clooney was singing.

They sat without speaking, both staring ahead.

Anna, aware of Martin's frustration, wondered how long she could hold him off.

"When will I meet your family?" he asked.

She evaded, as usual. "Soon."

He turned her to face him. "What's the problem? Don't you think they'll like me?"

"Oh, they'll like you. It's just . . ."

"What?"

She picked up his hand, braiding her fingers through his. "Two things. You're not Italian and you're not Catholic."

"You really think that'll matter?"

"Of course it will."

"Does it matter to you?"

"You know it doesn't." She nibbled her lip. "Well, it

would help if you were Catholic. I mean, then you'd understand some things, I mean some behaviors that may be a little confusing to you . . . ."

"To say the least. For instance, your sister. It's inconceivable that a woman would choose to isolate herself from the world and devote her life to God the way Luisa did."

"That's what I mean. If you'd spent twelve years in a Catholic school, you'd understand." Or would he? she wondered. Anna herself didn't always understand. College had broadened her views, but left her with too many unanswered questions.

"I doubt it." He glanced at his watch and switched the ignition key, then cautiously backed out of the lane.

Anna laid her head on his shoulder and lightly touched his thigh. "We really should get married. That would solve one of our problems."

Martin frowned. "Sweets, we can't get married until I graduate and have a job and a few bucks saved. We should have a house and—"

"Other people start out in apartments."

"That's not my plan."

"Oh, you and your plans!"

Anna met Martin's family first, a few weeks later. The meal was quiet and dignified, unlike her family's noisy, sometimes raucous dinners. His parents and younger sister hardly spoke, and when they did, it was in soft voices, asking polite questions. His mother, a fastidious woman with a tight permanent, appeared shy. His father was an older, more dignified replica of Martin. Anna couldn't help but wonder if Martin at his father's age would have the receding hairline and the permanent lines above arched brows, like ripples in a brook following a thrown pebble. The thought of Martin and her growing older together appealed to her.

When she left, both parents hugged her. She was sure she'd made a good impression.

A few weeks later, Martin came to her home for dinner and what he termed *the interrogation*. Will they shine the light on me? he'd asked. Actually, the questions were subtle ones.

"And do you have any plans for the future, Martin?" her father asked.

Anna winced. He could have waited a bit for that one.

"I want to work at Ford," Martin said, spearing a black olive. "I've always admired Henry Ford and the Ford Motor Company."

Mike snapped to attention and studied Martin through his spectacles. "Ford, eh? I'm a union man myself."

"Yes, I know." Martin's gaze was forthright.

Anna swallowed hard in the ensuing heavy silence. Triple jeopardy: non-Catholic, non-Italian, and a company man to boot. But her father said nothing more. Perhaps, after divining Martin's determination and sense of purpose, her father would bend his convictions.

By the end of the meal, after Martin had complimented Mike on his tasty wine, her father seemed to like Martin despite his hereticism.

After Martin left, Chiara washed the dishes, stacking the good china carefully in the drainer. Anna was unusually silent.

Giving her daughter a sidewise glance, Chiara said, "I think you like this Martin very much."

Anna concentrated on scratching candle wax from the silver candlesticks with a pink-painted thumbnail. "Yes, I do."

Chiara steeled herself. "Do you love him?"

"I think so."

Frowning, her most dire suspicions confirmed, Chiara said, "There are so many nice Italian boys around. Why couldn't you fall in love with one of them?"

Anna lifted her eyebrows. "Ma, I fell in love with Martin. I couldn't help myself. Once you get to know him, you'll love him too."

Love. The young people always talked about love without the least idea of what it meant. The movies and television had trivialized the word.

"Do you think you'll marry him?"

"Yes."

Chiara shook her head. "You're young. Maybe you should wait awhile."

"Ma! I'm twenty-one. Most of my friends are married already, with a baby or two." Anna took a dish towel and began drying the dishes.

Chiara's voice fell to a whisper, as if she were telling a terrible secret. "But he's not Catholic."

"No, he's not. It's not the worst thing in the world."

"But without the same background, without the same ideals and attitudes . . ." Chiara sighed wearily and faced her daughter. "Would he convert?"

"I doubt it. He has strong beliefs too. And they're as valid as mine." Anna looked away. "I'm going to marry him, Ma."

"Problems." Her mother shook her head sadly. "You'll have problems. When your father and I got married—"

"Oh, for heaven's sake, Ma. It was an arranged marriage!"

"But we got along fine!"

"It was an accident. Think how many arranged marriages don't work out."

"We knew we had to make it work. That's the way it wa. That was *la via vecchia.*"

Anna looked exasperated. She rubbed a glass with the dish towel until it shone. "Wouldn't it have been nice to be in love, Ma?"

"Love. With the right conditions, love grows."

Anna touched her mother's cheek and said softly, "It's nice to start out with it, though. Loving feels good."

"It feels good," Chiara mimicked. "But there are times when love isn't enough."

"Ma, sometimes . . . sometimes we can hardly keep our hands off each other. I want to get married soon, before we have . . . problems."

Chiara blushed. She knew the feeling her daughter spoke of, the needy cry of the flesh. Hadn't she answered the siren call of desire?

She wiped her soapy hands on a cloth and pulled Anna close in a hug. "I know, *figlia,* I know."

Anna returned the hug and kissed her mother's cheek.

When her daughter left, Chiara sat at the kitchen table musing as she sipped coffee in the darkened kitchen. Young people thought they knew it all. There was so much she would like to tell her daughter. Anna was wrong about her parents' successful marriage being an accident. It was no accident, but the result of tenacity and determination, as well as love. Anna needed to know about hanging on in the bad times—and there would be bad times; she knew of no marriages without them. And there was another sort of love, one she couldn't talk to

Anna about. Chiara thought of Stewart and their abiding relationship.

There was so much for her daughter to know. But Chiara supposed Anna would have to learn it for herself.

The next day, as Mike read the paper, he looked up suddenly. "Stewart Austin, remember him? The guy who set me up for the job at Ford. He was in an accident. Pretty serious, I guess."

"What? An accident? Let me see." Chiara snatched the paper from Mike's hands. The article was short: *. . . suffered a broken leg, fractured ribs, and internal injuries when the automobile driven by his wife hit an embankment. He is listed in serious condition at Henry Ford Hospital.*

A spasm clutched her stomach. Stewart in pain, seriously injured. She wanted to see him, to tell him . . . What? What could she possibly say to this man who had been lover and friend, who had remained in the recesses of her mind for all these years, whose face still appeared in fragments of dreams vaguely remembered in the light of morning?

She had to see him.

The next day Chiara left the shop early. At Henry Ford Hospital a gray-haired receptionist said gently, "I'm sorry, ma'am, only family can visit Mr. Austin. His wife's up there now. You can wait in the lobby and see her when she comes down, if you like."

Chiara leaned over, focusing on the number the receptionist's red nail pointed to. Third floor, room . . . The nail covered the room number.

She murmured a thanks and turned toward the exit, then made a circle to the elevators. On the third floor she wandered past the nurses' station, wondering how she could find Stewart's room. Walking down a hall picked at random, she peered into one room after another, then turned back toward the nurses' station. A door opened behind her and Audrey Austin's unmistakable high-pitched voice said clearly, "It's all my fault, Sonny. He'll never forgive me."

A male voice answered softly, "He'll forgive you, Mother. He always has. I only hope he survives to do so again."

Chiara speeded her steps past the elevators, to a door with "Exit" written in bold red letters. She darted through the door and rested against it. When she felt sure the two had left in the elevator, she inched the door open. Hurriedly she returned to the room from which they had emerged.

Stewart lay still and white. His head was bandaged and one eye was circled in a shade of purple-blue. One leg, in a cast, was suspended from a pulley. Was he breathing? She moved closer. His eyes opened.

He managed a weak smile. "Chiara."

She bent over the bed, bringing her face close to his. "My poor Stewart. How are you?"

"I'm right as rain. Especially now that you're here." His voice was thin. His eyes closed again and she thought for a moment he had fallen asleep.

She laid her hand upon Stewart's. In a raspy whisper he said, "We should have been together. You know that."

"It wasn't meant to be." How could it have been different? They were worlds apart, their paths crossing by a twist of fate.

"We should have had that child."

Chiara averted her eyes. The small wound in the corner of her heart ruptured and throbbed as it always did when she thought of the child that would have been hers and Stewart's. Softly she said, "That also wasn't meant to be."

"Ah, but you do love me, don't you, Chiara?" His words were barely a whisper.

Chiara swallowed. She had a husband; a husband she loved. She had a family to whom she was devoted. Her eyes welled up and a tear escaped down her cheek. Love. She and Anna had talked about love.

"It's all right. I understand. I know you love me." Stewart sighed. "I've loved you from the very first. You knew that."

"Yes." Of course she knew. In her heart of hearts, she knew that she loved him too, with a secret love that had been consummated in a passionate moment, and later, untended, unnurtured, had flowered.

Though it had happened more than twenty years ago, she remembered as if it were yesterday their desperate need for each other and the intensity of their passion. She remembered his sorrow on learning of their unborn child's fate. Yet he'd understood, and she had felt his concern for her from that day forward. His protection was abiding, a palpable thing, ever at the fringe of her awareness.

She remembered her guilt too.

Must one feel guilty for loving? No, she thought not.

Thankfully, Mike had never known. And it hadn't taken away from her love for her husband. Or had it? Who could know?

Stewart opened his eyes. "Admitting it doesn't alter anything, you know. We were destined to meet, to love, to part. Sounds poetic, doesn't it?" He coughed, wincing.

"Shh, you must rest. I shouldn't even be here."

"I'm glad you came." His eyelids dropped again, slowly. "I probably won't ever leave this place."

"You mustn't say that. Of course you'll leave." He was so still she thought he must be sleeping. "Stewart?"

His brows lifted first, then his lids, as if it took all his strength.

Chiara took his hand and put the back of it to her lips. Then she kissed his brow and said very softly, "I do love you."

Grateful tears glinted in his eyes.

The door swung open, sending a shaft of light across the polished floor.

"What are you doing in here? Out! Out!" A squat nurse jabbed her thumb toward the door. "No visitors allowed. Mr. Austin is very ill."

Chiara rose swiftly. "I was just leaving."

With a curious stare, the nurse rustled past Chiara to examine her patient, scolding on the way, "The very idea. This is a sick man. I don't know how you got in here . . ."

Sunday was Chiara's favorite day. Early Mass, then preparations for the traditional Sunday dinner, which she loved cooking. From the window she could see Mike out back, tending the vegetable garden. She cranked open the window and shouted, "Mike, you're stepping on my parsley!"

He gave her a dismissing wave and she shook her head.

She opened the oven door and leaned over the two chickens browning in the big enamel pan. Tipping the pan, she basted the chickens in their own juices, then arranged quartered potatoes and sliced carrots around the fowl.

Tina, who loved the funnies, sat at the kitchen table reading *Li'l Abner* aloud to her mother.

Chiara smiled dutifully, but as was often the case, the humor escaped her. "Don't leave the paper a big mess, or your father will get mad," she said, closing the oven door. "And set the table for dinner."

Luisa entered the kitchen and picked up a section of the newspaper. "Look at this man, Ma." She pointed at a small picture of a distinguished-looking man. "Isn't he the one who was in your shop that day when I came with Pa to pick you up?"

Chiara closed the oven door and straightened to peer more closely at the photo. The color drained from her face and her heart skipped a beat. Stewart.

"It says he died yesterday," Luisa went on. "He worked at Ford. I'm sure he's the one. You looked as though you were good friends that day. You were shaking hands or something, I remember."

Chiara leaned against the table, trying to regain her balance. Her voice sounded faint and faraway as she said, "Yes, he's the one." She hung the dish towel on a rack and walked slowly from the room and up the stairs.

She glanced around her bedroom with its new walnut furniture and peach-shaded spread with matching drapes. On polished wood floors, beige throw rugs blended with the walls, which held prints of Venice and Rome. Standing before the dresser, she touched the articles lying on a starched doily—a shiny silver brush and comb, covered jars with various creams, a dainty atomizer.

Things. In the past several years she had accumulated *things.* Along the way she had accumulated people too—people she cared about. Now one of those people was gone. None of the *things* mattered. People mattered. Stewart mattered.

Always, like a rosy glow in the background of her consciousness, there had been the awareness that Stewart cared deeply for her, that he was watching over her, that if she ever needed a friend, he would be there. It had been, always, a source of sustenance in trying times.

Now Stewart was dead.

She threw herself on the peach bedspread and cried.

Chiara bit the thread and squinted as she threaded a needle. They were making the needle eyes smaller these days. Here she was, at the very last minute, putting the finishing touches on Anna's wedding dress. With all the other things she'd had to do to get the new shop in Birmingham organized—instructing workmen, hiring seamstresses, ordering fabrics—there'd been little time for anything else. If only Luisa were still home, she could help with the new shop. It was the sort of thing Lou enjoyed. Ah, well, God wanted her for his own work; Chiara could understand that. But she would never stop missing Luisa.

Chiara jammed her needle into the tomato-shaped pin-cushion and shook out the white silk wedding gown. She couldn't imagine why the young people were so impatient to get married. Well, yes, she could imagine. But couldn't they have waited a little longer, until they had more money saved, until Anna had a steady job? At least Martin was working. He'd found a job immediately after graduation a month ago, in the finance department of the Ford Motor Company. She wished it could have been any other auto company but Ford. Martin's attitude toward unions wasn't favorable, and every so often he and Mike argued, not seriously, but even so . . . Well, Mike still thought of Ford as the enemy, and probably always would.

Anna said there would be plenty of time to look for a job after the wedding. She had a degree in psychology. Chiara could barely pronounce it, much less understand it. Why couldn't she have been a teacher like her friend Agnes? No, that was her Anna, stubborn, determined to go her own way.

"Is it finished?" Anna asked when Chiara brought the wedding gown to her bedroom.

"Yes, finally."

The reflection in the mirror showed mother and daughter, side by side, so different, yet, in some indiscernible way, alike; about the eyes, maybe, or simply the attitude, the posture. Physically, Anna had always favored her father. How lovely she was, Chiara thought, standing there in her white satin slip, her hair a dark halo around her peachy face, eyes bright and happy, her hands a little fluttery.

Chiara's chin quivered as tears threatened and finally spilled over. Her daughter, her firstborn girl, getting married.

"Mother." Anna turned to hug her. "You're not crying, are you?"

"Yes, I can cry on my daughter's wedding day, can't I?"

Anna patted Chiara's back.

"Anna, I . . . I want you to be happy."

"I am happy."

"There's so much I should have told you."

"Don't worry, Ma," Anna said softly. "I know what I need to know."

"I suppose you do. Look at you; you're almost the same age I was when I got married. But I was such a baby, so innocent." Chiara sat heavily on the bed. "I look back now and think about how I was always going to say things, and tell you about life, and about men and . . ." She dabbed her eyes. "Well, the time's gone by and I still haven't said much at all. Why is it so hard to talk, mother to daughter?" She pressed a tissue against her face and snuffled into it, thinking about her own mother and her own wedding day.

"I don't know. Maybe we know what's in each other's hearts."

"Just be happy, *figlia,* just be happy."

Anna hugged her mother. "I will."

Tina knocked and called through the door, "Ma, fix my sash. It's all twisted." She dashed in with Flora and Maria following behind. The two *comari* hovered over Anna like protective fairy godmothers while Chiara patiently tied Tina's rainbow-hued sash. Her Tina, at eleven, had begun to blossom with the early ripeness of Italian girls. She showed promise of a keen mind when she applied herself, but too often she was interested in other than her school work. Would she, like her older sister, insist on college?

"Where's Lou?" Anna's voice interrupted her thoughts. "She should be here by now."

"She's in the backyard, having coffee with your father." His was laced, Chiara knew, with a healthy dose of Seagram's Seven. She'd never seen Mike so nervous. Chiara went to the window and saw Luisa, in her postulant's black habit, sitting on a lawn chair next to Mike, the lilac bushes providing a screen from the sun. Well, if anyone could calm Mike down, Luisa could. Ah, Mike was handsome in his white dinner jacket. His hair, though gray, was still thick, his figure only slightly paunchy.

In her own room Chiara slipped the beige dress over her head. Anna had chosen the flattering design with an empire waist, V neck, and cap sleeves. Chiara touched her stiff hair. At Anna's insistence she had it done at the beauty shop, but it felt and looked fake. Impetuously Chiara grabbed her brush and yanked it through her hair, then let the natural waves wing back from her face. That felt much better, looked better too. Let Anna rant if she wanted.

Amazingly, they all arrived at church on time. It warmed Chiara's heart to see the look of love between Anna and her father when Mike tucked his daughter's hand into his arm for her trip down the aisle. The two were closer than ever. Mike's eyes were suspiciously moist when he took his place beside Chiara. The ceremony was a simple one, not a nuptial Mass, because Martin wasn't Catholic. Chiara's own mother and father would never have approved such a union, not in the old days, and not now either.

Fredo took movies outside the church, and afterward the wedding party went to Belle Isle for pictures. There was a dinner reception at the Whittier Hotel, on the Detroit River, for fifty people; then the couple left for Niagara Falls. It was all over so quickly, Chiara hardly had time to collect herself. "Don't forget to call when you get there," she yelled as the car sped away, its crepe-paper flowers dancing in the breeze.

Her tears had been shed before the wedding, and now she felt easier about the union. Anna and Martin obviously adored each other. Martin gazed so lovingly upon Anna, his hands straying often to touch her. They would be happy.

When would that devotion, that passion, dissipate? After the third child, the fourth? Perhaps they would be more fortunate than most. At least they'd had a chance to know one another before the ceremony, not like she and Mike, who'd hardly been allowed to talk, much less touch. Even so, what did anyone really know about another? It took a lifetime to understand, and even then there were mysteries, hidden corners in the mind. Chiara had her secrets and probably Mike had his. Indeed, she even had secrets from herself, unfathomable quirks of mind, attitudes, and posturings that made up her persona, twists in her behavior, puzzle pieces that she was still, at age forty-nine, trying to squeeze into place.

The young innocent girl who had married Michele Marcassa twenty-seven years ago was a different person from the mother who stood waving as the borrowed and bedecked Buick rolled away from the curb toward a beginning.

——Epilogue——

1963

Mike twisted his tie into place and dashed a bit of Vitalis on his hair, which was liberally sprinkled with silver. Well, at sixty-four, he should be gray. He'd earned every one of those gray hairs. He sighed, thinking: I'm old enough to retire. More and more lately he found himself saying things like: *when I was your age,* and *what do you punk kids know about the union? I was almost shot, almost arrested, I got beat up* . . . What the hell, they didn't care. It was past history to them, if they thought of it at all.

It seemed that he had lived his life on the edge of disaster, and had providently escaped damage, unlike both Reuthers. Walter's arm had been torn by gunshot, Victor had lost an eye. The two of them, along with their brother, Roy, lived with bodyguards nearby. Mike prayed those stalwarts would not die by the sword. Walter was at the height of his career, having been elected president of the CIO in 1952. No one worked harder or deserved recognition more.

Union work was dangerous and never-ending, for just when one hurdle was cleared, three more appeared. Old wounds healed, new ones erupted. Mike had learned to downplay his role for the sake of the family. They never knew how many near-misses he'd had.

For Mike, the season of discontent had begun when he went to the negotiating table against Ford, and there, sitting across from him, was Martin, his own son-in-law, *on the opposite team!* Life wasn't fair. He couldn't help it, the bile that rose, just thinking about his own son-in-law collaborating with the enemy. The strange thing was, Mike really *liked* Martin. He was bright and ambitious. But he was too young to know the whole story. Hell, Martin's father was a union man too. But that didn't matter to the kids today. What did they know about the forging of a great union? They had no idea of the kind of guts and bravery it took, not to mention bloodshed. But there he was, going off again, reliving the old days, painful as they were. Chiara had warned him, "You're starting to sound like an old man when you say, 'When I was your age . . .' "

Roma Hall was crowded. Chiara toyed with her wine-glass and turned to smile at Mike. She was ill-at-ease sitting at the head table surrounded by family and friends. Why the children had decided to celebrate their parents' thirty-fifth wedding anniversary in this manner was beyond her. It must have been expensive, as well as time-consuming. How had Anna arranged this party with all her other jobs—managing the shops and the twin boys and baby Theodore?

Chiara hadn't realized that she and Mike had so many friends. She gazed past the floral centerpiece, over the sea of nodding and smiling faces. There was Fredo with his wife. His girth had increased as his hair decreased.

The rumor was that Fredo was involved in a numbers racket. Sitting beside them were Dino and Rosa and their nine children.

Mike nudged Chiara. "Look, there's Sophia."

The midwife blew them a kiss and glanced around the hall with a self-satisfied expression.

"She's probably counting all the children that she coaxed into the world," Chiara said. "Her babies have babies of their own now, and even grandchildren."

Scattered among the crowd were neighbors, some from the old neighborhood, some from the new, and customers from many different ethnic origins.

Mike's associates were there, men who had been instrumental in the union movement. The Reuthers waved and smiled. Chiara recalled the ill-fated birthday party and May Reuther's kindness as she tried to put Chiara at ease.

Chiara left her place to greet Mortimer and Laurelia. They smiled widely, their dark faces showing little signs of age. Chiara gripped Laurelia's hand. "You were the first neighbor to welcome me to the flat on Chene Street. I'll always remember that."

Mike called her back to the table. "They're making toasts, Chiara. Can you stop talking for five minutes?"

A waiter poured wine, Mike's own, a deep garnet, sparkling, pure. Toasts were made by the children, and even Martin spoke, making jokes about how difficult it was to assimilate into an Italian family. There was more truth than fiction in his stories.

The guests clanged their silver against their glasses, signaling for a kiss.

Dismissing the insistent clatter with a wave of his hand, Mike said, "Ah, that's for newlyweds."

Chiara prodded him with her elbow. "They won't stop the noise until we kiss." She pointed her pursed lips in Mike's direction and he had no choice but to give her a perfunctory kiss.

"Oh, you kids!" said someone at Chiara's elbow.

"Penny!" Chiara hugged her first American friend.

"This is Frederick, my husband," Penny said, hanging on to the arm of a rangy, smiling man.

Penny had divorced Jimmy many years ago. In the old

days Chiara would have been critical, but now she was, if not approving, at least tolerant of divorce. Life was short; one must make the most of it. She couldn't quite believe God intended for his children to resign themselves to lives of misery.

When Penny and her husband returned to their table, Chiara said, "Mike, I almost forgot, I have a present for you." From the silver lamé bag that Tina had given her, Chiara pulled an envelope. Carefully she drew out a document and, unfolding it, pressed out the creases. She handed it to Mike.

"What's this?"

"Read it."

Mike's eyes darted across the page; then he looked at his wife with astonishment. "Your citizenship papers."

"I thought it was time. It's my gift to you."

Mike took her hand and squeezed it tight. "After all these years!" She thought he might cry. "You did this for me?"

Chiara shrugged. "For me too."

"Grandpa, Grandpa." Anna's six-year-old twin sons, Brian and Matthew, ran to their grandfather, diverting his attention.

Fondly Chiara watched Mike as he pushed back his chair and gathered the two little boys to him. He spoiled them, but why not? He finally had the boys he had always wanted. It was the one regret of her life, that she hadn't given him another son.

Anna strode up to them, the baby balanced on her hip, and admonished her boys to behave. She was a dynamo, her Anna, organizing, directing, making sure everything worked out smoothly. Anna collared Tina and gave her snappy instructions, to which Tina responded with a rolling of her eyes. Tina's skirt was too short, her eyes rimmed in black makeup, her once-lovely wavy hair teased up into a huge pouf. It was hard to believe Tina was a college sophomore.

Luisa joined the others. She had dispensed with her habit in favor of street clothes. It was a crime how they changed all the rules in the church, dispensing with hats and Latin, playing guitars and singing tunes that bore no resemblance to hymns. Chiara remembered with nostalgia how Luisa at twelve years of age had crowned the Blessed Virgin in the May celebration, the thin, high voices of the children in the background singing "O Mary, we crown you with blossoms today . . ."

What was next? Had Luisa made the right choice? Did she have twinges of regret that she would never have a man in her life, nor the pleasure of cradling her own child in her arms? Sometimes she didn't seem quite happy. Ah, well, one found both pleasure and sorrow down every path of life.

Anna and Martin seemed happy. Strange how things worked out. The newlyweds had returned from their honeymoon to learn that Chiara had had an emergency hysterectomy. Anna stepped in and took over the opening of the new shop, and to her surprise, she found she liked it and was reluctant to return the reins to her mother. So it was decided they would open a third shop in Redford Township. Anna had hardly been set up there when she made plans for a fourth. Now there were six.

How fortunate that Flora had been there to step in when Anna's twins were born. It was like history repeating itself. For Flora it was a blessing, as she had begun to live more and more in her memories, though she was hardly old, only fifty-eight.

Now the dinner was finished and Maria took the seat Mike had vacated next to Chiara. Flora sat on the other side, and the three of them reminisced.

Chiara said, "Flora, I'll never forget when we got off the train, and there you were, with Eduardo, waving, with that silly little hat with the red feather . . ."

"I still have that hat hidden away somewhere. It *was* a silly hat."

"On the ship, when you stopped to talk to me," Maria said, "I had no idea we would begin a friendship that would last so long."

Chiara teared up. "You were both there at my side, through laughter and sorrow, my dearest friends. . . ."

"I was thinner then." Flora held her ample sides and laughed.

"What stories we could tell," Chiara said. "What stories."

All my friends are here, she thought as she and Michele bade good-bye to their guests. Well, not all. Chiara's face softened. Stewart. He'd given her more than friendship, and his death had left a void that could not be filled.

Back home, only the family members remained, sprawled out in the living room, yawning as they reviewed the party, voicing surprise at this one's early aging, that one's unexpected success, another one's plumpness, another one's bitterness. Soon the children—Chiara still called them that—began recalling comic tales of their childhood. Some of the stories that had been upsetting when they happened, seemed to gain humor with each retelling.

Chiara glanced around the comfortable room. This house has survived many a crisis, she thought. Mike had tried again and again to convince her to move to Grosse Pointe, but she had refused. She didn't need a "good" address. This house was a family house. It held memories of shared times, good and bad.

Chiara realized Mike wasn't in the room. Often he sat alone in the kitchen, drinking wine, reflecting. But he wasn't there, nor in the yard. She called his name, then went upstairs, following the strange scuttling sounds from their bedroom. When she pushed the door open, she saw Mike standing on a chair in the closet, scrounging through boxes and cartons.

"What are you doing in the closet at two o'clock in the morning?"

"Never mind. When I find it, you'll know."

"You're making a mess in there."

Mike stacked a flowered hat box atop a red-lettered carton that proclaimed "Contadina Tomato Paste," and swore softly when a shoe box dislodged and fell on his head. Finally he shouted victoriously, "Ah-ha!" With a triumphant smile he hauled out his old guitar.

He jumped from the chair, holding the guitar aloft. Gently he caressed the curved light-wood sides and with an index finger traced the curlicue design along the frets.

Softly Chiara said, "You haven't played in a long time."

Sitting on the edge of the bed, he cradled the guitar as

though it were a baby. Gingerly he plucked one string, then another; then methodically, with his head tipped toward the instrument, he tightened each key with an accompanying hum. Finally assured the guitar was in tune, he began strumming. Very quietly, in almost a whisper, he sang a soulful accompaniment. *"O Sole Mio,"* a lullaby when he began, gradually gained momentum, and by the end, was the robust love song that its creator intended. With hardly a breath, he moved on to *"Torna a Sorrento,"* singing with his eyes closed, as if, indeed, the craggy outline of hilly Sorrento were unreeling behind his lids. Then he began another old song, so obscure Chiara didn't know the words, and then another. He continued playing and singing the old songs, the almost forgotten melodies of Italy, belting them out, one after another, with an intensity Chiara hadn't seen in a long time. He strummed, not always in key, and crooned with the emotional breaks and quivers of the old-country style. Gradually the children filed into the bedroom one by one and, barely noticed by their father, sat on the floor. They listened intently, joining in occasionally when they remembered the words.

Mike went on, song after song, eyes closed, oblivious of his audience, a look close to pain fixed upon his face.

Finally he stopped playing and laid the guitar across his lap, immobile, silent, his eyes, unseeing, fixed on a spot near the ceiling. No one spoke, seeming to sense a reverence in the hushed moment.

Luisa finally stirred herself to action. Rising from the floor, she went to Mike and kissed his cheek. Tina, then Anna, followed suit, and Martin, last in line, grasped Mike's shoulder.

When Mike blinked, Chiara saw tears, and her own tears prickled behind her lids.

The children left as quietly as they had come, and Chiara sat beside her husband.

"Let's go home," he said. A tear rolled down his cheek.

"Home?"

"To Italy. To live. We could settle someplace near Dante's town and see him once in a while."

Chiara was puzzled. Dante's name hadn't been mentioned in many years, not since the trip. What had happened to Mike? Chiara wondered. Why this sudden nostalgia?

Mike put his hand on hers. "What do you think? You always talked about going home again. Remember how you hated the cold winters? How you wanted to feast your eyes again on the Adriatic? We could do it now. I'm ready to retire. We have plenty of money. What do you say?"

Chiara's brows raised while her eyes closed slowly in a gesture of resignation. "Mike." She took his hand in both of hers. "What can you be thinking of, wanting to go to Italy after all these years? I'm not ready to retire. I have the stores. There's lots of work to do."

Mike rubbed his forehead. "I don't know, Chiara, I guess I got carried away by the old songs. I feel old all of a sudden, maybe a little bit useless. I want to see my old home, go back to my roots, see my . . ." He broke off, and his thumb strummed a slow chord on the guitar, and another. A sigh rose from deep in his chest.

"Mike. We've lived through a lot. We lost some things, gained some things. When I left Italy I thought the idea of *la via vecchia*, holding on to the old ways, was good. In some ways, it is good—the belief in family and friends, in loyalty and honor, in making your own way—those are valuable ideas."

Mike laid his guitar on the floor. "Those are the things we've passed on to our children."

"Yes. I like to think we took the good things from the old country and left behind the others." Chiara laid her hand on Mike's. "I used to dream of going back to the old country, Mike, but I don't think I could be happy there. This is where our children are. It's our home."

About the Author

Lucy Taylor began her writing career after raising eight children. She is the daughter of Italian immigrants and resides in Michigan with her husband. *Avenue of Dreams* is her first novel.